The Spid

Fergus Hume

Alpha Editions

This edition published in 2024

ISBN : 9789361472176

Design and Setting By
Alpha Editions
www.alphaedis.com
Email - info@alphaedis.com

As per information held with us this book is in Public Domain.
This book is a reproduction of an important historical work. Alpha Editions uses the best technology to reproduce historical work in the same manner it was first published to preserve its original nature. Any marks or number seen are left intentionally to preserve its true form.

Contents

CHAPTER I. ....- 1 -

CHAPTER II. ....- 11 -

CHAPTER III. ....- 22 -

CHAPTER IV. ....- 33 -

CHAPTER V. ....- 46 -

CHAPTER VI. ....- 56 -

CHAPTER VII. ....- 68 -

CHAPTER VIII. ....- 79 -

CHAPTER IX. ....- 91 -

CHAPTER X. ....- 101 -

CHAPTER XI. ....- 110 -

CHAPTER XII. ....- 120 -

CHAPTER XIII. ....- 131 -

CHAPTER XIV. ....- 141 -

CHAPTER XV. ....- 153 -

CHAPTER XVI. ....- 164 -

CHAPTER XVII. ....- 174 -

CHAPTER XVIII. ....- 183 -

CHAPTER XIX. ....- 195 -

CHAPTER XX. ....- 207 -

CHAPTER XXI. ....- 220 -

CHAPTER XXII. ....- 232 -

CHAPTER I.

A POSSIBLE PARTNERSHIP.

The exterior of The Athenian Club, Pall Mall, represents an ordinary twentieth century mansion, which it is; but within, the name is justified by a Græco-Roman architecture of vast spaces, marble floors, painted ceilings, and pillared walls, adapted, more or less successfully, to the chilly British climate. The various rooms are called by Latin names, and the use of these is rigidly enforced. Standing outside the mansion, you know that you are in London; enter, and you behold Athens--say, the abode of Alcibiades; listen, and scraps of speech suggest Imperial Rome. Thus, the tastes of all the members, whether old and pedantic, or young and frivolous, are consulted and gratified. Modern slang, as well as the stately tongue of Virgil, is heard in The Athenian, for the club, like St. Paul, is all things to all men. For that reason it is a commercial success.

Strangers--they come eagerly with members to behold rumoured glories--enter the club-house, through imitation bronze gates, into the vestibulum, and pass through an inner door into the atrium. This means that they leave the entrance room for the general conversation apartment. To the right of this, looking from the doorway, is the tablinum, which answers--perhaps not very correctly as regards the name--the purposes of a library; to the left a lordly portal gives admittance into the triclinium, that is, to the dining-room. At the end of the atrium, which is the neutral ground of the club, where members and strangers meet, swing-doors shut in the pinacotheca. Properly this should be a picture-gallery, but, in deference to modern requirements, it is used as a smoking-room. These three rooms, spacious, ornate, and lofty, open under a colonnade, or peristyle, on to a glass-roofed winter garden, which runs like a narrow passage round the three sides of the building. The viridarium, as the members call this cultivated strip of land, extends only twenty feet from the marble pavement of the peristyle, and is bounded by the side-walls and rear-walls of adjacent houses. It is filled with palms and tropical plants, with foreign and native flowers, and, owing to a skilful concealment of its limitations by the use of enormous mirrors, festooned with creepers and ivy, it really resembles vast pleasure-gardens extending to great distances. The outlook from tablinum, pinacotheca, and triclinium is a triumph of perspective.

Below the state apartments on the ground floor are the kitchens, the domestic offices, and the servants' rooms; above them, the cubicles are to be found, where members, both resident or non-resident, sleep when disposed on beds more comfortable than classical. Finally, on the top floor, and reached by a lift, are billiard-rooms, card-rooms, and a small gymnasium for those who require exercise. The whole scheme is modelled on a larger scale from the House of Glaucus, as described by Bulwer Lytton in "The Last Days of Pompeii." A perusal of this famous story suggested the novelty to an enterprising builder, and the Athenian Club is the successful result.

The members of such a club should have been classical scholars, but these were in the minority. The greater portion of those who patronised this latest London freak were extremely up-to-date, and defended their insistent modernity amidst ancient artificial environment by Acts xvii. 21: "For the Athenians and strangers which were there spent their time in nothing else, but either to tell, or to hear some new thing!" And certainly they acted well up to the text, for all the scandal and novelty of the metropolis seemed to flow from this pseudo-classical source. Plays were discussed in manuscript, novels on the eve of publication; inventors came here to suggest plans for airships, or to explain how the earth could signal to Mars. Some members had brand new ideas for the improvement of motor mechanism, others desired to evolve colour from sound, detailing with many words how music could be made visible. As to politics, the Athenians knew everything which was going on behind the scenes, and could foretell equally truthfully a war, a change of Government, the abdication of a monarch, or the revolt of an oppressed people. If any traveller arrived from the Land-at-the-Back-of-Beyond with an account of a newly-discovered island, or an entirely new animal, he was sure to be a member of the club. Thus, although the interior of the Pall Mall mansion suggested Greece and Rome, Nero and Pericles, the appointments for comfort, for the quick dispatch of business or pleasure, and the ideas, conversation, and dress of the members, were, if anything, six months ahead of the present year of grace. The Athenian Club was really a mixture or blending of two far-apart epochs, the very ancient and the very modern; but the dark ages were left out, as the members had no use for mediæval ignorance.

Over the mosaic dog with his warning lettering, "Cave Canem," strolled, one warm evening in June, a young man of twenty-four, whose physical appearance was more in keeping with the classical surroundings than were his faultlessly fitting dress-clothes. His oval, clean-shaven face was that of a pure-blooded Hellene, his curly golden hair and large blue eyes like the sky of Italy at noon, suggested the Sun-god, and his figure, limber, active, and slender, resembled the Hermes of the Palestra. He was almost aggressively handsome, and apparently knew that he was, for he swaggered in with a haughty lord-of-the-world air, entirely confident of himself and of his capabilities. His exuberant vitality was as pronounced as were his good looks, and there was a finish about his toilette which hinted at a determination to make the most of his appearance. He assuredly succeeded in accentuating what Nature had done for him, since even the attendant, who approached to remove the young man's light overcoat, appeared to be struck by this splendid vision of perfect health, perfect beauty, and perfect lordship of existence. All the fairies must have come to the cradle of this fortunate young gentleman with profuse gifts. He seemed to be the embodiment of joyous life.

"Is Mr. Arthur Vernon here?" he asked, settling his waistcoat, touching the flower in his button-hole, and pulling a handkerchief out of his left sleeve.

"In the pinacotheca, sir," was the reply, for all the attendants were carefully instructed in correct pronunciation. "Shall I tell him you are here, Mr. Maunders?"

The gentleman thus named yawned lazily. "Thanks, I shall see him myself;" and with a nod to the man, he walked lightly through the atrium, looking like one of Flaxman's creations, only he was more clothed.

Throwing keen glances right and left to see who was present and who was not, Mr. Maunders entered the pinacotheca. This was an oblong apartment with marble walls on three sides and a lordly range of pillars on the fourth, which was entirely open to the gardens. Beyond could be seen the luxuriant vegetation of the undergrowth, whence sprang tall palms, duplicated in the background of mirrors. The mosaic pavement of the smoking-room was strewn with Persian praying-mats, whose vivid colouring matched the pictured floor. There were deep armchairs and softly-cushioned sofas, all upholstered in dark red leather, which contrasted pleasantly with the snowy walls. Many small tables of white metal and classical shapes were dotted here, there, and everywhere. As it was mid-June and extremely close, the fireplace--looking somewhat incongruous in such a place--was filled with ferns and white flowers, in red pots of earthenware, thus repeating the general scheme of colour. Red and white, snow and fire, with a spread of green in the viridarium--nothing could have been more artistic.

Under the peristyle, and near a fountain whence water sprang from the conch of a Triton to fall into a shallow marble basin with prismatic hues, were several copper-topped tables. Near them, basket chairs draped with brightly-hued rugs, were scattered in picturesque disorder. One of them was occupied by a long, slim man of thirty. With a cigarette between his lips and a cup of coffee at his elbow, he stared straight in front of him, but looked up swiftly when he heard Maunders' springy steps.

"Here you are at last!" he remarked somewhat coolly, and glanced at his watch. "Why didn't you turn up to dinner as arranged? It's close on nine o'clock."

"Couldn't get away from my aunt," replied Maunders, slipping leisurely into an adjacent chair. "She seemed to have the blues about something, and wouldn't let me go. Never was there so affectionate an aunt as Mrs. Bedge, and never one so tryingly attentive."

"Considering that she has brought you up in the past, supplies you with money at present, and intends to make you her heir in the future, you might talk more kindly of her."

Maunders shrugged his shoulders. "Oh, the Eton-Oxford education was all right; she did well by me there. But I don't get much money from her now, and judging from that, I may be heir to very little."

"You ought to be glad that you are an heir to anything," said Vernon frowning, for his friend's light tones jarred.

"Why?" asked the other. "My parents are dead long since. Aunt Emily is my only relative, and has neither chick nor child. If she didn't intend to leave me her money she should not have brought me up to luxury and idleness."

"It would certainly be better if she had made you work," assented the host contemptuously; "but you were always lazy and extravagant."

"I was born sitting down; I am a lily of the field and a rose of Sharon."

"Likewise an ass."

"You think so?" said Maunders drily. "Well, I hope to change your opinion on that point before we part."

"It will take a deal of changing. But all this talk is beside the purpose of our meeting. You made this appointment with me, and----"

"Didn't keep it to the minute. I'm nearly two hours late. Well, what does it matter?"

"Everything to me. I am a busy man," snapped the other sharply.

"So you say." Maunders looked very directly at his host. "Some fellows don't think so. Your business----"

Vernon interrupted. "I have no business; I am an independent man."

"And yet a busy one," rejoined Maunders softly; "strange."

There was that significance in his tone which made Vernon colour, although he remained motionless. He certainly was about to make a hasty observation, but his guest looked at him so straightly and smilingly, that he bit his lip and refrained from immediate speech. Maunders, still smiling, took a cigarette from a golden case and lighted up. "You might offer me a cup of coffee."

Vernon signalled to a passing attendant. "A cup of coffee for Mr. Maunders."

"With a vanilla bean," directed the other man. "I don't like coffee otherwise. And hurry up, please!" Then, when the servant departed, he turned suavely to his host. "I forget what we were talking about."

"So do I," retorted Vernon coolly.

Maunders, smoking delicately, rested his wrists on the copper edge of the table and looked searchingly into his friend's strong face. And Vernon's face was strong--much stronger than that of his companion. He likewise had blue eyes, but of a deep-sea blue, less shallow and more piercing than those of Maunders. His face was also oval, with finely cut features, but more scored with thought-marks; and his hair was as dark, smooth, and short-cropped as that of the other's was golden, curly, and--odd adjective to use in connection with a man--fluffy. Both were clean-shaven, but Vernon's mouth was firm, while the lips of Maunders were less compressed and betrayed indecision. The former had the more athletic figure, the latter a more graceful one, and although both were well groomed and well dressed, Vernon was less of the dandy in his attention to detail. Poetically speaking, one man was Night and the other Day; but a keen observer would have read that the first used strength of body and brain to achieve his ends, while the last relied more on cunning. And from the looks of the twain, cunning and strength were about to try conclusions. Yet they had been child-friends, school-friends, and--so far as their paths ran parallel--were life-friends, with certain reservations.

"You were always as deep as a well, Arty," said Maunders, finally removing his eyes from the other's face and turning to take his cup of coffee.

"Don't call me Arty!" snapped Vernon irritably.

"You were Arty at Eton, when we were boys, tall and short."

"We are not at Eton now. I always think that there is something weak in a man being called by his Christian name outside his family--much less being ticketed with a confounded diminutive."

"You can call me Conny if you like, as you used to."

"I shan't, or even Constantine. Maunders is good enough for me."

"Oh is he?" The fair man glanced shrewdly over the coffee-cup he was holding to his lips. "You hold to that."

"I hold to the name, not to the individual," said Vernon curtly.

"You don't trust me."

"I don't. I see no reason to trust you."

"Ah, you will when I explain why I asked you to meet me here," said Maunders in his frivolous manner.

"I daresay; go on."

His friend sighed. "What a laconic beast you are, Arty."

"My name is Vernon, if you please."

"Always Vernon?" asked Maunders in silky tones. The other man sat up alertly. "What do you mean?"

"I mean that I want you to take me into partnership."

"Partnership!" Vernon's face grew an angry red. "What the devil do you know?"

"Softly! softly! I know many things, although there is no need to swear. It's bad form, Vernon, deuced bad form. The fact is," he went on gracefully, "my aunt keeps me short of money, and I want all I can get to enjoy life. I thought as I am pretty good in finding out things about people that you might invite me to become a partner in your detective business."

Vernon cast a hasty glance around. Fortunately, there were no guests under the peristyle, and only two men, out of earshot, in the pinacotheca. "You are talking rubbish," he said roughly, yet apprehensively.

"I don't think so. Your father died three years ago and left you with next to nothing. Having no profession you did not know what to do, and, ashamed to beg, borrow, or steal, you turned your powers of observation to account on the side of the law against the criminal." Maunders took a card from his waistcoat pocket and passed it along. "'Nemo, Private Enquiry Agent, 22, Fenella Street, Covent Garden,' is inscribed on that card. Nemo means Nobody, I believe; yet Nemo, as I know, means Arthur Vernon of The Athenian Club."

The man addressed tore the card to pieces and threw them amongst the flowers. "You talk rubbish," he said again, and still roughly. "How do you connect me with this private enquiry agent?"

"Ah, that's too long a story to tell you just now." Maunders glanced at his watch. "I am due at a ball in an hour, and want the matter settled before I leave here."

"What matter?"

"The partnership matter." There was a pause. "Well?"

"I have nothing to say," said Vernon firmly.

Maunders rose. "In that case I'll cut along and go earlier than I expected to Lady Corsoon's ball."

"Lady Corsoon!" Vernon changed colour and bit his lip.

"Yes. She didn't ask you to her ball, did she? She wouldn't, of course, seeing that you are in love with her daughter Lucy. That young lady is to marry money, and you haven't any but what you make out of your detective business. Perhaps if I tell her that you are doing well as Nemo, she might----"

By this time Vernon was on his feet. "Don't you dare, don't you dare!" he panted hoarsely, and the perspiration beaded his brow.

"Oh!" Maunders raised his eyebrows. "Then it is true, after all."

"Sit down," commanded Vernon savagely, resuming his own seat. "We must talk this matter out, if you please."

"I came here for that purpose. Only don't keep me too late. I am engaged to Lucy for the third waltz, and must not disappoint her."

Vernon winced. "You have no right to call Miss Corsoon by her Christian name."

"Why not? She's not engaged to you. I love her, and, as yet--as yet, mind you, Vernon--I have as good a right as you to cut in."

"I understood that you were as good as engaged to Miss Dimsdale."

"Oh!" Maunders lightly flipped away a cigarette ash. "The shoe's on the other foot there. She loves me, but I don't love her. Still, there's money in the business if Ida becomes Mrs. Maunders. Old Dimsdale's got no end of cash, and Ida inherits everything as his only child. But he wants her to marry Colonel Towton---you know, the chap who did so well in some hill-tribe extermination in India. But Ida loves me, and Towton's got no chance, unless I marry Lucy Corsoon and give him a look in."

"You're a cynical, conceited, feather-headed young ass," said Vernon with cold, self-restrained fury, "and I forbid you to speak of Miss Corsoon in that commercial way, much less call her by her Christian name. She loves me and I love her, and we intend to marry, if----"

"If Lady Corsoon permits the match," finished Maunders, stretching out his long legs. "It's no go, my dear fellow. She doesn't think you rich enough for the girl."

"I never heard that Constantine Maunders was a millionaire," retorted the other man bitterly.

"My face is my fortune, old chap, and there are various ways of getting Lady Corsoon's consent."

"What ways?" asked Vernon suddenly and searchingly looking at his friend.

"Ah, you ask too much. I am not your partner yet."

"That means you have some knowledge about Lady Corsoon which you can use to force her to consent."

"Perhaps. I know a great deal about most people. Every one has his or her secrets as well as her or his price."

"Are you a private enquiry agent also?" sneered Vernon, leaning back.

"Ah!" Maunders seized upon the half admission. "Then you _are_ Nemo?"

"Yes," assented the dark man reluctantly, "although I can't guess how you came to know about my business. I wish the fact kept dark, as it would be disastrous for me in Society."

"Probably," admitted Maunders lazily. "One doesn't like to hob-nob with an Asmodeus who goes in for unroofing houses."

"Yet you propose to join Asmodeus," chafed Vernon uneasily.

"Oh yes; I think it's a paying business, you see, and I want money. How I learned about the matter is of no great consequence, and I don't think any one else will connect you with this Nemo abstraction. And when in partnership, I shall, of course, keep it dark for my own sake."

"I daresay," sneered Vernon, secretly furious at having to submit. "And on what terms do you propose to join in the business you despise?"

"Half profits," said Maunders promptly.

"Really. You seem to set some value on yourself."

"No one else will if I don't," replied Maunders good-humouredly. "See here, Arty--oh, then, Vernon if you will--your business as a private enquiry agent is to find out things about people, and----"

"I beg your pardon, but you talk through your hat," interrupted Vernon acidly. "My business is to assist people to settle business which the general public is not supposed to know. I don't find out people's business. They come to me with difficult cases, and I settle them to the best of my ability."

"Yes, yes," said Maunders leniently, "you put the best complexion on it, old man, but it's dirty work all the same."

"It is nothing of the sort," almost shouted Vernon; then sank his voice to a furious whisper; "my business is perfectly honest and clean. The nature of it requires secrecy, but I take up nothing the doing of which would reflect on my honour. I have precious little money and also a logical way of looking at things. For that reason I trade as Nemo."

"Under the rose, of course," laughed Maunders. "You don't put your goods in the shop window. However, I understand perfectly, and I am willing to come in with you. Oh, make no mistake, my dear chap, I am worth having as a partner, as I know heaps about Tom, Dick, and Harry, which they would rather were kept out of the newspapers."

"I don't run a blackmailing business," said Vernon passionately.

"What a nasty word, and wholly unnecessary. I never suggested blackmailing any one, that I know of. All I say is, that, having a goodish acquaintance with the seamy side of Society life, I can earn my half of the Nemo profits by assisting you."

"And if I refuse?"

"I shall hint--mind you I shan't say anything straight out--but I shall hint that you are a professionally inquisitive person."

"I don't know if you are aware of it," said Vernon slowly, "but you are a scoundrel."

"Oh, dear me, no; not at all," rejoined the other airily, "I am simply a young man with the tastes of a duke and the income of a pauper. Naturally I wish to supplement that income, and your secret business seems to offer advantages in the way of earning immediate cash."

"And if I don't consent you will do your best to ruin me socially?"

"That's business," said Maunders promptly. "Get a man into a corner and skin him at your leisure. Well, do you consent?"

"I can't do anything else, that I can see," said the other bitterly. "However, you must give me a week to come to a decision."

"Take a month," answered the visitor generously. "I'm not in a hurry to skin you, old man. You can't get out of the corner, you know. And see here, if we make a fortune out of this business, I'll give you a chance with Lucy, and take Ida Dimsdale with her ten thousand a year."

"Will she have that much?"

"Oh, certainly. I made inquiries," said Maunders coolly. "It's no use jumping in the dark you know. Old Dimsdale--his Christian name's Martin--was a Police Commissioner in Burmah some years ago, and shook the pagoda-tree to some purpose. Now he's retired, and lives in a gorgeously glorified bungalow, which he built at Hampstead. He's not a bad chap, and Ida is uncommonly good-looking. I might do worse."

"What about Colonel Towton?"

"I'll cut him out. He's a very young colonel of forty-five, handsome and smart, but with precious little brain about him. He's got an ancient country house in Yorkshire, and--but here, I'll be talking all the night." Maunders jumped up. "And Lucy is waiting for me. You can take a month."

"Thank you," said Vernon frigidly. "I shall give you my answer then."

"It will be 'yes,' of course; you can't say anything else. I say"---Maunders threw a laughing glance over his shoulder--"by this time you must have changed your opinion as to my being an ass," and he departed still laughing.

Vernon ran after him and touched his shoulder. "Not an ass, but a scoundrel," he breathed with suppressed passion, and Maunders' laughter increased.

CHAPTER II.

A CONFIDENTIAL COMMUNICATION.

When Maunders passed into the atrium, Vernon returned slowly to his seat under the peristyle. Here he ordered a fresh cup of strong coffee to clear his brain, lighted another cigarette, and sat down to recall the late conversation. As a preliminary to a thorough consideration of the situation, he ran over in his mind what he knew of the man who wished to become his partner. His memories showed Maunders to be an exceedingly unscrupulous person, who was ready to do anything to gratify his appetite for pleasure.

Vernon's recollections carried him back to a Berkshire village of which his father had been the squire. Mrs. Bedge, the widow of a Levantine merchant, had taken a house in the neighbourhood, and there had settled with her nephew, Constantine Maunders. It seemed that her sister had married a naturalised Greek, hence the boy's Christian name. As the parents were dead, Mrs. Bedge, being without offspring, had adopted the orphan. From what Vernon remembered, Maunders had always been a handsome and charming little boy, who usually got his own way by sheer amiability and good looks. But he had inherited more from his Greek father than a classical face and a Christian name which smacked of old Constantinople, for he was crafty and clever, and utterly without moral principle. He could conceal his feelings admirably, he could scheme for his wants very dexterously, and he told a lie or the truth with the utmost impartiality when either suited the end to be gained. Posing as an innocent angel-child, he deceived everyone, and although outwardly he appeared to be an unsophisticated babe, he was in reality a little monster of egotism. Even when they were children together, Vernon--from bitter experience--had always mistrusted Constantine, and had judged his character more accurately than grown-up people. Those were invariably taken in by the brat's cherubic aspect.

At Eton, Constantine fared less happily. He was ten years of age when his aunt sent him there, and, as Vernon then was fifteen, she had asked him to look after her darling. But all Vernon's chivalry could not save Constantine from well-deserved kicks and thrashings. Schoolboys are not to be taken in by angel-children, so Constantine did not have a happy time. However, he was so diplomatic and unscrupulous that he managed to scramble through school life fairly well. At Oxford--whither he went some years after Vernon--he got on better, and became a general favourite because of his general pliancy of disposition. By means of that same pliancy he usually secured his selfish ends, under a guise of consistent amiability. Being quick-brained and clever, if somewhat shallow, he secured his degree, and left the University with an excellent character. Since then he had been a man about town, supported by his aunt's money. Mrs. Bedge had settled in London at Constantine's request, and could refuse him nothing. Yet--as Vernon judged from what the young man had said--even Mrs. Bedge's generosity could not supply Maunders with sufficient money to gratify the selfish desire he had always had for pleasure. Only the income of a Rothschild could have entirely satisfied his cravings for the delights of existence.

Vernon had been less lucky in life. His father had speculated rashly, and three years prior to the meeting of the young men at the Athenian Club had died a comparative pauper. Thrown on his own resources and without a profession, Vernon had utilised his observant and logical faculties to set up in private practice as a detective. For two years he had carried on the trade with success and without having been found out. But now that Constantine had come on the scene, Vernon felt that there would be trouble. Of course, by taking him as a partner an exposure could be avoided, but only temporarily. Maunders was so ready to make mischief that Vernon felt he would take all he could get out of the business, and when prosperous by marriage with Ida Dimsdale, would not hesitate to tell the truth. The sole safeguard lay in the fact that, being tarred with the same brush, Maunders for his own social sake might hold his tongue. He was always clever enough to avoid the publication of any facts to his disadvantage. It really seemed, on these grounds, that it would be judicious to admit him as a partner. But Vernon shivered at the prospect. At the best, such a business as he was engaged in, was a delicate one and decidedly unpopular. With Maunders' unscrupulous methods it might degenerate into a series of shady transactions.

"But I'll take the month and think it over," thought Vernon, when he had finished his coffee and cigarette. "Much may happen in thirty days which may enable me to get out of the difficulty." Then he took out his watch and noted that it was ten o'clock. "Just time to see Dimsdale," he yawned.

When putting on his light overcoat in the vestibulum, Vernon thought it was a strange coincidence that Maunders should have mentioned--incidentally, of course--the name of the man with whom he had an appointment at half-past ten o'clock. Earlier in the day Vernon had received a pressing note asking him to meet the writer at Colonel Towton's chambers, Ralph Street, St. James's, at that hour. So, as a matter of fact, two names pertinent to the situation had been mentioned, Dimsdale and Towton. Vernon wondered as he walked along Pall Mall what the reason could be. He did not believe in coincidence, and had sufficient experience of life to doubt the existence of chance, so the mention of the names taken in conjunction with the appointment must point to some problem being worked out. Vernon believed--as every thoughtful man must believe--that everything was worked out in the unseen world before it became a factor in the visible plane, and he was quite prepared to find, on this assumption, that the meeting with Dimsdale in Towton's chambers was more important than it appeared to be on the surface. Subsequent events proved that he was right in his conjecture.

Meanwhile--as he was a one-thing-at-a-time man--he sauntered leisurely along towards his destination, wondering what Dimsdale wished to see him about. The ex-police-commissioner was one of the very few people who knew of the business in Covent Garden. Dimsdale had been a life-long friend of Vernon's father, and had welcomed the young man with open arms to his home. It was odd that Vernon had not fallen in love with Ida, as nothing would have pleased Dimsdale better than to have given his daughter and her money to his old friend's son. But Fortune in her freakish way had decided that Vernon should fall in love with Lucy Corsoon, where every obstacle would be placed in the way of a successful wooing, so Ida and Arthur had settled contentedly down into a brother and sister relationship.

Dimsdale was annoyed that his pet project of a marriage could not come to pass, but there was no help for it, as he could not govern the young man's affections. Also he was annoyed because Vernon, when the death of his father occurred, would not let the elder man assist him. However, he told him his plans about the private inquiry office, and although the ex-police commissioner did not wholly approve, he judged from his knowledge of the young man's detective powers, that it was the best use he could put his talents to. More than this, he managed to bring him clients, and to spread the fame of Nemo by dexterous allusions. Vernon therefore was doing very well in the line he had struck out for himself, and felt duly grateful to Dimsdale for his assistance. He thought as he walked along Ralph Street that probably the old gentleman had found him a fresh client. But it was odd that Colonel Towton's chambers should have been chosen as the meeting place, since Dimsdale belonged to several clubs. And the matter, whatever it was, must be very important, else Dimsdale would have waited until Vernon paid his weekly visit to the Hampstead bungalow.

It was only a quarter-past ten o'clock when Vernon arrived, and he thought that he would have to wait. But Towton's servant intimated that Mr. Dimsdale was watching for his visitor in the Colonel's particular sanctum, and ushered the young man into the room, after relieving him of his coat and hat. The Colonel himself did not appear to be present, but Martin Dimsdale was smoking in a deep arm-chair, and jumped up in his boyish way to shake hands warmly. He always had a great regard for Arthur Vernon.

The room was an ordinary apartment, comfortably furnished, but in a strictly bachelor fashion. The scheme of colour was deep green and deep red, so that it appeared somewhat sombre. Trophies of Towton's sporting instincts in the shape of skins and heads appeared on the walls and on the floor. There were many military portraits and groups about, reminiscent of the Colonel's army life. The two windows were open and the curtains were pulled back, so that the room was fairly cool, while on the table stood a syphon, some glasses and a decanter of whisky, together with a box of cigars. These were at Mr. Dimsdale's elbow. He had evidently been passing the time in smoking and drinking pending his young friend's arrival.

"I'm glad to see you, boy," said the ex-police commissioner, pointing to a chair. "Sit down and make yourself at home. Towton gives me full permission to play in this yard. Have a peg and a cigar."

"Not too strong, please," warned Vernon, accepting a cigar and sinking into the indicated chair. "I haven't so steady a head as yours."

"It's a cleverer head," said Dimsdale, squirting in the potash. "Else I should not have asked you to meet me here--Nemo."

"Oh!" Vernon placed the glass beside him. "I thought it was a Case. But why did you ask me to meet you in Towton's rooms, and where is Towton?"

"At my sister's ball along with Ida and Miss Hest."

"Lady Corsoon's ball?"

Dimsdale sat down and nodded. "Yes. It's a swell affair, as Sir Julius wants to make an impression on some Australian people he desires to rope into his schemes for making money. Something to do with mines, I believe. I didn't feel inclined to go, although I daresay I'll have to look in later to fetch Ida and Miss Hest home. I wished particularly to see you." His manner assumed a portentous gravity. "So I asked Towton if I could come here and make the appointment."

"But at your club----"

"What I have to say is sacred and secret," interrupted the old gentleman. "A club has many eyes and many ears. Better be on the safe side. Oh, that's all right," he added with a nod, on seeing Vernon's eyes stray to the open window. "Those only look out over the roofs of houses. No one can hear us. Whisky all right; cigar drawing well? Very good. Now then!" He settled himself for an exhaustive talk.

The old Indian officer had certainly not been dried up by the hot climate where he had spent the greater part of his life. He was a round, tubby, rosy-faced little man, all curves and gracious contentment. His face was clean-shaven and his head was bald, while his sharp grey eyes twinkled behind golden-rimmed pince-nez, balanced on an unimportant nose. With his round head and round body--sphere super imposed on sphere--and short legs, he looked like the figure of a Chinese mandarin, and nodded his head like one when he wished to emphasise a point. There was nothing military about him in any way, and Vernon wondered how so natty and neat an old gentleman ever came to have command of men appointed to hunt down Dacoits in the jungles of Burmah. Yet Dimsdale's official career had been a stirring one, and he had done good service in pacifying the country after the war. Now he had beaten his sword into a plough-share, and, with a considerable fortune, was spending his amiable old age under his own fig-tree. When Vernon looked at the rotund little man with the round rosy face, he saw before him a perfectly contented human being, and a very kind-hearted one to boot.

"Well, sir," he said, leaning back comfortably, "we're tiled in, as masons say, so I shall be glad to hear what you have to tell me. Also, I am obliged to you for seeking out this especial case for me."

"Two special cases, my boy, two special cases," said Mr. Dimsdale, wagging his head and looking more like a Chinese mandarin than ever. "One has to do with me--I'll tell you about it later; the other has to do with Mrs. Bedge and her adopted son."

"Maunders!" cried Vernon, astonished to find that his premonition was coming true. "You don't mean Constantine?"

"Yes, I do, Arthur; of course I do. Young Maunders. I never did like that boy somehow in spite of his good looks and polite manners. After all, he's half a Greek, and I don't like the Greeks either. They're nearly as tricky as the Armenians, and that's saying a lot. All the same, I'm sorry for the sake of Emily. I'm an old friend of Emily. Ha, ha! I was in love with her before she married Bedge. He was a Levantine merchant, you know, dealt in currants and cherry jam and all the rest of it. Not a bad chap, from what I remember of him, but far too old a husband for Emily----"

"Do you mean Mrs. Bedge?" asked Vernon, vainly endeavouring to stem the flow of the old man's speech.

"Of course I mean Mrs. Bedge. I call her Emily because--ha! ha!--I was in love with her. She was a handsome girl in those years, and a good one. Why, look how she adopted that rascal--I can't help thinking young Maunders a rascal, though he does want to marry Ida, which is not to be thought of. Yes, yes! Emily always was good. I don't believe a word of it, not a word." And Mr. Dimsdale, bringing his fist down on the table, glared at his companion through his pince-nez.

"You don't believe a word of what?" asked Vernon soothingly.

"I'm coming to that; I'm coming to that. Don't worry me and hurry me." Mr. Dimsdale rubbed his nose in a vexed manner. "Young Maunders, now. Eh, what? Have you seen young Maunders lately?"

"It's odd you should ask that," said Vernon slowly, "because I have just parted from him at the Athenian Club."

"Don't have anything to do with him, Arthur; he's a bad lot, a very bad lot indeed. Oh, it's nothing that he has done. I wouldn't say to anyone else what I am saying to you. But I can read character, and I have observed Master Constantine. He's so selfish that he would boil Emily for his own gratification, if it pleased him. And she would let herself be boiled, too; she's as silly over the scamp as he is selfish towards her. Why do you cultivate his society? Eh, what? It's wrong and stupid; yes, yes, stupid and wrong."

"I haven't seen so very much of him since we left Oxford," objected Arthur, "and certainly I don't cultivate him, as you put it, for I admire his character as little as you do."

"And on more tangible grounds, perhaps? Eh, what? Tell me."

"No; I have not much to go on. At school and at college, and when we were children together in Berkshire, I never wholly liked Constantine. He's too selfish and too unscrupulous, although he always keeps on the right side of the law. Still, if he could do anything for his own benefit against the law without being found out and made to pay the penalty, I believe he would have little hesitation in doing it."

"I daresay; no doubt you speak the exact truth from intuition. He's a snake that young man, a pretty, curly, insinuating snake; he's poison in a well-shaped and well-coloured bottle. Poor Emily! poor Emily! silly woman, but goodness itself. She's a Mrs. Lear with a thankless adopted child, sharper than a serpent's tooth. Bless her, and damn him for a rogue, though, bless me, I can't bring any actual charge against the young beast. Ha, no! but when one sees smoke, one guesses fire."

"Did you tell him that I was Nemo?" asked Vernon bluntly.

Dimsdale grew furiously red and furiously angry, so angry indeed that he rose to stamp about the room. "How the devil can you ask me such a question, and how dare you, if it comes to that? Am I an ass, an idiot, a babbler? I wouldn't tell Maunders that I had eaten my dinner, much less inform him of a secret which it is to your advantage to keep. Why do you ask? Hang you, for thinking me a traitor and a gossip."

"Forgive me," said Vernon with an apologetic air. "I am quite sure that you have preserved the secret of how I earn my money. But I know that Constantine haunts your house, and thought you might have let drop a casual hint, which he is clever enough, as we both know, to take advantage of. But the fact is he had found out about Nemo, and threatens unless I take him into partnership--he has given me a month to turn over the proposition--that he will make Society too hot to hold me."

"The young rascal, the young blackmailing scoundrel," cried Dimsdale, stamping again. "It's just what he would do. He haunts my house to make love to Ida, and I would rather see her dead than as his wife, especially now that I know what I am about to tell you."

"What is it?"

"Later on I shall explain. Meanwhile, don't beat about the bush, but tell me exactly what Maunders threatens."

Vernon detailed the conversation, and Dimsdale returned to his seat to hear the narrative. When it was ended he nodded with compressed lips. "Very clever on the part of Master Snake. He has you in his power right enough, since he is ready to betray you if you don't obey his commands. Well, then, I am going--to a certain extent--to put him in your power."

"What? Have you found out----"

"I have found out nothing," said Dimsdale testily. "Don't interrupt. Do you know of a blackmailer called The Spider?"

Vernon half rose and then sat down again with an effort at self-control. "I have come across his work on several occasions, and so has Scotland Yard. No one knows what he is or where he lives or anything about him. He gets his name from the fact that he always signs his blackmailing letters with the stamped representation of a spider."

"Go on," said Dimsdale, quite calmly for him, "tell me more."

"There is little to tell, sir. The Spider learns people's secrets somehow, and in a way which no one can discover. He then writes to this or that person and threatens unless a certain sum of money is paid to publish the secret by means of postcards sent to the private address and sometimes to the club of his victim. Of course, there is no combating this mode of procedure, so most people pay quietly, although some have kicked."

"Why isn't the reptile arrested when he comes for his money? Tell me that, sir. Tell me that."

"Sometimes the money is sent to a given address, and at other times The Spider, masked and cloaked, meets his victim personally. He is not arrested because he always tells his victim that if the police are brought into the question, and he is jailed, the especial secret will be published all the same to the world by a hidden accomplice by means of postcards. So you can see, Mr. Dimsdale, that if any person wishes his or her secret to be preserved they cannot risk an arrest. Still, I have been employed by one or two victims to learn the truth, and I have failed. I can't lay hands on The Spider, nor can any of the official detectives."

Mr. Dimsdale nodded. "He's a clever animal," said he grimly. "You have described his mode of procedure extremely well, my boy. It's just the way in which he is tormenting Emily."

"Mrs. Bedge. Is he blackmailing her?"

"Of course he is. Don't I tell you so?" said Dimsdale crossly. "She asked me to come and see her yesterday, and showed me three letters, with the figure of a spider at the foot of the writing. The reptile wants five thousand pounds, else he will send cards to her private address and to her friends stating that Constantine is her illegitimate son."

"What?" Vernon leaped from his chair aghast.

"Of course, it's an infernal lie," said Dimsdale warmly. "Emily is a good woman, even though she jilted me to marry a man old enough to be her father. She was true to him; I swear she was true to him, and simply adopted the son of his partner Maunders--his real name was Constantine Mavrocordato--because the boy's father and mother were dead."

"There is no grounds for this assertion on the part of The Spider?"

"Absolutely none. Confound it, sir, you know Emily," raged Dimsdale. "Can you know her and doubt for a moment but that this viper has made a most iniquitous accusation? She has the boy's certificate of birth, and can prove the truth, and moreover can call evidence on the part of friends who knew about the adoption when it took place. But you know that mud sticks, Arthur, however innocent a person may be. Emily simply can't stand up against this blackguard attempt. If she refuses to send the five thousand pounds to the address given within a fortnight, The Spider says he will send cards making his lying assertion to all her friends. Even if she rebutted it--as she can--there would always be shrugged shoulders and raised eyebrows and cold looks, and no-smoke-without-fire remarks."

"True!" Vernon looked thoughtfully at his cigar tip. "Plenty of innocent people do not care to face publicity on that account. Human nature is so prone to believe the worst, even in the face of the very plainest evidence. What does Mrs. Bedge propose to do?"

"She wanted to send the money, but I suggested that she should let me place the matter in your hands."

"Thank you. I'll do my best. But it's a difficult case, as The Spider is so hard to find."

"On this occasion I don't think he will be," said Dimsdale with grim humour, "since I propose to work with you."

"I don't understand----"

"Don't I speak plainly?" asked Dimsdale tartly. "I said there were two cases, didn't I? Answer me, sir; answer me?"

"Yes, but----"

"There is no but about the matter, Arthur. I shall make a full explanation after I have asked a simple question."

"And the question?"

"You see, don't you, how this information places Maunders, young beast, in your power?"

"No, I don't," answered Vernon very plainly and somewhat aggressively; "if you mean that I am to use my knowledge of his falsely being accused of illegitimacy as a threat to keep him from worrying me into a partnership."

"I don't mean that in the least," cried Dimsdale warmly. "Confound you, sir, would you make me out to be no better than this spider reptile. What I mean is that you can say to Maunders that you will receive him into partnership if he hunts down The Spider and clears the character of his adopted mother. Not that Emily's character requires clearing in my eyes, mind you. But we must consider the limitations of human nature, my boy, and place Emily, like Cæsar's wife, above suspicion. Now do you understand? Eh, what? Reply, sir."

Arthur nodded. "I understand. And if Maunders hunts down The Spider he will be worth engaging as a partner."

"No, I don't mean that. But you are setting him to achieve an impossibility, and unless he fulfils your wish he cannot hope to be a partner. In the meantime, you and I hunt down The Spider. Then when we have him jailed, Maunders, not having done what you asked of him, can't expect to become a partner."

"I think he will in any case?" said Vernon grimly.

"I think not, sir," said Dimsdale very distinctly. "Of course, Emily is all right, and this blackmailing accusation is a lie. All the same, Maunders, who is anxious to secure a position in Society and marry Ida--confound him, he never shall with my consent--will not wish the slightest breath of his being a possible natural child to get about."

"I should say nothing," said Vernon stiffly.

"Quite so. I never expected you would. But the mere probability of the business becoming known will make Maunders careful. He won't worry you again, as, judging you by his own iniquitous self, he will think you capable of betraying him. _Now_ can you see?"

"Yes. But Constantine knows that I would never speak."

"I daresay, because he thinks the bribe isn't enough. He believes as Peel did--or Walpole was it?--that every man has his price. He won't worry you, I tell you, if you give the merest hint to him of the matter. Not that you need to, for he will know about this blackmailing letter to-morrow."

Vernon recalled how Maunders had said that his aunt had detained him, and how he had suggested that she had something on her mind. "He doesn't know it at present, anyhow."

"No. Emily saw me before speaking to him. However, listen to the scheme I have in my mind to catch this Spider wretch. He is trying to blackmail me."

"Oh!" Vernon sat up and laughed. "How ridiculous. You of all men cannot be blackmailed, since your life is so open."

"No man's life is open," said Dimsdale drily; "and mine has its dark pages as everyone else's has. I have a secret; not a particularly bad one, it is true. Still, one that I should prefer to keep to myself."

"What is it?"

"I shan't tell you or any man," snapped the ex-police commissioner. "It is sufficient to say that it is not a very bad secret, and that even if it were told to the world it would matter little. However, The Spider--hang him, I think he must have some acquaintance with my life in the East--has learned something I thought no one but myself knew anything about. He asks one thousand pounds, which is moderate compared with his demand on Emily. Shows that he knows my secret isn't so very deadly, or it would be worth more."

"Did he write to you?" asked Vernon alertly. "Of course he did, making the usual threat of exposure by postcards to self and friends. Now I am going to consent to his demands."

"And pay the money?"

"I didn't say that," corrected Dimsdale sharply, "but I am writing asking him to meet me in my library, and receive the money; also for him to hand over any documents to me which even hint at my secret. When he comes, you can be concealed in the room and we'll take him in charge."

"But then your secret will become known," objected Vernon. "The Spider always provides against arrest by leaving the evidence in the hands of others to publish."

"He can publish what he likes about me," said Mr. Dimsdale coolly; "don't I tell you that the secret is of little value. The Spider in his letter to me embroidered upon actual fact, and can make things unpleasant; but I can prove the exact truth of what he states, and so can save my bacon. There may be a few cold shoulders, but I shan't care for that, especially when my own conscience is clear. Now, don't ask me to tell you my secret, for I shan't. It has nothing to do with you or anyone else. All you have to do is to come to-morrow or the next day to my house at Hampstead, and I'll sketch out the plan of campaign."

"What about Mrs. Bedge?"

"She has a fortnight to consider the payment. We shall catch the scoundrel before then--you understand. Eh, what? Good! Now I must be off to Julia's ball. Are you coming?--not asked! Of course; you love Lucy, and that will never do for Julia, who wants her to make a titled match. Good-night! Ha, ha! You have plenty to think about. Don't get brain fever. Good night!"

Then the oddly-assorted pair parted for the time being.

CHAPTER III.

HOW THE TRAP WAS SET.

As Martin Dimsdale had spent the greater part of his sixty years in Burmah, he naturally retained an affectionate remembrance of that most fantastic country. This he showed by calling his house "Rangoon;" and, as a further concession to what might almost be termed his native land, the house was built after the fashion, more or less accurate, of a bungalow. On arriving some ten years previously in England, Mr. Dimsdale had purchased an ancient Grange with its few remaining acres, situated on the verge of Hampstead Heath. In spite of the fact that the mansion was historic and famous, this Vandal pulled it down, amidst the protests and to the grief of various antiquarians. On the cleared ground he erected the rambling one-storey building which reminded him of the Far East. It was not an entirely Indian house, nor a wholly Burmese house, nor an absolutely English house, but a bastard mixture of all three, as the chilly northern climate had to be taken into consideration. But Dimsdale looked upon it as a genuine reconstruction of the bungalows to which he had been accustomed, and would hear no argument to the contrary. This was just as well for those who differed from his views, as he was a peppery little man, voluble in speech.

From the wide road, which flanked this corner of the Heath, the grounds were divided by a tall and thick-set laurel hedge, which must have taken years to attain its present stately beauty. At right angles to this, red-brick walls, old and mellow, ran back for a considerable distance to terminate in another hedge of mingled holly and oak saplings and sweetbriar and hawthorn. A gate in the centre of this gave admittance to a well-cultivated kitchen-garden of two acres. Beyond, and divided from the garden by a low stone wall, stretched the meadows, encircled by aggressive barbed-wire fences. The whole, consisting of eight acres, belonged to the man who had built the bungalow, and was a very desirable freehold for a well-to-do middle-class gentleman.

In the first square between the hedges and brick walls stood the house, looking quite dazzling in the sunshine by reason of its white-tiled walls and the raw hue of its red-tiled roof. Round three sides ran a deep verandah, and the fourth side--at the back--bordered the cobble-stone yard, at the sides of which were the stables and outhouses. Everything here was neat and trim and sweet-smelling, as Mr. Dimsdale would tolerate no litter, and was fidgety about the drainage. This was just as well, seeing that the stables were over-near the dwelling. Some judicious person had earlier pointed out to Mr. Dimsdale that it would be advisable to erect them beyond the kitchen-gardens and in the meadows, but the little man, out of sheer obstinacy, refused to entertain the idea, and built them cheek by jowl with the house.

On either side of the bungalow, trellis work covered with creepers shut off the yard from the front garden. This last, consisting of smooth lawns bordered by brilliantly coloured flowerbeds, stretched to a rustic-looking, white-painted gate set in the laurel hedge. To this, a broad walk, sanded to a deep yellow tint, ran from the shallow steps leading up to the front verandah. Two noble elms--the sole survivors of a once well-wooded park--sprang one on each side of the path, from the trim lawns.

The building itself looked most unsuitable to the chilly English climate, with its spotless walls and French windows. These, of which there were many, opened directly on to the verandah, which was paved warmly with red bricks, rectangular and thin. Each window was provided with green shutters, fastened back during the day and tightly closed every night at dusk. On entering the front door Mr. Dimsdale's visitors beheld a square hall, and the first object which struck the eye was a large gong, held shoulder high by two fierce-looking Burmese warriors carved in unpainted wood. Darkly blue Eastern draperies, glittering with tiny round looking-glasses, veiled the left door, which led into the library, and the right door, through which the dining-room was entered. Passing between curtains of similar texture and style, hanging straightly from the ceiling, the visitor came into a spacious room with a slippery polished floor and a high glass roof, which lighted the apartment, since, occupying the centre of the bungalow, there could be no side windows. Folding valves of carved sandalwood on either side gave entrance into two long narrow passages, broken by many bedroom doors. The bedrooms themselves looked on to the side verandahs through French windows, as has been described.

At the end of the middle apartment--which, like the Athenian Club antrium, was the general meeting place of those in the house, and served the purpose of a drawing-room--was another draped portal, admitting Mr. Dimsdale's male guests into a large billiard-room and a comfortable smoking-room; also his lady guests into a boudoir and a music-room. Beyond these, and shut off by another narrow passage at right angles to those at the sides, were the kitchen, the servants' quarters, and the domestic offices. As the stables, in the opinion of many people, were too near the house, the kitchen was too far distant from the dining-room. But Mr. Dimsdale, who was fond of delicate fare, prevented the cooling of the food in transit by having it brought to the table in hot-water dishes. He secretly acknowledged to himself that he was wrong as regards both stables and kitchen, but would never admit any oversight to his friends. As he had been his own architect, he believed "Rangoon" to be almost perfect in construction, design, beauty, and in its blending of Indian charm and English comfort. And in the main he was not far wrong.

The house was filled with quaint Eastern curios, and draperies and contrivances and furniture, although of this last there was comparatively little, since Mr. Dimsdale did not care to overcrowd his rooms, as is the English fashion; perhaps it was this sparseness which gave the house its foreign look. The library was furnished with tables and couches and chairs and bookcases of black teak, elaborately carved, while the central apartment contained nothing but bamboo chairs and tiny bamboo tables, all of which were covered with brightly-hued draperies. The dining-room was the most English-looking part of the house, as it was decorated and furnished in the Jacobean manner, and looked massively British. But the French windows--three in the front and three at the side--uncurtained and pronouncedly bare, admitted too great a glare into an apartment sacred to eating, which, for some traditional reason, is always supposed to have rather a twilight atmosphere. But Mr. Dimsdale loved plenty of light and fresh air and all the sunshine he could get, hence the many windows of the bungalow. It would have been easier to have removed the walls dividing the rooms from the verandah, and to have given them the full publicity of Eastern shops. And perhaps only the climate prevented Mr. Dimsdale from going this length. He was a fanatic in many ways, and had the full courage of his cranky convictions.

As a police commissioner, Mr. Dimsdale had been secretly in partnership with a Chinese merchant, who traded from Singapore to Yokohama, and from Canton to Thursday Island; that is, he supplied the capital and Quong Lee managed the investments. Thus the astute Englishman was enabled to return to England with an ample income, and proposed to spend the rest of his earthly life in enjoying it. The bungalow was his hobby, and he never grew weary of improving its beauties or of showing them to admiring friends. As he was a widower--Mrs. Dimsdale occupied a lonely grave in the Shan States--he had no one to coerce him into spending his money in any other way. It is true that Ida, his only child, was handsome and marriageable and light-hearted; but, having comparatively simple tastes, she did not yearn over-much for a fashionable life. Certainly she knew many in the great world, and sought society to some extent during the season, created by man; but, for the most part, she preferred the home-life of "Rangoon," which was assuredly lively enough and not wanting in interest even to the insatiable appetite of the young for pleasure. Her father, like many Anglo-Indians, had been accustomed, save when he had been stationed in lonely places, to much society, and was also gregarious by instinct. He invited Far East friends to sit at his hospitable board in the Jacobean dining-room, and made many new ones, who were ready enough to welcome an amusing, experienced old traveller for the sake of his society if not of his money. Dimsdale knew many people in the neighbourhood of Hampstead, and also a considerable number in the West End. His sister, Lady Corsoon, and her husband, Sir Julius, were his sponsors as regards this last locality. Besides, Mr. Dimsdale belonged to several clubs, took an interest in politics and the doings of the younger generation, which had matured during his exile, spent his money freely, and was always an amusing, chatty companion. With such qualifications it was no wonder that he possessed a large circle of friends, and was everywhere welcome. It must be admitted, however, that some frivolous people thought he was rather a bore, especially when he held forth about Rangoon.

Then there was Miss Hest--Frances Hest--who was so frequently staying in the bungalow, and was so sisterly with Ida that she might almost be regarded as another daughter of the jolly ex-police-commissioner. Her brother, Francis Hest, of Gerby Hall, Bowderstyke, Yorkshire, was a comparatively rich and superlatively far-descended north-country squire, who was quite a rural king in his own parochial way. But as his sister found the rustic life somewhat dull, she had come to London, after quarrelling with her brother, who did not approve of her leaving home. To force her to return he allowed her next to nothing to live on, and, not having a private income, she had earlier been in great straits. But being a clever girl of twenty-five, and gifted with the dramatic instinct, she had turned her talents to account very speedily. A retired actor with the odd name of Garrick Gail, who termed himself a professor, had polished her elocutionary powers, and she had obtained engagements to recite at various "At Homes." During the three years she had been in London, she had improved her chances so much that she made quite a good income. She was seen everywhere and knew everyone, and being a handsome, well-dressed girl of good family--no one could deny that--she made the most of her opportunities. Of course, Francis Hest resented her behaviour; but, always mindful that she was his sister, he extended a grudging hospitality to her for six months of the year, if she chose to accept it. Miss Hest did, but not in its entirety, and simply ran down to Gerby Hall when she felt inclined. She also had a flat in Westminster, but for the most part spent her days and nights at "Rangoon" in the company of Ida Dimsdale. The two girls, who had met by chance at a fashionable "At Home" two years previously, had struck up a sincere friendship, and saw as much of each other as possible.

Some few days after the conversation between Vernon and Dimsdale in Colonel Towton's chambers, the two girls were together on the verandah of the bungalow, busily engaged in sending out invitations for a ball. In honour of her birthday--she was now twenty-three--Ida had prevailed upon her father to allow her to give a masquerade in the central apartment. That was to be cleared for dancing--not that it needed much clearing, so sparsely was it furnished--and all those expected were told to wear masks and dominoes. At midnight all the guests were to unmask, and supper was to take place. Ida limited her guests to the number of one hundred, and, with the assistance of Miss Hest, she was weeding out undesirable people. With a bamboo table between them and a screen to keep off the hot sunshine--it was now the end of June and extremely sultry--the young ladies were too intent on their agreeable work to notice that a stranger was advancing up the yellow-sanded path. And yet, as the newcomer was Arthur Vernon, he could scarcely be called a stranger, seeing that he was a friend of the house and a weekly visitor.

On this special occasion he had called to resume with Mr. Dimsdale the conversation about The Spider, and, in his anxiety to complete the business--which included the setting of a trap for the blackmailer--would have passed by the girls in order to interview his old friend. But Frances, who seemed to have eyes at the back of her head--as Vernon had noticed on several occasions--drew Ida's attention to him at once. "Here is Mr. Vernon, dear," she said, pushing back her chair and straightening her tall, imperial form. "Let us ask him to suggest someone."

"Good-day, Miss Hest; good-day, Ida," said Vernon advancing easily, and looking very smart in his Bond Street kit. "Someone for what?"

Ida shook hands in her friendly, sisterly way and explained. "In a week we are giving a masked ball in honour of my birthday, and just now Frances and I are making out the invitations. Only a hundred people, Arthur, as the house won't hold any more comfortably. Here is the list--ninety-five names, as you see. So we thought----"

"That you might suggest a few other people," finished Miss Hest, leaning gracefully on the back of her chair. "We want gentlemen more than ladies."

"Isn't a week's notice rather a short one to give for an entertainment of this sort?" asked Vernon, running his eyes over the submitted list.

"Why should it be?" demanded Ida, opening her eyes. "There is no fancy dress to get ready, and I don't expect that everyone will be engaged on that particular night."

"It's the mid-season, you know, Ida."

Miss Hest nodded her approval. "I told Ida that. Everyone may be engaged."

"Well, I can't change the date of my birthday, dear, and I didn't think of a masked ball until yesterday. If we send out invitations for one hundred and fifty guests, that number will be sufficient. Everyone can't have other engagements on that especial night."

"I don't know so much about that," said Frances in her deep voice, which was of the contralto species. "People work desperately hard during the season."

Vernon laughed and handed back the list. "Who was it said that life would be endurable if it were not for its festivals?" he remarked, smiling. "I never see the weary faces of pleasure-seekers during the season but what I think of that saying."

"Well, never mind." Ida tapped her white teeth with the pencil she was using, and cast her eyes over the list of guests. "Can you suggest four gentlemen, Arthur?"

"There are two who would certainly come, and whose names you have unaccountably omitted."

Miss Hest raised her strongly marked eyebrows. "Why unaccountably?"

"I am thinking of Colonel Towton and Mr. Maunders."

"There," said Frances, turning gravely to her friend, "I told you everyone would notice that you had left them out."

"Am I supposed to be everyone?" asked Vernon, smiling again. "But why have you left Maunders and Towton out, may I ask? I thought they were such friends."

Ida sat down and coloured through her fair skin. "I wished to ask Conny Maunders, but my father won't hear of it. Why, I don't know."

Vernon reflected that he knew very well, since Dimsdale objected to Maunders paying undue attentions to his daughter. But he kept this knowledge to himself, and inquired about Colonel Towton. "Your father and he are such great friends."

"Of course," said Ida petulantly, "and as they've both been in the East and are both of an age, they should be friends."

"There's a difference between forty-five and sixty odd, dear," said Frances mildly.

"And between twenty-three and forty-five," retorted Miss Dimsdale, whose cheeks were growing even more scarlet. "And Colonel Towton is such a nuisance. He's always--don't laugh, Arthur."

"I beg your pardon, but I guessed what you were about to say," said Vernon with mock gravity. "But why do you object to Colonel Towton, who does not look more than thirty and who is a distinguished soldier, to say nothing of his being well-off and handsome."

"I don't know that he is so very well off," retorted Ida, defending herself; "he has only that old place in Yorkshire."

"I know," nodded Frances wisely, "it's a Grange at Bowderstyke, three miles from my brother's place. Colonel Towton is of a very old family, and I know for a fact that he has at least one thousand a year. You might do worse, Ida."

"I don't wish to marry money," said Ida in vexed tones; "and I don't love Colonel Towton, who is old enough to be my father."

"He is worth a dozen of Maunders," put in Vernon pointedly.

Ida stamped. "You take the privilege of our friendship to be rude and presuming," she said angrily. "My private affairs have nothing to do with you."

"Ida! Ida!" reproved Miss Hest, "don't----"

"I will," said the young lady crossly; "and I shan't ask Colonel Towton to the ball, when father won't let me ask Conny."

"You call him that?" asked Arthur, with a shrug. Ida looked at him indignantly, evidently with a conscience ill at ease. "I shall never speak to you again," she said in an offended tone.

"Not if I get your father to let Maunders come to the ball?"

"Oh, can you; can you?" she asked, in a girlish, delighted tone on this occasion. "I wish you would. Father likes you so much. And you can tell him," she added handsomely, "that if he will let me ask Conny I shall invite Colonel Towton. There--that's fair."

"You are playing with fire," warned Frances gravely. "Better not invite Mr. Maunders. You can never marry him."

"It's indelicate to speak of my marriage in the presence of a stranger," said Ida with some heat.

"I am not a stranger, I hope," remarked Vernon quickly.

"Yes, you are, when you are horrid," and with a rosy face of sheer annoyance she flitted to the end of the verandah. Ida was rather like Titania, being sylph-like, golden-haired, and blue-eyed, whereas Miss Hest resembled Judith with her strongly-marked handsome face and black eyebrows.

"Who is horrid?" asked a voice at this juncture, and Mr. Dimsdale appeared on the threshold of the French window, which was behind the table. "Ah, Arthur, is that you? I have been expecting to see you. Come into the library."

Vernon obeyed at once, as Frances had hurried after the petulant girl to pacify her. Miss Hest treated Ida as a wilful child, and by scolding and coaxing and cajoling managed to get her to behave like a reasonable being. It must be confessed that Dimsdale had spoiled his golden-haired darling, and even the boarding-school she had attended could not supply the place of the mother, who was dead. The old man turned to Vernon when they entered the drawing-room through the French window. "Who is horrid?" he asked again.

Vernon laughed and slipped into a chair. "It's a storm in a tea-cup," he explained easily, and accepting a cigar. "Miss Hest advised Ida to give up Maunders, and I supported her. Then Ida----"

"I know, I know," broke in Dimsdale sadly. "She is wilful and is quite infatuated with the scamp. Arthur, Arthur, I should have married again, so that Ida could be trained by a good woman. I can't manage her."

"I think Miss Hest can," said Vernon significantly; "and she has sense enough for two. A most masculine young person. But do you think you are wise forbidding Maunders to come to this masked ball?"

"Yes, I do. Ida is crazy about him."

"Opposition will only make her more crazy," warned Vernon, shaking his sleek head. "It would be better to let them come together, and then she would get sick of him. Maunders is so shallow that she would find him out sooner or later, for Ida has plenty of common sense if it was not obscured by this persistent frivolity, which, after all, is only a youthful fault."

"But if Maunders wants to marry her----"

"He doesn't, Mr. Dimsdale. I can vouch for that. He wants to marry your niece."

"What!" Dimsdale, who was lighting a cigar, wheeled round with an astonished air. "Why, I thought you loved Lucy?"

"So I do," replied Vernon earnestly, "and she loves me. But Maunders is a fascinating fellow and a dangerous, unscrupulous rival."

"I quite believe it. Eh, what? The fellow's a scoundrel," grunted Mr. Dimsdale crossly. "He should be tarred and feathered. Still, if things are as you say, I don't mind Ida asking him to the ball. But she must ask Towton also," he added with sudden determination.

"She will do so, although she dreads his love-making. However, she may grow sick of Maunders when she finds he is running after Lucy Corsoon, and Towton may catch her heart in the recoil."

"Hope so; hope so," muttered Dimsdale, turning his cigar in his lips. "I want to see my little girl safely married to Towton, who is as good a fellow as ever breathed."

"But not a young fellow. However, it is wiser to let events take their course for the present, Mr. Dimsdale. Opposition, as I say, will only make Ida more wilful, since she is filled with romance natural at her age."

"Ouf," breathed the old man, wiping his brow with a bandanna handkerchief. "What a handful women are! But there," he dismissed the subject with a wave of his hand, "let us leave these trivialities and talk business. Have you heard anything more about The Spider?"

"Well, I made enquiries at Scotland Yard, and find that he is very much wanted by the police."

Mr. Dimsdale grunted. "Humph! The police are always wanting and never getting."

"The Spider is too clever for them," protested Vernon anxiously. "He won't be too clever for me," said the elder man with sudden ferocity, and slapping his hand on the table. "Eh, what? Am I to be blackmailed by an infernal scoundrel who swears that he will tell a parcel of lies if I don't pay him one thousand pounds. Hang him."

"If it is merely lies, why pay?" asked Vernon drily.

"There is a grain of truth in the lies," admitted Dimsdale crossly. "The absolute truth I can face, but the lies make me out to be a very queer person indeed. I shall tell you all when we secure this man."

Vernon looked up astonished. "How do you propose to secure him? If you arrest him, his accomplice will spread the lies you talk of, by postcard amongst your acquaintances, as is usually the case in The Spider's business."

"I'll risk that, sir; I'll risk that," said Dimsdale with a defiant air; "but I'm hanged if he'll get a penny out of me. I shall set the trap, and you will be in this room behind a screen to rush out and seize him when I give the signal. Understand? Eh, what? Understand? Come, come! Speak up."

"What sort of trap do you propose to lay?" asked Arthur cautiously.

"Well," Dimsdale leaned back, twisting his half-smoked cigar between his fingers. "It was the masked ball--this silly form of entertainment, which Ida insists upon having for her birthday--which gave me the idea. You see, with the chance of being masked and mingling amongst my guests, The Spider will be the more ready to come, and will suspect nothing. I am writing to him to-morrow, telling him about this ball, and am suggesting that he should come wearing a mask to enjoy it. Then, at eleven o'clock, say, he can secretly meet me in this room to receive the money."

"Cash?" echoed Vernon significantly. "Of course. The fellow's too clever to risk cheques. They would put the police on his track; would put the police on his track, my boy."

"But do you intend to pay the money?"

"No, no, no, no! How stupid you are, Arthur. Use your brains, use your brains, boy. I shall offer to pay the money, and then you, concealed behind the screen--that Japanese one up in the corner--can rush out and----"

"But I have no authority to arrest him," interrupted Vernon impatiently. "Why not post a policeman, or a plain-clothes detective, to catch the beast?"

"I don't want any policeman in my house," retorted Dimsdale gruffly; "and you are detective enough for me. If he blackmails me, you will be the witness, and we will have every right to hold him. Then you can take him away and hand him over to the Hampstead police."

"He may show fight."

"Then have a revolver with you," snapped the old man. "I don't want a scandal and a row on Ida's birthday, and in my house."

"It seems to me that you are going the best way to have one," said Vernon deliberately; "much better let me inform the police and have the thing done in an orderly fashion."

"No, I tell you." Dimsdale again slapped the table. "I'll do it my own way or not at all. If I catch the beast by laying this trap, both myself and Mrs. Bedge and many other people will be safe. But if we call in the police, however secretly, The Spider--who seems to have ears and eyes all over him--will get wind of the ambush."

Vernon nodded. "There's something in that," he assented. "Perhaps on those grounds it will be better that we should engineer the job together. Well," he stood up straight and slim, "I shall come here on the night of the ball--by the way, when does it take place?"

"Monday week. It's a short notice, but Ida only thought yesterday of this way to celebrate her birthday."

"Are you quite sure," asked Vernon, taking up his tall hat, "that it is advisable to lay this trap on the night of the ball?"

"Yes, I do; yes, I do," said Dimsdale in a fussy manner. "The mere idea of masks, which will enable the scoundrel to hide his infernal face without comment, will recommend itself to him. He will think that he is exceptionally safe, not dreaming that I intend to fight."

"You will fight, then?"

"Am I not laying a trap into which he will walk?" inquired Dimsdale with much exasperation. "Of course I fight, as my secret is not such a very bad one. I can defend myself, and I am willing to risk that being known which I had rather were kept silent, for the sake of saving other people from being blackmailed by the beast. Eh, what? Am I not right?"

"Yes, I think you are. But I wish you would tell me your secret."

"After we have captured this scamp I shall do so, and then I shall tell you the absolute truth together with his embroideries. Don't look so grave, boy. I haven't committed a murder or stolen from the till."

"I never thought of such a thing," said Vernon hastily, "but----"

Dimsdale good-humouredly pushed him towards the window. "I know your doubts, my boy, but later I can satisfy them. Meanwhile let us settle that I am a scoundrel, and look on this trap as one set by a thief to catch a thief. By the way, does Maunders know of the threat made by The Spider against his mother. She intended to tell him, you know."

"I am not aware, sir. Maunders has not been near me since that night at the Athenian Club--the same night when I met you at Towton's rooms. Well, I shall come to the ball. Meantime, let me know----"

"I'll advise you if I hear from The Spider. There, get out. Good-bye, unless you'll have a cup of tea or a glass of wine."

Vernon declined and departed. The girls were no longer on the verandah or even in the garden.

CHAPTER IV.

WHO WAS CAUGHT IN THE TRAP.

Vernon had his doubts as to the success of Mr. Dimsdale's scheme. The Spider, as the authorities very well knew, was a wary individual, and in all dealings with his victims had been careful to provide for his own safety. He certainly met them at duly-appointed places, disguised as an old woman or a young man, as a navvy or as a foreigner; but none of those he intimidated dared to call in the police. The reason was that The Spider invariably advised them beforehand by letter that his accomplice held the evidence of the secrets for which they were being blackmailed, and that any proceedings being taken would result in the publication of these by cards being sent to their friends and relatives and acquaintances. It therefore can easily be guessed that no one had the courage to lay the rogue by the heels.

But, as it appeared, The Spider had, in Mr. Dimsdale, stumbled on a man who was not averse to his secret being known. Vernon wondered what the ex-police-commissioner had done that he should have one at all, and looked forward eagerly to being told. Dimsdale was such a very respectable old gentleman, and so very open in his speech and actions and entire life, that it seemed incredible he should conceal anything. However, as The Spider had learned in some extraordinary way, he did possess some secret, and therefore was being threatened. It was lucky for Dimsdale in particular and the public at large that he cared so little for the revelation of whatever shady doings he had been concerned in, since by trapping The Spider an end would be put to the dangerous career of this social pest. Whatever Mr. Dimsdale's secret might be, he well deserved to be forgiven for the service which he was rendering to everyone.

But it was questionable, in Vernon's opinion, if The Spider would meet his victim in a house filled with company, where there was every chance of a hue and cry being raised. Certainly the scamp, well protected by mask and domino, would be able to mingle with the company unobserved. Even if unmasked, he could not be discovered, other than as an uninvited guest, since no one knew his actual appearance. And then he might choose to come as a cabman or a chauffeur or as a waiter at the supper. Of course, if he kept the appointment in the library his identity would be proved beyond all doubt when he made his blackmailing demand. This, The Spider, although confident, for the usual reason, of the silence of Dimsdale, might not choose to risk, since many people being in the bungalow, he might be overheard. Vernon looked at the whole affair as a somewhat forlorn hope, until he, three or four days later, received a letter from Mr. Dimsdale.

The old gentleman wrote that The Spider had agreed to meet him in the library at "Rangoon" at eleven o'clock in the evening, and requested he, Vernon, to enter the room earlier, so that he could be concealed behind the screen. "I have not," Mr. Dimsdale went on to say, "advised the police, as it is unnecessary for us to talk until we have trapped our bird. But once he is in your grip he will see the folly of resistance, and will probably agree to walk quietly to the Hampstead Police Station. Failing that, we can shout for assistance, of which, it is obvious, there will be plenty to hand. But, you will understand that I wish to effect the capture as quietly as possible, so as not to alarm my guests."

In the latter part of his letter Dimsdale stated that Maunders had been calling at the bungalow during his--the writer's--last interview with Vernon. He was, in fact, round the corner of the house, nearest to the library when Vernon stepped out of the French window. Dimsdale had found him there on the verandah in the company of the girls, and had promptly told him that he was not wanted, in his usual peppery way. There had been a row, as Maunders had been grossly insolent, but Miss Hest--a very capable girl, as Mr. Dimsdale wrote--had induced him to depart. Confirmation of this report was received by Vernon from Maunders himself, when the two met by chance in Piccadilly.

"The old man was most insolent," complained Maunders indignantly; "There is no crime in loving Ida, so far as I can see."

"Since you love Miss Corsoon, and only run after Ida for her money, I think Mr. Dimsdale has every reason to forbid you the house," said Vernon drily.

"Oh, rot. I know what I'm about. As to forbidding me the house, I received an invitation to the masked ball on Monday, and I'm going."

"Ida only extorted permission from her father to ask you. If you're a gentleman you will not go to be received on sufferance."

Maunders chuckled coolly. "Ida won't receive me in that way," said he with superb insolence, "as she really loves me, and the old gentleman doesn't matter. I love Lucy, but she has no money, so I expect I shall have to sacrifice myself by marrying Ida."

"If Mr. Dimsdale will allow you," chafed Vernon.

"Oh, he won't; but Ida can defy him."

"If she does she will lose her fortune."

"That remains to be seen," said Maunders airily. "Hang old Dimsdale, what objection can he have to me?"

"Your aunt might tell you," said Vernon significantly. The blood rushed to Maunders' cheek, and he looked searchingly at his friend, but not agreeably. "What do you mean?"

"I mean that I can only consent to take you into partnership if you succeed in capturing The Spider," said Vernon slowly and somewhat evasively.

"Who is The Spider?"

"I think you know, if not from the newspapers, then from Mrs. Bedge."

Maunders looked at the ground. "So old Dimsdale told you?"

"Yes. He wished to enlist my services on behalf of your aunt to capture this blackmailing beast."

"Oh; and do you intend to?"

"No. I intend to leave the capture to you."

Maunders opened his eyes. "But, my dear chap, I know nothing about The Spider, as you call this man, to say nothing of detective business."

"Yet you wish to become Nemo's partner," said Vernon, very drily. "See here, Maunders, it's no use beating about the bush. I shan't take you as my partner unless you catch this man and so prove your capability."

"And suppose I tell everyone who Nemo is?" asked Maunders with an ugly look.

"You can do so if you like," rejoined Vernon coolly, "for then there will be no Nemo. I shall simply leave England and seek my fortune in Africa. And, after all, I don't see why you should refuse this test. It's to your own advantage that he should be caught, unless you want your aunt to pay five thousand pounds."

"Bosh! What The Spider says is a lie."

"I daresay; but it won't be pleasant for Mrs. Bedge to know that her friends receive cards stating you are her natural son."

"It's an infernal lie," raged Maunders, the blood flushing his cheek and making him look handsomer than ever. "I am not a bit like my aunt in any way. It is true that her sister was my mother, but I take after my father."

"Constantine Mavrocordato!"

"Dimsdale told you that; he seems to have imparted a lot of my private affairs to you," observed Maunders acidly.

"They are quite safe with me as Nemo. I don't use my private discoveries to blackmail people."

"Do you believe this lie of The Spider's?"

"No, I don't, for one moment. Mrs. Bedge is a good, kind woman, far too good for you, Maunders. She has brought you up and educated you, and allows you money, and altogether has behaved like a trump. For her sake, if not for the sake of becoming my partner in a paying business, you ought to hunt out this brute who asperses her fair fame."

The other man stared again at his neat boots. "I'm not such a rotter as you think, Vernon," he said, in a voice filled with feeling; "and, of course, I appreciate my aunt's kindness. We'll let the partnership business stand over for the present. I give you my word that I shan't tell a soul you are Nemo. Also, I'll go to work on my own, and see if I can't catch The Spider. He's not going to get five thousand pounds of my money if I can help it."

"Your aunt's money," corrected Vernon gently. "It will be mine some day," said Maunders with a shrug; "but you can see that I have some conscience, badly though you think of me."

"I don't think so very badly of you," replied Vernon hurriedly and somewhat untruthfully, "you have your good points, Constantine, but you are so given over to pleasure that you stop at nothing to gratify it."

"I stop on the right side of the law, however," retorted Maunders, again becoming his callous self, after the momentary softening. "There will be no chance of Nemo catching me. Well, good-day. I'll do what I say, and perhaps when I meet you at the ball, I'll have something to tell you."

"You intend to go, then, in spite of Dimsdale's behaviour?"

"Yes, I do," said Maunders doggedly; "and I intend to marry Ida with her thousands a year. So now you know." And he walked off abruptly, leaving Vernon to congratulate himself that he no longer had a dangerous rival in the affections of Lucy Corsoon.

"Though I don't believe old Dimsdale will consent to the marriage with Ida," thought Vernon, as he resumed his interrupted walk.

During the few days that still remained until the night of the masked ball, Vernon saw nothing of Maunders or of Martin Dimsdale. But on the Monday morning, when having luncheon in the triclinium of the Athenian Club, Colonel Towton made his appearance. He glanced round the room, and catching sight of Vernon, walked up to his table.

"'Day," he said in his sharp, military way. "I'll join you here, if you have no objections."

"Delighted, Colonel," replied Vernon, and passed along the menu. He wondered why Towton was making such a palpable advance towards friendship, for, as a rule, he was somewhat stiff, with a reserved manner, after the way of army men.

The Colonel seemed to be in no hurry to explain, but fixed his eyeglass to examine the card, and order his luncheon. He was a tall, slim, dry-looking man, perfectly groomed and perfectly dressed and perfectly master of himself. In spite of his forty-five years, his close-cropped hair and smartly-twisted moustache were without a grey hair. Dark and knightly-looking, with alert eyes of Irish blue, he looked as juvenile as any of his subalterns. He was one of those men who ripen young, so to speak, and who remain in that condition for the rest of their lives. Towton was an admirable soldier, with several letters after his name, and it was a pity---as everyone said--that he had retired so early from the army. He should certainly have remained in order to attain to the rank of a general. But it was generally known that family reasons connected with the inheritance of a Yorkshire estate had necessitated the Colonel sending in his papers. Outside his profession he was not talented, but had a considerable fund of common sense, which is a rarer commodity than people imagine.

"I want to have a private talk with you, Vernon," said the Colonel, after he had selected his dish. "Luckily there's no one within earshot." He glanced round the room to note that he and his companion were isolated in a secluded corner. "You don't mind my having a private talk, do you?" he jerked, staring through his eyeglass and twisting his moustache.

"I am at your service," said Vernon, wondering what was coming.

"I am going to be rather personal, both as regards your affairs and my own," went on Towton very directly and honestly. "Rather odd in a man who is a mere acquaintance, eh?"

"Not at all," said Vernon politely; "I can only repeat that I am at your service, Colonel."

"Fact is, I wouldn't say a word, but that I know you're a good sort; plenty of chaps say that. And again," Towton unfolded his napkin rather nervously, for him, "you are a great friend of the Dimsdales."

"Yes, I am," acknowledged Vernon, guessing somewhat of the business which had brought the Colonel to his table.

"And a friend of young Maunders."

"We were at school together."

"And a friend of the Corsoons," pursued Towton, distinctly ill at ease, as if he felt that he was taking a liberty.

"See here, Colonel," remarked his companion straightly; "I guess what you are driving at from your coupling of those names. May I speak out?"

"Yes." Towton nodded away the waiter who had brought his soup.

"You are in love with Miss Dimsdale, and Maunders is paying her attentions."

"Quite so. May I add, on my part, that you are in love with Miss Corsoon, and that the same gentleman is your rival?"

Vernon nodded and pushed away his empty plate. "I think we have cleared the ground for action," he said significantly.

"I am obliged to you for your candour," said Towton courteously; "and I knew from your reputation that you would meet me half-way. It is not easy for an elderly man, such as I am, to speak of his love for a young girl. But as I am devoted to her, and you are devoted to Miss Corsoon, it seemed to me that we might join forces against that handsome young scamp, who is playing fast and loose with the affections of both the girls. On this ground, I ventured to take the liberty of speaking to you on so private a subject."

"I am very glad that you did so, Colonel. Our united actions may be of great service to the ladies in question. Maunders----" He hesitated generously.

"I know," interrupted Towton abruptly, "that young gentleman's reputation is as bad as yours is good. Even if I did not love Miss Dimsdale, I should feel justified in doing my best to save her from that scamp. You can tell him that I said so, if you like."

"What? Give our plans away to our common enemy," said Vernon jokingly. "That would scarcely be wise. Maunders is as clever as the devil."

"And as unscrupulous. But let us be frank. Which of these girls does he love, in your opinion?"

"What love he can spare from himself he gives to Miss Corsoon; but he is after Miss Dimsdale's fortune."

"I thought so. She is infatuated with him, worse luck. And Miss Corsoon?"

"She and I understand one another," said Vernon with some reserve. "I am not afraid of Maunders in that quarter, although he has good looks and a great charm of manner. We are talking of very delicate matters, Colonel."

"I know we are; I know we are." Towton flicked his napkin irritably. "Ladies' names shouldn't be mentioned between gentlemen. I am rather a Turk in that respect; but as this young gentleman will make both of them miserable, and is a thorn in your flesh as in mine, we must between ourselves put delicacy on one side. What do you propose to do?"

"I don't know," said Vernon, crumbling his bread dismally. "Lady Corsoon certainly will not let her daughter marry a poor man such as I am. What are your plans, Colonel?"

"I don't know," repeated Towton, equally dismally. "Miss Dimsdale is crazy about Maunders, and will not cast a glance at me. The father is on my side, however, so I have some chance."

"You may take it as certain," said Vernon with decision, "that Dimsdale will never consent to his daughter becoming Mrs. Maunders."

"She may defy him."

"There is that possibility, certainly."

"Hang him," muttered Towton, referring to Maunders. "Why can't he marry Miss Hest and have done with it."

"Miss Hest has neither the money nor the looks to attract such a gay spark."

"Oh, come now, she's a handsome girl."

"Not in Maunders' way. He likes a weak woman, whom he can bully; and Miss Hest is much too firm and managing a wife for him to risk. By the way, are you going to the ball to-night?"

"Yes." Towton's face lighted up with ridiculous pleasure. "It may give me a chance to----"

"No, don't propose, Colonel. You will only be refused. Take my advice, and wait for a week or so. Maunders may be out of your way by that time!"

"What do you mean, exactly?"

"I am not at liberty to say. But I advise you to wait." Towton played with his bread and cheese. "All right," he said at length. "I place myself in your hands, although I am hanged if I can see what you mean."

"Well," confessed Vernon, rising, "to tell you the truth, I am not very sure myself what I do mean. But I have a kind of instinct that if both of us play a waiting game, Maunders will get the cold shoulder."

"From Ida--I mean from Miss Dimsdale?"

"Yes, and from Miss Corsoon. Come into the pinacotheca and smoke."

The two conspirators went there and discussed the matter further. As Vernon had confessed, he had no clear idea in his mind as to why he advised the Colonel to wait. But, in some vague way, he fancied that this business of The Spider might occupy Maunders' time and prevent his paying his usual attentions to Lucy and Ida. In that case both the girls would probably feel offended. Then Vernon intended to bring them together in some as yet unthought-of way, so that they might mutually discover how Maunders was courting both of them indiscriminately. Lucy, of course, in any case would have nothing to do with the young man; but Ida's pride, taking fire, might induce her, on making this discovery, to listen to the Colonel's wooing. Everything in Vernon's brain was vague and undecided, but he faintly felt that if events happened in some such way Maunders might be eliminated as a stumbling block. All these possibilities, however, being still in the clouds, he did not reveal them to Towton. The conversation in the pinacotheca resolved itself into the two men consoling one another regarding their doubtful love affairs. Arranging to meet at the masked ball, they parted on more than friendly terms and with quite a feeling of intimacy. This was natural, considering what they had been discussing.

But the proposed meeting at "Rangoon" never came off. The unexpected happened, as Vernon might have guessed it would. But, with all his experience of life, he was never so much astonished as when a telegram was handed in at his rooms with the name of Lucy Corsoon attached. "Come to No. 34, Waller Street, West Kensington," ran the wire, "at nine o'clock. Trouble with M.----L. Corsoon."

"Now what the deuce does this mean?" Vernon asked himself.

Undoubtedly the letter "M." referred to Maunders, since there was no one else with that initial to cause trouble. But what the trouble might be, or why carefully-guarded Lucy Corsoon should be in West Kensington it was hard to say. Lady Corsoon rarely let her daughter out of her sight, and on this night both were due at "Rangoon" to enjoy the masked ball. But, as Vernon rapidly reflected, there could be only one reply to so urgent a wire, and that was to stand on the doorstep of No. 34, Waller Street, West Kensington, at the appointed hour. He glanced at his watch. It was after eight, so he had only time to drive from Bloomsbury to his destination. Vernon, for obvious reasons connected with his income, lived in old-fashioned rooms in that middle-class district, and was more comfortable than if he had lived in Mayfair, both as regards space and rent.

His domino and mask were lying on a chair, ready to be slipped into a brown leather bag. He had intended to drive in a taxi to Hampstead, because of the bag, as it was too much trouble to carry it by train, since in that case his journey would be broken. As he was thinking what was best to be done, the landlady's husband, who acted as his valet, came with the information that the cab was at the door. Vernon made up his mind at once to act the part of a knight-errant, in spite of being due at the ball, and, without troubling about the domino and mask, put on his overcoat. Unless something serious was wrong--and the telegram gave little information--he could return, get the bag and drive on to the ball. But if Lucy was in dire trouble he would not go at all to "Rangoon." Mr. Dimsdale would have to manage with The Spider as best he could. Always provided that that astute individual walked into the trap, which was doubtful.

All the way to West Kensington Vernon puzzled his brains as to what could be the matter, and why Lucy Corsoon should be in a West Kensington house. Ridiculous as it seemed, he entertained the idea that she might have been kidnapped by Maunders, and had contrived to send the wire to the lover upon whom she could rely. But then Maunders--as he had said--always kept on the right side of the law, and kidnapping was an indictable offence. But if he had acted thus rashly, as Vernon reflected with a thrill, he was simply playing into his rival's hands. "If I rescue Lucy, Lady Corsoon will certainly let me marry her out of gratitude," thought the young man.

However, the whole affair was so mysterious that until he saw Lucy there was little chance of a reasonable explanation. He therefore possessed his soul in patience until he arrived in Waller Street. Here he sprang out, and telling the cabman to wait, ran up the steps of a semi-detached house of the suburban villa residence style. The night was brilliant with moonlight, so he easily saw the number on the glass over the door, and also the long, dull street of similar houses. It was some minutes before the appointed time, but that mattered very little. There seemed to be no light in the house, and Vernon wondered more than ever why Lucy should be in so unusual a locality.

Shortly the sound of light footsteps was heard, and a light appeared, against which the numerals on the glass above the door stood out black and distinct. Then the door itself was opened cautiously, and the white face of a woman looked out. "Is Miss Corsoon here?" asked Vernon abruptly.

"Are you Mr. Vernon?" questioned the woman in a frightened whisper. "Yes. I received a wire from----"

"Come in, come in," breathed the woman, and held the door open sufficiently for Vernon to slip in. "I am so glad you've come," she went on, still below her breath, and apparently much afraid. "It's as much as my life's worth to admit you. But the poor young lady----"

"Is she here?"

"Yes. They've got her in the cellar below. Only because she cried so much did I dare to send that telegram to you, and----"

"What the devil does it all mean?" demanded Vernon fiercely and gruffly.

"Hush, hush! Don't raise your voice. Follow me on tip-toe. They will hear."

"Who are they?" asked Vernon softly, and obeying.

But all the woman said was "Hush, hush!" So, wondering at this strange adventure, which seemed genuine enough, the young man went after the woman down some wooden stairs which led from the hall to the basement. As he followed he saw by the light of the candle which his guide carried that the hall was dusty and unfurnished. She led him along a dark passage and opened an end door with an air of mystery. "The young lady there," she said softly, and handing him the light. "Take the candle, and for heaven's sake don't say that I betrayed them."

"Them? Who?" asked Vernon imperatively.

She clutched his arm. "They'll hear you," she whispered, pointing upward, and pushed him towards the open door. "She's drugged--in there."

Vernon uttered a loud ejaculation, which made his guide shiver, and stepped into the dark room, holding the candle above his head. The next moment the door closed quickly behind him. He turned sharply, but already the key had clicked crisply in the lock. He was a prisoner. "And it's a plant; a plant," cried Vernon in a cold fury. "I'm trapped."

He certainly was, for there was no sign of the girl who had been supposed to send the telegram. All the terror and whispering of the woman had been a comedy to inveigle him into his prison. The place was a small kitchen, dusty and forlorn and unfurnished. There were no plates on the rack or on the shelves of the open cupboard, and no fire in the rusty grate. The room had not been occupied for many a long day, as the roof and corners were thick with dust and cobwebs. An iron-barred window glimmered straight before Vernon, and there was a small door near it. Through this he went, to find himself in a tiny scullery also lighted dimly by an iron-barred window. The door through which he had entered was fast locked, and he had no means of opening it. There was no doubt that he was a prisoner, decoyed to this lonely, unfurnished house by means of the false telegram.

"What the deuce does it all mean?" Vernon asked himself, and sat down on the dusty floor to think out his position. To save his dress clothes he made a cushion of his light overcoat, and sat on it, hugging his knees, with the candle beside him. The position was dismal enough, and decidedly mysterious, as he confessed. "What does it mean?" he repeated mentally.

The next instant the obvious answer flashed into his mind. "The Spider," cried Vernon, leaping to his feet and addressing the bare walls. "Yes, this must be The Spider's trickery."

And the more he thought of it the more certain he felt that he had, at the first blow, hit the right nail on the head. In some way The Spider had learned of the arranged trap, and had sent the wire purporting to come from Lucy Corsoon as a decoy. It had proved only too successful, and now here he was safely locked up in an underground room with no chance of escape, while Mr. Dimsdale, at "Rangoon," was left to face the ingenious scoundrel alone. "But that's all right," Vernon soliloquised, as he sat down again. "If I am not on the spot other people are, and when The Spider makes his demand, Mr. Dimsdale will probably raise the alarm. The Spider is not so clever as I thought."

This was poor comfort. The Spider, at all events, had been clever enough to ensnare a private detective who prided himself on his astuteness. One trap had been set by Mr. Dimsdale, and here was another set by The Spider, out of which it was impossible to escape. The bars of the windows were too strong to twist, the door was too stout to break down, so there was nothing for it but to wait. It was impossible that he could be kept in his dungeon for ever, and sooner or later he would be released. Besides, someone would have to bring him food, and if it was the white-faced woman who had so cleverly led him into the trap, Vernon promised himself grimly that he would seize her at the first opportunity and make her aid his escape. Finally, the taxi was still at the door, and the driver might become sufficiently alarmed if his fare did not reappear to speak to the nearest policeman. It was ridiculous that a man should be captured in guarded London in such a way. Vernon was angry with himself for having been tricked. But until the abrupt closing of the door he had never suspected that anything was wrong.

Meanwhile, he guessed that The Spider, having got him out of the way, was keeping his appointment with Dimsdale in the library. It was not probable that the blackmailing would succeed, as Dimsdale was quick-tempered, and as likely as not would simply seize the creature when he demanded his money, shouting meanwhile for assistance. Vernon wished that he was at his appointed post behind the screen; but he comforted with the reflection that Dimsdale would be able to deal with the matter unassisted. So far as he was concerned, being helpless, he could do nothing but wait.

For the next hour or so--he did not pay much attention to the time--Vernon wondered how The Spider came to know of Dimsdale's trap, and how he had so cleverly laid his own. The blackmailer seemed to know everybody's business, as his profession required, so in some way he had managed to learn of Vernon's love for Miss Corsoon. Only such a message from such a girl would have lured the lover into such a predicament, and The Spider had not only been clever enough to know this, but had been clever enough to utilize his knowledge. For the moment--it was a wild thought, and passed in a flash--Vernon wondered if Constantine Maunders had anything to do with the matter. But the idea was ridiculous, since The Spider was attempting to blackmail Mrs. Bedge, which Maunders certainly would not countenance. But if not Maunders, who could it be? Certainly Dimsdale might have talked to someone else about the proposed trap, since he was extremely frank and injudicious in his speech. Vernon resolved to question him on this point when next they met, and hoped from his reply to learn who had lured him to No. 34, Waller Street, West Kensington. Having arrived at this conclusion, he rested his head on the overcoat and tried to sleep, since it was foolish to waste his strength in beating his wings against the prison bars. After a time, so tired was his brain with hard thinking, that he actually fell asleep.

How long the sleep lasted he did not know, but he woke from a troubled dream with the idea that he heard soft retreating footsteps. The candle was burnt to the socket and the room was extremely dark, so Vernon sat up in a confused way, trying to recall his position. With alert ears he hearkened for the presumed footsteps, but as there was no sound save his own laboured breathing, he decided that he had been dreaming. It was lucky that he had a box of lucifers in his pocket, for the lighting of one enabled him to see the time. His watch revealed that it was one o'clock in the morning, and as he had arrived at nine he must have been imprisoned for four hours. His limbs felt stiff as he rose to his feet, and with a yawn he stretched himself.

"I can't stay here all night," he muttered desperately. "I'll try what shouting will do;" and shout he did with all the power of his lungs, only to receive no response.

Feeling that he was losing both time and temper, Vernon groped his way in the thick darkness towards the door. Gripping the handle he gave it an angry, despairing twist. To his surprise the door proved to be open. Apparently the footsteps he had thought dream-sounds were real, and his prison door had been quietly unlocked at the moment of his awakening. Picking up his overcoat, he felt his way along the passage and up the stairs and into the front hall--slow work in the gloom of an unknown locality. There was no noise to be heard, although he held his breath to listen. So far as he could judge, the house was empty. Finally, intent upon getting assistance, he tried the handle of the front door, and found that there was no difficulty in getting clear. In two minutes he was in the quiet street, looking up and down for a policeman.

The road being isolated and the hour late, there was neither vehicle nor pedestrian to be seen, nor did any light gleam from the windows of the silent houses. Vernon shivered in the cold breath of the night, then walked swiftly up the street to seek assistance. Shortly he found a burly constable at the corner, and breathlessly detailed all that had happened to that somewhat sceptical officer. A shrill whistle brought another policeman to the spot, and with the two Vernon returned to No. 34, the door of which he had left ajar. This somewhat convinced the officers, and they took his name and address, promising to search the house, and also to watch it. Vernon himself, on fire to reach Hampstead and to learn what had occurred, could not wait to see what discoveries might be made. The policemen wished to detain him, but finally he got away, and raced towards the more public part of West Kensington to find a cab.

As luck would have it, he picked up a belated taxi that had just taken home a fare. The chauffeur demurred about driving out so far as Hampstead, but a treble price promptly offered overcame his scruples, and in a short time Vernon was spinning towards his much-wished-for destination. All the way he was trying to conjecture how The Spider had contrived to overhear the arranging of the trap, for he must have done so, else there would have been no reason for the imprisonment. But by this time Vernon's brain was weary, and he fell into a doze. When he woke the taxi had pulled up with a jerk, and he found himself on the Heath before the gate of "Rangoon." With a sudden spasm of fear he noted that a policeman was standing at the entrance, apparently on guard.

Stumbling out of the cab, Vernon staggered towards the man. "I have come to Mr. Dimsdale's ball," he said hurriedly.

"It's over, sir," said the policeman, touching his helmet.

"Over--so early!"

"Early in the morning, sir, you mean. But the fact is, there's trouble."

"Trouble!" Again a cold chill struck Vernon.

"Yes, sir, and the ball came to an end."

"Mr. Dimsdale?"

"Dead, sir. Murdered, as you might say."

"Dead!" echoed Vernon, quite dazed.

"Strangled," said the policeman bluntly.

CHAPTER V.

AFTER THE TRAGEDY.

The news was as horrible as it was unexpected. Vernon had anticipated blackmail, he had even believed that in the absence of a third person The Spider might show fight. But he had never dreamed that murder would take place, as such a crime was entirely contrary to The Spider's methods. With a gasp he pulled himself together.

"Have they caught the man?" he demanded anxiously.

"What man?" questioned the constable suspiciously.

"The murderer."

"No, sir; it's not known who killed Mr. Dimsdale. He was found strangled in his library, some time after eleven o'clock. The alarm was given, the police were called in, and the ball came to an end. Now, sir," added the man in a friendly way, "I haven't any right to tell you more, and as what I have told you will be in the papers to-morrow, no harm's done. You go home now, sir, and you'll learn all about your friend when the inquest takes place."

Vernon thought for a second. "Is your Inspector in the house?"

"Yes, sir, but you can't see him."

"I must see him, and at once. I believe I know who killed Mr. Dimsdale."

"Oh, you do, do you?" said the policeman with a subtle change of manner. "Then you come along with me."

"Wait till I pay my cabman," muttered Vernon, and, the policeman making no objection to this, he gave the chauffeur the promised fare. When the vehicle had disappeared down the road, diminishing blackly in the moonlight, he returned, to find that the constable was holding open the gate.

"What name am I to give?" asked the man gruffly, for it was evident that he regarded Vernon with suspicion owing to what he had admitted.

"My name doesn't matter; the Inspector does not know me," said Vernon impatiently. "Hurry up, man! hurry up! Every moment is of value."

Impressed by his imperious manner, the policeman knocked at the closed front door, which was immediately thrown open by a second constable on guard in the hall. By this individual Vernon was introduced into the Jacobean dining-room, after a few hurried words of explanation. Inspector Drench--the constable had informed Vernon of the name--was seated at the table taking notes, and Miss Hest, looking pale and anxious, stood at his elbow. She was the first to speak.

"Mr. Vernon," she exclaimed hoarsely, "you have come at last. Poor Mr. Dimsdale was asking for you all the night. And now----" she broke down.

"How did you get in, sir?" questioned Inspector Drench imperiously, and nodding to the policeman that he should leave the room. "I gave orders that nobody was to be admitted."

"I insisted upon seeing you," said Vernon quickly. "This evening--or rather yesterday evening--I had an appointment with Mr. Dimsdale in his library, but I was decoyed to an empty house in West Kensington, and have only managed to get away."

Inspector Drench stared. "What do you mean by all this, sir?"

"What I say," rejoined Vernon tartly, for his nerves worried him. "I understand that Mr. Dimsdale is dead."

"Mr. Dimsdale has been murdered," cried Miss Hest, clasping her hands and speaking in a thick, emotional voice. "Murdered in his library. No one knows who strangled him."

"I know."

"You!" Drench stood up alertly. "Take care, sir. Anything you say now will be noted," and he shuffled his papers like a pack of cards. "Who is guilty?"

"The Spider."

"The Spider!" echoed Miss Hest. "Who is The Spider, or what is The Spider?"

She looked puzzled, but the Inspector, better informed, looked open-mouthed at the young man. "Do you mean to say that The Spider perpetrated this crime, sir?" he asked, scarcely able to speak from sheer amazement.

Vernon, thoroughly worn out from what he had undergone, dropped into a chair listlessly. "Yes."

"But this Spider?" broke in Miss Hest volubly; "I don't know who he is or what he is. Tell me if----"

"Allow me," interrupted Drench sharply. He was a military-looking man, something after the style of Colonel Towton, and spoke aggressively.

"Allow me, for I am in charge here, miss. The Spider is the name--if you may call it so--of a well-known blackmailer, for whom the police have been looking, and are still looking. Perhaps, Mr. Vernon--I think you said that this gentleman's name is Vernon--will explain how he comes to be possessed of such precise information."

"There is no difficulty in explaining," retorted Vernon, annoyed by the suspicious looks of the officer. "Listen!" and he rapidly detailed all that he knew, all that had taken place from his interview with Dimsdale in Towton's chambers to the moment when he leapt from the taxicab to be met by the constable at the gate with the news of the murder. As the recital proceeded Drench tried to conceal his amazement, but scarcely managed to do so, while Frances Hest, for once startled out of her self-control, uttered ejaculations. It may be noted that Vernon suppressed for the moment the fact that The Spider was blackmailing Mrs. Bedge, as he did not wish to spread scandal. But Inspector Drench and the lady were put in possession of all other facts.

"What was Mr. Dimsdale's secret?" asked Frances curiously.

"I can't tell you, as I don't know. After the capture of The Spider he promised that I should be told. Now I shall never know."

"This comes," said the Inspector bitterly, "this comes of amateur detective business. If I had been informed of the appointment I should have made arrangements to capture The Spider."

"If you had been informed," retorted Vernon heatedly, "The Spider would never have kept the appointment."

"Why not? He was ignorant of my plans?"

"He learned mine easily enough, and would have learned yours. You seem to forget, Mr. Inspector, that we are dealing with a genius in the way of criminality. The Spider, whomsoever he may be, seems to know everything. I believe that he is the head of a gang and has his spies all over London. No one person could be so well posted up in secret arrangements otherwise."

"How did he come to know of the secret arrangement between yourself and Mr. Dimsdale?" asked Drench abruptly.

"I can't say, unless Mr. Dimsdale, who had rather a loose tongue, revealed his plan of the trap to someone else. I said nothing."

"Mr. Dimsdale gave no information to anyone in this house," said Frances decisively; "if he had, either I or Ida would have known. As it is, he apparently met this dreadful person in the library at the agreed time. And, now that I think of it," she mused, "I wonder that I did not suspect something of the sort. Mr. Dimsdale told Ida and myself that we could have all the rooms for the ball save the library, as he wished that to himself."

"There's nothing unusual in such a wish," remarked Drench easily. "When a house is upset by a party a man naturally wishes one of his rooms left undisturbed so that he can have peace."

"What happened exactly?" asked Vernon with an air of fatigue.

Inspector Drench signed that Miss Hest should explain, and glanced at his notes as she spoke, to be certain that she was repeating what she had already told him prior to Vernon's entrance.

"It is hard to tell what took place to a minute," protested the lady. "Our guests arrived just before ten o'clock, and everything was going splendidly."

"Everyone was masked, I suppose," said Vernon quietly.

"Oh, yes. But Mr. Dimsdale stood in the Hall until nearly eleven, receiving our guests, and made everyone unmask before they entered the ballroom."

"Why did he do that?" asked Drench suddenly.

"Can't you guess?" put in Vernon impatiently. "Mr. Dimsdale expected The Spider, and wished to see if he would come."

"But he didn't know what The Spider was like. No one knows."

"I daresay. But Mr. Dimsdale knew those whom his daughter had invited to the ball. If an unknown person had unmasked he would have jumped to the conclusion, and perhaps truly, that he was The Spider. Well, Miss Hest?"

"Everyone who unmasked were people we knew," she continued, "for I stood with Ida near Mr. Dimsdale, receiving the guests. At a quarter to eleven Mr. Dimsdale went to the library."

"Alone?"

"Certainly. No one, to my knowledge, entered the library during the whole of that evening until Ida, in search of her father, insisted upon going in, notwithstanding the prohibition, at a quarter to twelve. Then she found Mr. Dimsdale seated in his chair, quite dead."

"Were the windows open?"

Inspector Drench arose. "Come and see the room, Mr. Vernon," he said, moving towards the door. "Nothing has been disturbed, not even the corpse. Everything remains as Miss Dimsdale found it at a quarter to twelve."

"And Ida fainted," whispered Frances in Vernon's ear as the trio crossed the hall to enter the library. "Poor child! It was no wonder, when the sight was so horrid. She's in bed now, crying her heart out. Inspector," added Miss Hest, raising her voice, "you won't want me any longer? Let me return to Miss Dimsdale, as she needs every attention."

"Very good, miss. I shall continue your examination in the morning."

"I have told you everything I know."

"One moment," said Vernon, laying his hand on her sleeve as she moved away. "I want to know if any guest arrived after Mr. Dimsdale went into the library."

"Two. But Ida and I made them unmask. We knew them quite well. Mr. and Mrs. Horner from Finchley. And I may tell you, Mr. Vernon, that Mr. Dimsdale came out of the library at five minutes to eleven for a single moment to ask if you had arrived."

"I wish I had arrived," said Vernon bitterly, "I might have prevented this tragedy. Are you sure, Miss Hest, that no strangers were at the ball?"

"Well," she said thoughtfully, "it is difficult to say, since all were masked. But no stranger was there to my knowledge, and when the crime was discovered everyone unmasked. We knew all the guests, as we had known them when they arrived; still, some stranger might have slipped in. But I must go to Ida. I'll tell you anything else you wish to know in the morning."

Vernon nodded and released his grip of her sleeve. She flitted away into the central room on her way to Ida's bedroom. Vernon mused for a moment, then followed Drench into the library, where the Inspector, indeed, had already preceded him. The first glance Vernon threw around showed him that one of the French windows was open.

"I thought so," he said pointing out this to the Inspector. "The Spider did not come as a guest, but watched his opportunity and slipped in at the window. At what time is Mr. Dimsdale supposed to have been strangled?"

"The doctor we called in says--so far as the state of the body shows--that the crime was committed about a quarter past eleven. Miss Dimsdale discovered it at a quarter to twelve, thirty minutes later."

"The appointment was for eleven," said Vernon nodding, "so The Spider was fifteen minutes late. But he came in there"--he pointed to the French window--"and he escaped in the same way."

"With the thousand pounds?" asked Drench drily. He did not like to be shown his business by this young man.

"I don't think so," replied Vernon musingly, and cautiously feeling his way, as it were, to a decision. "You see, Dimsdale never intended to pay the money, and therefore was not prepared with the specie from the bank. The Spider, for once, went without his booty, and did worse work for nothing than he ever did for reward."

"Yes," said the Inspector carelessly; "I believe this is the first time murder has been connected with his name--publicly, that is. Who knows what assassinations he may not have to answer for privately? However, here is the room and the corpse. What do you make of both?"

The other man looked round slowly. The room blazed with the full power of the many electric lights, which the Inspector had turned on; also, as the apartment was square and sparsely furnished, there was no nook or cranny that could not be seen at a glance. The three windows had neither blinds nor curtains, in accordance with Mr. Dimsdale's craze for fresh air; but round the desk, which was on the right side of the room, near the fireplace, a high screen was drawn, the same which the girls had used on that morning when they were selecting the guests for the fatal ball. In a chair, turned sideways from the desk, drooped the form of the dead man. He was arrayed in evening dress, but his shirt-front was crumpled, and his face was swollen and discoloured. There was no disorder round about the desk; the Persian mat had not even been kicked out of the way.

"Yes," said Drench in answer to a look from Vernon, "there could not have been any struggle, since all is in order. In my opinion The Spider--if it was that chap, as you seem to think--must have come silently behind his victim, and strangled him with the handkerchief before he had time to call out. He came to kill as well as to rob."

"A handkerchief?" asked Vernon interested. "I thought he did it with his hands, Mr. Inspector?"

Drench shook his iron-grey head. "There are no marks of hands on the throat, Mr. Vernon; only a cruel black line, which shows that a cord or handkerchief must have been used--and used with great force. Though, to be sure," added the Inspector reflectively, "Mr. Dimsdale was so short and fat in the neck that a slight pressure must have caused apoplexy."

"Did he die of that?"

"And strangulation; a mixture of both. But it's odd, Mr. Vernon, that with those uncurtained windows he should have been murdered without anyone seeing the performance. There must have been many guests in the front garden, as people always do wander outside between the dances to get fresh air."

Vernon pointed to the screen. "That served the purposes of both curtain and blind, Mr. Inspector. Behind that the crime could be committed without anyone being the wiser, even if anyone had been on the verandah."

"Provided there was no noise," insisted Drench.

"Exactly; so that makes me believe that your surmise is correct. The Spider, for some reason, may have come to kill, as well as to blackmail. Perhaps, as he learned about the trap--which he must have done to arrange for my absence--he dreaded lest Dimsdale should prove a dangerous person, and so got rid of him. If that mirror"--Vernon pointed to a long, broad looking-glass which covered one side of the fireplace, and which reflected desk and chair and screen and seated figure--"could speak it would tell how the crime was committed. I can guess myself," he ended.

"Perhaps you will let me hear your guess," said Drench sceptically.

"The Spider, I fancy, stole in quietly through the French window, which was open, and came suddenly upon Dimsdale seated at his desk waiting to keep the appointment. Before the old man could turn The Spider had the handkerchief or cord round his neck and quietly choked him. There would be no noise and no struggle. Then he looked for the money"--Vernon pointed to the desk, several drawers of which were pulled open--"but not finding any he stole out again through the window."

"The guests in the garden would have seen him leave the room."

"What if they did? No one anticipated a crime, and no one but Miss Hest and Miss Dimsdale knew that the library was forbidden territory. Moreover, The Spider may have chosen his time to escape when another dance was in progress, the chances being that everyone would return to the ballroom. And you may be sure," added Vernon with emphasis, "that The Spider made use both of mask and domino, so that he might be taken for a guest, and might escape notice."

"But Miss Hest said that everyone unmasked----"

"Who entered the house as a guest," followed on Vernon quickly; "just so, Mr. Inspector. But The Spider entered as a stranger by the window, not wishing, perhaps, to take any chances. And, of course, we are agreed that he is infernally clever, and well posted in necessary details."

"I'm with you there," murmured Drench mournfully, "but it's a pity you and Mr. Dimsdale did not warn me of your trap. I should have caught the man easier than you amateurs."

"I am not an amateur," said Vernon unexpectedly; then, when the Inspector looked at him interrogatively, he added, "I trade as Nemo, of Covent Garden."

"Ah, yes; I've heard of you," replied Drench in a less supercilious tone. "So you are Nemo, are you, Mr. Vernon? I was told that you had solved several mysteries. In fact, a friend of mine at the Yard said you'd a head on your shoulders."

"I'll need it," said Vernon with a shrug, "to unravel this mystery."

"It's no mystery," said Drench quickly, "since you say that The Spider murdered this poor chap."

"The Spider himself is a mystery, and one which the police would give much to solve. I intend to hunt him down--not alone on account of my poor dead friend here, but because he so cleverly decoyed me out of the way."

"Ah, your pride is up in arms?"

"Well, yes; I suppose you can put it that way. But I wish to ask you two things, Mr. Inspector: first, that you will not reveal my trade as Nemo to anyone in society."

"Oh, I promise that easily, especially as I don't go into society, and I can guess that you want it kept quiet. And the second thing?"

"Will you permit me to place my services at your disposal?"

The dexterous way in which Vernon put his request as a favour to be granted pleased the Inspector, especially as he knew from what he had heard of Nemo that such services would be of value. "I shall be very pleased to let you work with me, Mr. Vernon," he said cordially. "What do you propose to do first, may I ask?"

"This house in West Kensington is an empty one, and must have been taken by The Spider for my temporary prison. I must ascertain from the landlord who took it, and thus we may learn something about the looks of The Spider."

"You think he took the house himself: applied to the landlord, that is?"

"Yes, and no; he may have done so, or one of his gang may have rented the house. But if we can catch the person who _did_ see the landlord, we may learn something about The Spider, if indeed the tenant was not the man himself."

"Well"--Drench scratched his head thoughtfully--"there is something in that, Mr. Vernon. But The Spider is so clever that you may be sure he has made himself safe. You think he heads a gang?"

"I am certain, and the woman who played such a clever comedy to inveigle me into the kitchen is one of the gang."

"Perhaps The Spider himself, in disguise?"

"You may be right, as, of course, since I was captured about nine o'clock, there was plenty of time for him to change and get to Hampstead by eleven."

"Moreover, he was a quarter of an hour late," suggested Drench, "but it puzzles me, sir, to think how your trap business came to his ears."

Vernon looked regretfully at the dead man in the chair. "Perhaps Mr. Dimsdale may have talked," he remarked. "I said nothing. But we shall never know now----"

"Until we lay hands on The Spider and force him to confess," ended Drench, nodding. "By the way, I suppose some reward will be offered for his apprehension by Miss Dimsdale? I understand she is rich."

"It's very probable, as she inherits her father's money--about ten thousand a year, it must be."

The Inspector whistled. "That's a tidy fortune," he said meditatively. "I expect the reward will be a large one."

"I expect so also," rejoined Vernon, understanding clearly what was meant, "and if we learn the truth about this crime and capture The Spider you can have the reward all to yourself."

"But you're a professional, Mr. Vernon, and have to make your money."

"I don't want it in this case. The Spider made use of a certain lady's name to inveigle me to West Kensington, and I mean to be even with him."

"Miss Corsoon. I think you mentioned Miss Corsoon."

"Yes, only you needn't talk about it outside your office," said Vernon hastily. "I don't want her to be mixed up in this business. Also, I am not very proud of having been trapped in this way."

"Only the police will know," Drench assured him, and led the way out of the room, after turning out the lights. "You'd better go home now, Mr. Vernon, as you have done quite enough to-night, and look worn out."

Vernon nodded. "When will the inquest take place?"

"To-morrow; the sooner it's over the better. We can work on the clue of The Spider which you have supplied. We'll catch him."

Vernon shrugged his shoulders. He was less confident of success than Drench, since for nearly two years The Spider had entirely baffled the police.

CHAPTER VI.

TWO CONVERSATIONS.

The inquest duly took place, but no evidence was forthcoming likely to lead to the capture of the assassin. That he was The Spider there, of course, could be no doubt, since the declaration of Vernon went to show that the late Mr. Dimsdale had made an appointment with the blackmailer. Naturally, the whole story had to be told at the inquest, and the public became aware, through the medium of the newspapers, that the dead man had a secret. It could not have been a dishonourable secret, was the general opinion, else Mr. Dimsdale would scarcely have risked a revelation. Using it, whatever it might be, as a decoy to lure The Spider into a trap, he had lost his life in the attempt to capture the famous criminal. And if The Spider had been celebrated before, he was still more celebrated now, and in a more sinister way. Formerly the police had wanted him as an extortioner; now he was inquired for as a murderer.

The "Rangoon" crime--as it came to be called--made a mighty sensation, as there was that about it which appealed to the somewhat jaded taste of the public. That a man should be strangled in his own library, and in the very house where nearly one hundred people were dancing, was truly wonderful, when the sequel was that the assassin had escaped. The windows of the library had neither blinds nor curtains; guests had been talking and walking in the garden; on the other side of the tall laurel hedge cabs and carriages with attendants had been waiting in the road, yet The Spider had come and gone like a shadow. Behind the frail concealment of the screen a terrible crime had taken place, and, far from hurrying his departure, the criminal had actually lingered to search for the money he hoped to get. It was proved at the inquest that he did not get his plunder, for enquiries at Mr. Dimsdale's bank showed that the thousand pounds had not been drawn. Undoubtedly, since the dead man had intended to defy the blackmailer, the secret could not have been one to be ashamed of. But what the secret was the public never knew.

Vernon, as he had stated to Inspector Drench, was not proud that he had been so cleverly tricked into temporary imprisonment by The Spider, and would fain have kept that episode to himself. But for the rounding off of the case, it was necessary that it should be told, and thus sensation was piled upon sensation. Vernon, however, contrived to keep the name of Miss Corsoon to himself and Drench, and it was vaguely stated in the papers that Vernon had been inveigled to West Kensington on the plea of helping a woman. Inquiries proved that the landlord had never been applied to as regards the letting of Number 34. The Spider had simply seen that the house was empty and had gained access thereto by means of a skeleton key. For one single evening he had utilised the house as a prison; and when the police searched the same, which they did from cellar to attic, they found no trace of The Spider or of the white-faced woman who had played so clever a comedy. The daring evinced in connection with the West Kensington house was amazing; the escape of the assassin from "Rangoon" scarcely less so; and the whole formed a case unexampled in the annals of crime for cool audacity. And the outcome of the affair was extremely unsatisfactory.

Nothing could be discovered concerning the whereabouts of The Spider, and whether he belonged to a gang or worked single-handed no one could say. The man defied both detective and policeman, and laughed at the attempts of the law to lay him by the heels. Letters were written to the papers and leading articles appeared, clamouring that immediate action should be taken against The Spider, who was a menace to civilisation. The police did all that was possible, and hunted London in the vain endeavour to lay hands on the rascal, but without success. The Spider left no tracks behind him, and could not be followed to his lair. A verdict of "Wilful Murder" was brought against him, and a reward of one thousand pounds was offered at the instance of the murdered man's daughter for his apprehension, but nothing further came of the matter. The crime was a nine-days' wonder, but as the days grew into weeks and weeks into months, public interest dwindled. It seemed likely that the murder of Martin Dimsdale would have to be relegated to the list of undiscovered crimes. Even Inspector Drench despaired of success, and gloomily shook his head. Only Vernon remained firm in his intention to solve the mysteries of the murder and The Spider, and he said as much to Mrs. Bedge two months after Dimsdale had been laid in his grave.

Maunders' aunt was a thin, aristocratic, pale-faced old lady, prim in her dress and manners. She occupied a quiet, unpretentious house at Hampstead, not far from "Rangoon." A note from her had brought Vernon to see her, and now the two were seated in a pointedly antiquated drawing-room, talking earnestly. Everything about the house and its owner was prim, and the whole atmosphere suggested early Victorian days. It seemed strange that so dismal and old-fashioned a house should be the home of an intensely modern young man like Constantine Maunders. But, as Mrs. Bedge informed Vernon, her nephew gave her very little of his society, as he had engaged rooms in town and lived in them the greater part of the week.

"He only comes from a Saturday to a Monday to stop here," sighed Mrs. Bedge, folding her lean mittened hands on her drab-hued dress, "yet he knows how fond I am of his company."

"Constantine was always selfish," remarked Vernon bluntly.

Mrs. Bedge protested with the foolish fondness of an old woman. "Oh, indeed, you must not say that. Constantine is high-spirited, and I daresay that he thinks this place somewhat dull. But when he is here I invariably find him thoughtful and affectionate."

This was very probable, since Mrs. Bedge had money, and Maunders expected to be her heir. It was not likely that so astute a person would risk the loss of a fortune. Something of this sort must have revealed itself in Vernon's eyes, for Mrs. Bedge, with the swift instinct of a woman, guessed what he was thinking about.

"No," she said in her plaintive way, "it is not greed of money that makes Constantine love me, but his own sweet nature which gives affection, unasked. Constantine knows that I have spent a great deal on his education and in fitting him out in life. Now I have very little money left: this house, the furniture, and a few hundreds a year. When I die he will receive very little, poor boy. I thought it best that he should enjoy the money while he was young, and without waiting for my death."

"Constantine ought to work," said Vernon, wondering at the blindness which could describe Maunders as unselfishly affectionate.

"He intends to, when he can find something to his mind. And then, he is so handsome that he may make a rich marriage. I thought Ida Dimsdale would have taken him," sighed the old lady; "she has ten thousand a year and is also a very charming girl. But there is no hope for Constantine there."

"You astonish me," said Vernon, and meant what he said. "I understood from Mr. Dimsdale himself that his daughter was in love with Constantine."

"She was; she seemed to be quite crazy about him, but that was before the terrible death of her father two months ago. Since then she has shut herself up with Miss Hest at 'Rangoon,' and when Constantine has seen her, she has been quite different. She loves him no longer, and as good as told the poor boy so. It nearly broke his heart."

"I don't think Constantine's heart is so easily broken," said Vernon grimly, and relapsed into silence. It struck him as strange that Ida should cease to love the handsome scamp, considering how infatuated she had been with him for months. But, if things were as Mrs. Bedge stated, there was a chance that Colonel Towton's warm devotion would be appreciated; there was also the chance--and Vernon winced when he thought of it--that, having no opportunity of marrying Ida, the pleasure-loving Maunders would prosecute his wooing of Miss Corsoon with renewed vigour; in which case, and in spite of Lucy's pronounced liking for him, Vernon thought dismally that there would be little likelihood of his own success. A more dangerous rival than Maunders, when he really put his heart into love-making, can scarcely be imagined. Mrs. Bedge broke in upon these meditations.

"And what we have been speaking about brings me to the reason why I asked you to come and see me," she said, smoothing her dress and arranging the old-fashioned bracelets she wore. "You see, as I tell you, I am not rich, and as I have informed you, Ida does not love Constantine as she used to. Now, I want you to consider if it could possibly be arranged that I could become Ida's companion."

Vernon started with astonishment. He did not think that Mrs. Bedge would prove a very cheerful companion to a young girl, and moreover it seemed strange that, at her age, she should wish for such a position. She must be poor indeed, and considering how Constantine had drained her, this was scarcely to be wondered at. "Miss Hest acts more or less as Miss Dimsdale's companion," remarked Vernon with some hesitation.

"I think she is a most dangerous woman," said Mrs. Bedge, a warm colour flushing her faded cheeks; "she is a public reciter. I may be old-fashioned, but I do not think it is right that a young girl like Ida should be so friendly with a woman who appears on the stage."

Vernon laughed at this echo of early Victorian prudery.

"Miss Hest only recites at concerts and 'At Homes,'" He explained; "she can scarcely be called an actress."

"I look upon her as such," said Mrs. Bedge primly. "I have known Ida for years: when her father was in Burmah he sent her to school in England, and she always spent her holidays with me. That is how Constantine came to fall in love with her. It has been the dream of my life to see them married, especially as Ida is rich and needs a man to look after her money. I wish to become Ida's companion, not only because I am one of her oldest friends and need to supplement my income, but because I hope to influence her again in my boy's favour."

"I understand." Vernon smiled quietly as he thought that if Maunders looked after Ida's money there would be little of it left in a few years. But he quite understood, as he had acknowledged, the affectionate scheme of the fond old woman, who was a slave to her adopted son. "I can scarcely advise you, Mrs. Bedge. Miss Hest is a lady--there can be no doubt on that point--and her character is above reproach; also, she is clever and strong-minded, the kind of companion Miss Dimsdale wants. For I should not think," he added after a pause, "that Miss Dimsdale was capable of managing her large fortune. I have seen very little of her since the funeral. I suppose the will was proved and she is in possession of her money?"

"There was no will," said Mrs. Bedge unexpectedly. "Constantine learned that from Ida herself. She merely inherited as next of kin, which is the same thing. Why poor Martin--I call Mr. Dimsdale, Martin, because I knew him for years and years," she explained in parentheses--"why poor Martin never made a will I can't say, but he did not."

"Strange," reflected Vernon musingly; "so business-like a man would certainly have made a will, I should have thought. However, as Miss Dimsdale has inherited as next-of-kin it doesn't matter; failing her, the money, I presume, would have gone to Lady Corsoon?"

"Certainly; but Ida, as a daughter of poor Martin, takes precedence of Julia as the sister. But think of all that money, Mr. Vernon, being at the mercy of an adventuress like Miss Hest."

"I don't think she is an adventuress, Mrs. Bedge, and I can't see how the money is at her mercy."

"I see it very plainly," said Mrs. Bedge with asperity. "Miss Hest has a most extraordinary influence over Ida, and not a healthy one, since she has permitted her to shut herself up for weeks."

"The natural grief of Miss Dimsdale----"

"There are bounds to grief," interrupted the old lady sharply, "and the young recover from sorrow quicker than do the aged. Poor Martin was a good father, and Ida does right to mourn him; but not to the ridiculous extent of shutting herself up for two months with that woman."

"You don't seem to like Miss Hest."

"No, I don't. Oh, I haven't a word to say against her character. I daresay she is a lady and perfectly correct in her behaviour: but she is not the companion for Ida. Besides, she comes and goes from 'Rangoon' at her will, and is not a regular companion, such as the girl should have. Miss Hest, so Constantine tells me, lives at Isleworth with a horrid old retired actor and his wife."

"Professor Garrick Gail. Yes; she told me that herself."

"So brazen," sniffed Mrs. Bedge, more prim than ever; "it's not right, I tell you, Mr. Vernon. Someone should interfere."

"No one can, Mrs. Bedge. Miss Dimsdale is her own mistress, being over age, and has her own money. She has a right to live as she pleases."

"Not in my opinion, Mr. Vernon; it's not respectable. Could you not see her and suggest that she should sell or let, 'Rangoon' and come here to live with me as her paid companion? Also, she could help to keep up this house."

Vernon almost laughed, so selfish was the proposition, and thought it very unlikely that Ida would surrender the charming residence of "Rangoon" and the intellectual society of Miss Hest, to shut herself up with a buckram old dame in a stuffy, second-rate dwelling. "I am not intimate enough with Miss Dimsdale to suggest such a thing."

"But you are searching for the assassin of her father," persisted Mrs. Bedge with the dogged obstinacy of age; "out of gratitude she should adopt your suggestion. Besides, you would be glad to see your old schoolfellow Constantine settled for life."

It was on Vernon's lips to say that he would be sorry to see any woman, let alone Ida Dimsdale, tied to a selfish creature like Mr. Maunders, but out of pity for the infatuated old lady he refrained. Besides, since she believed Constantine to be an angel, no one would ever be able to argue her out of that fancy. "Other people are searching for The Spider also," he said gently, "so Miss Dimsdale has no particular reason to show me any gratitude, especially as she has offered the reward of one thousand pounds."

"I know. Constantine is trying to earn it."

"The deuce he is?" sprang from Vernon's lips.

Mrs. Bedge drew up her spare form and folded her hands. "I do not like slang, Mr. Vernon." Then, when he apologised, she continued: "Constantine wants to earn the money, and also, if he catches The Spider, Ida will surely marry him out of sheer gratitude."

"I think he has a stronger reason to catch The Spider," said Vernon drily.

Mrs. Bedge coloured and looked aside. "I guess what you mean, as I asked poor Martin to speak to you on the subject of that attempted blackmail. It was scandalous, was it not? However, I have heard no more from the wicked creature, and I don't think I shall. After committing this crime, it is not likely that The Spider will dare to continue in his wickedness."

"Well," said Vernon, standing up to take his leave. "I certainly have not heard of anyone being blackmailed lately. Perhaps The Spider thinks that he has gone too far, and is afraid. I suggested myself to Constantine that he should capture The Spider if he wished to become my partner in--that is," broke off Vernon in some confusion, "he might----"

"I understand," said Mrs. Bedge quietly; "I know that you are Nemo. Poor Martin revealed your private business when he suggested that he should consult you about The Spider's attempt to blackmail me. But you can be perfectly satisfied. I shall not betray your secret, having," she smiled faintly, "one of my own."

He looked at her inquiringly. "I don't understand."

"I refer to the accusation The Spider brought against me," went on Mrs. Bedge, her eyes glittering feverishly and her breath coming and going in gasps. "Oh, it was shameful that a man should dare to accuse me of immorality--yes, there is no need for us to mince words, Mr. Vernon--of immorality. Why, the only man I ever loved was Martin himself. Then he went to India and I was worried by my family into marrying Mr. Bedge; my sister married his partner, Constantine Mavrocordato."

"Maunders, I understood the name was."

"That was the English name he took, and that is why his son--my adopted boy, but really my nephew--comes to be called so. I never liked Mavrocordato, and to think that this Spider should accuse me--me----" She clenched her thin hand and all the primness fled. She was no longer a precise old lady of a precise epoch, but an angry and insulted woman. "If I could find this man, Mr. Vernon, I should strike him across the lips. I urged Constantine to hunt him down, both to gain the gratitude of Ida by punishing the murderer of her father and because I wish The Spider to be punished for the insult he put upon me. Should you find him, Mr. Vernon, don't spare him."

"I can promise you that," said Vernon very grimly, for the decoying still rankled in his breast. "Still, as yet we can find out nothing about him. If he blackmails you again, let me know. Then we can arrange a trap."

"So that I may be murdered like poor Martin. No, thank you."

"I'll see that such a thing doesn't occur a second time. But I fancy you can set your mind at rest, Mrs. Bedge. The Spider is too much wanted for him to continue his little games: the risk is too great. I daresay he'll turn his attention to America or to the Colonies."

Mrs. Bedge followed him to the door. "Then you think that he has left England?" she inquired eagerly.

"I don't think so; I think--well, I scarcely know what to think. Leave things as they are, Mrs. Bedge, and sooner or later I hope to capture the rascal. Now I must leave you."

"Will you see Ida and suggest my scheme to be her companion?"

"I don't know her well enough to suggest it bluntly. But I shall see her some day and hint at your idea."

"And please keep your eye on Constantine. I fear he is ruining his health with society."

"I see very little of Constantine, Mrs. Bedge, and I fear he would not take any well-meant advice I might offer him."

Finally he got away from the prim house, although Mrs. Bedge was anxious to keep him in conversation. When on the Heath, breathing the widely-blown air, he drew a long breath to refresh his lungs. He did not wonder that Maunders remained as little as possible in that tomb, for it was nothing else. To a pleasure-loving, lively young man, accustomed to be petted by pretty women and welcomed by monied men, the society of his aunt and the atmosphere of her stuffy house would naturally be abhorrent. And Constantine was not the individual likely to deny himself a merry life for the sake of attending on the woman to whom he owed so much. He had absolutely no idea of the meaning of the word "gratitude." Most people--and Maunders was one of them--do not know that there is such a word in the dictionaries.

Walking along musingly, Vernon remembered how Dimsdale had spoken of Emily Bedge, and how he also had stated, as she had done, that they were in love when young. Now Dimsdale was dead, and the girl he had so admired was a faded old woman, cherishing a foolish affection for one who would never return the same, and who had no intention of returning it. Considering the lonely life and sad history and dismal present position of Mrs. Bedge, the young man began to think that, after all, it would be a charity to persuade Ida Dimsdale to take her as a companion. In the society of the girl Mrs. Bedge might grow youthful again. Of course, her presence might be dangerous, as she would certainly do her best to persuade Ida into marrying Constantine, and assuredly the infatuation of Ida might revive. Vernon wondered how it had died away, and what causes had been at work to make Ida regard with indifference the handsome face of the scamp. From the hint given by Mrs. Bedge, he began to believe that this was the work of Miss Hest. If so, it was no wonder that the old woman spoke ill of her. Of course, Mrs. Bedge was biassed, for Vernon himself believed Frances Hest to be a clever, capable woman, who was likely to prove a tower of strength to Ida, since the girl's character, although sweet, was not particularly firm. But then there was always the chance that Miss Hest might become a tyrant.

Thinking in this way, Vernon suddenly stumbled against a man coming from the opposite direction, also deep in thought. They looked up with a mutual apology and both burst out laughing. The newcomer was Colonel Towton, and he explained himself as they shook hands.

"I have just been to see Miss Dimsdale," said the Colonel crisply, "and she gave me so much to think about that I was in a brown study."

"And I have come from Mrs. Bedge, who also made me think," observed Vernon with a smile, "hence I ran into you. Where are you going, Colonel?"

"Back to town," said the military man promptly, "but I am walking. I always walk as much as possible in London for the sake of necessary exercise. Perhaps you would rather drive?"

"No. I prefer to walk. I am glad to have met you, Towton, as I wished to speak with you privately."

"Curious," said the Colonel, screwing his glass into his eye. "I had you in my mind when I ran into you. Let us walk down the hill and talk: there is more privacy in the open air than anywhere else. Well?"

"Well," echoed Vernon, as they turned their faces towards London, "what do you wish to say?"

"I'll come to the point circuitously," retorted the Colonel smartly. "So you have been to see Mrs. Bedge? Poor old Dimsdale told me about her. My rival's aunt, I believe?"

"Yes. A quaint old lady of the Albert period."

Towton shuddered. "I know the style, Vernon. Stiff and prudish and dowdy. H'm! rather a contrast to our young friend. He's devilish handsome and infernally modern. I suppose the old lady gives him plenty of money: he always seems to be in the forefront of things. Yet I don't like him somehow: his voice doesn't ring true; but there, perhaps I am prejudiced, since he courts Miss Dimsdale. I'm a man, and not a saint, so I feel jealous."

"You have no need to be, Colonel."

"Eh! what?" The Colonel stopped abruptly and his eyes sparkled. "Do you mean to say that he has ceased to court Miss Dimsdale? Well, well," he went on, without waiting for a reply, "I shouldn't wonder. I might have guessed as much, for three or four times I have been to the Corsoons, and Maunders was always there, making furious love to that pretty Lucy of theirs. You had better look after her, if you intend to make her your wife, Vernon."

"Lady Corsoon always receives me so coldly, that I scarcely dare call," confessed the young man dismally. "I daresay Maunders has put a spoke in my wheel in that quarter."

"Yes; but, hang it, he can't mean to marry both girls?"

"You forget what I hinted just now, Towton. Mrs. Bedge assured me, and with great grief, as she wants the marriage to take place, that Miss Dimsdale has ceased to care for her nephew."

Only military self-control prevented the Colonel from throwing his tall hat in the air. "I thought she was kinder to me to-day," he said jubilantly, "and she never mentioned Maunders' name, now I think of it. Do you believe that I have a chance, Vernon?"

"A better one than ever you had," replied Vernon heartily, "and you may be sure I shall endeavour to aid you in every way. But, by the way, how is Miss Dimsdale? I have seen her only once since the burial of her father, and, of course, then she was overcome with grief."

Towton thought for a moment before replying. "To tell you the truth, Vernon, I don't think that dark-browed young woman is a good companion for her in any way."

"Why not?" Vernon was rather struck that Mrs. Bedge and the Colonel should unknowingly agree on this point. "She is clever?"

"Oh, I daresay, and, if you ask me, a sight too clever," grumbled the Colonel, shouldering his thin umbrella like a gun. "Ida--well, I can call her Ida to you, since we have become so friendly--Ida is a charming girl, but not strong-minded. I shouldn't seek her for my wife if she were, as I hate masterful women. Miss Hest is of that sort, and she seems to have too much control over Ida. In fact--I may be wrong, and I wouldn't say this to anyone but yourself--but it's a kind of hypnotism."

"H'm. Do you remember what the Concini woman said about her supposed magical influence over Marie de Medici: that she only used the influence of a strong mind over a weak one?"

"Oh, I don't think Ida is weak-minded," said the Colonel hastily; "she is a sweet, loving, delightful girl, who would make any man happy. But Miss Hest is what I call a cat: yes, an amiable cat, so long as things go to her liking, but I'm sure she could show her claws if necessary."

"Does she support Maunders?"

"She supports no one but herself. It seems to me that she finds that the reciting doesn't pay, and so hopes to become Ida's companion for life. If Ida married she'd be nowhere. I fancy for that reason she wishes to keep Ida single, and so doesn't countenance either Maunders or myself."

Vernon mused. He remembered how he had fancied that Miss Hest might have been the person to undermine Maunders' chances. Now Towton was saying the same thing. However, he said nothing, while the Colonel, walking and talking vigorously, continued his speech.

"Besides," said Towton, "there's a queer strain in the family. Gerby Hall, where the brother lives, is three miles from my place. Brother and sister are twins and exactly like one another, but they don't hit it off together. Gerby Hall is supposed to be haunted, and people think the Hests to be mad, or queer, or--the deuce knows what."

"Frances Hest doesn't seem to be mad," said Vernon drily.

"Well, I don't know. Her head seems to be screwed on all right, but she believes in occultism and all that sort of thing. Her influence is unhealthy, for she induced Ida to go to Diabella, who----"

Vernon nodded. "I know. Diabella is a fortune-teller in Bond Street and is supposed to be very clever. What did she tell Miss Dimsdale?"

"Ah, that I couldn't find out. But it made her ill; gave her a headache or something. Ida said very little; seemed averse to speaking about her visit, and Miss Hest supplied all the information. She was full of the wonderful things which Diabella had told Ida."

"What wonderful things?"

"I can't say. I told you that Ida refused to speak about the matter. But I intend to find out something about this Diabella, and therefore I am going to call on her. I have an appointment in three days."

"She'll tell you nothing about Miss Dimsdale."

"Of course not. But I shall be able to see what kind of a woman she is. I don't want Ida to get under another bad influence. That of Miss Hest is quite enough. I am clever enough to read this Diabella's character, and if possible, I shall try and prevent Ida from seeing her again."

"It's just as well. Tell me what you hear from this fortune-teller."

Towton shrugged his shoulders. "Oh, it will be the same old rubbish about love and money and marriage. I don't believe in these mercenary occult people myself, although I have every faith in the genuine sort I have met with in India. Now, one of those, Vernon, would soon spot this damned Spider."

"Why not ask Diabella?"

"I shall do so. Gad! it's an idea. But, then, I don't think occultists who take money are the real truth-tellers. However, it can do no harm asking her, so I shall do so. By the way, Vernon, have you heard if the police have stumbled on the track of that rogue?"

"Not yet. Drench tells me that nothing has been discovered. I am trying to hunt him down myself."

"You? Pooh! Pooh! Pooh!" said Towton good-humouredly. "Why, it needs a trained man to do that. The Spider is as clever as the devil, hang him. To think that I was at the ball, and in the next room, when our poor old friend was being-strangled by that beast. I tell you what, sir, the strangling put me in mind of the Thugs."

"What do you mean?" asked Vernon quickly.

"It's only an idea. But this Spider strangled the old man so cleverly and so quietly that I wondered if he was some nigger who had known Dimsdale in India or Burmah and so had learned his secret, whatever it might be."

"It's a queer way of looking at it," murmured Vernon thoughtfully, "and Dimsdale's secret has to do with the East, I fancy. There may be something in what you say. I'll think it over."

"Do," said Towton cordially, "and I'll come to your rooms to report on my proposed interview with this Bond Street Witch of Endor."

On this understanding they parted, having had a most interesting conversation on important subjects.

"There may be something in Towton's idea," thought Vernon.

CHAPTER VII.

LADY CORSOON'S APPEAL.

Since the tragic death of Dimsdale, Vernon had seen very little of Maunders. Certainly--since even London is parochial in bringing the same people in the same set constantly together--he had met him casually at the houses of mutual acquaintances, but beyond a few careless words, nothing had passed between them. It seemed as though Maunders, after deciding to leave the partnership with Nemo in abeyance, had drifted knowingly apart from his old schoolfellow. Vernon did not care much, as he mistrusted a man who was willing to sacrifice everything and everyone to his greed for pleasure.

Maunders reminded Vernon in many ways of Lucien de Rubempré in "Lost Illusions." Egotism was the keynote of the real person as of the fictitious; but where Balzac's hero drifted weakly with the tide, Maunders struck out against it for a landing of his own choosing. As Lucien was drawn, handsome, clever, and unscrupulous, so was Maunders in actual life, and an insatiable love of pleasure was common to both. Overindulgence might well wreck Mrs. Bedge's darling, as it had wrecked the lover of Madame de Bargeton.

It was the conversation with Colonel Towton which sent Vernon in quest of the man whom he would otherwise have avoided like poison. He wished to learn clearly the attitude of Maunders with regard to the two ladies he was so audaciously wooing. Much as the man loved Lucy Corsoon--and Maunders' love in this quarter really seemed to be the most honest part of him--he loved himself more; and it seemed incredible to Vernon that so egotistic a person would risk losing the world of pleasure for a genuine passion. Sir Julius Corsoon was wealthy and Lucy was an heiress, but if she married Maunders, who was no favourite with the baronet, her father would probably cut her off with the proverbial shilling. It really seemed wiser for Maunders to stick to Ida and the ten thousand a year of which she was sole mistress. But then, if Ida had truly overcome her infatuation, Maunders had little chance of success in that quarter. A desire to learn the true state of affairs brought Vernon to Maunders' chambers in Planet Street, Piccadilly, at eleven o'clock in the morning, two or three days after that enlightening conversation with Colonel Towton.

Vernon naturally expected to find the sybarite housed like Solomon-in-all-his-glory, and he was not disappointed. The rooms were beautifully decorated and sumptuously furnished. No expense had been spared to make them worthy of this fastidious young gentleman, who was only content with the very best which civilisation could afford. He received his friend in a delightful Pompadour apartment, airy and bright, and gracefully frivolous. Recalling the sombre, shabby house at Hampstead, and Mrs. Bedge's revelations regarding a diminishing income which made her anxious to seek at her age the post of a paid companion, Vernon could not think how Maunders managed to provide himself with such gorgeous surroundings. He had no settled income, and, like the lilies of the field, he neither toiled nor spun. But he welcomed Vernon in a maroon-coloured velvet smoking-suit which must have cost a considerable sum in Bond Street, and asked him to partake of a delightfully tempting breakfast, set out with all the delicacies of the season.

"Though, I daresay," said the handsome scamp in his languid, insolent manner, "that you breakfasted at cock-crow. You were always aggressively virtuous."

"I certainly have been up some hours," replied Vernon coldly. "While you eat I can smoke, with your permission." He sat down and lighted a cigarette carefully. "I have called to see you----"

"An unexpected pleasure," murmured Maunders, pouring himself out a second cup of coffee. "Yes?"

"To ask you if you are engaged to Miss Dimsdale," finished Vernon pointedly.

"Perhaps I am."

"In that case you will have given up all pursuit of Miss Corsoon?"

"Perhaps I have."

"Oh, hang your evasions. What do you mean?"

"I don't recognise your right to ask me questions about my affairs."

"They are mine also, confound you," snapped Vernon energetically. "I love Miss Corsoon, and if you would leave her alone she would probably accept me."

"What good would that do?" asked Maunders lightly; "Her mother wouldn't."

"Would Lady Corsoon accept *you*? After all, you have nothing but your good looks to offer the girl."

"Ah, but the girl has a fortune to offer me."

"You aren't worth it. And let me remind you that however much Miss Corsoon may be taken up with your looks, her mother will certainly disapprove of the match."

Maunders shrugged his shoulders. "You can't be sure of that."

"I am sure of one thing, that Sir Julius will cut his daughter off with a shilling if she marries you."

"Now that's very clever of you, my dear boy," said Maunders gracefully, "for Sir Julius _is_ the stumbling-block. He's a purse with a gaping mouth, which goes about on two legs, and has no sympathy with romance."

"Romance! Why, you don't know what it means," said Vernon scornfully. "You want to marry money, and either Miss Corsoon or Miss Dimsdale will serve your turn. The last is in possession of her money, whereas the first may not inherit her expected fortune, which will certainly be taken away from her if she marries you. Why not stick to Miss Dimsdale?" Maunders rose and went to the window. "Because I really love Miss Corsoon, much as you may doubt it," he said impetuously. "I have a heart----"

"Which is for sale to the highest bidder. See here, Conny----"

"Conny?" Maunders lifted his eyebrows. "I thought you barred pet names?"

"I am appealing, not to the man-of-the-world, but to my old schoolfellow, if you put it in that way. See here, I love Lucy Corsoon, and, if you would only clear out of the gangway, she would really love me. She does--I have seen it in many ways."

"Bosh! If she really loved you she wouldn't listen to me."

"I don't know. You have good looks and a kind of magnetic power which influences women against their will: hard women of the world, too, much less an innocent girl such as Lucy is. It's a great power to have, and you make bad use of it."

"Just because I happen to cross your track. Thanks."

"Oh, hang your dodging. I came here to receive a plain answer to a plain question. Are you going to marry Miss Corsoon or Miss Dimsdale?"

"I haven't made up my mind."

"You would if Miss Dimsdale would listen to you," snarled Vernon. "If I asked her to be my wife she would accept at once," retorted Maunders.

"No, she wouldn't. Your aunt told me that she had lost all love for you since the death of her father."

Maunders' face grew black. "I wish the old lady would keep her ideas to herself," he said angrily, "for it is an idea and nothing more. Naturally, as her father came by his death in so terrible a manner, Ida is grieved and can't think eternally of me. All the same, she loves me."

"I doubt that."

"On what grounds?"

"On what Mrs. Bedge said."

"Pooh! Pooh! Pooh! What does my aunt know about it?" said Maunders lightly and with superb insolence. "She's a dear old thing, but several centuries behind the age. Ida is mine if I choose to have her, and I would have her if my silly heart did not stand in the way."

Vernon jumped up in a royal rage. "I forbid you to make false love to Miss Corsoon. I love her and she loves me, and it is only your infernally magnetic personality that draws her heart away from me. If you meant well by her, and I thought she would be happy, I would withdraw; but you only mean to marry her for her money, which she may never get."

"I love her, I tell you; I love her," said Maunders as violently as Vernon had spoken, "and money or no money I shall marry her if I choose. You have no chance. Lady Corsoon hates you."

"I don't believe it. She shows signs of yielding, and has asked me to go to tea at her house this afternoon. If she hated me she would not ask me in so friendly a way."

An almost imperceptible smile passed over the full lips of Maunders, and he shrugged his shoulders. "Go to her house by all means and hear what she has to say," he sneered. "I'll risk your visit."

Vernon was baffled by all this fencing and evasion. The man would neither say "yea" nor "nay," and it was impossible to tell what he intended to do. "If you will leave the field clear for me with Miss Corsoon I will take you into partnership," he said at last, entreatingly.

"I am not sure if I wish to be taken in," retorted Maunders contemptuously; "it is not a respectable business."

"You are a liar! My business is perfectly respectable, and I earn my money honestly." Vernon caught up his hat and looked round the elegant room. "I doubt if you can say the same."

"What do you mean by that?" demanded Maunders furiously.

"I mean that you haven't a sixpence, that your aunt can't allow you much, and that you are living far beyond your means. Where do you get the money?"

"That's my business," said Maunders coolly, "and my aunt is wealthy."

"So wealthy that she desires the post of a paid companion to Miss Dimsdale," sneered Vernon, making for the door. "She told me so herself, although I'm bound to say that she desires to further your interests by inducing Miss Dimsdale to love you again."

"I can manage all that for myself," said Maunders decisively; "my aunt has no business to interfere with my affairs."

"She brought you up, and----"

"And I am to be her slave for the rest of my life. Nonsense! All that filial feeling is out of date," said Maunders lightly. "However, I shall tell my aunt what I think of her talking to you in this way. As to the rest of it, you keep out of my way, Vernon, or it will be the worse for you."

"Ah!" Vernon faced round at the door. "Now you speak clearly. Is it to be peace or war between us?"

"War," snapped Maunders. "You can't hurt me and----"

"War let it be," interrupted Vernon, opening the door. "Good-day," and he walked out smartly, leaving his friend, or, rather, his enemy, now that war had been declared, rather surprised by his abrupt departure. But when the door closed Maunders' face grew black and his brow wrinkled.

"Perhaps I shouldn't have driven Arty to such a declaration," murmured the young man thoughtfully. "He's a fool, but a clever fool. After all, although I love Lucy it will be better for me to marry Ida since she has the money. I wonder how Aunt Emily found out about Ida's change towards me? It can't last, however, if I only take trouble to see her often enough. It's Lucy who holds me back. I'm a fool, as I know that Lucy doesn't care for me as she does for Arty. I wish I hadn't fought him now; but he can't harm me, he can't." Maunders glanced round the luxurious room. "He shan't. There's too much to lose. Damn him, I'll fight him and beat him. There!"

While Maunders was coming to this conclusion Vernon was walking swiftly along Piccadilly, in the direction of Covent Garden, as he intended to go to the office wherein he carried on business as Nemo. Now that Maunders had openly declared himself as an enemy the situation was somewhat adjusted, and Vernon felt that he could deal with it. He made up his mind to tackle Lady Corsoon that very day and ask if he might be permitted to pay attentions to Lucy. Then in an interview with the girl herself he might manage to brush aside this semi-hypnotic influence which Maunders' fascinating personality seemed to exercise over her. If he could only get the mother on his side all would be well. Lady Corsoon did not know that he was Nemo, which was just as well; but she did not know also that he had expectations from a bachelor uncle who could leave him a title and a fortune of three thousand a year. If this were set before her she might be induced to welcome him as a suitor, although both Sir Julius and Lady Corsoon were said to desire nothing less than a duke for their only child. But if this was the case, Vernon wondered why the lady tolerated Maunders, who was poor and without position. However, when he called that afternoon he might be able to learn the reason. At all events, his expectations, against Maunders' mere good looks, would probably carry the day.

At the office a surprise awaited him. His clerk, a dry-as-dust, lean old fellow, as silent and wise-looking as an owl, met him in the outer room with a mysterious face and informed him that a lady had been waiting an hour for the appearance of Nemo. She had refused to give any name, and had declared her intention of remaining until she saw the detective. Vernon, in his business capacity, was used to people who came and went without giving names, as their business was generally shady, so he did not pay much attention to the matter. Hanging up his coat and hat and laying aside his gloves and cane, he passed into the inner room. Then he received the surprise aforesaid. His client was none other than Lady Corsoon herself.

She arose, perfectly self-possessed, and did not appear to be surprised to see the young man. "How are you, Mr. Vernon?" she asked, holding out a gracious hand, "or perhaps I should call you Nemo here--Mr. Nemo."

Vernon, violently red and inwardly greatly upset by this recognition, accepted the gloved hand timidly. "How did you find out that I----"

"Oh, your enemy told me," finished Lady Corsoon, sitting down.

"My enemy?" stammered the unfortunate man nervously.

"Mr. Constantine Maunders, who----"

Vernon interrupted her and struck a hard blow on the table. His eyes flashed dangerously. "Then, in spite of his promise, he told you what I so much desired to keep secret?"

"Yes," said Lady Corsoon drily. "It was his desire to put me against you, so that he could philander with my daughter. But his shot failed to hit the mark. I was delighted to hear that you were Nemo; I have heard something of Nemo's doings and cleverness, and so the information brought me here, as you see."

"To forbid me your house?"

"I asked you to afternoon tea to-day, and that invitation was issued after your enemy betrayed you. Sit down, Mr. Nemo, and become business-like. We have much to talk about."

Considerably surprised by this attitude, Vernon sank into his chair before the desk and stared at Lady Corsoon in the dim light which filtered through the dingy window of the room. She was well worth looking at, in spite of her age, as her dress was perfect and her looks still displayed the remains of considerable beauty. She was somewhat stout, it is true, but her complexion--whether due to art or nature--was that of a young girl, and her sparkling brown eyes revealed an intellect of no mean order. A clever woman was Lady Corsoon, within limitations, and she would have been even more a power in the fashionable world than she was had she not been so dominated by the powerful personality of her husband. Sir Julius was of long descent, but in his youth of ruined fortunes, owing to a spendthrift father. Being an inborn financier, however, he had built up an Aladdin's palace of gold on the ruins, and was extremely wealthy. Yet he had the heart of a miser, and allowed his wife and daughter only sufficient to keep up their position with care and difficulty. This mean behaviour explains the reason of Lady Corsoon's visit to Vernon in his _avatar_ of Nemo, as he speedily understood. But as yet he had not overcome his surprise at thus finding his mask torn off.

"Come! Come!" said Lady Corsoon, tapping his arm with her sunshade. "I have come to see a business man and not a dreamer. Wake up, Mr. Nemo."

Vernon winced on hearing her pronounce his trade name. "I am at your service," he said in a low voice.

"And in my hands," rejoined Lady Corsoon briskly. "What would the world say if it knew that Arthur Vernon was a private inquiry agent, making his money out of people's secrets?"

"You take me for The Spider, apparently," said Vernon with spirit, and anxious, through pride, to repel the odious accusation. "I make money by helping people to keep their secrets, not by betraying them. I am on the side of the law, not of the criminal. Upon my word, I can't see that a man who carries on an honest business to preserve secrets and to save unfortunate people from blackmail is worse than--if indeed as bad as--a City rogue who trades unscrupulously on people's weakness for gambling."

Lady Corsoon changed colour at the last words, and evidently was about to make a remark thereon. However, she checked herself sharply and replied with feigned carelessness, "Very well argued, Mr. Vernon. But people are prejudiced against those who seek to know secrets."

"Because everyone has a turned-down page in his or her Book of Life," cried the young man. "I--in my business--prevent that page being read by those who wish to be paid for the reading. I don't want my business known, but I am not ashamed of it."

"Why did you take it up?"

"Because my father lost all his money, and I had scarcely enough to live upon," retorted the young man quickly and proudly.

"You have expectations?"

Vernon started. "How do you know that?" he demanded sharply. Lady Corsoon tapped his arm again. "In my own way I have been doing a little detective business. You were so persistent in following Lucy from house to house, and so decidedly refused to receive my 'No' for her answer, that I made inquiries to see why you could have the courage to offer a young girl a ruined fortune. I learned, indeed, that you were ruined by your father, but I learned also that Sir Edward Vernon, of Slimthorp, in Worcestershire, is your uncle. He has a good income and no wife and is eighty years of age. The chances are that you will succeed him."

"He cannot keep me out of the title," said Vernon bitterly, "but you should have gained more information, Lady Corsoon. My uncle hated my father because my father married the woman he loved, and he hates me because I am the son of that woman. I do not hope to inherit the money, and what is a title without money? I did not explain what you have discovered, else I should have done so, since it seemed useless to put forward all that as a plea for an engagement to your daughter."

"My dear man, a title is better than nothing. You are too modest. Besides, Lucy will have plenty of money."

"I know, if she marries as you and her father wish. But I hear," Vernon smiled bitterly, "that you want a duke."

"I want an honest man, upon whom I can depend," said Lady Corsoon with energy, "and for that reason I have come to see you."

"In spite of the fact that I am Nemo?"

"For the very reason that you are Nemo," she retorted with a lightning glance. "My dear boy, Mr. Maunders thought to do you a bad turn by telling me of your secret business, and thought that I would certainly forbid you my house and finally end your dangling after my daughter. As it is, he has done you a good turn, as you are the man I want."

"For Lucy?"

"And for myself. If you can carry out safely the business I have come to see you about I shall encourage your addresses to Lucy, and, so far as I can influence so iron-natured a man, I shall win Sir Julius to your side. Come, is it a bargain?"

"Oh," Vernon caught her hand joyfully, "of course it is; I never dreamed of such happiness. But now I know why Maunders smiled when I told him that I was due at your house this afternoon."

"When did you see him?"

"Immediately before I came here. I went to ask whether he wished to marry Miss Corsoon or Miss Dimsdale, but he refused to say. But he smiled--ah! he thought that, having told you I was Nemo, you intended to dismiss me for ever from your house when I called this afternoon."

"I daresay, but he will learn that instead of enemies we are friends, and that instead of his marrying Lucy, you shall. It is just as well," added Lady Corsoon quietly, "as she loves you, although she is more or less fascinated by that--that--that gentleman, shall we say?"

"But you are fascinated yourself, Lady Corsoon, else you would scarcely have tolerated a penniless man dangling after your daughter."

"I tolerated it, as you say, because Mr. Maunders knows my secret."

"Your secret?" In a flash Vernon recalled the conversation with the young man under the peristyle, in which Maunders had hinted that he knew something which would enable him to manage Lady Corsoon.

"What is your secret?"

"I have come to tell you, so don't interrupt until I have finished," said Lady Corsoon coolly. "I come to you because I know in a hundred ways that you are, what Mr. Maunders is not, an honest gentleman, and also the private detective that I need. I have one great vice, Mr. Vernon, I am a gambler, and for the last two years I have lost a heap of money at bridge. To pay my debts, since Sir Julius kept me always very short of money, I pawned certain family jewels. If Sir Julius finds that out he is capable of causing a scandal by forcing a separation. For Lucy's sake, as well as for my own, I don't want such a thing to take place."

"But how can he find out?"

Lady Corsoon fished in a green and gold bag which was slung on her arm and produced an elegant sheet of writing paper. "Read that," she said quietly.

Vernon started, and suppressed a cry. At the foot of the writing he saw a purple spider impressed clearly--the well-known sign manual of the scoundrel who had murdered Mr. Dimsdale. Glancing his eyes over the pages, he read that The Spider had learned about the pawning of certain family jewels and, moreover, had managed, by forged tickets, to get the same into his possession. He was willing to sell them back for two thousand pounds, to be paid in gold on a certain date and at a certain place, to be arranged when he received Lady Corsoon's reply. The reply was to be put in the agony column of the _Daily Telegraph_, when further arrangements would be made for the payment of the sum and the handing over of the jewels. Failing consent, The Spider intended to apply to Sir Julius and to reveal Lady Corsoon's gambling propensities. The whole of this precious epistle, written very elegantly, ended with the ideograph of the purple spider.

"What do you think of it?" asked Lady Corsoon when Vernon finished reading.

"What can I think of it, but that the man is a blackguard. You want me to deal with this?"

"Yes. I can't pay the two thousand pounds, as I have not got it. My husband keeps me very short. You see that I am candid; but then I trust you, as I doubt Mr. Maunders."

"Why do you doubt him?" asked Vernon suddenly. "Because he followed me one day to a pawnshop and learned my secret. Not in so many words, but by unmistakable hints he gave me to understand that my open house to him and my encouraging of his love for Lucy was the price of his silence. Things have gone from bad to worse, and I feel that I am under his thumb, until the jewels are got back again and all proof of my madness is destroyed. I am keeping a brave face, Mr. Vernon, but I am truly in despair. Sir Julius is a hard man, and the revelation of what I have done means disgrace. My husband will not spare me."

"For his daughter's sake?"

"No. He would remove Lucy from my care and cast me off with a small income to live on. He can't get a divorce, but he will insist upon a separation, as I feel certain. You alone can save me, and, if you can, I agree to your marriage with my daughter. Oh," she cried, struck by a strange look in Vernon's eyes, "don't think I am selling Lucy to you. But she loves you, and now that I know you will some day have a title, the money doesn't matter, as Sir Julius may be persuaded into accepting you as his son-in-law. At all events, if you will be my friend I shall be yours. Is it a bargain?"

"Yes," said Vernon, gripping the hand she held out; "for more reasons than this one do I wish to track this blackmailing beast to his lair. Agree, by a line in the _Daily Telegraph_, to pay the money in a month. That will give me time to turn round."

Lady Corsoon drew a long breath of relief. "Thank God I came to you. As for Mr. Maunders, I really believe----" She hesitated.

"What?" asked Vernon looking up quickly.

"That he is The Spider himself."

CHAPTER VIII.

THE GRIEF OF IDA.

Vernon was not the man to let the grass grow under his feet when there was anything to gain by hurry. And in this case the happiness of his whole life was at stake. The visit of Lady Corsoon to enlist him on her side with the bribe of supporting his suit for her daughter was one of those unexpected cards which Fate deals us to win in the game of life. It was a veritable ace, with which Vernon hoped to trump Maunders' trick. Hitherto the handsome scamp had had everything his own way. Now he was to find serious obstacles in his path. With Lucy's love and her mother's support, the course of true affection might run smoother. The father might be gained over by playing on his instinctive dislike to Maunders and by the news, which Vernon had hitherto not thought worth imparting, namely, that he had a chance of becoming a baronet.

Moreover, since war had been declared between the two schoolfellows, Maunders would undoubtedly make himself disagreeable in any case. Already, acting treacherously, he had informed Lady Corsoon of the way in which Vernon earned his money, and it was probable that now he would inform others. Of course, the young man wished to prevent this, for, in spite of his defence of his profession, he was aware that the world does not look amiably on one who lives by learning the secrets of weak humanity, even when the aim is to preserve those same secrets from use by villains. But the difficulty was to seal Maunders' mouth, as the moment he noticed-- and he certainly would, speedily--that Vernon was favoured by Lady Corsoon, he would spread the scandal with a zeal born of the knowledge that his empire was slipping from him. Also, he would strive to intimidate Lady Corsoon more openly, and it could not be denied but what her position towards her aggressively upright husband was a delicate one. Thus Maunders was the enemy both of Lady Corsoon and of Vernon: to crush him they therefore formed a secret partnership. In this unity lay their strength.

The weapon Vernon proposed to use towards his dangerous foe was that supplied by the chance remark of Lady Corsoon that Maunders might be The Spider. When she departed with the assurance that there was nothing to be afraid of for at least one month, Vernon sat silently in his chair, thinking over what had been said. After all, it did not seem impossible that Maunders should be this arch-scoundrel, for whom the police were so eagerly seeking. To Vernon's own knowledge, the young man did not receive large sums from Mrs. Bedge, and he had no other source of income. Yet, as Vernon had seen, he contrived to live like a prince on nothing a year. Perhaps, like the amiable and talented Mrs. Rawdon Crawley, he managed to keep up his princely appearance by spending other people's money--that is, by getting deeply into debt. But Vernon knew that Maunders did not owe one penny.

He came by the information by having, at the request of the late Mr. Dimsdale, searched into Maunders' private life some months previously. The old ex-police-commissioner, seeing that his daughter was infatuated with the young man, hoped to learn something to his discredit, and so asked Vernon--whom he knew already as Nemo--to make an examination. Of course, Vernon did not guess at the time that Mr. Dimsdale wished to find something to the discredit of an undesirable suitor, and merely thought that the old man was anxious to learn if Maunders was a fit husband for his daughter. In fact, Vernon believed that he was doing his old schoolfellow a good turn in probing his life. He certainly learned that Maunders owed nothing and always settled his debts scrupulously--presumably on money allowed by Mrs. Bedge; so he presented his report to Dimsdale with the remark that Maunders, at all events, was an honest man. Now the case assumed a different aspect with Mrs. Bedge's confession of poverty--a confession which was supported as true by her anxiety to become Ida's paid companion. Since Maunders paid his debts and lived like a millionaire in embryo, how did he manage to fill his purse? Lady Corsoon had provided a very reasonable reply to this serious question. He was The Spider.

"But, hang him, he's not clever enough," muttered Vernon, rising to pace the narrow confines of his office at this point of his meditations. "He's cunning and smart and observant and unscrupulous. But The Spider is a genius and manages his affairs in a far-seeing way, which does not suggest Maunders. Conny is shallow in many ways, and for the present would sacrifice the future. No, The Spider never does that. He waits and plans and arranges his operations in such a way that he can never be captured. No, feasible though it seems, I can't see Constantine as that master-criminal."

But again Vernon reflected that when the trap had been arranged between him and the dead man the window of the library had been open, and, as Mr. Dimsdale had mentioned in his subsequent letter, with wrath, Maunders had called at the moment. In fact, he had been round the corner of the bungalow nearest to the library with the two ladies. Now, it was not impossible that in passing the library, light-footed as he was (and Maunders trod like a cat), he might have lingered at the sound of voices. Thus he might have gained the necessary knowledge of the trap, which he had afterwards utilized to inveigle Vernon to the West Kensington house. That is, presuming he was The Spider; and the name of Lucy Corsoon used in the wire was the very name which Maunders, knowing Vernon's love for the girl, would employ. Finally, Maunders had been at the ball, and it would have been easy for him, masked and cloaked as he was, to steal into the library and commit the crime, afterwards mingling with the guests in all apparent innocence. On these grounds Vernon began to believe that Lady Corsoon might be correct in her assumption. But always there came the doubt that Maunders was too shallow to be the arch-rogue. He was clever, but certainly not a genius, whereas The Spider was a Napoleon amongst the criminal fraternity.

"In one way I can prove something," said Vernon to himself. "If Maunders did enter the library he must have been absent from the ballroom for some time. I shall go to 'Rangoon' and ask questions without letting it be seen why I ask them. Then I can learn for certain about his movements on that night. Moreover, I can interview Miss Dimsdale and learn how she is disposed towards the Colonel. Finally, I'll see if he is right in thinking that Miss Hest's influence is harmful to her in any way."

Having come to this decision, he repaired the ensuing day to Hampstead, fully determined to set his doubts at rest. A glance at the agony column of the _Daily Telegraph_ had assured him that Lady Corsoon had carried out his suggestion. Under the initial "X," she asked for one month's time to consider the matter of "S." This undoubtedly would be accorded to her, as it was The Spider's policy never to hurry his victims. He robbed them in a most graceful and easy-going fashion, and so dexterously, that his victims rather congratulated themselves that they had so honest a criminal tradesman to deal with. So Lady Corsoon's secret was safe for a month. Before the expiration of that period Vernon hoped to lay hands on the rogue who had baffled the police for so long. But in his heart he did not expect to find Maunders in the grip of the law.

At first Vernon was refused admittance by the butler, but on insisting and on sending in his card he was shown into the central hall. Shortly Miss Hest made her appearance with a smiling but somewhat serious face. She looked extremely tall and handsome in a black-browed way as she advanced towards the visitor.

"How are you, Mr. Vernon," she said, shaking hands politely; "is your business with Miss Dimsdale very important? She is not well to-day. I have just been bathing her forehead with eau-de-cologne."

"Oh, I have just come to make an afternoon call," replied Vernon easily. "I am sorry to hear that Miss Dimsdale is ill."

Frances sighed. "She has never been the same since her poor father's terrible death. She loved him as dearly as he loved her, you know, Mr. Vernon, so the shock was great."

"I quite understand. Still, after two months' more or less of quiet she surely must be recovering. At her age one does not remember for ever."

"No. At our age one has longer memories, Mr. Vernon. But it is kind of you to call. Ida likes you very much, especially as you were such a friend of poor Mr. Dimsdale's. I think you might come in for a quarter of an hour."

Vernon hesitated. "I don't wish to disturb Ida," he said doubtfully, "if she wants to be quiet."

"Oh, she left the decision to me when we got your card. I am acting as a kind of nurse to the poor darling. Ida is just like my sister, you know."

"But your professional engagements?"

"They don't matter. I have made a good deal of money in one way and another, Mr. Vernon, you know. I can afford to take a rest. I want Ida to come down to Bowderstyke with me and stop at the Hall."

It flashed into Vernon's suspicious mind that perhaps Frances wished Ida to fall in love with her brother. Ten thousand a year would be very acceptable to Mr. Hest, if Colonel Towton's story was to be believed. According to him the brother was not a millionaire, and what money he had he spent lavishly in helping the parish. He remarked about this to Frances as she led him through the door at the end of the hall and into the boudoir, where Ida was lying.

"I hear from Colonel Towton that your brother is quite a philanthropist."

Frances laughed. "Oh, the Colonel has been talking, has he? My brother would be quite annoyed, as he never liked to be praised."

"Then he's not human," said Vernon bluntly.

"He's human enough to be annoyed with me because I chose to earn my own living," said Frances bitterly. "However, let us see Ida, and then I'll tell you all about my brother. In fact, I want to ask your advice."

"Why should you think I was capable of giving advice, Miss Hest?"

"Oh, you are so grave," she replied with a smile and halting at the door of the boudoir, "and Mr. Dimsdale, poor man, always said that you were so clever in making suggestions. Besides, you don't know the opinion Ida has of you. Ida, dear," she passed into the room, "here is Mr. Vernon."

"Arthur," said the girl, who was lying on a couch near the window, "oh, I am so glad to see you. I'm glad Frances did not send you away. She's such a tyrant as my nurse."

"Perhaps you need a tyrant to manage you, Ida. You were always too impulsive and reckless of your health."

"I think I have changed since poor papa's death. I don't feel reckless in any way now. I shall never get over it; never."

Frances, who had taken some knitting to sit in a near chair, frowned as the girl spoke. "That's the way she goes on, Mr. Vernon. Isn't it foolish? I want her to go out and enjoy herself."

"As if I could when poor papa is dead only two months," cried Ida sighing.

"Oh, I don't mean you to lead a gay life. But you shouldn't stay here day after day without sunshine."

"I think Miss Hest is right, Ida," said Vernon, gravely scrutinising the pale face of the girl; "you are not looking well."

"I don't feel at all well," she replied peevishly.

"There's nothing organically wrong," put in Frances quickly. "The doctor said that Ida was perfectly healthy, and only needed to go out and lead a happy life to become quite strong."

"I shall never be happy again," said Ida with determination. Visitor and nurse--as Frances might be called--looked at one another. The girl evidently had made up her mind to be miserable.

This was not a sensible attitude to adopt, but then Ida was not a particularly sensible girl. She assuredly was not brilliantly clever, although she possessed a certain amount of brains. Pretty in a doll-like way, with her golden hair and blue eyes and creamy-pink complexion, she was an excellent type of a charming, modest, playful English girl, who would make a good wife and a devoted mother. But there was nothing original about her, and, being the spoilt darling of an elderly father, she was subject to moods. She was sick or well, merry or sad, just as the fit took her. At one time she would fatigue herself with theatres and dances and tennis-tournaments, and again, with a revulsion of feeling, would lie on the sofa all day, reading novels. Poets would have called her an April lady, of sunshine and rain, but an ordinary human being would have found her trying. It said a great deal for Miss Hest's true affection that she put up with so whimsical a being. A weathercock was nothing in comparison with Ida Dimsdale.

Why a sober, elderly, military man like Colonel Towton should desire to make such a featherhead his wife was a problem which Vernon was trying to solve as he stared at the girl on the sofa. Ida's mood since the death of her father had been to play the invalid. Certainly she had suffered a shock, as was natural; but time had softened the memory of the tragic death, and Vernon approved of Miss Hest's desire to get the girl away to Yorkshire.

"You ought to go to Gerby Hall, Ida," he remarked after a momentary silence; "a few weeks in the open air would do you all the good in the world."

"That's what I tell her," said Frances severely; "but she won't come down to Yorkshire, as I suggest. I shall end in going away altogether."

Ida stretched out a pretty hand and caught that of Miss Hest. "Oh, no, Frances, darling; you know that I cannot live without you. I must have a companion."

Vernon thought that this was a good opportunity to advance Mrs. Bedge's request which he had promised to bear in mind. "There is a charming old lady who offers to become your companion," he said gently. Ida stared and shuddered.

"I don't like old ladies. Who is she?"

"Mrs. Bedge. She asked me to speak to you because she has lost a lot of money, and is therefore willing to accept a salary as your companion."

Frances laid down her work and clasped her hands.

"Why, Ida, it's the very thing for you, dear. Mrs. Bedge is so old and so sedate. Then I can attend to my business, knowing you are all right."

"Frances," Ida sat up on the sofa and looked reproachfully at her friend, "how can you talk so? I like Mrs. Bedge, who has always been very kind to me, but there is no denying that she is extremely dull. Besides, I have told you that you can have whatever salary you like to ask to make up for losing all your engagements."

"And I replied that I wished to be independent," said Miss Hest stiffly; "I don't like living on anyone. That is why I left Gerby Hall. But about Mrs. Bedge, dear; it is really a capital idea."

"I shan't entertain it for one moment, and when Mrs. Bedge comes I shall tell her so--with thanks, of course," added Ida as an afterthought. "Why couldn't she speak to me direct?"

"Well," Vernon laughed, "it is rather a delicate subject. However, if you won't have her you won't, so there's no more to be said. And might I suggest, Ida, as you really are looking better with the colour that has come into your cheeks at the suggestion, that you should pull up the blind and make the room look more cheerful."

Ida jumped up lightly and did as he asked. Her mood had changed with the advent of this tactful young man. "Is there anything more your lordship requires?" she asked with a saucy curtsey.

"I should like a cup of tea; you are not hospitable," replied Vernon, delighted by the change in her manner.

Ida touched the button of the bell. "You were always greedy, Arthur." Then, when the footman appeared, she gave the necessary orders. "I believe you called less to see me than to get your tea," she ended, laughing quite in her old girlish fashion.

"Ida, I don't believe you are ill at all," said Vernon, scrutinising her.

"Her imagination makes her ill," put in Frances, who was knitting industriously. "She believes that she is sick, and therefore she _is_ sick."

"That is Christian Science," laughed Ida, sitting in a chair instead of returning to lounge on the sofa. "Perhaps you are right, dear. Of course, I have fretted a great deal over poor papa's death, but fretting will not bring him back," she ended with a sigh, and her face clouded over again.

"What you want is bright society," Vernon assured her hurriedly.

"And you suggest Mrs. Bedge," was Ida's ironical retort.

"No. I never thought that she was the right companion for you, as she is too staid and solemn; but I have discharged my conscience by putting her request to you. I never for one moment thought that you would entertain it."

Ida looked at him inquiringly. "You think that I am right?"

"Yes, I do. Miss Hest is a much better companion." Miss Hest bowed to the compliment with a grave smile.

"Oh, I mean what I say, my dear lady. Take Ida down to Gerby Hall and play the tyrant as much as possible by forcing her to keep in the open air all day. She will return quite cured."

"I don't think I should mind going to Yorkshire," said Ida pensively, as the tea was brought in; "and from what Frances says Gerby Hall must be a delightful old place. But then, my sojourn would be disagreeable, as Frances is not on good terms with her brother."

"Say that he is not on good terms with me," said Miss Hest coolly. "I have nothing against Francis, save that he objects to my being independent. But he is very just, and does not wish me to remain always absent from the Hall. I can go down, and can take any one down, on conditions."

"What are they?" asked Vernon, accepting a cup of tea.

"That I, and anyone I bring, bother Francis as little as possible. In fact, when I am at the Hall Francis usually goes to York while I remain; and even when he returns he sees almost nothing of me, as I keep out of his way. He isn't a bad fellow, and of course I should speak well of my twin brother."

"Are you very like one another, Frances, dear?"

"Extremely, in face and form. We can mystify anyone when we are seen together, but in disposition we are quite unlike one another. I am more egotistic than Francis. He is a philanthropist and devotes all his money to improving the parish. Six or seven villages owe everything to him."

"He keeps them all going, you mean?" suggested Vernon, idly leaning back.

"Not exactly. But two years ago there was a great dearth of water, which has frequently occurred during the dry weather. Francis determined that it should not occur again, so he obtained permission and engaged a clever engineer to construct a reservoir at the top of Bowderstyke Valley."

"That was a big work to undertake, and must have cost heaps of money."

"Francis can afford it," said Miss Hest indifferently. "Our grandmother, from whom he inherits the estates, left a lot of ready money, and Francis is a clever speculator. He works hard at stocks and shares and is always in touch with his broker in London. But all the money he makes he spends in improving the parishes around. He has repaired several churches, and has built a poorhouse, and also a small hall for entertainments. He and the vicar work hand in hand. Then, of course, this reservoir is his crowning work, as it supplied water to at least six villages."

"Oh, what a good man he must be," said Ida thoughtfully. "Here am I, with all my money, doing nothing."

Bearing in mind that he fancied Miss Hest wished to marry Ida to her brother, Vernon quite expected to hear her endorse this praise. Miss Hest, however, received the tribute very coolly. "Francis is vain," she remarked, "and desires public applause. Perhaps that is why he spends all his money in public charity."

"Does he never take any pleasure in other ways?" asked Vernon.

"I think he finds his pleasure in his home and surroundings. Still, he goes away to York and London and Paris for weeks at a time, and enjoys himself in some dull way. I am sure it is dull, as Francis hasn't got any spirit for a lively life. However, if Ida comes down she can judge him for herself. But I don't think we'll see much of him, and for my part I'm very glad. I always escape from Francis's society whenever I can. We don't get on well together at all; rather odd, isn't it, considering we are twins?"

"Oh, I don't know, Miss Hest. Twins often are the opposite in disposition as they are the replica of each other in looks."

Frances looked up with an approving smile. "You have described my brother and I to the life," she said nodding.

"Colonel Towton has a place near Gerby Hall, I believe?"

"Yes. The Grange, it is called, a quaint old mansion, three miles distant from my brother's property. Higher up the valley, in fact, and on a rise to the right of the reservoir. Colonel Towton wasn't pleased with the construction of the dam, as it spoilt the view from his house, and then he always declares that if the dam broke the valley would be swept from end to end by the force of the water. But I don't think any accident of that sort will happen," ended Frances emphatically; "The dam is extremely solidly built and will last for many a long day."

"I think I should like to go to Bowderstyke, if only to see Colonel Towton's house," said Ida unexpectedly; "He told me such a lot about it."

"I thought you didn't like Colonel Towton?" said Vernon smiling.

"There!" exclaimed Frances, dropping her knitting, while Ida flushed. "Didn't I say that Mr. Vernon would remark how fickle you are, Ida?"

"Fickle?" echoed the young man, looking puzzled.

"You know that Ida was in love with Mr. Maunders," went on Miss Hest, while Ida still blushed and appeared embarrassed. "She never gave her poor father any peace and always wanted to marry him. Well, since the death she has taken a positive dislike to him and can only find good in the Colonel."

"Ah!" said Vernon meaningly, "that would have pleased poor Mr. Dimsdale. He greatly desired to see Ida the Colonel's wife."

"I begin to think papa was right," said Ida in a low tone and turning away her face. "I did like Mr. Maunders very much. I suppose I really was in love with him in a way. But since papa's death he has scarcely been to see me and has not acted at all sympathetically. Now, the Colonel has called constantly, and has been so kind and so sweet that I--I----"

"That you love him," ended Miss Hest coolly.

"I'm not sure. He's awfully nice and is devoted to me. I daresay if I saw much of him I might--I might----"

"Well," Miss Hest interrupted again, "I hope you will, as I am sure Colonel Towton would make you an excellent husband. He is handsome and distinguished and sensible enough to guide you. My dear," Frances laid her hand on Ida's knee, "I shall be glad when you become Mrs. Towton, as then I shall be free to go back to my work. People are sure to say, if I stay with you, that I am actuated by mercenary motives."

"What nonsense," said Ida quickly; "why, you will not even let me give you a present."

"I can buy presents for myself," said Frances obstinately, "and, since I left Gerby Hall to be independent, I certainly don't intend to play the part of a bribed or paid companion."

Ida's eyes filled with ready tears. "How cruel you are, Frances," she wailed.

"I am sensible and reasonable," said Frances firmly, knitting with an obstinate mouth. "I really love you, dear, but I can't sacrifice my independence to be a hanger-on. All the same, until you have a husband I don't feel justified in leaving you, so feather-headed, to your own devices."

"I am not so weak-minded as you think," flushed Ida crossly.

"Yes, you are, my dear. You can't say whether you love Colonel Towton or Mr. Maunders. You don't know your own feelings."

"Yes, I do. I really believe I love Colonel Towton. I know that I did before Constantine appeared. Then I took a fancy to him. Now that fancy has gone, and I again love the Colonel. Yes," Ida paused meditatively, "I am sure that I love the Colonel."

"Pooh! Pooh! Just what I said: you don't know your own mind."

"I wish you would carry out your first impulse, Ida, and marry Colonel Towton. He's a good man and Maunders isn't." This came from Vernon.

"I feel that," muttered Ida, "but he fascinates me. And, after all, he is trying to learn who killed my father."

"So am I," said Vernon drily, "yet you don't love me. Not that I want you to," he added hurriedly and colouring. "But about Maunders; has he ever said anything to you likely to reveal the name of the assassin?"

"No. Why do you ask?" inquired Ida, and even Frances stopped knitting to look steadily at Vernon.

"Do you suspect that Mr. Maunders knows more than he admits?" asked Miss Hest.

"No! No! No! Of course I don't," answered Vernon hastily and leading cautiously up to the purpose of his visit; "but he was in the house when the murder took place and might have seen some stranger present who would be The Spider."

"I don't think so, and I don't see how he could, seeing that everyone was masked. If he had seen any suspicious character I certainly should have known of it at once."

"Why you, rather than anyone else?" asked Vernon quickly.

"Well, you see, Ida was in one of her freakish moods on the night of the ball and gave Mr. Maunders the cold shoulder, consoling herself with the Colonel all the evening."

"I did so because papa did not wish me to pass my time with Constantine."

"I daresay, Ida," responded Miss Hest rather acidly, "but you asked him to the ball notwithstanding your father objected. At all events, Mr. Vernon, as Mr. Maunders was cold-shouldered he came to me and I had the burden of him from ten o'clock up to the time Ida discovered the murder, at a quarter to midnight. Mr. Maunders never left me alone all that time, so if he had seen anyone suspicious he would have told me."

"Quite so, quite so," murmured Vernon absently and thinking that here was a very good _alibi_ for Maunders, and the stronger since it was given unconsciously by one who did not know the reason for putting it forward. "I daresay The Spider came in by the window," he remarked in louder tones.

Miss Hest made a significant gesture. "I don't know how he came or how he went," she said, nodding towards Ida, who had grown pale, "and the police seem to be able to discover nothing. But you might see Mr. Maunders and learn if he had any suspicions that a stranger was present."

"That would be useless in the face of what you tell me. He would have spoken to you had he been doubtful," said Vernon courteously, "and----"

"There, there! Don't say anything more. Don't you see that Ida is on the verge of fainting?"

Miss Hest caught Ida's hands. "Poor child, they are quite cold. You had better go, Mr. Vernon."

"Yes." He rose promptly. "I am sorry that I spoke of the murder. Don't think anything more about it, Ida, but go to Yorkshire and recover your health." Ida nodded faintly. "Yes; I shall go. It is best for me to get away from this tragic house." And Vernon quite agreed with her.

CHAPTER IX.

WITCHCRAFT.

While Vernon was having his interview with Ida and her companion Colonel Towton went on a little expedition of his own. Ever since the discovery that Ida had been to Diabella, Towton had been anxious, in his turn, to pay a visit to the famous Bond Street fortune-teller. Ida, as the Colonel had told Vernon, apparently was suffering from the effects of what she had been told by this fashionable Witch of Endor, although what had been said Towton could not find out. Miss Hest and the girl had both held their peace on the subject, notwithstanding that the former had talked generally on the wonderful powers of the woman. In fact, she had seriously advised Colonel Towton to interview Diabella and search out the future for himself. The soldier had laughed, as he was not given to dabble in occultism. Nevertheless, he had made up his mind to seek out the seeress, if only to discover indirectly what those methods of devilry were which had so strongly impressed Miss Dimsdale. Towton, to put it plainly, went less as a client than as a spy.

Considering that Ida had no very strongly-marked personality, it was wonderful that the Colonel should be so deeply in love with her. He was clever in his own way, and not without brain-power inside and outside his own particular military profession. His bravery was undeniable, his tact considerable, and he had left the Army on account of family affairs with the name of one who had cut short a brilliant career unnecessarily. Towton assuredly would have risen to be a general had he not retired when the family estates came into his possession. But now that he had abandoned his profession his one aim was to marry and lead a quiet domestic life. He did not wish for a clever wife, or a wealthy wife, or a particularly lovely wife, as he was too matter-of-fact to be romantic. His dream was of a peaceful hearth and a house perfectly managed by a gentle wife. In Ida he believed that he saw the helpmate he so greatly desired: one who would make her husband's will her law, and who would be a cheerful companion. Her moods he believed to be the result of lack of guidance, and he flattered himself that when she became Mrs. Towton he would be able to render her less freakish. Ida's nature was so impressionable that he thought it could be easily moulded, and in this he no doubt was right. Many of the girl's faults were due to the over-indulgence of her father, and to the lack of a firm hand to lead her in the right way. She would have welcomed a master, having one of those natures responsive to suggestion. And, in an unconscious way, the Colonel appealed to her as a strong, kind-hearted man, who could shelter her from the storms of life better than any one else could. In point of fact, the two were made for one another, and, but for the intrusion of Maunders, their course of true love would have run smooth.

However, Colonel Towton was extremely obstinate, and, having decided that Ida was the very wife he desired to preside over his dinner-table, he was determined not to let her be snatched from him by any rival. He admitted with some dread that Maunders was a formidable wooer, and moreover guessed, with the keen instinct of a man in love, that Frances Hest had too much control over the girl. For one thing, she had induced Ida to go to Diabella, a thing Towton would never have permitted had he been able to help it. He knew from his Indian experience only too well that there is truth in occultism, and that an impressionable being--such as Ida truly was--could easily be obsessed by strong suggestion. He had no reason to doubt Miss Hest, and did not think for one moment that she was his enemy in any way: but, with the assistance of suggestions from Diabella, she might lead Ida into unhealthy ways. And all those dealings with the unseen with which psychics have to do were unhealthy in the Colonel's very material eyes. Already, as he had seen for himself, the visit to Diabella had upset Ida; so, whatever the harm done might be, it was necessary to undo it by proving the woman to be a fraud. Towton therefore ascended the stairs to the consulting-room of Diabella with the intention of learning if the fortune-teller was a humbug. Once assured of that, he resolved to explain her methods to Miss Dimsdale and so prevent her trusting as truth whatever the woman had said. Then Ida's indignation at being duped, as the Colonel believed she had been, would probably shake Miss Hest's position. Towton felt certain that Frances was more friendly to Maunders than to himself, and at one sweep he hoped to get rid of both. Afterwards Ida would be more willing to become his wife.

Diabella's offices, as they might be called, consisted of two rooms: a small outer one entered directly from the passage, and a spacious inner one which overlooked the street. As Towton tapped at the door of the prophetess his thoughts suddenly flew back to his many years of sojourn in the Far East. For the moment he could not think what had detached him so unexpectedly from England until, on stepping across the threshold of the now open door, he became aware of a strong, pungent scent, impossible to describe. At once he noted it as that smell of the bazaars, which runs without a break from Port Said to Hong Kong. Perfume is the strongest of aids to memory, therefore Towton's thoughts had flashed back over many years to various Indian experiences. His body was in England, but his soul was in the East: nor did the sight which met his eyes dispel the illusion. The room he entered and the attendant who welcomed him were both Egyptian in looks.

The small apartment resembled an ancient tomb, as the walls and ceiling were painted vividly with hieroglyphics, glowing in crimson and blue and yellow and emerald green. Through a stained-glass skylight overhead a dim, coloured light streamed just sufficiently to reveal the weird looks of the room. It was faked, of course, but very cleverly faked, as the Colonel secretly admitted; even to the attendant, who, apparently a true Eastern, was attired in a garb which one of Pharaoh's fan-bearers might have worn appropriately. The floor was covered with linoleum painted to resemble marble, and there was a quaintly-shaped table of ebony, two or three antique and uncomfortable chairs, copied from furniture of the XIX. Dynasty, and a weird-looking teak sofa, covered with bright yellow cushions. What with the grotesquely-painted walls, the sparsity of furniture, the dim light, the scented atmosphere, and the strangely-dressed attendant, who salaamed profusely, Colonel Towton felt as though he had stepped at one stride across the Mediterranean to a resuscitated Memphis.

The man was a slim, straight native, with handsome, haughty features of the Brahmin type, and Towton wondered that he had broken caste to cross the Black Water. He had keen, black eyes, which took in the looks of the English sahib in a single flash, notwithstanding that he stood with crossed arms and downcast eyes. Towton wondered if he spoke English, and, for the sake of an experiment, addressed him in Tamil. The dark-skinned man replied in very fair English, with an inquisitive glance at this stranger who spoke the Indian dialect so glibly.

"Is your mistress in?" enquired the Colonel, speaking Tamil.

"Within, sahib, and she waits," was the reply in Anglo-Saxon.

Immediately following these few words Towton was led into the inner room, and the attendant closed the door after him, leaving the client alone with Diabella. The room was decorated much in the same tomb-like fashion as the other one, but there were mummies standing round the wall at intervals in their richly adorned coffins, and the two windows looking on to Bond Street were draped with rich Eastern stuffs to entirely exclude the light of day. But several lamps, burning perfumed oil, dangled from the ceiling, and the room was filled with a mellow radiance, eminently suited to the object for which it was used. Towton shrewdly surmised that the peculiar decorations, the exclusion of daylight for the use of artificial illumination, and the highly-scented atmosphere which prevailed even more strongly here than it had done in the outer room, were all meant to daze the senses of Diabella's clients so that they might more readily credit her assertions. It was all cleverly conceived and carried out.

The woman herself was seated at the end of the room under a kind of canopy on an uncomfortable ebony-wood chair inlaid with ivory. Before her was a tiny square table of the same sombre wood, with twisted legs, and on this stood a large crystal the size of a small orange. Diabella was seated in a hieratical attitude with her hands on her knees, like some stone god, and wore a stiff straight robe of mingled black and yellow, which made her resemble a viper. But her face struck Towton most, as she apparently wore an entire mask modelled in wax from some actual Egyptian mummy. This was surmounted by the well-known head-dress of harsh black ringlets, combed straightly to the shoulders. The mouth of the mask was partially open, so that the fortune-teller could speak easily behind it. With her dead-looking face and motionless attitude, Diabella looked exactly like the mummies which flanked her right and left. And right and left also, in tall iron tripods, flamed some spirits, which cast weird lights on her uncanny appearance. Nothing better could have been designed to impress the weak-minded; and in that Temple of Illusion and from the lips of such a strange creature the boldest might be excused for believing the impossible. Even Colonel Towton felt an unaccustomed shudder, as though he were in the presence of the Unseen.

"You wish to consult those who dwell in darkness about the future?" asked the sorceress in a strange, metallic voice, as unhuman as were her looks.

Towton smiled scornfully and twisted his moustache. He had quite recovered his momentary obsession by that perfumed atmosphere, and sat down with a cool air. "You should speak Egyptian to be perfect," he scoffed.

Diabella disdained to notice the jeer. "Would you have me look in the crystal, or spell the cards, or read the hand."

"None of the three, thank you," said Towton drily. "Do you really possess the power of reading things?"

"I can read the past, the present, and the future;' I can tell all that is permitted to be told by the Powers. You are an unbeliever."

The Colonel chuckled. "Wrong, first shot. Having seen a good deal of this sort of thing; although," he glanced round the room, "scarcely so dressy a place, I believe that some gifted people have certain senses at command, if not under control, with which they can foretell things. I quite appreciate your remark about the Powers permitting and forbidding, as I am aware that such is the case."

"I did not say that you were an unbeliever generally," said Diabella, trying to recover her lost ground, "but that you did not believe in me."

"You did not put it precisely in that fashion," retorted Towton. "However, I may as well have my guinea's worth. Is there any reason why I should believe in you?" he demanded contemptuously.

The quiet voice replied indifferently. "Yes. I have not held your hand nor have I contacted your atmosphere closely. Still, I am sufficiently in touch with you to state that you bring a woman in your aura."

"In my what?" asked the Colonel, wilfully dense.

"The aura of your magnetism streams from you radiant as a rainbow. In it is standing the thought-form of a girl. She is not very tall, she has blue eyes and golden hair, and you love her. Am I right?"

"I shan't say," replied the Colonel, secretly surprised to hear this description of Ida and the statement of his feelings towards her. "Humph!" He made a half unwilling admission, "you have some psychic powers, after all. Tell me more."

"Give me your ring," commanded Diabella imperiously. "It is impregnated with your magnetism and will thus suggest your colour."

"My colour?" repeated the Colonel interrogatively and removing his signet ring to place it on the ebony table.

Diabella picked it up and held it in the hollow of her right hand. "Every human being in the unseen world around has a colour which is the prevailing hue of the karmic body, tinted by desire. I can thus recognise you as you appear on the astral plane, and so can read your karma of the past, which appears in the astral records. Thence I can deduce your future for good or evil, in a great measure correctly."

"Then you can't be certain that what you tell me is true?"

"No. Under certain circumstances, when the High Ones permit, the future is revealed beyond all doubt, but those circumstances are connected only with spiritual enlightenment. Otherwise those who have the sight merely deduce what will happen by reading the karma of the past, which can be discerned in the astral light."

"Your claims are certainly more modest than I expected," said Towton somewhat interested, "and if you can tell me my past life correctly I shall credit more or less your prophecies. You know my name?"

"Richard Towton."

"Ah--you got that from my letter asking for an appointment. But I have a middle name which I don't use. What is it?"

"Richard Henry Towton is your full name."

"Correct. Where was I educated?"

"At Wimperly Public School, and then at Sandhurst."

Towton nodded. "You might be certain of Sandhurst, as I am a soldier, but Wimperly is good. Go on."

"You joined your regiment twenty-five years ago, and shortly after joining it was ordered to India. You were stationed at Bombay, afterwards at Travancore. You fought in Burmah, where you met Martin Dimsdale, and became intimate with him. You won a D.S.O. in the Vikram Expedition, and----"

"All that," interrupted the Colonel politely, "with the exception of my meeting with Dimsdale, you might have read in the newspapers. Why did I retire from the army?"

"Your cousin died and left you The Grange at Bowderstyke, in Yorkshire. You gave up your profession so as to get the estates in order: they had been sadly neglected by your cousin, who was a drunkard."

"That is impolite, but true," said Towton with a grimace. "Go on."

"You wish to marry."

The Colonel shrugged his shoulders. "Every man wishes to marry."

"You wish to marry a girl called Ida Dimsdale," went on the passionless voice, and Diabella refrained from making any comment on the remark.

"Ah! Now you are becoming interesting. Why do I wish to marry Ida Dimsdale?" The reply was unexpected. "You desire to get her money in order to recover certain lands sold by your late cousin."

"That is a lie." Towton grew a trifle red and spoke sharply. "I love Miss Dimsdale, and would take her without a penny."

"That is how you will have to take her," replied Diabella coldly and without insisting upon the truth of her previous statement.

"Nonsense! Miss Dimsdale has a large fortune."

"You think she has ten thousand a year. She has nothing."

Towton felt an astonishment which he could scarcely conceal, and wondered if Diabella had spoken in this way to Ida. "What do you mean?"

"I mean that this girl is not the daughter of Martin Dimsdale."

"What!" Towton rose in his surprise; "How dare you say that?"

"I am only reading what I see," said Diabella wearily. "Your fortune and this girl's is connected, therefore I know of her past."

"Past! Past!" fumed the Colonel, sitting down again. "She has no past in the sense you mean. She was born in Burmah, and her mother died shortly afterwards. Dimsdale sent her home to relatives, and afterwards she went to school at Hampstead. Five years ago he returned to settle in England and she has been with him ever since."

"Quite true; but you are foolish to tell me so much, as now you will say that I merely echo what you have mentioned."

"I have certainly not mentioned that she is not Dimsdale's daughter."

"No. Yet it is true. Her name is Ida Menteith, and her father was a major in a native regiment. Menteith was with his wife in Burmah at a hill station called--called--wait until I get the name." Diabella stopped for one moment, then spoke out triumphantly, "It was called Goorkah Station, and was besieged by the Dacoits?"

"Yes. I remember the station, but not a man called Menteith."

"This happened before you went to India."

"What happened?" asked Towton bluntly. "What I am about to tell you. Dimsdale was then a police-commissioner. He loved Mrs. Menteith, who returned his love, and hated the husband."

"I don't believe that for one moment. Dimsdale was a good fellow, who would never make love to another man's wife."

"Many good fellows do that," said Diabella sarcastically; "and Dimsdale did love Mrs. Menteith: so deeply that he did not save the husband's life when he could have done so."

"That's an absolute lie," insisted Towton angrily. "How dare you malign a dead man who cannot defend himself!"

"Martin Dimsdale's friend, George Venery, who is a merchant at Singapore, can prove the truth of what I say."

"Rubbish! How do you know?"

"I read all I am telling you in the astral light," said Diabella. "If it displeases you I need tell no more."

"It does not so much displease me as make me wonder at your imagination."

Diabella still preserved her immobility. "Write to George Venery and you will find that I have spoken the truth."

"It seems incredible," muttered Towton doubtfully. "Of course, I know that there is great truth in occult matters. But what you say is too precise to be anything but what you must have learned--perhaps from this man."

"No," replied the fortune-teller. "I never heard the name of Venery before, and I have never been to Singapore or even to Burmah. I only read what I see. How else should I know?"

The Colonel made a gesture of disbelief. Although he believed in the unseen, from various Indian experiences, he could not credit the story of this masked woman. "Go on, and tell me more," he said at length; "later I can write to Mr. Venery and verify your statements."

"Ida Dimsdale is Menteith's daughter," said Diabella quietly. "She was born in Rangoon when her father was being besieged in Goorkah Station. Dimsdale was in the neighbourhood with a force and hastened to relieve his friend. But he purposely delayed his approach so that the station might be taken and Menteith killed."

"I don't believe that for one moment. Dimsdale would not act so wickedly."

"He did act in that way, as Venery can tell you. It was his behaviour that caused a breach between them. Dimsdale hoped to get rid of Menteith and so marry the wife. His plan of delay was successful, and the station was taken by the Dacoits. Menteith was crucified and his perfidious friend arrived when he was dying. Menteith was buried at Goorkah Station and Dimsdale returned to Rangoon, hoping to marry Mrs. Menteith now that the obstacle was removed. Mrs. Menteith, however, weak after the birth of her child, died in a few days. Then Dimsdale was stricken with remorse and brought up the child as his own. She has passed for his daughter and, as his next-of-kin, inherits the money. But she is no relation, since Dimsdale did not leave a will and----"

"How do you know that Dimsdale left no will?"

"I might have seen it in the papers," said Diabella coolly; "but I did not, for to my sight the hidden things of Dimsdale's life are revealed. But you can understand that if you marry Ida you will get no money with her. The truth will be made known and Lady Corsoon will inherit it, as it is but right she should do."

Towton rose so hurriedly that he knocked over his chair. "I can't stand any more of this," he declared impetuously; "all your occult business is a sham, and you are making up lies. I insist upon your removing that mask so that I may know who you are."

Diabella rose, tall and straight and stiff, but did not seem disturbed. "Beware, Colonel Towton. If you advance a step it will be the worse for you."

The military man laughed and stepped forward. "I must know who you are, as I intend to make you pay for telling these falsehoods."

"They are true."

"They are lies. Now I know why Miss Dimsdale was agitated because of her visit to you. You told her this story also."

"What if I did? The truth----" she flung up a hand as the Colonel took another step forward. "Stand back, I tell you."

"Take your mask off," he insisted, and stretched out his hand.

Diabella swerved to one side and avoided his grasp. Then she dropped into her chair, pressing the arms of the same hard. Immediately from the mummies set round the room came a most unearthly crying, which confounded the Colonel, not expecting such a tumult. The weird room rang with thin wailings and dismal cries. It was evident that some mechanism connected with the chair produced these noises. The place was filled with clever contrivances to intimidate nervous people. But Colonel Towton was not nervous, and after his first startled pause he sprang forward again to seize the seated figure. At all costs he was determined to unmask the sorceress and learn who she was. Then he might hope to find out how she had become possessed of these facts concerning Dimsdale's past life, or whether those same facts were simply lies designed to perplex and mystify.

Diabella never moved as Towton came towards her, and the Colonel soon knew why she was thus certain of her safety. Before he could reach the hither side of the ebony table, rapidly as he moved, he was gripped from behind by two gigantic hands and twisted round sharply to face a tall and burly Hindoo arrayed in a white robe and wearing a white turban. "Let me go, you dog!" muttered Towton in the Tamil dialect, and set his teeth.

Diabella clapped her hands and the two men closed in a fierce struggle. As they swayed round the room the ebony table was upset and the woman cried out a sentence in an unknown language in her metallic voice. The next moment the native unloosened his grip on the Englishman and stepped back.

"Will you go now?" demanded Diabella quietly and addressing Towton.

"No," he cried fiercely. "I want your mask removed."

Whether Diabella gave a sign or not Towton was never able to say, but she must have given a signal, for just as the words left his mouth the native sprang forward with the leap of a tiger and the next moment Towton found a silk handkerchief round his neck. It flashed across him that in this way had Dimsdale been killed, and then, with the tightening of the handkerchief, came almost insensibility, or, rather, a dazed feeling, which bewildered his brain.

He had a faint feeling of being led out of the room and of hearing a door closed. When he recovered his senses he found himself seated on the floor of the passage quite alone. His first thought was to tell the police what had occurred, his second to conceal the adventure.

"I shall consult with Vernon," he thought, and walked unsteadily down the stairs, feeling his neck somewhat sore, but otherwise uninjured.

CHAPTER X.

MYSTERY.

It was quite three days before Colonel Towton was enabled to have an interview with Vernon. He certainly wrote to him at once, but on receiving no reply he telephoned, only to learn that his friend had been unexpectedly called from town on the same evening. Towton therefore had to possess his soul in patience, and remained in his rooms recovering from the assault. And this took some little time.

The attempt at strangulation by the burly Hindoo--who was a different person to the slim doorkeeper--had caused the Colonel's neck to swell, as the flesh was bruised and chafed. His windpipe also felt painful owing to the strong compression, and for twenty-four hours he had found it difficult to swallow with ease. Towton recognised only too uneasily that he had been within a short distance of actual death, and perhaps would have been strangled outright had not Diabella, as he verily believed, stopped her too zealous servant. Naturally, she did not wish for a client's death lest the police should interfere and put an end to her lucrative trade, which was assuredly a very paying one.

Meanwhile the Colonel received a letter from Ida saying that on the ensuing day she was going down to Yorkshire with Miss Hest. There, breathing air like champagne, and enjoying perfect rest, undisturbed by callers, she hoped to recover her spirits and health within a month, the time of her proposed stay. But what pleased Towton most in the letter, and what caused him to blush like a girl, was the hope Ida expressed that he would come down to his country seat while she stayed at the Hall. "You have often told me of your beautiful home," wrote Ida amiably, "and one of my reasons for staying at Gerby Hall is to see The Grange. If you should take a fancy to run down, perhaps you will show it to me yourself, as I hear from Frances that the house is full of historical interest." There were a few lines more to the same effect, and it really seemed as though Ida wished to become acquainted with her future home. At least, Towton looked at the matter in this way and his spirits rose accordingly. Maunders apparently was out of favour, and Ida had returned to her first love. Without being unduly conceited Towton was very well satisfied that the girl had loved him before the handsome scamp had come on the scene. Then the latter's looks and charm of manner had infatuated her to an alarming extent. Now, and the Colonel sincerely hoped that such was the case, her momentary aberration, as it might be called, had passed away, and she was holding out the olive branch of complete reconciliation.

But that Towton still felt unwell after his rough and tumble encounter with the Hindoo, and but that he wished to consult Vernon about the matter, he would have gone down to Yorkshire at once so as to bask in the sunshine of Ida's eyes. But he put a restraint on his feelings and decided, not without a struggle, to remain where he was. In connection with various ideas which had occurred to him since his visit to the Bond Street fortune-teller, it was imperative that he should consult with someone and ventilate various theories, which might, or might not, elucidate various mysteries. Therefore Towton read and smoked and played patience in his comfortable rooms, watching the passing of time with open eagerness.

On the third evening, and that was a Saturday, Vernon made his appearance at eight o'clock. He entered with perfect coolness, and found himself facing a very impatient man.

"Did you wish to see me, Colonel?" he asked quietly. "I found a note at my chambers requesting me to call at once."

"Do I wish to see you?" echoed Towton jumping to his feet and wringing Vernon's hand heartily. "Why, my dear fellow, I have been sitting here on pins and needles for the last few days. What the deuce took you out of town so unexpectedly? I beg your pardon, I should not enquire into your private business. Sit down and have a cigar. The whisky and potash is on the table at your elbow."

"Oh, my business is not private," replied Vernon, taking a comfortable chair and a very excellent cigar. "All the world will know in a week or so."

"Know what?"

"That my uncle, Sir Edward Vernon, is dead, and that I am a titled, well-to-do man, worth knowing."

"I never knew you had an uncle," said Towton staring.

"It's not unusual for men to have uncles," said Vernon drily. "I didn't buck about the relationship, as we were not the best of friends. A family quarrel between my father and Sir Edward, you understand? However, when I returned from a visit to Miss Dimsdale I found a letter from my uncle asking me to come to Slimthorp, near Worcester, as he was very ill. I packed up and went by the evening train, and there I have been for the last three days."

"Humph! I suppose I ought to congratulate you?"

"Well, you may. Sir Edward can't last more than a week, and he leaves me heir to his title, his mansion, and a few thousands a year. He's not a bad old fellow, either," went on Vernon meditatively, "and I am sorry he is dying. I don't deny, however, that his death will make a great change in my fortunes for the better, as is obvious."

"It will enable you to marry Miss Corsoon," said the Colonel nodding.

"Yes." Vernon thought of his interview with Lady Corsoon and replied briefly. "Uncle Edward is eighty years of age," he added apologetically, "so he can't be said to have been cut off when he was green."

"He's not cut off yet," answered Towton with a shrug. "I don't want to throw cold water on your prospects, Vernon, but these old fellows have wonderful recuperative power."

"I shall be glad if he gets better," said Vernon emphatically; "and now that we are friends I may be able to make his life more cheerful. He has a dismal time all alone in that barrack of a house. But I don't see why I should bore you with all this family history."

"I do," said the Colonel unhesitatingly. "It's because you and I have been drawn into closer friendship by our common acquaintance with Maunders, who is playing fast and loose with the two girls we love. We have had to make common cause against the enemy, and so are forced to speak freely. Besides, you are a good chap, Vernon, and I don't wish to work alongside a better man," and, leaning forward, the Colonel gave his friend's hand a grip.

"Would you do that, would you say that, if you knew that I was a private detective, or, to soften the term, a private enquiry agent?"

"What!" Towton nearly jumped out of his chair. "As I had no money when my father died," explained the young man steadily, "and my uncle would have nothing to do with me, I turned my powers of observation to account by setting up as Nemo, of Covent Garden, to hunt down criminals and to help people to keep their secrets when threatened by blackmailers. Mine is a perfectly honourable profession, I assure you, Colonel, but you may have your prejudices."

"Well," said Towton after a pause, "I don't deny that I care little for detectives, who are too much the bloodhounds of the law. But I am quite sure that you were driven to take up the business, and I am also quite sure," added Towton emphatically, "that the business as conducted by you is all that can be desired in the way of honour. Why did you tell me?"

"If I hadn't, probably Maunders, when he found that we were working together, would have told you. It struck me as a wise thing to take the wind out of his sails."

"There's something in that," admitted the Colonel, twisting his moustache. "And I am glad that I heard of your profession from yourself. But how did your friend Maunders find out what you kept secret?"

Vernon shrugged his shoulders. "Who knows? He seems to have a wonderful nose for smelling out things to his advantage."

"To his advantage? Come, now!"

"I assure you, Colonel, it is so. He wished to become my partner. Lately, however, he has changed his mind and he promised to hold his tongue. To my cost," went on Vernon slowly, "I found that he has not done so, as he told Lady Corsoon."

"The devil he did! Then good-bye to your chances of the daughter."

"Do you think so, when I shall soon be Sir Arthur Vernon, with an eligible country seat and three thousand a year, more or less?"

"No. That alters the case; it whitewashes you, as it were. Ho! ho!" Towton laughed maliciously, "that will be one in the eye for Mr. Constantine Maunders. And serve him right! Why the deuce does he play the lover with two women at once? I congratulate you, Sir Arthur----"

"Colonel, you are premature."

"Never mind. It's just as well to take the bull by the horns and time by the forelock. I congratulate you, Sir Arthur, for you will marry Miss Corsoon and wipe our friend's eye. He won't have either girl."

"Certainly not Lucy, if I can help it," said Vernon hotly; "but what about Miss Dimsdale? I rather think, from what I saw at our interview of three days ago, that she inclines to you, Colonel."

"Ah! Miss Dimsdale." Towton nursed his chin in the cup of his hand. "It is about Miss Dimsdale, amongst other things, that I wish to see you."

"What other things?" demanded Vernon bluntly.

"Diabella for one."

"The fortune-teller? Have you seen her?"

Towton put his hand to his neck with a wry smile. "Yes, the jade. She nearly had me strangled."

Vernon dropped his cigar. "Strangled!"

"Yes." The Colonel unloosened the white silk scarf he wore round his throat and leaned forward to show a fading black mark round it. "You see!

I assure you I have scarcely been able to swallow since I saw you last. That damned Hindoo nearly did for me."

"Hindoo! Did a Hindoo attempt to kill you?"

"Rather, and jolly nearly succeeded."

"But why?"

"Because I wished to tear off the false face worn by Diabella: a waxen or papier-mache sort of face, which makes her look like an Egyptian, so as to be in keeping with her room, I suppose."

"Why did you wish to tear it off?"

"Because she--well, she said certain things, and----" Towton stopped as Vernon rose quickly and began to walk about the room. "What's up, now?"

"Colonel, do you remember how you gave it as your opinion that Dimsdale had been strangled by a Thug?"

"Ah!" said Towton drily, "the same idea strikes you also, I see. Well, Diabella may have something to do with the matter. I asked you to see me in order that we might thresh it out. Now that I know you are Nemo I am all the better pleased, as your professional knowledge may link this and that together."

"This and that?"

"Bond Street and Hampstead," said the Colonel impatiently; "that is, you may see a connecting link between this beastly nigger attempting to strangle me and the actual strangulation of poor Dimsdale in his library."

"I can't see the link," said Vernon thoughtfully. "Diabella knows nothing about Dimsdale."

"On the contrary, she knows a great deal. By the way, didn't you tell me that Dimsdale was being blackmailed by that confounded Spider?"

"Yes." Vernon stared and wondered why the question was asked. "He had a secret, which The Spider learned, and intended to tell it to me after the capture of the beast. But The Spider killed him, and so----" Vernon shrugged.

"I wonder if what Diabella told was the secret," muttered Towton, stroking his chin. "Did Dimsdale ever give you to understand that his secret, whatever it might have been, was a disgraceful one?"

"On the contrary, he said that he didn't mind any one knowing what it was," said Vernon promptly; "only he added that The Spider had embroidered actual facts and so might make things hot for him were the added facts to become known to the world at large."

Towton nodded. "I thought so."

"Thought what?" asked Vernon impatiently.

"That Diabella and this mysterious Spider are in league."

Vernon dropped into his chair, placed his hands on his knees and stared very hard at the lean, brown face of the soldier. "What do you mean?"

"Listen, and I'll tell you. I am quite sure that you will come to the same conclusion," and Towton in an incisive manner related what had taken place in the fortune-teller's weird apartments.

The effect on Vernon was to produce an extraordinary emotion of mingled dread and relief: dread, because he saw deep and dangerous villainy at work, and relief as now he espied a gleam of light in the darkness surrounding the "Rangoon" crime. He made no remark either during Towton's recital or after it, so that the Colonel grew impatient.

"Well, what do you make of it?" he asked sharply.

"I agree with you that Diabella and The Spider are in league. Perhaps," he rose, much agitated, "perhaps Diabella is The Spider all by herself."

"The Spider I always understood to be a man."

"It is presumed so, but who knows. Diabella may be the real originator of these crimes and may employ men to collect her fees. Then, of course, as a popular fortune-teller, she has every opportunity of learning people's secrets, for those who consult such creatures always give themselves away. A few skilfully put questions and a few dexterous prophecies would make people loosen their tongues. Then a clever woman, putting two and two together, would soon make the four, which means blackmail."

"But how the deuce could she learn this secret of Dimsdale's?"

"Well, the secret is connected with the Far East and you say that Diabella employs two Indians in her fortune-telling business. She may have learned it from them since the older man, the one who attempted to strangle you, may have been a soldier in the Burmese War and so may have been connected with Dimsdale. Then, again, Diabella may herself have been in the East and may have learned about Ida not being Dimsdale's daughter."

"Do you think it is true?"

"I fear so, as the secret of her birth and adoption by Dimsdale is not one that any man would mind being made known. But the embroidery to which our poor dead friend alluded consists of this assertion: that he wilfully delayed coming to the assistance of Menteith and for the sake of the man's wife acted in a David-and-Uriah-the-Hittite manner. That embroidery is indeed worth blackmail. But it isn't true. I believe Dimsdale's assertion rather than Diabella's story. She knew the facts, and improved upon them in the way I have mentioned."

Colonel Towton nodded. "Then Ida, not being Dimsdale's daughter, and there being no will, cannot inherit her presumed father's money as next of kin?"

"I think not. It will go to Lady Corsoon, as Diabella asserted. She is Dimsdale's sister and only relative. It will be a good thing for Lady Corsoon," murmured Vernon, thinking of the gambling debts, "as it will make her independent of her miserly husband."

"There is another thing to be thought of," said the Colonel gravely, "and that is the blackmailing of Ida."

"Oh. Do you think that her health is suffering from that?"

"Yes, I do. She went to the fortune-teller, and what she heard has made her ill. She probably was told the same story as I heard and knows that she is keeping the ten thousand a year wrongfully from Lady Corsoon. This being the case, and Ida being a sensitive girl, it is no wonder that she is disturbed and ill. Her conscience is fighting between keeping the money and giving it up. Then Miss Hest may be forcing her to keep silence; otherwise, as she is the sweetest girl in the world, I feel sure she would speak out and give up the fortune."

"She may not believe the story."

"Certainly she may not; but it must have sown doubts in her breast, and if left to herself she would perhaps come to me or to you, asking us to resolve these doubts. But Miss Hest----"

"Colonel! Colonel! I don't think you are altogether just to Miss Hest. She is really a kind-hearted, decent woman, and is not after Ida's money, as you imagine. She wants Mrs. Bedge to become Ida's companion, or for Ida to marry you, so that she can go back to her reciting."

"Does she want Ida to marry Maunders?" asked Towton shrewdly.

"No. I think she fancies you will make Ida a better husband. No, Colonel, Miss Hest's conduct is above reproach, and if she knows about this wild story told by Diabella she will advise Ida for the best."

"In what way?"

"Well, it is no use Ida telling you, or I, or anyone else the tale, unless she is sure of the truth. According to Diabella, this man Venery, in Singapore, can substantiate the story, so, under the guidance of Miss Hest, provided, mind you, she knows the story, Ida may have written to Venery. If Venery says that Ida is not Dimsdale's daughter I daresay the girl will see her supposed aunt and surrender the fortune. Miss Hest, undoubtedly, as you say, exercises a certain amount of control over Ida's weaker mind, but she is a good woman and assuredly is not a fortune-hunter."

"It may be as you say," assented the Colonel grudgingly. "However, it is plain that Diabella knows something of The Spider and something of the murder, since she is aware of Dimsdale's secret."

"You don't think she read it in the astral light? I know you believe in occult matters."

"To a certain extent," said Towton drily, "but I don't believe that the Unseen ever furnished so detailed a story. Communications from the next world are apt to be scrappy. What's to be done?"

Vernon quickly decided. "We'll divide the burden," he said promptly. "You write to-night or to-morrow to George Venery, of Singapore, asking how much of this yarn is true, and I shall call on Diabella."

"Why not consult Inspector Drench and have her arrested."

"It wouldn't be a bad idea," pondered Vernon, "and yet it is not wise to act with too much haste. After all, we can't get a search warrant, as you have no witness to your assault, and the woman can easily deny the story of Dimsdale which seems to connect her with The Spider. I shall go on my own and secure more evidence upon which to get a warrant, if not for her arrest at all events for a search through those rooms of hers. Some evidence regarding The Spider--if indeed she is connected with him, as seems extremely probable--may be found concealed there. I'll call to-morrow morning," ended Vernon rising, "in the character of a superstitious client."

"And I'll write the letter to Venery, of Singapore."

In this way the matter was decided and the burden was divided. Vernon went away with the conviction that by chance the Colonel had struck upon the much-wished-for clue which would lead to the identification of the famous Spider. Certainly, he might be jumping to a conclusion, but, taking all that was known into account it looked extremely probable. And if it was true it behoved him to act cautiously lest The Spider at the eleventh hour should slip through the fingers of the police. For this reason, and until he was positive, Vernon did not think it wise to call in the assistance of the law. First it was necessary to prove the collusion of Diabella and The

Spider, so that if she were not the scoundrel herself she would at least be able to identify him beyond all doubt. Second, even if his identity were proved it would be no easy task to arrest so slippery a criminal. Like the celebrated fox in the fable, The Spider had a thousand tricks, which he could use to better advantage than the animal. The fox in the story of Æsop was caught, but it was probable, unless the very greatest care were used, that The Spider would escape. Already the police had experienced his subtlety, and regarded the arch-scoundrel as a very wary and dangerous bird who was not to be caught by putting salt on his tail.

Colonel Towton, being less experienced in the trickery of the criminal classes, was more hopeful of success, and next morning settled down to write the letter to Venery, of Singapore, quite confident that all the mysteries were on the eve of solution. He quite expected to hear from his correspondent that Ida was not Dimsdale's daughter, but he was quite sure that the embroidered facts of the pointed delay in the rescue of Menteith were false. Assured of this, he was quite willing to marry Ida, as the daughter of a poor soldier, and to hand over the fortune to Lady Corsoon. Love was everything to the Colonel at this moment, and nothing else mattered.

But just as he reached the second page of his letter Vernon burst into the room with a half-vexed and half-triumphant air. He told his news without any delay. "I believe you are right about Diabella being connected with The Spider, Colonel," he said; "she has shut up her rooms and has cleared out bag and baggage."

CHAPTER XI.

THE NEEDLE IN THE HAYSTACK.

It was big news, which meant more than at first sight appeared, since the implication was of depths below depths and veils behind veils. To be quite plain, the unexpected flight of the fortune-teller, for it was nothing else, hinted at the truth of Towton's suspicions. Had there been nothing but the mere assault Diabella could have faced that and could have even counted upon the Colonel doing nothing, since an unbiassed witness was lacking. The flight was not caused by the incident which had taken place in the Bond Street rooms, but by the fear that something dangerous might peep out from behind it. And what could this something be--on the grounds of Diabella's story and the Hindoo's attempted strangling--but a dread lest The Spider should be traced?

"I am perfectly certain that you are right, Towton," said Vernon, sitting sideways on the table and swinging his legs. "Only the fear of her connection with that blackmailing scoundrel being traced could have scared her into disappearance."

"She has really gone?"

"Really and truly. Remember, she had three days to make herself scarce, but so afraid was she lest you should take action that she decamped on the morning of the second day."

"How decamped?" questioned Towton, laying down his pen.

"She sent the Hindoo to surrender the lease. Bahadur his name is."

"The native who tried to choke me?"

"No; the doorkeeper. I was precise to ask if he was lean or stout. The lean one came to surrender the lease."

"And his name is Bahadur. Well, that's something worth knowing. But how did you get your informant to talk, and how did you find any person in authority to explain matters?"

"That was easy." Vernon slipped off the table and into a chair. "I called on the plea of wanting my fortune told by Diabella. Instead of Bahadur opening the door a neat little maid-servant made her appearance and informed me that Diabella had retired from the business, which had been taken over by a certain American prophetess. I asked to see the lady, and I did."

"You don't think she was Diabella unmasked?"

"Not from your description. You told me Diabella was tall; this woman was short, and the voice, instead of being metallic, as you described it, was rather musical, although disfigured by a Yankee twang. This new sorceress, from New York City, as she told me she was, could never have spoken English without the twang."

"It might have been assumed."

"Not it. I can tell the true from the false," said Vernon emphatically. "Mrs. Hiram G. Slowcomb is a genuine American, sure enough. Besides, her ideas of surroundings and those of Diabella differ. The last desired weird decoration and furniture, a mask, an Egyptian dress, Oriental attendants, and so forth. Mrs. Slowcomb's idea is that people should not be frightened, but should have their future told in a motherly, old-fashioned way amidst rural-fireside-granny-scenery. She intends, so she told me, to transform the Egyptian rooms into the semblance of a rustic cottage interior, with a cat and a humming tea-kettle, rafters with strings of onions, and flower-pots on the ledges of Bond Street windows turned into casements. It's rather a clever dodge," reflected Vernon, "as people will be at their ease directly and so will talk freely and listen comfortably."

"And Mrs. Hiram G. Slowcomb herself?"

"A motherly old thing in a mob cap and a stuff dress with a voluminous apron and a woollen shawl over her shoulders. I daresay she has dressed for the old cottage interior part, for she was seated in a wooden chair which didn't fit in with the Memphis decorations, and knitted a homely stocking."

"What did she tell you about Diabella?"

"Very little, because she knew very little."

"Do you believe that?" asked the highly suspicious Colonel.

Vernon shrugged his shoulders. "Everyone tells such lies nowadays that I never believe anyone. But Mrs. Slowcomb seemed to be genuine enough. However, I'll soon prove that, as I intend to have her watched by a man upon whom I can depend. I shall learn in that way if she has business relations with our masked friend."

"What did she tell you?" asked Towton again.

"Well, it seemed that she heard about Diabella wishing to retire from business and went to see her. Diabella denied that the rumour was true, but promised Mrs. Slowcomb the first refusal of the rooms and goodwill, though how one can transfer fortune-telling clients beats me. However, Mrs. Slowcomb retired and left her address--somewhere in Pimlico, where she was wasting her talents on maid-servants and suburban people. Diabella sent Bahadur to her there and the lease was duly transferred for a sum of money. I believe Bahadur took Mrs. Slowcomb to the City and interviewed the landlord's lawyer. However, it was all done fair and square."

"But Diabella must have signed the consent to the transfer?"

"So she did, under the name of Isabella Hopkins, which may or may not be her real name. At all events, she took the rooms as Miss Hopkins and signed that name on the transfer. Mrs. Slowcomb never saw her--at least, without the mask. She was as you saw her when Mrs. Slowcomb called at the rooms, and didn't show in the lawyer's office."

"But the lawyer must have seen her?"

"Well, he did, and I went to see him. He's a stiff old buckram creature, who declined to impart anything about Miss Isabella Hopkins as he wanted to know why I wished to know; and, of course, on the face of it, you can see, Towton, that I couldn't gratify his very natural curiosity."

"But why not, if we are to catch Diabella?"

"We haven't got enough grounds to go upon," said Vernon, shaking his head. "I think it is best to let her fancy we don't suspect anything and then we may be able to capture her unawares. She's connected with The Spider, if not that gentleman himself, I am sure, and your visit and behaviour, which led to the strangling attempt, have given her a fright. But if we keep silent her suspicions will be lulled and she may reappear."

"Surely not."

"Oh, I think so. Fortune-telling is an invaluable way of learning secrets, and Diabella must be very useful to The Spider, or to herself, if she is him. She won't surrender her position without a struggle. It's too paying all round, my dear fellow."

"But she did surrender it."

"Only because she lost her head for the moment and thought you might bring the police on the scene for the assault. That would lead to unpleasant questions being asked, which might result in heaven knows what revelations. Fortune-tellers are not in good odour since the campaign of a certain halfpenny paper against them."

The Colonel leaned back in his chair, reflecting, while Vernon rose to walk up and down the room for the purpose of stretching his long legs. He lighted a cigar and went on talking lightly.

"You never saw such a heap of clever dodges as this Diabella has to impress the weak-minded. Those mummies--they are all faked, by the way--have reeds inside them leading to their mouths, and Diabella, by pressing on the arms of her state chair, could send a stream of wind along to make them squall."

"And they did squall," said Towton musingly. "I never heard such a devilish row in my life. What else?"

"Oh, some arrangement by which when the room was darkened the interior of the painted walls were illuminated to reveal the Egyptian figures as walking and sitting skeletons. Then there's an apparatus to make thunder, and flashlights for lightning, to say nothing of ingeniously arranged draughts calculated to make anyone's hair rise in the necessary darkness when he or she felt a cold breath fanning him or her. I wonder Diabella didn't send her clients stark, staring mad."

"It sounds like a fraudulent spiritualistic medium, Vernon, and only confirms my suspicions that Diabella was not a genuine occultist."

"But do you really believe anyone has such powers?" asked Vernon curiously.

"I really do," said the Colonel promptly, "strange as it may appear. In India I have seen too much of the Unseen to doubt. There are certain gifted people who can see and who can control forces of which the average person knows nothing. Oh, yes, I believe, and--but what's the use of talking? I can never make you believe, and I don't want to."

Vernon shrugged his shoulders again and buttoned up his coat. "As you say, it doesn't matter," he answered. "However, Diabella has vanished with her two satellites, so there's nothing more to be done at present."

"You give up the hunt?"

"I said, at present. No. I shall lie quiet until Diabella reappears."

"She won't, if she's wise."

"She will--if she's daring, and I shrewdly suspect that she is."

"Do you believe her to be this Spider?"

"I do, and I don't. I really can't say. But if not the rose, she is near the rose. All I can assert with safety, Colonel, is that if we can lay hands on this witch in grain we'll learn who murdered poor Dimsdale."

"God grant that."

"Amen! to that pious prayer," was Vernon's reply as he left the room. Towton duly finished his letter of inquiry to Venery, of Singapore, and having posted it went cheerfully about his usual business of pleasure--that is, as cheerfully as a man in love well could do. At the Colonel's age love was rather a serious matter, since he had taken the disease badly, as is invariably the case with middle aged men. Some individuals constantly let their emotions trickle out to expend themselves in trifling love affairs, amusing for the moment; others dam up the passions for years until they burst through the barrier, to sweep everything before them irresistibly. Colonel Towton was one of the latter. But, not being entirely blinded by his late-born infatuation, he did not deem Ida perfection, as a hot-headed youth would have done, and he foresaw that, as Mrs. Towton, she would need guidance and firm control. Hitherto, for want of both, she had run wild; but the materials were there, out of which, as Towton put it to himself, he could build a model wife. That she was frivolous, rather than strong-minded, was a point in her favour, as the Colonel desired to mould wax rather than to hammer iron. So if Ida only consented to marry him he hoped for a calm and contented domestic existence, undisturbed by aggressive romance. And with his home-loving, self-controlled nature, Towton infinitely preferred the outlook from an unemotional point of view.

As to the money, he cared little for the possible loss of that, although he could not deny but what Ida's yearly thousands would have come at the right moment to effect improvements on the Bowderstyke estate. Towton was too prosaic and level-headed to despise the power of the purse, but on the other hand he was not at all grasping, and was quite satisfied to marry a girl with no dowry but her beauty and sweet nature. All the same, he intended to inform himself fully of the truth by inquiring, as he had done, from the man Diabella had mentioned as her authority. The Colonel had no notion of letting Ida's money benefit Lady Corsoon if he could help it. Of course, if it was proved to be legally hers he would be the first to see that she had her rights. On the other hand, should Ida turn out to be Dimsdale's daughter, Towton made up his mind that the ten thousand a year would be joyfully used for the improvement of his family property. With these thoughts to employ his mind he waited very patiently in London, considering that he was a man of actions rather than a dreamer of dreams. Later on, when Vernon had coaxed Diabella from her hiding-place, Towton intended to travel to Bowderstyke-to see his beloved. He had every belief that during his absence Vernon could manage the affair which interested them both so greatly.

For the next few days the Colonel saw nothing of Vernon, but, while in the tablinum of the Athenian Club, he unexpectedly came face to face with Mr. Maunders. The scamp looked singularly handsome, and was dressed carefully, as usual; but the sight of a snake would have been more pleasing to the worthy Colonel. He did not like Maunders, and, moreover, resented him as a somewhat dishonourable rival, for no one could respect a man who pointedly wooed two women at one and the same time. Towton therefore nodded coolly and crossed to the central table to pick up a Service Magazine. As he did so Maunders sauntered to his side and slipped into a chair near to that one which the Colonel had taken.

"Have you had any news of Miss Dimsdale?" asked Maunders amiably.

"No," retorted Towton, opening his magazine as a hint that he wished to be left alone.

"She is still in Yorkshire with Miss Hest," persisted Maunders.

"So I understand," was the stiff reply.

"I believe she will remain there for one month."

"Possibly she will."

Maunders was not discouraged. "Have you any message for her," he asked.

"Why do you ask?" demanded the Colonel, sitting up abruptly.

"Because Francis Hest--you know, the brother of Miss Dimsdale's friend--has asked me down to Gerby Hall. I am going there at the end of the week for a few days. I thought you might have a message for Miss Dimsdale."

"There is such a thing as the post," said Towton, exasperated by the young man's cool assurance. He took up the magazine again, then hesitated and threw it on the table. Averse as the Colonel was to discuss his private affairs with anyone, and least of all with Maunders, whom he so frankly hated, he felt that he ought to take advantage of this chance to learn exactly what was Maunders' attitude towards Ida. "Am I to understand that you are engaged to Miss Dimsdale?" he asked sharply.

"Why should you think that?" asked Constantine negligently.

"Why, indeed! Considering that one day you profess to be paying attentions to Miss Corsoon and the next pay your addresses to Miss Dimsdale. But as you are going down to Gerby Hall it looks as though you inclined to marry the latter young lady."

"No," said Maunders indolently and looking at Towton through half-closed eyelids. "I am going to see Francis Hest, who is a friend of mine. But I daresay Miss Hest and Miss Dimsdale find it dull, so I may be able to amuse them a trifle."

"I am quite sure of that," said Towton sarcastically; "your social qualifications are well known. But I asked you if you were engaged to Miss Dimsdale."

"No, I am not, nor am I likely to be."

This was good news, but Towton could not be sure if Maunders was speaking honestly. "Then you intend to marry Miss Corsoon?" said the Colonel.

"I do. But I don't see why you should trouble yourself about my private affairs," said Maunders, insolently cool.

"It was not I who sought this interview. But as you chose to speak to me I have every right to mention a subject which concerns us both."

"And concerns Vernon also."

"Precisely," said Towton with great emphasis. "It is useless to disguise the fact, Mr. Maunders, that we are rivals, and----"

"Pardon me, no," interrupted the young man quickly. "I have been refused by Miss Dimsdale, so the field is open to you."

"Ida refused you?" muttered the Colonel stupefied. "Strange, is it not?" replied Maunders lightly, "but such is the case. I asked her to marry me and she hinted at a previous attachment. I presume she meant-----"

Towton threw up his hand and coloured through his bronzed skin. "We will not mention names, if you please."

"I don't mind. But you know how the land lies--so far as I am concerned, that is. But you will have to reckon with Francis Hest."

"Miss Hest's brother?"

"The same. Francis and Frances--twins, with twin names, you might say. She is devoted to this more than brother, and wishes him to marry money."

"Do you mean to say that Miss Hest has taken Miss Dimsdale down to Gerby Hall so that she may meet Mr. Hest?"

"Yes. He's not a bad-looking fellow: exactly like his sister, who is handsome in an imperial way, as you have seen. In fact, if you see Frances you have seen Francis. The brother isn't very well off, as he has spent all his available cash in philanthropic works, and constructing some confounded dam to supply water to several villages has nearly ruined him. Miss Dimsdale's money will therefore come in very acceptably. But I fear Hest will waste it in helping the poor; he's ridiculously crazy about doing what he calls good."

"It's ridiculous," muttered the Colonel crossly. "Miss Dimsdale doesn't know this man Hest."

"Frances will see to that. Now that Miss Dimsdale is at the Hall she will have every opportunity of seeing him. Miss Hest will throw them together on every occasion. Upon my word," Maunders rose and stretched himself, "were I you, Colonel, I should go down to Gerby Hall and look after matters."

"Thanks for your advice," said Towton picking up the magazine again, "and good-day to you, Mr. Maunders."

"This is what comes of my trying to help you," observed the young man with a shrug. "I do what I can and you throw my philanthropy in my face."

"No! no!" Towton's conscience smote him, for really Maunders had done him a distinct service, and also he had announced that Ida had refused him, which was excellent news. "I thank you for what you have told me. It is probable that I shall go down to Gerby Hall at the end of the week."

Maunders nodded. "I may meet you there," he yawned, and sauntered away with a bored air, which was rather overdone. As a rule he was alert and full of life, so it looked as though this languor was assumed for some purpose, and not a good one, if the man's selfish nature was to be taken into account.

It wanted three days to the week-end, so Towton really intended to take the northern journey. He had never trusted Miss Hest, and it was quite probable that as she had discouraged the wooing of both himself and Maunders her intention was to secure the heiress for her too philanthropic brother.

Of course, if Towton could prove to the twins that Ida had no money it was possible that no further plans would be laid to entrap her. Money was what Francis Hest required for his lord-of-the-manor schemes, and money was what the sister desired to secure for him. But, considering that Frances did not get on well with her brother and that they rarely met, it was strange that she should be so anxious to serve him; unless, indeed, the two had come to an agreement that if Francis married the supposed heiress Frances should share the income. On the whole Towton thought it would be just as well to go down to The Grange for a week or so and pay a neighbourly visit to Gerby Hall. He would at least learn how much of Maunders' tale was true, and perhaps might induce Ida to accept him, since she had refused his handsome rival.

"Gad! I'll go down on Saturday," decided the Colonel.

And it happened that before Saturday he received a letter which made him even more anxious to visit his family seat. It came from Ida, and she pointedly asked him to come down and see her. Amongst other things, she wrote that Francis Hest had gone away and that she had only seen him twice at Gerby Hall. "Frances and her brother don't get on well together," went on Ida in her letter, "and are rarely together. When he is in she is out, and _vice versâ_, like the little old man and woman in the weather cottage. I only saw Francis for a few minutes each time and I don't like him much, although he greatly resembles Frances. But he is more gloomy and is quite a misanthrope. Nor do I like Frances so much as I did, as she seems inclined to take the upper hand with me, and wants me to do exactly as she wishes. Lately she has been urging me to marry Mr. Maunders, and told me that he was coming down to stop for a time. Besides, there is a housekeeper, Miss Jewin, who is a double-faced woman, I am sure, and looks quite dangerous. She fell in ecstacies over a photograph of Mr. Maunders, which he gave Frances, and told me, presumptuously, that she thought we made a handsome couple. In fact, I don't like this place at all, and I wish you would come down and stand by me."

At this point the Colonel laid down the letter to think. Apparently Maunders was lying when he stated that he did not wish to marry Miss Dimsdale, and that Frances wished to secure the heiress for her brother. He told one story, and Ida another; and of the two Towton preferred to believe that of the girl. The letter went into general details about the beauty of the country and the dismal gloom of the Hall. Towton gathered indirectly that Miss Hest was keeping a close watch on Ida, and that the girl was beginning to resent this over-emphatic influence. In fact, throughout the letter there sounded a note of alarm, as though Ida was both uncomfortable and uneasy. She certainly pointedly asked Towton down to stand by her, and when he had finished the epistle he was quite decided about travelling by the Saturday train as he had arranged. But the contradictory stories told by Ida and Maunders puzzled him greatly. More than ever he mistrusted Miss Hest, who seemed to be playing a deep game for the winning of Ida's fortune. But the Colonel chuckled to think of her disappointment when she learned that Ida was not entitled to the money, always provided that Diabella had spoken the truth.

As two heads are better than one, and as Towton was working in consort with Vernon, he promptly sought out his friend and laid the letter before him. Also he detailed what had taken place in the tablinum of the Athenian Club between himself and Maunders. Vernon heard the Colonel's narrative with great attention, then gave his opinion after some reflection.

"There is some devilry under all this," he said, laying a finger on the letter, "and Miss Hest seems to be working in conjunction with Maunders. He says one thing and Ida another, so it is difficult to know exactly how matters stand."

"I believe Ida."

"Well, on the whole, so do I. I think," Vernon paused, then added abruptly, "I don't trust Maunders, you know."

"Neither do I."

"In that case, let us act exactly opposite to the way in which he suggests."

"How do you mean?" questioned the Colonel doubtfully. "Maunders wants you to go to Yorkshire. As he is going himself he would naturally want a clear field, if indeed Miss Hest is supporting him in this design on Ida's fortune. Therefore he has some reason--and you may be sure that it is a bad one--to get you down."

"I can look after myself," said Towton sturdily.

"Quite so; but we have to look after Ida. Don't go to Yorkshire."

"But Ida wants me to go. See how urgent her letter is."

"I understand. All the same, I think it wiser for you to remain."

"Until when?"

"Until I can corner Diabella," replied Vernon, and ended the conversation.

CHAPTER XII

A TEMPTING OFFER.

Naturally, under the pressure of Ida's imploring letter, Colonel Towton was not anxious to remain inactive in London. He wished to go to Bowderstyke himself and learn the exact truth. Maunders said one thing and Ida another, so if the two were confronted the absolute facts of the case would certainly come to light. Towton assuredly believed Ida rather than Maunders, but it seemed strange to him that Miss Hest should champion Constantine, and strange also that Maunders should wish him to come down to Gerby Hall, where, if Ida spoke correctly, his presence would not be welcome either to Miss Hest or her co-conspirator. And Maunders was far too clever a man to do anything without having some object in view. What that object might be Colonel Towton as yet could not fathom.

For this last reason, and because his rival so pointedly advised him to go to Gerby Hall, the Colonel remained in London. Whatever Maunders' plans might be, they would assuredly be thwarted by the absence of Towton, and, later, the Colonel determined to go, even before Vernon lured Diabella from her hiding-place. Meanwhile, as Maunders had stated that he was himself going to Gerby Hall on the invitation of Miss Hest, the Colonel sought the young man's rooms on Sunday afternoon in order to see if he had kept his promise, as he fancied that the proposed visit might be some trick. On inquiry, however, the Colonel learned that Constantine had departed on the previous day and had left notice with the caretaker of his chambers that he would not return until an entire week had elapsed. Evidently he had meant what he said, namely, to accept Miss Hest's hospitality.

This knowledge, however, only made Towton the more anxious to go also, as the idea that Maunders was having it all his own way and was subjecting Ida to persecution made him restless. He wished to ride forth like a knight of old to rescue his lady-love, who certainly, if her letter was to be believed, seemed to be in great peril. It said a great deal for Towton's disciplinarian instincts that he obeyed Vernon, as one more professionally clever at such cases, rather than his own desires. In the meantime, having satisfied himself with regard to Maunders' whereabouts, the Colonel took up his usual life for, at all events, a week. He relieved his mind by writing to Ida saying that he would come down to The Grange at the termination of that period.

Vernon had not thought fit to impart to Towton how he proposed to inveigle Diabella into the open for the very simple reason that he was puzzled himself how to act. Several times he had been to the Bond Street rooms, only to find that they were in the hands of decorators, rapidly transforming the weird Egyptian hall into a cosy English cottage. Mrs. Hiram G. Slowcomb was already advertising that "Granny!" would foretell the future after the fashion of the renowned Mother Shipton, and already had seen several of Diabella's old clients, desirous of novelty. To these she told wonderful things in a strong American accent, which did not suit the thrum cap or the tartan shawl or the general looks of an ancient rustic dame. However, she was succeeding very well, and there was no doubt that when her _mise-en-scene_ was prepared that she would become the fashion for a few months. She professed to know nothing of Diabella, and as she was quite frank in answering questions Vernon saw no reason why he should not believe a story which certainly appeared, on the face of it, to be true. The lawyer of the landlord still refused to say anything about Isabella Hopkins since Vernon declined to state why the knowledge was required. And, of course, as he was suspicious rather than certain he could say absolutely nothing.

In this dilemma, and wondering how he was to come face to face with the woman, Vernon decided, on the Sunday when Towton went to seek Maunders, to pay an afternoon call. This errand took him into the luxurious drawing-room of Lady Corsoon. By this time the month of grace allowed by The Spider was nearing its end, and Vernon, having accomplished nothing definite, considered it necessary to reassure the millionaire's wife. Naturally, he expected to find her haggard and hysterical, but was truly surprised to behold a perfectly composed person, comely and content. Her brown eyes sparkled when the footman announced the newcomer, and she swept forward--the word is necessary to exactly describe Lady Corsoon's imposing gait--to welcome him with ill-concealed eagerness.

"How are you, Mr. Vernon?" she asked in her best society manner, and then dropped her voice to a confidential whisper, "I should have called at your office to-morrow had you not come."

"I am quite well, thank you," replied Vernon, for the benefit of the surrounding guests, and lowered his voice likewise: "Any news, good or bad?"

"Yes; both. Wait till everyone goes," she said softly, and again spoke gracefully in her character of hostess. "You poor man, you really must have a cup of tea. Go to Lucy and ask nicely."

Vernon needed no second command, but thrust his way through a crowd of well-dressed people to find a bamboo table covered with tea-things, over which a pretty, fresh-coloured damsel presided. She received him with a shy blush, which made her look like a dewy rose. Lucy Corsoon could not be called lovely, nor would she have attracted attention in any marked degree. A bright, sweet English girl was all she claimed to be, and, having the bloom of youth, she really appeared more charming than she really was. In a very plain white frock and without a single ornament, she looked like a modest violet, almost hidden by its leaves. The ardent gaze in her lover's dark eyes made her blush more than ever as she handed him a cup of tea.

"Without sugar," she said in a gentle voice; "I know your tastes."

"Who else should?" inquired Vernon smiling, and sipped his Bohea. "This tea is delightful and exactly what a thirsty man requires."

"I hope you are hungry also. Mr. Hest, please pass the cakestand to Mr. Vernon."

The lover wheeled when the name was mentioned, to find himself facing the counterpart of Ida's companion. He would have guessed the relationship even if Lucy had held her peace. Mr. Hest smiled at the amazed look of the young man, and swung forward the bamboo cakestand with a soft laugh.

"Don't say what you are going to say, Mr. Vernon," he remarked pleasantly. "I know exactly how astonished you are to see that I am so like my sister."

"You are indeed," breathed Vernon, mechanically taking bread and butter. "I should have taken you for Miss Hest in disguise but for----" he hesitated.

"But for this scar?" finished Hest, laying a finger on a cicatrice which ran in a thin crimson line from the right temple to the corner of the mouth. "I got that in Paris years ago; the knife of an Apache scored me in this way. It is just as well, if only to distinguish me from Frances. I rarely come to London, but when I do everyone stares at me, as you did." Mr. Hest shrugged his shoulders. "It's rather a nuisance being a twin."

"You are not so tall as your sister," ventured Vernon, while Lucy laughed at the idle jest of the Yorkshire squire.

"There's very little difference. Frances looks taller because she wears petticoats. If I dressed in her clothes and could hide this," he laid his finger again on the scar, "you would not be able to tell the difference."

"Your voices are different," said Vernon after a pause.

"I really begin to think you must be a detective, Mr. Vernon, since you are so very observant. Yes, our voices are different and in the wrong way."

"The wrong way?"

"Ah, you are not so observant as I thought. Yes; Frances has a deep contralto voice, somewhat heavy for a woman, whereas my voice, as you hear, is rather thin in quality. Nature mixed up the voices as we are twins, maybe."

It was as he said. Hest's voice had not the volume or the richness of his sister's, but it certainly had a less serious note. Vernon, recalling what Towton had told him of Ida's remark in her letter as to Francis being dismal and misanthropic, wondered that she could have been so mistaken. He was really more cheerful than Frances, and did not seem to treat life in her aggressively sober manner. Besides, that he was a philanthropist was in itself an argument against his being of a gloomy disposition. Vernon judged that Mr. Hest was much more of an optimist than was his sister, and that he lacked in some measure that sterling common sense which, to put it plainly, made her company rather dull. If Frances had been the man and Francis had been the woman their temperaments would have suited the change of sex ever so much better. But, perhaps, as Mr. Hest had just observed, since the two were twins nature had got mixed.

Vernon would rather have spoken to Lucy, but could not do so, and every now and then fresh guests came to be served. He was therefore left to the society of Hest, and took advantage of the opportunity to learn if the man was in love with Ida. "Did you leave Miss Dimsdale in good health?" he asked.

"Oh, yes. She is ever so much brighter, Mr. Vernon. The air of our Yorkshire moors has picked her up wonderfully and has brought colour to her cheeks."

"And your sister?"

Hest shrugged his shoulders again. "Oh, Frances is always in robust health, Mr. Vernon. I find her company too exhausting for my health. She always wants me to be doing something or saying something, and is never at rest."

"You do a good deal yourself in the way of philanthropy?"

"Well, I do," said Hest, his dark face lighting up, "but it is really selfish on my part. There is nothing I love so well as to help the unfortunate. I have quite changed the parish of Bowderstyke, and instead of being a Rip Van Winkle sort of place it is now in lively touch with the twentieth century. If you are ever down our way, Mr. Vernon, come and stop at the Hall and you shall see my _opus magnus_--the Bolly Reservoir. Miss Dimsdale was quite amazed when she beheld the strength of the dam."

"I have heard of that great work from your sister. She was quite enthusiastic over the enterprise."

"What! Frances enthusiastic over anything of that sort? You surprise me, Mr. Vernon, you do, indeed. Frances cares nothing about such things. Poetry and society and a general aimless life is her idea of living, But then she is a woman, and we must not be hard on women."

"It's strange," said Vernon, musingly, with his eyes on Hest.

"What is, if I may ask?"

"The life you mention would suit your nature rather than hers, I should think, considering what I have seen of both of you. You are not so serious as Miss Hest, so far as I can judge."

Hest laughed. "Well, you see, Frances takes her pleasures seriously and in a very ponderous manner. I take my work lightly and as a hobby. That is all the difference, save that I am sure I get more amusement out of life than she does. Wait till you hear us argue."

"You are stopping in town long?"

"Only for a few days. I may go to Paris or I may return to Gerby Hall. It all depends upon Miss Dimsdale."

Vernon looked surprised. "On Miss Dimsdale? In what way?"

"Well," Hest hesitated, "it's rather a private matter to----"

"Oh, I beg your pardon."

"Not at all. You know Frances and Miss Dimsdale so very well that I don't mind telling you. The fact is my sister thinks that I ought to be married at my age--I shan't tell you how old I am because that would give away Frances, who, like all women, doesn't want her age to be known. But the long and short of it is that she wants me to marry Miss Dimsdale. I saw very plainly that Miss Dimsdale didn't want to marry me, so I ran away."

This explanation appeared to be clear enough, and Vernon drew a long breath of relief. Ida had been right; Frances had wished her brother to marry the girl and secure the fortune. Now that Francis declined to entertain the idea Miss Hest had invited Maunders down to try his luck. But Vernon could not see what interest the former could have in bringing about the marriage with the latter. He lifted his eyes from the carpet to again address his companion, but found that Mr. Hest had slipped away to talk to an old lady with an ear-trumpet.

"You might speak to _me_," hinted a low voice at his ear, and he turned to smile at Lucy's injured face.

"You are so busy."

"There is a lull now in the tea-drinking. Why haven't you been to see me lately, Arthur?"

"I have been very busy, also I have been out of town."

"You should be with me--always," pouted Miss Corsoon.

"What would your mother say to that?" he asked, smiling broadly.

"She would be annoyed," returned Lucy promptly.

Vernon started. "Surely you are mistaken," he said anxiously, stopping to almost whisper in her ear. "Your mother gave her consent, and when I was last here she said in your presence that she did not mind my----"

Lucy interrupted with a flush. "I think she has another opinion now. For some time she appeared to be pleased that we should marry, but the day before yesterday she hinted that there might be obstacles."

"Ah, your father?"

"No. Mother can manage father in any way not connected with money. Mother has changed her mind on her own account."

"But for what reason?" asked Vernon, much perplexed.

"I wish you could find out," mourned Miss Corsoon. "She refuses to tell me in any way. But I love you, and I won't give you up. I'd run away with you if you were not so poor."

"Shortly I'll be poor no longer," said Vernon quickly, "and then we can run away whenever you like."

"You will be poor no longer?" questioned Lucy doubtfully.

"No, dear. My uncle, Sir Edward Vernon, of whom we spoke when I was here last, has become reconciled to me and has made me his heir. I shall have the title and something like three thousand a year."

"Oh, how delightful. But perhaps it's wrong to say that since it means your uncle's death."

"I think Sir Edward will be glad to go," replied Vernon candidly. "He has lived a long life, and the latter part of it is very weary and dreary. He told me himself that he was looking forward to the great release."

"And then you will be rich?"

"Yes; and you will be Lady Vernon."

"It seems too good to be true."

"I don't think so, dear. Even your father can scarcely object to our marriage when I have an assured position."

Lucy looked down at the tea-cups. "It's mother I'm thinking about."

"I shall see Lady Corsoon before I leave," said Vernon compressing his lips, and sending a glance in the direction of his hostess. She caught his eye and smiled graciously: so graciously indeed that he bent again down to Lucy.

"You must be mistaken, darling," he whispered. "Your mother is quite friendly, and I am sure will not object in any way."

"She has changed her mind," answered Miss Corsoon obstinately, "at least, she told me not to count on marrying you."

"Strange. She gave no explanation?"

"None, and was quite cross when I asked for one."

This view of Lady Corsoon's attitude was supported by the fact that on seeing Vernon conversing so earnestly with Lucy she called to the girl to come to her. Ostensibly this was to present her daughter to a fashionable countess who had lately arrived, but Vernon guessed that she really wished to end the _tête-à-tête_. This was curious, considering the conversation which he had held with his proposed mother-in-law at the office of Nemo. It was evident that she had changed her mind once more, and as Lady Corsoon was not a weathercock, Vernon wondered what powerful cause could have brought about the alteration. However, he gave up speculation as he wandered about the room, speaking to his friends, and promised himself a full explanation when the company departed. As Lady Corsoon had asked him to remain it was evident that she intended to let him know what was the matter. And Vernon determined not to leave the house until he _did_ know. Shortly the young man was captured by a flippant lady, voluble and somewhat silly, who gave him a surprising piece of information. "Oh, Mr. Vernon, I am so glad to see you," she babbled gushingly, "you really must come to the--the bazaar--the great bazaar."

"Never heard of it, Mrs. Crimer."

"You silly man; don't you read the papers? One of the Princesses is to have a stall, and no end of actresses and society people. It's to be held at The Georgian Hall in aid of Homeless Hindoos."

"Really!" said Vernon idly, "why are they homeless?"

"Oh, I don't exactly know," gushed Mrs. Crimer vaguely; "it's a flood, or a fire, or a blizzard."

"I don't think they have blizzards in India."

"Perhaps they don't; how clever you are, Mr. Vernon. But all I do know is that the poor things want money, and we hope to make heaps by this bazaar. There will be lovely things sold, and games and flower stalls and sweets and fortune-telling," babbled the flippant lady incoherently.

"Fortune-telling?" Vernon, paying little attention, only caught the last word with any degree of clearness. "Of course. What would bazaars be without fortune-telling? And this time it's really genuine. Diabella----"

"What!" Vernon spoke so loudly that several people jumped, and the flippant Mrs. Crimer put her gloved hands to her ears with a pretty gesture of pain.

"You dreadful man, how you bellow! Yes; Diabella has a tent in the grounds at the back of The Georgian Hall--we hope it will be a sunny afternoon, you know--and intends to charge everyone ten shillings. You know, she usually charges a guinea, but we think we'll get more by asking less."

"But I thought," Vernon carefully commanded his voice, "I thought, that Diabella had retired from business?"

"So she has. That delightful Granny has taken her business. I'm going to see her and ask about my Affinity."

"Your husband?"

"Oh, no," said Mrs. Crimer airily; "he's only my husband, you know. But I must have an Affinity: someone who is a spiritual lover. And Granny----"

Vernon ruthlessly cut her short. "How did you get Diabella?"

"Really, I don't know," murmured Mrs. Crimer vaguely. "Someone asked her, or she asked herself. I don't know which. But she is to be there in her Egyptian dress and wearing an Egyptian mask and in an Egyptian tent. Do go and have your fortune told."

"I shall," said Vernon grimly, and inwardly rejoicing over the chance that was placing Diabella in his power. "And do you----"

"No." Mrs. Crimer spread out her hands with a shrug. "I really can't talk to you any more. Everyone is going and I have heaps and heaps of dear, delightful people to see. Good-bye! so glad you will come to the bazaar. Quite angelic it will be--quite--quite." And the flippant lady babbled her way to the hostess, who was now taking rapid leave of her various guests. Lucy had disappeared, as Vernon soon learned by a glance round the room, so he sat down and waited until Lady Corsoon could give him her promised ten minutes' explanation. He would have liked to have had a chat with Sir Julius, if only to enlist him in favour of the marriage by dropping a hint regarding the expected inheritance. But the financier rarely put in an appearance at his wife's "At Homes," finding them far too frivolous for a man of his capacity. So Vernon decided that if Lady Corsoon's explanation did not prove satisfactory he would interview Sir Julius and formally ask for the hand of Lucy. With the credentials of a soon-coming title, a lordly mansion and three thousand a year, he hoped to have his proposals well received. At a former interview the baronet had scoffed at his pretensions; but now things were changed for the better, and the chances were that all would go well.

"Now, Mr. Vernon," said Lady Corsoon, when the last guest had shaken hands and departed, "we are alone and can have a talk. What news of your search?"

"I have no news," replied Vernon placing a chair for the lady. "The Spider cannot be found."

"Only seven days remain and I must give my answer then, Mr. Vernon. You know the terms: either I pay two thousand pounds or my husband," she winced, "is informed that I sold those family jewels to pay my Bridge debts."

"I am sorry, Lady Corsoon, but as yet I have not caught the man." She made a gesture of despair. "Oh, what is the good of being sorry? I came to you as a practised detective," this time it was Vernon who winced; "at least, Mr. Maunders assured me that you were," she hastened to say.

"Very kind of Mr. Maunders," said Vernon sarcastically. "Go on."

"Well, I came to you for assistance, and you have done nothing."

"I have done everything that I could do," said Vernon drily, "but The Spider is too clever for me. As he has baffled the entire police force it is no shame for me to confess as much."

"What do you intend to do?"

"I can't say," said Vernon, thinking of a possible meeting with Diabella at The Homeless Hindoos' Bazaar. "In a few days I may have news."

Lady Corsoon shook her head. "I can't afford to wait, since the time is so short. Of course, you know that your marriage with Lucy depends upon your getting me out of this unpleasant position?"

Vernon felt inclined to say that she had placed herself in the said position, but he restrained himself, as it was useless to make an enemy of her, and merely bowed.

"Very good," went on the lady sharply, "if you don't catch this Spider and close his mouth and regain those jewels which he got from the pawnshop you don't marry Lucy. In any case you are not a good match."

"I am now, Lady Corsoon. My uncle has been reconciled to me and has made me his heir. Soon I shall be Sir Arthur Vernon, with a good income."

"Oh, my dear man," Lady Corsoon waved a jewelled hand impatiently, "there are plenty of baronets and knights with moderate incomes who would be glad to marry Lucy for herself, let alone her expectations from her father. My conditions are that you should get me out of this trouble. Can you?"

"I shall try; I can say no more."

"Then listen to me," said the lady firmly. "A few days ago I received a letter from The Spider."

"Ah!" Vernon nursed his chin and swung his leg. "So that is why you have changed your mind with regard to my wooing of Lucy?"

"Who told you that I had changed my mind, sir?" she asked abruptly. "Lucy hinted something, and then I saw that you separated us in----"

"There, there! I understand." Lady Corsoon waved her hand again. "You are right. I have changed my mind, as The Spider has given me another chance; but, of course, if you can catch him and make him hold his peace and can recover the family jewels I pawned, I am willing to keep to my agreement with you and support you in marrying my daughter."

"The Spider has given you another chance," repeated Vernon sitting up. "And what may that be? Have you the letter?"

"It's locked away. As I did not expect you to-day I did not put it in my pocket. But I can tell you what he says."

"The Spider?"

"Yes, of course," said Lady Corsoon quickly. "He tells me that if I will pay him ten thousand pounds in twelve months he will place me in receipt of that amount a year by proving that I am entitled to my late brother's money. Strange, is it not, since my niece Ida is Martin's daughter?"

"Very strange," replied Vernon mechanically. This news proved to him more conclusively than ever that Diabella was connected with The Spider, and, if not the blackmailer herself, worked in concert with him. But until he could lay hands on the woman he determined to say nothing to Lady Corsoon about the matter. "How long does he give you to answer this new demand?"

"Two months," said Lady Corsoon, triumphantly; "so at least I have gained time, and much may happen."

"As you say, much may happen. How does he propose to place you in possession of this income. Does he say?"

"No." Lady Corsoon wrinkled her brows. "He simply makes the offer. Certainly Ida inherits as next-of-kin, but it may be that this Spider--who seems to know everything--has found a will giving the income to me. Then," she hesitated, "there is another condition."

"What is it?"

"One you won't like. If I get this money I am to consent to the marriage of Lucy with--with----"

"With whom?" asked Vernon jumping up. "Don't keep me in suspense."

"With Constantine Maunders," said Lady Corsoon coolly.

CHAPTER XIII.

THE BAZAAR.

For the next few days Vernon vainly grappled with the new problem which Lady Corsoon's information had supplied. That The Spider should offer the millionaire's wife a fortune of ten thousand pounds per annum on condition of receiving the income for the first year scarcely surprised the young man, for he already suspected The Spider to be connected with Diabella, if, indeed, the creature was not that famous individual herself. But it seemed odd that the arch-criminal should interest himself in Maunders' affairs, even to assisting to bring about the marriage with Lucy. Could it be possible that Maunders was one of the gang?

Vernon recalled that after Mrs. Bedge's confession of poverty he had suspected Maunders in this respect, since the young man apparently contrived to live like a prince on nothing a year. He did not receive much from his aunt and he did not earn an income, so it was possible that in some shady way he managed to become possessed of sufficient money to gratify his extravagant tastes. Maunders also being in the vicinity of the library on the occasion of the conversation with the late Mr. Dimsdale, must have heard the suggested arrangement of the trap. But then, as Vernon recalled, Miss Hest had stated in quite an innocent way how Maunders had been with her all the evening and could not thus have had anything to do with the crime at "Rangoon." Vernon's suspicions had been banished by Miss Hest's assertions, but they now revived in full force after Lady Corsoon's communication. He had made her show him the letter, and it proved to be similar to the earlier epistle of The Spider, even to the ideograph at the end. Apparently it was genuine enough, and, if genuine, Maunders must be connected in some way with the blackmailer. No other explanation was feasible.

Had Maunders been in London Vernon would have gone straight to tax him with his possible complicity, but the young man was at Bowderstyke and so, for the moment, could not be questioned. But, sooner or later, he would return to London, and then Vernon intended to force him to explain. Meanwhile it seemed best to seek out Diabella at the Bazaar for the Homeless Hindoos and threaten her with arrest unless she explained how she had come to let The Spider know Martin Dimsdale's secret. Also, she might supply the connecting link between The Spider and Maunders. Vernon was rather surprised at Diabella's daring in thus making a public appearance, but he supposed that his ruse had been successful, and that the fortune-teller, not having been openly searched for, presumed that Colonel Towton had taken no steps. If she had learned that Towton was to be at the fête she might have declined to risk exercising her profession; but she had no reason to believe that he would be present, and thus dared the danger. But, never suspecting Vernon, he could enter the tent and tear off her mask, which was what he intended to do at the first opportunity.

The young man hesitated whether to tell Inspector Drench or to remain silent until more satisfied as to the hidden connection between Diabella and The Spider. After reflection, he decided to carry through the matter himself. By removing the waxen mask he would at least learn what Diabella was like, and perhaps, if brought to bay, she would speak out to save her skin. Then, when he knew more, he might venture to call in the aid of the police. It was a dangerous business, and perhaps Vernon would have been better advised had he taken more precautions against the woman's escape; but the evidence against her was so vague, and there appeared to be so much to clear up, that he doubted if Drench would be able to arrest her on the bare suspicion. At all events, after turning the matter over in his mind Vernon started by himself for the bazaar, resolved to act on his own initiative. He told no one of the second letter from The Spider to Lady Corsoon, not even Colonel Towton. So that military gentleman, ignorant of what was taking place, lingered in his chambers or idled at the Athenian Club, fretting over his inaction and longing for some chance to display his generalship. A very natural feeling, considering the Colonel's active mind.

The Georgian Hall was a huge repository of Hanoverian relics in South Kensington, and consisted of many moderately large apartments encircling a spacious central room. This was used for concerts, balls, meetings, fêtes, and such-like entertainments requiring ample scope for their celebration. The minor halls were dedicated to the display of objects connected with the rule of the House of Brunswick, and dating from the reign of the first monarch of the dynasty. Memorials of warfare on land and at sea were here, together with pictures of famous events, and collections of old-world things dealing with social life of the various epochs. One room was filled with figures representing the male and female garbs of the different reigns; another displayed china and silver and glass of the several periods; and a third room held quaint furniture, recalling the tales of Jane Austen. The political and social and military history of England was contained in the museums, and from this fact the hall took its name, since the objects dated only from The Act of Succession. It was an interesting place and well worth the patronage which it received from the idle public.

On this occasion the central room was filled with gaily-decorated stalls in divers colours, on which were displayed modern luxuries likely to appeal to the purses of the self-indulgent. Society beauties, charming actresses, and celebrated lady novelists presided over the booths of this Vanity Fair, and did a large trade by their fascinating personality alone. Vernon, accurately dressed, as became a young man about town, managed to elude these sirens, who would have cajoled every shilling out of his pocket, and walked into the grounds at the back of the Hall, where, Mrs. Crimer had informed him, the tent of Diabella was to be found. It was a sunny afternoon, as the flippant lady had desired, and the spacious gardens looked extremely pretty with flags and tents and flowers and general greenery. Games of all kinds were going on, and the place resembled a fair with its crowd of laughing people, who were enjoying themselves thoroughly. So far as could be judged, the Homeless Hindoos would benefit largely by the bazaar, as it apparently was a great success. No prettier function had taken place during the season.

"'I must see who you are,' cried Vernon, and pulled her hands away." Page 180.

Vernon saw endless friends and acquaintances, as many fashionable folk were present, but, taken up with his own anxious thoughts, he spoke to no one. However, someone spoke to him as he threaded his way amongst the throng, for a friendly touch on his shoulder wheeled him round, to behold Francis Hest. He looked more like his sister than ever, and decidedly handsome in his immaculate frock-coat, grey trousers, patent leather boots, and silk hat. The only fault which Vernon--always rather fastidious--could find in his general appearance was that he wore his hair much too long, which gave him the look of a poet or of a fashionable musician. And the full black locks added still more to his resemblance to Frances.

"I did not expect to find you here, Vernon," said Hest after a handshake. "Why not? It's one of the entertainments of the season, and everyone who is anyone is bound to patronise it."

"I should have thought it was too frivolous for you."

"Oh, I assure you I am a very frivolous person," said Vernon smoothly.

"Is Colonel Towton?" asked the other smiling; "and is he here?"

Vernon wondered why the question was asked. "Really, I can't say. Towton is certainly not frivolous, but he enjoys society and is usually to be found everywhere, enjoying himself. Do you know him?"

"No. I am an innocent countryman, who knows no one in the fashionable world except Lady Corsoon, who is a host in herself. I asked out of curiosity, as, having heard Miss Dimsdale speak of the Colonel, I should like to meet him."

"Oh! She spoke of Colonel Towton, did she?"

"Is that strange?" asked Hest, smiling again and showing his white teeth. "I rather think Miss Dimsdale admires the Colonel."

"He admires her and wants to marry her," said Vernon bluntly.

"So I should imagine. Another reason why I did right in running away from Gerby Hall and in declining my sister's help in marrying me to the lady. I think, however," added Hest significantly, "that unless the Colonel looks to his bride he will find she is likely to become Mrs. Maunders."

"I should be sorry to see that."

"Why? Don't you like Maunders?"

"Oh, yes. We were at school together. But I believe that Miss Dimsdale is in love with the Colonel. You know, of course, that Maunders has gone down to your place?"

"Certainly. Frances wrote me that he arrived on Sunday morning. That is why I advise Colonel Towton to look after Miss Dimsdale."

"Why does your sister wish Miss Dimsdale to marry Maunders?" asked Vernon in a pointedly blunt way.

Hest raised his thick, dark eyebrows. "Ask me another," he said lightly. "All I can say is that Frances is a great matchmaker. Failing me, she suggests Maunders as a suitor. He is younger than the Colonel, I believe."

"And much handsomer. But he has not Towton's sterling character. By the way, have you met Maunders?"

"Twice. Once in town and once at my own place. I confess that he doesn't attract me greatly. Handsome, yes; but there is something dangerous about him."

"Dangerous?" Vernon looked straightly at the speaker, wondering how he had chanced to hit on the very defect which spoilt Maunders' charm.

"It's the only word I can think of which describes him. But perhaps I am wrong. Frances would think so."

"I always thought that Miss Hest did not like Maunders."

"It may be so," said Hest indifferently. "Still, he is handsome, and Frances is a woman. It seems to me, however, that the word rests with Miss Dimsdale. If she loves Colonel Towton she will marry him, if Maunders, he will win her. A wilful woman will have her way."

"I do not think that Miss Dimsdale is wilful," said Vernon stiffly, then with an afterthought that Hest might help the Colonel to thwart the plans which Frances certainly appeared to entertain, he added, "Would you like to meet Towton?"

"Oh, yes. I shall be in town for a week before going to Paris. I have few friends here and like to be amused."

"Where are you staying?"

"At Professor Garrick Gail's, Isleworth."

"Oh!" Vernon could scarcely conceal his surprise. "I thought that you did not approve of your sister appearing as a reciter?"

"Nor do I," rejoined the other man with a frown, "but Frances asked me to deliver a message to Professor Gail, whom I met before and whom I like. He asked me to accept his hospitality while in London, so I did so, as I hope to induce him to get Frances to abandon this scheme of earning money by her talents--which by the way I don't deny--so that she may resume her proper place in society as my sister."

Vernon shook his head. "Miss Hest is of too active a mind to bear tamely the life of an ordinary country lady."

"She is singularly obstinate, if that is what you mean," said Hest with a curling lip. "However, that is my address, so if you can arrange a dinner with Colonel Towton I shall be glad to meet him and to give him the latest news of Miss Dimsdale."

"Thank you!" Vernon booked the dinner. "Say next Wednesday?"

"That will suit me capitally. The day after to-morrow? Well, and what are you going to do now?"

"Just wander round," replied Vernon evasively. He did not wish to disclose his plans regarding Diabella to the Yorkshire squire. "Good-day."

"Good-day," said the other in a friendly tone, and the two were soon separated by the ever-moving crowd.

It was growing late by this time and the gardens were not nearly so filled as they had been. Already there was a shade of twilight in the calm sky and several lamps had been lighted. It was necessary to see Diabella at once, for it might be that she would not be present in the evening. Vernon therefore went to seek for the Egyptian tent and soon found it standing in an isolated position at the far end of the ground. With some skill the canvas had been erected into the square form of a Memphis temple, and this, coloured like stone and adorned with gaudy hieroglyphics, looked a striking object in the waning light. Two imitation sphinxes guarded the doorway, and beside these on either side stood two men like bronze statues with folded arms. One was slender and the other burly, and both were natives of India in spite of their ancient Egyptian array. Vernon, knowing what he did know, had no difficulty in recognising Bahadur and the heavier man who had attempted to strangle the Colonel, until prevented by his mistress.

"Can I see Diabella?" he asked, approaching slowly and addressing Bahadur as the more amiable-looking of the two.

"One, two, three," said the man, showing his teeth and throwing up triple fingers. "Three to see mistress. Then you."

Vernon nodded and, resting on his cane, stared at the merry scene in an idle manner. But his thoughts were taken up with the probable scene which would ensue when he tore the mask from the woman's face. He wondered if she would make an outcry and would summon her attendants, and if so, would the sullen-looking wrestler attempt to choke him? But Vernon resolved at the moment he removed the mask to intimate that he knew of the assault on Colonel Towton, and so hoped that the woman would not risk unpleasant discoveries by making an outcry but would be willing to talk calmly. If so, then he hoped to induce her to state how she came to be possessed of Martin Dimsdale's secret. And here again, as it always did, came the thought that Diabela might be a disguise for The Spider, in which case she would surely decline to incriminate herself. If she did and refused to be frank there would be nothing for it but to see Drench and procure her arrest. For the moment, and now that he was on the very eve of the enterprise, Vernon regretted that he had not brought the Inspector with him so that he might be legally supported by the arm of the law. But it was too late for such regrets, and when he arrived at this point of his meditations Bahadur lifted the curtain which formed the door of the canvas temple to intimate that the stranger might enter.

The interior of the tent was adorned as an Egyptian Hall, much in the same way as the Bond Street rooms, save that the mummies were absent. Diabella, in the weird dress described by Towton, sat stiffly in a chair, with a small table at her elbow. The cards and the crystal and various charts bearing astrological figures were on the table, together with a boat-shaped lamp. This gave out a fairly strong light, and Vernon could see plainly the expressionless waxen mask which covered the face of the fortune-teller. She looked like a sphinx, solemn, calm, and passionless. Yet below that non-committing mask Vernon guessed was the face of the true woman, alive with passion and intrigue. He saw two glittering eyes scanning him curiously from the shadow of a black veil which the seeress wore draped over her Egyptian head-dress, and shivered a trifle at the uncanny look.

The sorceress saw the tremor. "Are you afraid?" she asked in her metallic voice, which was as expressionless as her mask.

"I am afraid of nothing," replied Vernon boldly and coldly; "but the night air strikes chill."

He thought that he heard a sarcastic laugh, but it was so soft that he well might have been mistaken. However, thinking that the prophetess was sneering at him he might have ventured on some angry remark, but that he recollected his intention and drew back with a grim smile. The laugh would be on his side when the mask was torn off.

"You wish to have your fortune told?" asked Diabella coldly and stretched out her hand. "Let me read your palm."

This was just what Vernon desired, as the grip brought him within snatching distance of the mask. There was a stool near at hand, upon which Diabella motioned that he should be seated; so shortly he was sitting, so to speak, at her feet, with his hand in hers. Shadows filled the corners of the tent and enhanced the grotesque looks of the figures painted on the canvas. The laughter and chatter of the diminishing crowd without had died away into a faint and confused murmur, and in the vivid circle of the lamplight sat the two figures. Diabella, holding back her veil, bent over Vernon's hand in silence.

"You are coming into good fortune," she said thinly. "Yes. Here is the line which foretells money and position. One near to you, if not dear, is on his death-bed and you benefit by his decease. Am I right?"

She raised her glittering eyes again to peer into his face. "If you are certain of your craft, there is no need for you to ask if you are right," said Vernon composedly. He was well aware of how fortune-tellers gain more knowledge than they impart by such dexterously-put questions.

Diabella gave a very modern shrug quite out of keeping with her dress and mien. However, she made no reply and continued her reading. "There is marriage here", she continued in a low voice; "but you have a rival."

"Will he be successful?"

"If he chooses to be."

"That is untrue," contradicted Vernon nettled; "The lady loves me."

"It is questionable--questionable," muttered the woman hastily. "Your rival is a formidable one and not easily turned from his purpose. Look at the break in the line yourself." She handed him a magnifying glass. "That means trouble before you achieve your heart's desire."

"Can you tell me what my heart's desire is?" asked Vernon after a glance through the glass.

"A lovely, wealthy wife and a happy home."

"Quite so; but I have a stronger desire."

"To do what?"

"Ah!" said Vernon sarcastically, "that is for you to say. But my second desire, which is marriage, is contingent on my first being realised."

"I see, I see," said Diabella raising her voice, which whistled shrilly like the wind through a crack. "You have to save someone from disgrace before you can marry the girl you love?"

"Is the someone a woman or a man?"

"A woman, and closely connected with the girl you wish to marry."

"Is there any chance of success?"

"None! none!"

"Then I shall not marry the----"

"You may marry, for the line of Venus is strongly marked," interrupted Diabella sharply. "The girl loves you, and may defy the person with whom she is so closely connected."

"And my rival also?"

Diabella shook her head. "He is too strong for her. He can force her to marry him when he chooses."

"Perhaps he may be forced to defend himself," said Vernon incautiously.

Diabella looked up quickly. "What's that?"

"Never mind. If you can read events you must guess what I mean."

"I can only read what is in your hand, and all that a man plans and thinks may not be written there. Still, you will be wise to leave your rival alone, for he is too strong for you."

"I don't think so, knowing what I know."

"What do you know?" Diabella's metallic voice sounded somewhat nervous, and she dropped Vernon's hand to clasp her own on her lap.

"I know," said Vernon, bending closely towards her, "I know that my rival will marry neither Ida Dimsdale nor Lucy Corsoon."

Diabella shrank back and gripped the arms of her chair. "The names are not familiar to me," she breathed in a low voice.

"Think again. The first name is familiar, surely?" mocked Vernon. "Why should it be?"

"Colonel Towton might be able to answer that."

Diabella rose suddenly, tall and straight, from her chair and threw out her arms with a repellant gesture. "I do not know the name of Colonel Towton."

Vernon rose slowly and measured his distance carefully. "You seem to forget a great deal, madame," he said softly, his fingers itching to tear off the expressionless mask.

"I never ask the names of my clients," she mumbled.

"How do you know that Colonel Towton was a client of yours? I never told you."

"I guessed--that is---- Ah! Help!"

She shrieked loudly and with good reason. Vernon's hand had shot out while he kept her attention engaged, and in a moment he had ripped the mask from her face. Head-dress and all came away in his grip, and Diabella covered her face with her hands. At her shriek the fold of the tent door was torn open and the burly Indian appeared. Vernon flung aside the mask and veil and head-dress and seized Diabella's wrists as the Indian ran forward to aid her. "I must see who you are," cried Vernon and pulled her hands away. "Maunders!"

He fell back a step and into the arms of the Hindoo. It was indeed Maunders whom he beheld, shrinking back into the shadows with a furious, shameful face, startled as a trapped animal. Vernon had no time to see more, for the Hindoo made a clutch at his throat, silent and venomous. Mindful of how Colonel Towton had been assaulted and Dimsdale killed, the young man turned fiercely to grapple with his assailant. As the two men closed in what promised to be a deadly struggle Maunders recovered his presence of mind sufficiently to dash over the lamp, and the tent became pitchy dark.

In that Cimmerian gloom the combatants swayed and swung and fought with silent earnestness. But the Hindoo was the stronger of the two, and Vernon felt the lean, long fingers grip his throat with vicious strength. He faintly heard Maunders, now at the door, hurriedly call to the native in an unknown tongue, and, fearful lest the two villains should escape, he tore himself away with a violent effort, crying as loudly as he could for assistance. The next moment his opponent flung himself forward and, picking him up as though he were a child, dashed him with gigantic force to the ground. His head struck the turf with a thud, and everything was swallowed up in blank insensibility.

CHAPTER XIV.

RUN TO EARTH.

In half an hour, more or less, Vernon came to himself slowly, and opened his eyes in a bewildered manner. He was in complete darkness, and for the moment could not remember where he was or what had taken place. Gradually memory returned to him and he sat up painfully to recall details. His head throbbed with the violence of the fall, and the short, sharp struggle had set his nerves jangling like ill-tuned bells. Rising to his feet with an effort he wondered why the Indian had not finished him off, then recollected the rapid words of Maunders in an unknown tongue. Probably he had been speaking Tamil and had ordered the man not to go to extremities. As in the case of Colonel Towton, when the creature had been warned by Diabella, or, rather, by Maunders, as in this instance, the native had stopped short of actual murder. In Maunders' desperate enterprise it was necessary that he should remain on the right side of the law.

Striking a match, Vernon ascertained that he was still in the tent, for its blue glimmer showed the figures and hieroglyphics weirdly flickering on the canvas walls. Apparently the criminals, for they were nothing else, had fled, leaving him insensible, and Vernon wondered that he had not been discovered. But when he walked outside he saw on the door a notice stating that the booth was closed for an hour, and guessed that in this way Maunders had provided time for flight. So warned, no one would enter the tent, and evidently both the noise of the struggle and his cry for assistance had passed unheeded. Vernon drew a long breath and stood where he was, watching the crowd of people merry-making under hundreds of coloured lamps, quite oblivious to the fact that a tragedy had nearly taken place under their very noses. He wondered what was best to be done.

It was useless to go to those in authority at The Georgian Hall as no one would credit his wild tale, although the flight of Diabella and her accomplices might lend colour to his narrative. Moreover, Vernon decided that more than ever was it necessary to hunt down Maunders in secrecy, as he wished for a full explanation from him before calling in Drench to assist. Likewise, for the sake of Ida, of Mrs. Bedge, and Lady Corsoon, Vernon wished if possible to avoid publicity, since any scandal would certainly bring their names into unpleasant notoriety. For these reasons the young man left The Georgian Hall without telling anyone what had happened. But he chuckled as he went to think how the public would be disappointed to find the tent of the sorceress empty. Also, how amazed those managing the bazaar would be to discover that Diabella had vanished with her takings for the day, which would be considerable. Vernon felt quite sure that a man so unscrupulous as Maunders would not hesitate to seize the till seeing that, having been exposed, and doubtful if his old schoolfellow would hold his tongue, he would want all the money he could get to assist his flight.

The question was to learn whither he had fled and what track to follow in order to hunt him down. It was close upon seven o'clock, and outside The Georgian Hall Vernon hesitated as to his next step. He wondered whether it would be better to go home and retire to bed, since he felt shaken by the struggle, or to seek out Colonel Towton and enlist him as a fellow-pursuer in the man-hunt. Finally he decided to take a taxi to the Colonel's chambers and relate what had happened, for he knew that unless he discussed the matter he would only worry the whole night over the catastrophe. He therefore fortified himself with a stiff brandy and soda at a near hotel and pulled himself together for a serious conversation. And serious enough it would be for Constantine Maunders, who could not be permitted to continue in his nefarious career.

As it happened, Towton, late in dressing for dinner, had not yet left his rooms for the Athenian Club. Vernon arrived at a quarter to eight, just as the Colonel opened the door. The two came face to face with mutual joy at meeting.

"My dear Vernon, I am glad to see you. I am simply dying to have a talk, as I can do nothing but think of the entanglement in which we find ourselves."

"You can't be more pleased than I am at having found you, Colonel. I have had an adventure with Diabella."

"The deuce. Have you learned who she is?"

"Who _he_ is, you mean. Yes. That mask concealed Constantine Maunders."

Towton sat down on one of the hall chairs and stared. "Do you mean to say that the young scamp has been masquerading as a woman?"

Vernon nodded and sat down wearily, for his bones ached. "I presume he thought that there would be less danger of discovery if he changed his sex. I expect he wore those long Egyptian robes over his ordinary clothes. When discarding them he would reappear as Maunders, and could easily escape without being noticed in the crowd. He's clever, is Constantine, and yet not clever enough."

"I don't know what you're talking about," said Towton gruffly and rising to his feet. "Suppose you come with me to the Athenian and tell me all about the matter."

"I'm not in evening kit."

"Oh, the deuce take that," said the Colonel cheerfully.

"And I'm rather knocked up with my fight."

"Fight? Did Maunders show fight?"

"No. Your Hindoo did. He assaulted me as he did you and left his job unfinished in the same way. It's a long story and I want your assistance. Go and have your dinner, Colonel, and I'll lie down on the sofa in your sitting-room until you return."

"Pooh! pooh! I can't eat with such news as this exciting me." Towton threw off his coat and hung his silk hat on a peg. "Come into the sitting-room and I'll send my man to the nearest restaurant for a meal. Meanwhile you'd better have a peg, for you look as white as a winter's day."

"No, thank you, Colonel. I had a brandy and soda just after leaving The Georgian Hall," said Vernon as they entered the sitting-room.

"Have you been there--at the bazaar?"

"Yes. Diabella had set up her tent there and was telling fortunes. I heard of this at Lady Corsoon's the other day, and so ventured to beard the lioness in her den."

"And the lioness turned out to be a lion," chuckled Towton throwing himself into a chair after making the sofa comfortable with cushions for his guest. "Well, we'll have the whole story after a makeshift dinner, for, hang it, your disclosure has taken away a very excellent appetite. Bendham!" The Colonel turned to the retired soldier who acted as his valet and who had just entered the room, "go round to the nearest restaurant and tell them to send in the best small dinner they have, for two. Look sharp, now. You can lay the cloth in the smoking-room; we'll make shift there."

Bendham saluted military fashion and took a speedy departure, while his master turned his head in the direction of Vernon. "Tell me all that has happened to you now," he said easily; "it will be some time before the dinner makes its appearance, and I'm on tenterhooks. The deuce, to think that our blackguard friend--for he is that, I swear--should be earning his money as a fortune-teller. It's worse than----" Towton hesitated.

"Than my profession of a detective, you would say, Colonel," finished Vernon languidly. "I should rather think so. I assist the law, and Maunders breaks it. But neither profession is tempting to a gentleman."

"Oh, hang your profession," said Towton impatiently. "You will soon enter into your kingdom when Sir Edward gives up the ghost. And it's just as well that you have some experience in thief-catching seeing what scoundrels we have to deal with. Maunders, by jove! Now we'll be able to find out how he came to know that Ida wasn't Dimsdale's daughter. No wonder he decided to give her up, seeing that he was after the money. What did he say?"

"Nothing. He cleared out of the tent as soon as I discovered his identity."

"Where is he now?" demanded the Colonel sharply.

"I don't know. That's what I wish to speak to you about. And, to make things quite clear, as I want your opinion, you had better hear the whole story."

Towton intimated his desire to be informed of what had taken place, and listened attentively while Vernon detailed all that had happened since Mrs. Crimer had informed him of Diabella's proposed appearance at the bazaar. He ended with a description of his recovering from insensibility in the deserted tent and his subsequent decision to consult the Colonel before taking any steps. "And my reason for wishing to move quietly is obvious," was the concluding remark of the young man.

"Yes! yes! I quite understand. We must keep Miss Corsoon's name and that of Miss Dimsdale out of the papers. By the way, what did this fellow mean by hinting in his confounded fortune-telling at disgrace to someone closely connected with Miss Corsoon? Does he mean her mother or her father?"

Vernon felt a trifle confused. In his interest in the recital he had unconsciously let slip more than he had been prepared to impart. Both as a detective and as a gentleman he was bound to keep Lady Corsoon's secret, and as the disclosure of it was not particularly pertinent to the matter in hand he brushed aside Towton's question with a scornful laugh. "Oh, I daresay that was all patter. Maunders knows that I love Lucy and thought to intimidate me by a threat that he had power to force the mother to support his preposterous claim to marry the girl. But after this exposure he will scarcely dare to come forward."

"The blackguard," cried the honest Colonel heatedly; "he blackens the character of both man and woman in his endeavours to earn his dirty money. But I thought he was supposed to be at Gerby Hall?"

"Oh, he doubtless arranged that so as to provide himself with an _alibi_."

"Why the deuce should he provide himself with an *alibi?*"

"Can't you see that Maunders must be The Spider?" said Vernon impatiently. Towton leaped to his feet and began to walk to and fro much perturbed. "Oh, impossible! I don't like Maunders; all the same, it seems incredible that he should be a murderer."

"I can't see that myself," said Vernon drily. "Maunders is half a Greek and is as wily a bird as ever had salt put on its tail. Whether he gets it from his Greek father or from his English mother I can't say, but he certainly has that strong criminal taint, which induces him to get money for his whims by illegal methods rather than by honest toil. Besides, we can't say if he killed Dimsdale, even though, as is apparent, he is The Spider. Miss Hest declared to me in all innocence, and not with any intention of defending him, that Maunders was with her nearly all the evening."

"Then he can't be The Spider," insisted the Colonel, "for undoubtedly The Spider killed poor old Dimsdale."

"So we thought; so everyone thinks; and yet--well, of course, it's not impossible that Maunders ordered this nameless native to get the money, and the man may have executed the murder without instructions."

"Or else," said Towton emphatically, "Maunders may have had his mask torn off by Dimsdale when he came for the money and murdered the old man to prevent discovery. It cuts both ways."

"Pardon me, no, if Miss Hest is to be believed."

"I don't trust that woman," said the Colonel abruptly.

"She is scheming to get Ida to marry her brother."

"I think she will fail there, as the brother is in London."

"What?"

"Yes. I met him both at Lady Corsoon's and at the Bazaar. He said that his sister _did_ wish to bring about the match, but that, not being desirous of marrying Ida, he ran away from the Hall."

"Leaving the field clear for Maunders?"

"You forget that Maunders is in town masquerading as Diabella."

"He may have come up for that purpose."

"Well, we can ascertain that from Mr. Hest. He declares that he left him at Gerby Hall, or that Maunders was expected, I forget which. But we'll see him to-morrow and ask."

Towton shook his head wisely. "He won't know of Maunders' movements."

"You never can tell. At all events, it will do no harm to ask him. Now I come to think of it," said Vernon musingly and searching his memory, "Hest told me to-day at the bazaar that he had received a letter from his sister saying that Maunders had arrived on Sunday morning. That was yesterday, so it is impossible to believe that Maunders went down and came up in such a hurry. It's my opinion that he never went to Gerby Hall at all."

"And I say, by jove!" cried the Colonel greatly excited, "Hest told a lie if he said that he received a letter saying that Maunders had arrived. Even if posted in Bowderstyke last evening it could not reach him before to-night, and you say he gave you the information this afternoon?"

"He may have received it at mid-day."

"No," said Towton decidedly. "Our post at Bowderstyke is very uncertain, as I know to my cost. This evening or to-morrow morning is the very earliest that Hest could receive a letter posted on Sunday, and as Maunders did not arrive until then Miss Hest could not have written before."

"I don't believe that he arrived at all, and I can't conceive why Miss Hest should tell a falsehood."

"I can. She is scheming for this money. However, I shall go with you to-morrow and we'll have it out with Hest. Where is he to be found?"

"He is staying with Professor Garrick Gail, at Isleworth."

"The deuce! Ida told me that he did not approve of his sister's reciting."

"Nor does he. But she asked him to give some message, and the Professor asked him to stop at Isleworth while he was in town. He did so, as he explained to me, so that he could persuade the Professor to induce Miss Hest to give up her career."

"A very lame explanation," said the Colonel grimly. "Gentlemen don't stay at such places for such weak purposes. I tell you, Vernon, that I don't believe in those Hests. I never did, although you defended the sister. They had a bad name at Bowderstyke as a wild family."

"Oh, I thought that Francis Hest was looked upon as a benefactor?"

"He is," admitted the Colonel reluctantly, "he's a crazy philanthropist, with his parish school-houses and Bolly Reservoir. All the same, there's a queer taint about them, and they live queer lives."

"I can't see that. Frances recites in London in a perfectly open and honest way, and Francis acts in a noble manner as a philanthropist."

"I daresay. All the same, I don't trust either brother or sister: they quarrel like mad, too."

"Most families do," retorted Vernon drily as he swung himself off the sofa, "and Frances is certainly trying to further her brother's interest by securing him an heiress. That doesn't look as though they quarrelled."

"Humph!" said Towton disbelievingly. "Probably the sister has learned that Ida isn't an heiress and wants to do her brother a bad turn. However, it's no use talking, as we get no further. Let us see Hest to-morrow, and then learn, if we can, the whereabouts of Maunders. All depends upon the confession of that scamp. But, I tell you what, Vernon, if our young friend is this poisonous beast of a Spider he will have left England by to-night's mail."

"Perhaps. But I could not stop him without consulting Drench, and that means the interference of the police, which we wish to avoid."

"It's a damned tangle altogether," muttered Towton savagely, "and--but here comes Bendham to announce dinner. Come and eat. To-morrow we can talk further."

Vernon was quite willing to drop the subject for the time being, as his head and limbs still ached with the struggle, and he felt more inclined to go to bed than to sit discussing criminal trickery, which required a very clear brain. Even at the makeshift dinner, which after all was dainty and tempting, he was unable to eat much, and excused himself to his host as speedily as he could consistently with politeness. After arranging to meet the Colonel next day at three o'clock at Waterloo Station he went home. A warm bath took the pains partially away, and he was so tired that almost as soon as his head rested on the pillow he dropped into a profound sleep. Not a single dream broke his rest, which was prolonged to ten o'clock the next morning.

While at breakfast, which he devoured with an excellent appetite, Vernon recollected that he had not Professor Garrick Gail's exact address. It was at Isleworth that he lived, but it was necessary to find the street and the number of the house. This was quickly learned from an _Era_, which he sent his servant to buy, and he ascertained that the retired actor dwelt in Siddons Villa, Petterby Road. Vernon rather regretted that he had not made the appointment with Colonel Towton earlier, since Mr. Hest might have gone out for the day. However, he comforted himself with the reflection that in any case Hest and Towton would meet at dinner on Wednesday. Meanwhile, there was always the chance that the Yorkshire squire might be at Isleworth, and in any case Vernon felt curious to see where Miss Hest lived when in town. Like the Colonel, he was beginning to mistrust that young lady.

Punctual to the moment Vernon arrived at Waterloo Station, but found Towton before him. They greeted one another cordially, and Towton congratulated his friend on his improved looks. And certainly a night's rest had done wonders for the young man. He felt, as the saying goes, as fit as a fiddle, and quite looked forward to the visit. "And I sincerely trust that Mr. Hest is at home," he said anxiously.

"We can wait for him if he is not," said the Colonel, shouldering his umbrella in soldier fashion. "I don't leave until I have seen him, that's all. In one way or another I intend to have these infernal mysteries cleared up. Upon my soul, sir," said the Colonel bluffly, "I feel as though I were bathing in dirty water."

"You are not used to the seamy side of life as I am," replied Vernon as they passed the barrier and stepped into the train.

"No, by jove, sir, I'm not. And once I am married to Ida I shall take care to leave all this sort of thing alone. Not the thing for a gentleman by any means. You chuck it also, Vernon."

"I intend to when my uncle dies. Once let Sir Arthur Vernon come into existence with a good income and Nemo vanishes for ever."

The Colonel nodded his approbation, and the two chatted about their errand on the way to Isleworth. But all they could do in the absence of positive fact was to theorise, which was unsatisfactory. But they hoped when they laid hands on Maunders--no very easy matter, since the scamp had taken the alarm--to have everything cleared up. Vernon still held that his former friend was The Spider, but Colonel Towton disagreed. "No! No! No!" said he decisively, "Maunders may be bad, but he isn't a murderer."

"He's anything that suits his purpose, so long as he isn't found out," was Vernon's retort. "He's clever----"

"And cunning, but he isn't bold, and would be sure not to bring himself within reach of the hands of justice by bloodshed."

"He has brought himself quite close enough in other ways," replied Vernon.

In this way they talked, and in due time arrived at the charming suburb of Isleworth, which looked quite countrified. The two descended the steps and passed along a narrow path which led out of the station into the road. An inquiry from a passing butcher-boy on a bicycle soon advised them of the whereabouts of Petterby Road, and shortly they found themselves facing a double-fronted house with a small and neglected garden between it and the quiet side-road.

"The sluggard's domain," said Towton with disgust, for, like most military men, he was excessively tidy. "Might be made pretty if attended to, by jove."

"I don't think retired actors go in much for gardening," said Vernon with a smile, as he reached for the knocker.

A stout woman, with the remains of heavy good looks, opened the door with the air of a tragedy queen, although her dress was scarcely regal. Vernon asked if he could see Mr. Hest and received a reply in the negative, as it seemed that Mr. Hest was absent. "But I anticipate that he will return at a comparatively early hour," said the lady grandiloquently.

"Can we see Professor Gail?" asked Vernon, determined to enter the house and wait for hours if necessary.

"Professor Garrick Gail," said the lady, giving him the entire name with the air of a Siddons, "is resting prior to going later to the Curtain Theatre. But if your errand is pressing----"

"Yes, it is. Please give the Professor my card."

"I am Mrs. Garrick Gail, formerly Miss Hettie Montgomery," said the lady in haughty tones, "and I do not convey messages. Maria!" she beckoned to a small servant whose not very clean face peeped under her substantial arm, "convey this intimation to your master. Gentlemen," she flung open the door grandly, "enter, and repose yourselves in the drawing-room."

Vernon smiled at the tinsel majesty of the actress, but the Colonel, without moving a muscle of his good-looking face, marched in stiffly. Shortly they found themselves in a tawdry room of no great size, crammed with theatrical photographs and furnished in a poor, pretentious manner, which revealed poverty, while it aped the genteel. Mrs. Garrick Gail, formerly Miss Hettie Montgomery, conducted them in with the air of one accustomed to the centre of the stage and then departed stating that her husband would shortly do himself the honour of waiting on them.

"What airs!" murmured Towton, recalling his Shakespeare indistinctly; "an intolerable quantity of sack to a pennyworth of bread."

"These actors and actresses are always in the glare of the footlights," said Vernon, sitting down cautiously on a shaky chair. "By the way, Colonel, if I do a little business with the Professor don't look more surprised than you can help."

"Business? What business?"

"I intend to ask if Miss Frances Hest is open to an engagement. It is necessary, since both you and I are beginning to mistrust that young lady, to be diplomatic."

"That means you mistrust this actor also and wish to throw him off the scent?"

Vernon nodded. "Exactly, and--hush----" He stopped and composed his features as the door opened and Professor Gail stalked into the room, like the Ghost of Hamlet's father.

Anyone could see at a glance that the man was an actor. He was tall, and lean, and solemn, yet with a twinkle in his deep-sunken eyes, which showed that he could play comedy as well as tragedy. His bluish jowl, from frequent close shaving, his long hair, his measured gestures, and his lordly gait all revealed one who was used to the world behind the curtain. His voice was deep and sonorous and his enunciation almost too perfect; nor did he clip his words colloquially, but gave them their full length and full meaning. Finally, he had a certain dignity, habitual to one who had played many a kingly part in his time, and who in ordinary life found it difficult not to relapse into blank verse.

"Colonel Towton--Arthur Vernon," he read from the pencilled card. "These are your names, I take it? And your business, gentlemen?"

"Well, we are killing two birds with one stone," said Vernon easily, as the actor sat down in a regal manner as though the arm-chair were a throne. "My friend here wishes to see Mr. Hest."

"He is absent for the moment, sir, but will return anon. Will you wait or will you leave a message."

"I prefer to wait," said Towton stiffly, as he did not like the atmosphere or the company. "When do you expect Mr. Hest back?"

"Well, sir, he may return in twenty minutes or in sixty, which is to say, on the hour. As my guest he has full freedom to go and return when he desires. I am content that you should remain, and if any refreshment----"

"Thank you, no," interrupted the Colonel hastily but politely.

"It is well. And you, sir?" The Professor turned to Vernon. "Nothing for me, thank you. I have called both to see Mr. Hest and yourself, sir, as I wish to engage Miss Hest to recite at the 'At Home' of a friend of mine. Lady Brankworth. Perhaps you know her?"

"Well. I know her well. I have superintended amateur plays in her drawing-room on more than one occasion. Ah! so she desires the services of my talented pupil? And on what date?"

"Thursday week, I think. But I am not sure. I shall have to see her again and then can let you know. Miss Hest is away, I fancy."

"In her ancestral home in Yorkshire," said the actor rolling his words out grandly, "but she returns shortly and will be delighted to accept of the engagement provided the fees----"

"Those will be all right, Professor. Lady Brankworth pays liberally."

"And so she ought, to secure the services of Miss Hest. I assure you, sir, that I have rarely come across a lady who recites so nobly. If she would only pay attention to her art instead of indulging in social frivolity with that unfortunate young lady who lost her father at Hampstead, she would become one of our greatest actresses."

"I fancy her brother does not wish her to go on the stage," said Vernon.

Professor Garrick Gail waved his hand and then thrust it into his coat in Napoleonic fashion. "He is prejudiced, prejudiced. I would he were on the stage himself, if only because he resembles his sister, my talented pupil, so closely. As Viola and Sebastian in 'Twelfth Night,' they would take the town by storm. Always provided," said the old actor with another wave, "that Mr. Hest has the same talent in measure as his sister has: a fact I am by no means sure of."

"They are very like one another," broke in Towton coldly.

"For that reason I wish both were on the stage to play in twin parts," replied the Professor in his most stately manner. "They are as like as two eggs, as you observe, sir. But Mr. Hest thinks little of our glorious profession, and is staying here in the vain hope of inducing me to persuade his sister, my talented pupil, to surrender the laurel wreath of the stage. Needless to say, I decline to commit so great a crime."

How long the Professor would have gone on descanting on the histrionic capabilities of Frances Hest it is hard to say, but his eloquence was cut short by the entrance of Mrs. Gail, who swept an apologetic curtsey to the gentlemen for her sudden appearance. She then whispered to her husband, and Vernon caught a word or two about "a bill--man at the back door--must have his money," etc. Gail looked perturbed and rose quickly.

"A small domestic concern, gentlemen," he said, stalking to the door followed by his wife. "Excuse me while I adjust matters. I shall return soon," and he made his exit with Mrs. Gail in a most approved stage fashion.

When they were alone the Colonel asked a question: "Can you get this engagement for Miss Hest?"

"Oh, yes. Lady Brankworth is a great friend of mine and is always giving parties. There will be no difficulty in my making good my word. The old man seems to be all right and his wife also. Whatever devilry the Hests may be up to, that worthy couple know nothing about it."

Scarcely were the words out of his mouth when the door opened quickly and a man entered the room in great haste. Vernon sprang to his feet.

"Maunders once more!" He cried; "The very man I wish to see."

And Maunders it was, looking like a trapped tiger, furious and despairing.

CHAPTER XV.

FACE To FACE.

Maunders recognised his peril in a moment and immediately turned to retreat. But Vernon was too quick for him and leaped between him and the door. When it was closed and Vernon had his back against it Maunders glanced desperately at the one window of the room. Here Colonel Towton, now on his feet, barred his way, so there was nothing for it but to surrender to a strength he could not fight against. With extraordinary self-control the scamp pulled himself together and demanded in a surly tone what his captors meant by behaving towards him in this way.

"Sit down," said Vernon without deigning to reply directly; "you have to explain matters before you leave this room."

"I have nothing to explain," muttered Maunders doggedly, but nevertheless judged it wise to obey. "You had better take care what you are about."

"I'll take care of myself and of you also," replied Vernon composedly.

"I ask you, Colonel Towton, if this is the way for one gentleman to treat another?" demanded the trapped rogue.

"Two gentlemen," corrected the Colonel coldly, "who are dealing with a confounded scoundrel."

"I'll make you pay for those words," threatened Maunders, biting his lips.

"I don't recognise your right to demand satisfaction as I only deal with gentlemen. Mr. Vernon and myself have run you to earth, and----"

"How did you find out that I was here?" interrupted Maunders curiously.

"We did not expect to find you here," said Vernon, still with his back to the door and keeping a watchful eye on his former friend. "We came down on other business, connected with Mr. Hest."

"With Hest?" Maunders appeared perturbed.

"What do you know about him?" asked Towton sharply, and noticing the change of expression.

"I know nothing, save that he is stopping here."

"And how do you come to be in this house?"

"That's my business," retorted Maunders doggedly. "Your business is our business," interposed Vernon quietly.

"I fail to see that."

"You fail to see a good many things; but don't be afraid, I shall make everything clear to you in good time."

"Are you here as my old school friend?" said Maunders, whining sentimentally, "or as Nemo, the detective?"

"You will soon learn. But of one thing you may be certain, that I am no friend of yours. Can you wonder at it, seeing what I discovered yesterday?"

"I can explain everything."

"Good! Colonel Towton and I await your explanation."

Maunders again cast a look at door and window and again saw that there was no hope of escape. "What do you wish to know?" was his sullen request.

"In the first place, how you come to be here."

"That's easy. I started on Saturday to go down to Yorkshire, as I told you how I intended to go. But news came that my aunt was ill and wished to see me at once. I turned back at the station and went to Hampstead. Then I met Hest at the bazaar yesterday----"

"Does he know that you are Diabella?" interrupted Vernon quickly.

"No, he doesn't. I met him before I went into the tent to do business. He asked me why I had not gone to Yorkshire, and when I explained he asked me down here. I came last night and remained the night. It's all fair, square, and above-board with me."

"That's a lie," said Vernon impulsively, "and Hest told me another one at the bazaar. He could not have seen you between the time I parted from him and came to you when you were masquerading as Diabella, yet he told me that he had received a letter from his sister saying you were in Yorkshire. And you didn't come down here, I take it, to talk Shakespeare and musical glasses. There is something between you and this man Hest, and between you and Professor Gail, no doubt."

Maunders rose suddenly and spoke with great earnestness. "I assure you that Gail knows nothing more than that Hest asked me to stay as his guest. He will be here soon, and I beg of you to say nothing to him of what you have discovered. I shall explain everything to your satisfaction before you leave this house."

"On that condition," said Vernon, making a sign that Towton should be silent, "we will say nothing to the Professor. I believe I hear footsteps, so no doubt he is coming." Vernon moved away from the door. "If you try to escape, Maunders, I'll break your leg with a bullet," and he pulled out a neat revolver which he kept concealed in his hip pocket.

"Rather melodramatic," sneered Maunders with a shrug; "However, you need not be afraid. I'll sit here quietly enough."

"You have more cause to be afraid than I have. Hush! Here is the Professor coming," and as he spoke the door opened to admit the old actor. "Mr. Maunders has just come in to keep us company while we wait for Mr. Hest," said Vernon in an easy tone.

"Yes," said Maunders, who by this time had recovered his composure. "We are old friends and have much to talk about, so don't let us keep you from your afternoon sleep, Professor."

"If you will not think me lacking in courtesy," said Gail in his stately manner, "I shall certainly retire. The brain," he tapped his forehead, "needs rest, and I have invariably found that sleep, as Shakespeare says, 'knits up the ravelled sleeve of care.' Wil you have any refreshment, gentlemen?"

"No, thank you," replied Vernon politely; "but it is growing dark, so perhaps you will order lights."

"Yonder lamp is ready for use," said the Professor, pointing to the corner near the fireplace, "and certainly it is growing unusually dark, although it is scarcely five o'clock. A fog is descending on the verdant earth." He went to the window and looked out. "Yes, a dense fog. Have you noted, Mr. Maunders, how rapidly these autumnal fogs descend on London?"

"Yes. But I should have thought that you were too far away to have them here," replied Maunders in an easy conversational tone, which did great credit to his powers of self-control. "No, sir; no. The fuliginous haze does not spare even our rural suburb, if I may so term it." He swept aside the curtain with a tragic gesture. "Mark how the cloudy mists, darkened with smoke, swallow up house after house and road after road; mark how a brown pall is drawn over the fair green looks of earth and how the----"

"One would have to be in a balloon to see all that," said Maunders rudely. "I hope you won't mind, Professor, but I have private business to discuss with my friends here. If Mr. Hest comes in, please tell him I shall see him in his bedroom as soon as my friends go."

"Do nothing of the sort, Professor," snapped the Colonel. "I have come here to see Mr. Hest, and he must meet me in this room."

But the speech of Maunders had offended the touchy old actor. "I have nothing to do with these things," he said, stalking towards the door, "and, in the good old English fashion, my guests are at liberty to act as they please. Mr. Hest need be told nothing, and when he returns he will certainly enter this room, as is his custom."

"But----" began Maunders, only to be cut short by the indignant Professor.

"You are not my guest, sir, but the guest of Mr. Hest," he said in his deepest tones, "and you have told me to leave my own room. These manners are suited to the Hyperboreans of the Far North."

"I wish to explain----"

"Explain nothing, sir," cried Gail in the ponderous manner of Dr. Samuel Johnson. "You may have a front like Mars to threaten and command, but I am no menial to be so hectored." He swept an imaginary mantle over his left shoulder and mouthed blank verse:

> "We must not stint
> Our necessary actions in the fear
> To cope malicious censurers."

"Therefore," ended Mr. Gail, returning to prose, "I shall retire to my couch, and so good-day to one and all."

When he had made his exit, for it could scarcely be said that he took his departure in a conventional manner, Maunders gave vent to a weak, tittering laugh, doubtless to cloak the real nervousness he felt. "The old fool," he observed with his characteristic shrug.

"Let us hope you will not prove to be a young one by withholding from us the truth of this shady business you have been engaged in," said Colonel Towton in a caustic manner, for his sympathies were with the retired actor.

"Thank you, I don't wish to receive any compliments," sneered Maunders, "and, for heaven's sake, let us get this business over at once. I have more to do than to explain my private affairs to interlopers."

Vernon laughed as he saw that under his air of bravado Maunders was intensely anxious about his position. "That cock won't fight," he said coolly. "You must be aware that you are in a very dangerous position."

"I am aware of nothing of the sort. I can justify myself----"

"Do so, as regards your masquerading."

"Is it a crime to earn an honest livelihood?"

"Honest!" said Towton with scorn, "but let that pass."

"Fortune-telling is as honest as your detective business," said Maunders insolently to Vernon. "I am Diabella. Why should I deny it?"

"You can't, or you would. But to dress up as a woman——"

"I didn't," denied Maunders with a scowl. "I simply wore those Egyptian robes over my ordinary clothes and the waxen mask to conceal my face. Also, all that rotten paraphernalia seems to be necessary to the business."

"I daresay, to deceive people," said Vernon drily. "Why did you act in this way, may I ask?"

"Because I couldn't get my mother to allow me sufficient money to live on."

"I thought that Mrs. Bedge was your aunt?" put in the Colonel quickly.

"So she is, but I am likewise her adopted son. She kept me short, and I had to earn my money somehow. For three years I have masqueraded as Diabella, and, although I don't want it known, I don't mind if you do tell, as no one can say a word against me."

"I can," said Towton grimly. "You employed your servant to strangle me."

Maunders shook his head violently. "I did nothing of the sort. Hokar——"

"Is that the native's name?" interposed Vernon suddenly.

"Yes. I had two native servants. Hokar and Bahadur, and they are both devoted to me. When you, Colonel, tried to pull off my mask naturally Hokar intervened to prevent your doing so. In the same way, Vernon, he punished you for using violence towards me. And I prevented the faithful fellow from strangling you both, so you have your lives to thank me for."

"Why didn't you prevent him from strangling Dimsdale?" asked Towton.

"I swear that Hokar had nothing to do with that murder, nor had I."

"Of course, you would say that for your own safety," said Vernon contemptuously; "but how was it that you became possessed of Dimsdale's secret?"

Maunders hesitated. "I am not bound to answer that," he said defiantly.

"If you don't answer me you will answer Drench," threatened Vernon firmly.

"Drench? You would not dare to bring him into this matter?"

"Why not? Dimsdale was blackmailed on account of a certain secret, and, because he would not pay, perished by violence. You know this secret, so the inference is that you----"

"That I ordered him to be strangled?" finished Maunders calmly. "How can that be when Hokar was never near Dimsdale's bungalow in his life, and certainly, as I was with Miss Hest nearly all the evening, I could not have committed the murder myself."

"That remains to be proved," rejoined Vernon, suppressing what Miss Hest had told him of the young man's movements on the fatal night. "And even presuming you are innocent of the actual crime, and that Hokar was not near the house, The Spider, who came to blackmail, must have learned from you the secret which he threatened to disclose."

Maunders was silent for a moment. "You can't prove that I knew about this secret," he said doggedly.

"Colonel Towton can swear that he heard it from Diabella, and I can prove that you are the fortune-teller. These facts only admit of one interpretation, Maunders. Either you are an accomplice of The Spider or you are The Spider himself."

"It's a lie, it's an infernal lie," cried Maunders greatly agitated.

"It's the truth, and you know it. Your face reveals the truth."

"How can you tell that when we are nearly in darkness with this fog?" asked Maunders between his teeth.

"I can see well enough, and the darkness is easily remedied. Colonel, will you please light the lamp while I keep an eye on our friend here."

Maunders cursed his former schoolfellow ardently, while Towton quietly lighted the tall lamp which stood in the corner. The light soon glowed through a rosy shade, adorned in a tawdry manner with artificial flowers, and Vernon stepped up to Maunders. The scamp met his scrutiny unflinchingly, and displayed a courage worthy of a better cause. He was pale with apprehension, for he well knew, in spite of his bravado, that he was in a tight place. But the crimson hue of the light filtering through the shade threw a delicate glow on his finely-cut face. Facing the two gentlemen, who knew him past all denial to be a scoundrel, he looked as handsome a lad as ever stepped in shoe-leather. It seemed a terrible pity that so fair an outside should mask such internal evil. Something of this sort occurred to Vernon as he stepped back with a sigh.

"I wish you were as decent a fellow as you look," he said in a regretful voice. "In heaven's name, Maunders, why can't you be an honest man? You have a handsome face, a fine figure, you have had the best education England can afford, and you hold a good position in the social world. Finally, your aunt, Mrs. Bedge, who adopted you as her son, loves you dearly, and if you have not sufficient self-respect to keep straight for your own sake you might behave like an honest gentleman for hers."

Maunders might have been moved by this discourse, or he might not. At all events, he showed little signs of feeling on his classic face. "It's all very well your talking," he said sullenly and looking down, a trifle ashamed, if indeed he could be said to display any emotion, "but I have been brought up to live like a prince. I have the tastes of a duke and the income of a pauper, so I must gratify my fancies somehow. I am no more proud of having had to take to fortune-telling for my bread and butter than you are in setting up as a private detective. Neither business is respectable, but the law can say nothing to you or me."

"Nothing to me, certainly," Vernon assured him coldly, "since I am, and always have been, on the side of justice. Your fortune-telling may be innocent enough in the main, since you prefer wringing money from silly people instead of taking up a good business. But it's your connection with The Spider that is dangerous to you."

"I am not The Spider, and I have no connection with the beast."

"In that case how comes it that The Spider offers to place Lady Corsoon in possession of her niece's fortune on condition that she permits _you_ to marry Miss Corsoon?"

The Colonel uttered an ejaculation of mingled wrath and horror, and Maunders grew a shade paler. "Is that true?" Towton demanded with a look of loathing at Maunders and then an inquiring glance at Vernon.

"Perfectly true," was the response. "I did not intend to say anything to you, Colonel, since the affair is a private one of Lady Corsoon's. But it seems necessary to be frank even at the risk of exposing a lady's secrets, much as I hate to do so. Lady Corsoon received an offer from The Spider to return certain jewels which she pawned to pay her bridge losses, and which he obtained possession of by means of forged pawntickets, on condition that she should pay one thousand pounds. Afterwards another letter was received saying that he would take ten thousand pounds--a single year's income of Miss Dimsdale's--and would place Lady Corsoon in possession of the fortune. She was to pay the money and consent to the marriage of our friend here with Miss Corsoon. How do you explain this interest which The Spider takes in you, Maunders, if you don't know him?"

The culprit moistened his dry lips and replied with insolent boldness: "I wrote that letter to Lady Corsoon myself--that is, the second letter. I know nothing about the first."

"Then you are The Spider?" cried Towton fiercely.

"No. Don't run your head against a wall," retorted Maunders coolly, and fighting for every inch of the disputed ground. "Lady Corsoon told me about the first letter and the threat. I advised her to consult Vernon in his character of Nemo, and did him a good turn."

"And yourself a better," said Vernon scornfully. "You hoped that Lady Corsoon on learning my employment would forbid me to think of her daughter."

"Yes, I did. However, I sent her to you to do business. Then I thought as she was committed so far with The Spider that there would be no harm in my trying to get her on my side so that I might marry Lucy. I knew that Ida was not entitled to the fortune, as there was no will and she was not old Dimsdale's daughter. I knew also that Lady Corsoon was kept short by her husband and would like to have her own money, if only to pay The Spider and recover the jewels so as to hide her fault from Sir Julius. For this reason I wrote the letter asking that Lady Corsoon should aid me to marry her daughter."

"And you asked for ten thousand pounds also," said Towton wrathfully.

"Only one year's income of the Dimsdale investments," retorted Maunders with great coolness; "a man must have some money for his honeymoon."

"And when Lady Corsoon died you guessed that your wife--which she never will be, you can rest assured--would inherit the whole Dimsdale fortune?"

"Quite so. I thought of everything. I suppose Lady Corsoon showed you the second letter as well as the first in your character of Nemo?"

"You are correct," replied Vernon with great composure, "and I noted that the second letter, like the first, was signed with the ideograph of The Spider."

"Naturally, it would be," said Maunders with a shrug. "I easily had an india-rubber stamp made. The thing, if done, had to be well done."

"You are a blackguard," said Colonel Towton, much disgusted. "And may I ask," requested Vernon with irony, "how many other people you have blackmailed by using this stamp?"

"None; nor did I blackmail Lady Corsoon. I simply made a suggestion."

"On the threat of telling her husband about her gambling and sale of the family jewels."

"The Spider used that argument first," said Maunders sullenly; "I simply endorsed it."

"I heartily believe that you are the scoundrel himself," snapped Towton.

"I swear I am not. Why, even my mother was blackmailed--my adopted mother, that is--on the plea that she is my _real_ mother. Would I have done such a thing as that?

"You would do anything to gain your own ends," said Vernon coldly, "always provided your villainy was not discovered."

Maunders grew furiously scarlet. "At least I would have spared my aunt. Mrs. Bedge would give me her last sixpence in my character as her adopted son. There was no need for me to attempt blackmail."

"Perhaps there was not. But all this does not explain how you came to communicate the secret of Dimsdale to The Spider."

"I didn't communicate it, and how he managed to learn it I can't say."

"How did you become possessed of it?" asked Towton very directly.

"I shan't tell you. And I'm not going to be ragged any longer. If I'd guessed for one moment that you were in this house I would not have put in an appearance."

"I can well believe that," said Vernon coolly.

"It's not that I'm afraid," Maunders hastily assured him. "As Diabella I have done nothing to which the law can take exception. The assaults on you and the Colonel were brought about by your own damned meddling and by the fidelity of Hokar. But I have given up playing Diabella----"

"Because you feared lest we should have you arrested," said Towton shrewdly.

"No. Had I been afraid I should never have appeared at the bazaar."

"Oh, yes, you would. You pretended to leave London so as to provide an _alibi_ in case of danger," said Vernon quietly, "and you did not think that Colonel Towton would be at the bazaar. Seeing me didn't matter, as you did not know that Towton and myself were working together. And when I think of the infernal rubbish you told me----"

"It was your own fault," said Maunders sulkily, "and I've had enough of this so, I'm off."

He moved towards the door, but Towton sprang forward and caught his arm. "If you leave this room you will be handed over to the police," he declared.

"He will be handed over in any case," said Vernon decisively.

Maunders turned ghastly pale and his knees shook. He was beginning to lose the courage which had carried him so far successfully. "Vernon, you would not disgrace your old friend," he pleaded piteously.

"You are no friend of mine," was the stern reply, "and your sole chance of escape from arrest is to reveal how you learned this secret of Dimsdale's."

"If I tell it will you let me leave this house free?"

"No, I shan't. I intend to keep an eye on you until this mystery of The Spider is cleared up. You are his jackal."

"I am not; I know nothing. I refuse to speak."

"Colonel, go out and fetch a policeman."

"No! No! No! No!" almost shrieked the wretched man, and flung himself on his knees. "Arthur, don't, don't. I swear I am innocent. I know nothing of Dimsdale's murder."

"Stand up, you cur, and speak out," said Vernon, more enraged by this exhibition of weakness than he had been by the man's insolence. "How did you learn this secret of Dimsdale's? Is it true or a lie?"

"It is true. It is true. I swear it is true. Oh, don't call in the police."

Maunders still grovelled and clung to the knees of Vernon with such force that the young man could not get away. Outside, the fog had rolled right up to the single window of the apartment, and the livid look of the atmosphere suited the situation much better than did the calm, rosy light of the lamp. Near the door knelt Maunders, weeping piteously and begging that the police might not be called in. Vernon stood silent, but Towton gave vent to an oath at the unmanly demeanour of the detected scoundrel.

"Who told you the secret?" he demanded fiercely. "I insist upon knowing, and if you don't tell I'll call in the police myself. A cur such as you are should be under lock and key."

"Come, Maunders," said Vernon sternly, "who told you?"

"Miss Jewin. She knew Dimsdale in India and Burmah," snuffled the kneeling man, desperately afraid.

"Who is Miss Jewin?"

"Hest's housekeeper at Gerby----"

"What!" Both men uttered the ejaculation simultaneously and looked at one another. Then ensued a silence, while the fog closed in thicker and darker, and only the weeping of Maunders could be heard. Suddenly from the hall came the sound of the door opening, and then a firm footstep. Maunders gave a wild cry and clung vehemently to Vernon's legs.

"It's Hest! It's Hest! He'll kill me for telling."

"Then Hest is The----"

"Yes! Yes! He's The Spider and----"

The door was flung open as the footsteps paused, and Francis Hest, wrapped in a heavy overcoat, stood on the threshold smiling. Maunders beat the ground with his hands and crawled to the newcomer's feet.

"I couldn't help it; I couldn't help it. I had to tell you were----"

"The Spider," cried Vernon, whipping out his revolver. "I arrest you in----"

He got no further. At the words of Maunders the villain's face had changed with the rapidity of lightning from smiles to desperate anger. He cast a furious look on his accomplice then suddenly lowered his head so as to get under the line of fire. The next moment Vernon felt Hest charge him head downward in the stomach. The revolver shot harmlessly to the roof, while the young man, taken by surprise, was dashed against the Colonel. Both men fell in a confused heap.

"Follow! Follow, you devil!" cried Hest kicking Maunders, still on his knees, and then he rushed out of the door. Maunders leaped up to race for his liberty and closed the door behind him. When the Colonel and Vernon got on their feet again they rushed into the hall to find it empty. The front door had crashed to with a noise like thunder, and they heard it being locked on the outside, to the accompaniment of a triumphal laugh.

"We've lost them," cried Vernon, tugging vainly at the door. "They'll get away easily in the fog."

CHAPTER XVI.

THE SEARCH.

While Vernon desperately tried to wrench open the front door Towton, with the quick foresight of an old soldier, ran back into the drawing-room and lifted the window sash. In less than two minutes he was outside and hastened to release his companion. Luckily, in his hurry Hest had been unable to extract the key from the lock, so a swift turn of the wrist soon removed the barrier. Vernon and the Colonel set off hot-footed in pursuit of the fugitives, and as they plunged into the fog caught a glimpse of Gail and his wife hurrying into the hall with scared faces, doubtless attracted by the ominous sound of the pistol-shot. But there was no time to explain as every moment was of value, and the two men put their hearts into the chase.

The sudden autumnal fog which had so unexpectedly descended had turned the atmosphere to thick wool, so that it was difficult to breathe, let alone to see. On all sides the gloomy mists shut in the prospect, and after racing vaguely for some minutes down the silent road, the pursuers halted by mutual consent to listen for possible flying footsteps. Not a sound struck on their ears; it might have been the middle of the night, so dense was the darkness and so silent the whole neighbourhood. They could not tell in which direction the two scoundrels had fled, and on the face of it pursuit was absolutely useless.

"We might make for the railway station," suggested the Colonel; "They may have gone there."

Vernon shook his head. "I doubt it. Maunders is too cunning and Hest too desperate to think of taking the train to Waterloo. But, in any case, I'll send a wire to the stationmaster asking him to detain them. Maunders can be recognised from having no hat."

"There are many men who wear no hat nowadays," said Towton dismally, "it is not a distinguishing mark worth much. But how the dickens are we to find a telegraph office in this fog?"

Vernon looked around and noted a weak flare of light illuminating the darkness. Followed by his companion, he walked towards it and found that it came from the windows of a grocer's shop at the corner of the road. Entering quickly, he asked for the nearest telegraph office, and learned to his great satisfaction that it was at the chemist's two or three doors down.

The worthy grocer looked somewhat alarmed at the entrance of two gentlemen without hats, for, in their haste, Vernon and his friend had forgotten to take them. But they gave the tradesmen no time to ask questions, and by closely skirting the shops round the corner managed to find that of the chemist. Here Vernon sent a wire to the stationmaster at Waterloo instructing him to detain two men, one dark and one fair, without a hat, who might possibly arrive by an early train. He added a meagre description of their dress, so that the telegram proved to be somewhat lengthy.

"But I fear it is useless," said Vernon as they left the shop and had handed the wire to the startled chemist. "They won't take the train, I'm certain, and even if they do my description is not clear enough, unless the Waterloo stationmaster happens to be singularly intelligent."

"We can but hope for the best, and we have done all we can," said Towton in a decided tone. "What's to be done now?"

"We must return to Siddons Villa, both to get our hats and to see Gail."

"How are we to retrace our steps in this fog?"

"Petterby Road is just round the corner, and by keeping to the railings of the gardens we are bound to find the house."

It was as Vernon said. They had raced in a straight line down to the grocer's shop at the corner and had not left Petterby Road until they went to the telegraph office. On recovering the bearings of the first shop they carefully felt their way up the road, reading on every gate the designation of each house. In this way, and after some ten or twelve minutes had elapsed, they managed to strike Siddons Villa and again found themselves at the front door. It was closed, as also was the window.

"I hope Gail has not run away also," said Vernon ringing the bell.

"Do you suspect he has anything to do with the business?"

"Who knows? On the face of it he looks innocent, and Maunders certainly swore that the old man was ignorant. But Maunders is a liar and----"

Here the door was cautiously opened, and the white face of Professor Gail became visible. "Who is there?" he asked in a trembling voice.

"Mr. Vernon and Colonel Towton," said the latter gentleman; "we have returned to get our hats and to explain."

"You won't fire any more pistols? My wife is almost fainting, and I don't like this sort of business. What does it----"

"Open the door, open the door!" cried the Colonel testily; "you shall have a full explanation."

Mr. Gail still seemed reluctant, as he apparently took them for robbers and dangerous rogues, so Vernon, losing patience, forced the door back and the old actor along with it. They faced the Professor in the hall and saw that he was holding an old-fashioned blunderbuss--probably a stage property used in "The Miller and His Men" and other out-of-date plays. In the distance, and sheltering herself behind her husband, was Mrs. Gail grasping a poker in her trembling hand. The pair seemed to be thoroughly frightened, and, considering the circumstances, it was small wonder that they were.

"I have sent Maria for a policeman," quavered Mrs. Gail, "and both my husband and myself are armed."

"I hope Maria won't lose herself in the fog," said Vernon good-humouredly, and in spite of his vexation at the escape of The Spider and his jackal.

"In heaven's name, what does it mean?" demanded the Professor somewhat recovering his dignity.

"Come into the drawing-room and we will explain," said Towton with some impatience, for he had small leniency for cowardice; "There's nothing to be afraid of. Mr. Vernon and I are honest men: you have got rid of the villains."

"The villains?" shrieked Mrs. Gail, trembling violently and dropping the poker.

"Maunders and Hest," said Vernon carelessly; "come in."

He preceded his friend and the Gails into the drawing-room, quite certain, from the way in which they had behaved, that they knew nothing of the wicked doings of Hest and Maunders. When the door was closed and everyone was seated Vernon proceeded to examine the actor and actress. The situation, as Professor Gail said afterwards, was highly dramatic.

"You must answer my questions frankly," said Vernon addressing the couple; "if you do not, the police may interfere."

"The police?" shrieked Mrs. Gail, turning as white as chalk.

The Professor silenced her with a gesture and spoke to Vernon with great dignity. "Young man," he said, striving to keep his voice from trembling, "I pay my rates and taxes, my bills to my tradesmen, and my rent for our home. Under these circumstances I cannot see why you should talk of the police."

"I speak of them in connection with what has taken place."

"And you may well do so, young man. To fire a pistol in a private house----"

"That was an accident," Vernon hastened to explain. "My revolver went off when Mr. Hest assaulted me."

"Why should Mr. Hest assault you?" demanded Mrs. Gail, much astonished.

"That's a long story. Tell me," Vernon turned towards the Professor while Towton held his peace and nursed his hat, "what do you know of Maunders?"

"Know of him?" said the amazed Gail, looking thoroughly puzzled. "I know no more than that he is a friend of Mr. Hest's who called last night and who was requested, by Mr. Hest and not by me, to stay the night. I have never set eyes on him before."

"Did Miss Hest ever mention him?"

"Yes, she did," broke in Mrs. Gail, who was listening intently. "She told me that he was a friend of hers in love with Miss Dimsdale, and mentioned that he was the only man she had ever seen handsome enough to play Romeo as Romeo should be played."

Professor Gail nodded his head graciously. "I agree with Miss Hest there," he said gravely; "Mr. Maunders is indeed handsome. But she never told us anything about him, Mr. Vernon, save what my wife has related."

"And Mr. Hest? What do you know of him?"

"Nothing more than that he is the brother of my talented pupil. He came with the message from his sister, who is at her ancestral halls in Yorkshire, to the effect that she would return in a month, or perchance earlier, to fulfil certain engagements which I have procured her. I invited him to stay here during his stay in town."

"Why did you?" asked the Colonel, speaking for the first time. Gail looked embarrassed, but Mrs. Gail spoke for him. "Mr. Hest, we know, is very rich," she said frankly, "and both my husband and myself wish to have a theatre of our own. We thought that if we showed him some hospitality he might finance us. I must say," she added, looking puzzled, "that I wondered that such a rich man was content to accept our humble lodgings instead of going to a swell hotel. But he seems to be easily pleased."

"It was not that, Hettie," said the Professor quickly. "Mr. Hest simply remained here so that he could persuade me to induce my talented pupil to give up reciting, as he dreaded lest she should go on the stage. And she ought to be an actress, in my humble opinion, for her capabilities are of a very high order. As Lady Macbeth, or in any of Sardou's characters, such as La Tosca, Fedora, and the rest, she would produce a sensation."

The speech of both man and wife seemed frank enough, and they appeared to be a couple of simple people devoted to their profession and quite ignorant of evil. Vernon glanced at Towton and saw from the expression of the Colonel's face that he thoroughly believed them. Still, so as to be quite sure of his ground, he asked another question: "Miss Hest as a reciter or an actress may be all that can be desired, but do you and Mrs. Gail like her personally; do you think she is what we call--well--er--straight?"

"Yes," cried the woman forcibly; "Miss Hest is one in a thousand. She is a kind-hearted lady who sympathises with those who struggle."

"Hettie is quite right," said the Professor with dignity. "Many a time has Miss Hest assisted us when tradespeople have worried. I am sure that she would have persuaded her brother to enable us to enter into management in the long run, as she has every confidence in my capabilities."

"And in mine," said Mrs. Gail jealously. "She said that my Emilia in 'Othello' was the best performance she had ever seen. But now, gentlemen," the actress rose to give effect to her words, "may I inquire why you ask these questions, and why you come here to fire pistols in a peaceful home?"

At the beginning it had been in Vernon's mind to tell the whole story right out and to tax the couple with complicity. But they really seemed to be entirely ignorant of Hest's true character, and evidently had only lately met Maunders. He therefore did not think it wise to reveal what he and the Colonel knew lest the Gails should gossip about the matter. And until he had consulted Drench the young man did not desire that this last unusual affair should become public. He therefore shot a warning glance at the Colonel and answered cautiously:

"It is only a private matter, Mrs. Gail, which is not worth explaining. The pistol-shot was an accident."

"But you said that Mr. Maunders and Mr. Hest were villains," she persisted. "Ah, I spoke somewhat harshly, being a trifle excited. They have treated me and my friend here very badly and we came for redress. How their consciences smote them you can judge from the fact of their flight. You will possibly never see them again. But if they do chance to return you must wire to me at once to the Athenian Club, Pall Mall."

"I don't like these hints and suggestions of evil, sir," said Gail, restlessly, "and certainly I should never think of telegraphing to you unless Mr. Maunders and Mr. Hest give me leave. And why, sir, should they not return?"

"Don't seek to know any more, Mr. Gail, but do as you are told," said Vernon in a peremptory tone, "and also it will be wise if you and your wife hold your tongues over what has happened and stop the servant from talking."

"Suppose we don't?" demanded Mrs. Gail aggressively.

"In that case you will get into trouble."

"How dare you--how dare----"

"See here!" Colonel Towton rose angrily. "We have reason to believe that these men are connected with The Spider."

Mrs. Gail shrieked and the Professor turned pale. Both knew that terrible name which was so freely mentioned in the papers. "Do you mean to say----"

"We say nothing," said Vernon sharply, "and my friend here has perhaps said too much. But it is as well that you should know the necessity of keeping silent tongues in your heads."

"We, knowing nothing of these matters, cannot be expected to----"

"I am quite aware that you are innocent of complicity," interrupted Towton, "but you both must promise to be silent until you have leave to speak."

"And if not?"

"Already I have told you that the police will interfere," observed Vernon coldly. "This business is concerned with The Spider, so, for your own sakes, hold your confounded tongues."

The Gails, however, were not so easily commanded. They wished to know how Hest and Maunders were connected with The Spider, and if they were in any way accused of being, as they termed it, "in the know." But the arguments and commands of Towton, together with those of Vernon, gradually induced the worthy couple to listen to reason. In fact, at the end of half an hour both were thoroughly terrified into thinking that their reputation might be ruined were it known that men connected with The Spider had been under their roof. Neither Gail nor his wife were averse to being mentioned in the papers or to securing an advertisement so as to add to their theatrical fame, but the publicity likely to be procured from the late episode was not the sort they desired. They therefore finally agreed to keep silence about the strange interview and the flight of their guests, and also declared that they would make Maria hold her tongue. Nevertheless, their curiosity remained unabated, and Vernon had to promise them that it would some day be satisfied.

"You shall know all when the time comes," he said when taking leave, "but keep silence until the appointed hour lest you get into trouble."

This speech, being somewhat stagey, sounded pleasantly in the ears of the couple, and Towton left the house with his friend, quite satisfied that Professor Gail and his wife and their servant would say nothing of what had taken place. "And now," said the Colonel, "let us grope our way to the station. After we reach town we can see Drench."

Vernon agreed, and by following the line of houses they finally managed, but with some difficulty, to get to the railway. Here they had to wait for a considerable time for a train, as the ordinary traffic was somewhat complicated by fog. It was eight o'clock before they reached Waterloo, and they learned from the stationmaster that nothing had been seen of the two men alluded to in the telegram, although each train and the barrier of the platform it arrived at had been watched by the police. Vernon was not surprised at this intelligence.

"I thought both Hest and Maunders were too clever to risk a wire to Waterloo Station, as they knew I would send it."

"What's to be done now?"

"Let us go to your rooms and send a telegram to Drench at Hampstead asking him to come down."

"The fog is still thick," said Towton as they stepped into a taxi; "perhaps he won't come. Hang it, every possible obstacle seems to be placed in our way. The blackguards will escape."

"Not out of England, at all events," said Vernon grimly. "When we explain everything to Drench he will have all the stations and all the ports watched. We'll catch them sooner or later."

But the young man spoke with more confidence than he actually felt, as he knew that Hest was extraordinarily clever in concealing himself. As The Spider he had baffled the police for years, and, being an arch-criminal, would be dexterous enough to escape even out of this tight corner. He began to consider what was best to be done after sending a wire to Inspector Drench, when his meditations were broken in upon by the Colonel.

"Do you really believe that Hest is The Spider?"

"Of course. Didn't you see his face change when Maunders spoke, and didn't he cut and run when he saw that the game was up?"

"It certainly looks like guilt. And yet it seems incredible. The man always has lived in Yorkshire, whereas The Spider is supposed to live in town."

"No one has ever known the whereabouts of The Spider," said Vernon coolly, "and it is as easy to write blackmailing letters in Yorkshire and post them in London as to live in town altogether for that purpose. Besides, his sister told me herself that Hest frequently went away for days and weeks at a time. Doubtless he was attending to his nefarious business in London."

"How do you reconcile this devilry with his philanthropy?"

"It seems odd, doesn't it? But we know that the worst criminals have their good points. There lives some soul of good in all things evil, you know."

"I rather think," said the Colonel grimly, "that Hest looks upon himself as a kind of modern Robin Hood, who takes from the rich to give to the poor. He blackmailed wealthy folk in order to build his Bolly Reservoir and his confounded school-houses. Robbed Peter to pay Paul, as you might put it."

"Rob Dives to help Demos is the way he would put it," said Vernon with a shrug. "However, we have made a great discovery and one which the police will thank us for making. When Hest is captured many a rich man will sleep the easier."

"Yes, when he is captured; but that won't be easy."

"I agree with you. The Spider is as clever as his father--the devil. Humph!" added Vernon thoughtfully, "I wonder if his sister knows anything about his infernal doings."

"No," said the Colonel decidedly. "I don't like Miss Hest, as I think she is too imperious and masterful and wants her own way too much. All the same, I don't believe she would have countenanced her brother's behaviour. Besides, she was always away from him, and he doubtless carried on his pranks without her knowledge."

"You defend her. I thought you didn't like her?"

"I admitted only a moment ago that I did not," snapped the Colonel as the taxi cautiously felt its way up Whitehall, "but I must be just to her. The poor woman will suffer as it is when her brother's criminality becomes known. It will ruin her reciting business."

"That's true, and there is no chance of keeping the matter quiet. Hest must be captured and imprisoned."

"Hanged, you mean. Remember, he murdered Martin Dimsdale."

Vernon shuddered. "I suppose he did," was his reluctant admission. "I am sorry for Miss Hest, as, contrary to your opinion, I think highly of her. She may be masterful, as you say, but Ida is so weak that it is just as well that she should have someone to lead her in the right way."

"Oh, Miss Hest has led her in the right way, no doubt," retorted the Colonel; "but I prefer to be the guide myself. See here, Vernon, come down with me next week to my place at Bowderstyke."

"What for? We have to hunt down Hest and Maunders."

"We can safely leave that to Drench and his underlings. I want to get Ida away from Gerby Hall. Sorry as I am for Miss Hest in having such a brother, I don't want Ida to continue under her protection any longer, especially as she wants to marry her to Maunders."

"Maunders will have no chance now," said Vernon with a grim chuckle. "But you are a bachelor, Towton, so Ida will scarcely be able to come to The Grange."

"I shall ask her aunt down as chaperon."

"Lady Corsoon? Good! And ask Lucy also, for my sake."

"With great pleasure. I think that the removal of Maunders from my path and yours will result in the courses of our love running smoother. Ah, here we are, and I'm glad, as I want drink and victuals."

After the long, cautious creeping through the fog the two gentlemen arrived at the Colonel's rooms, and Bendham was sent out for food. Having dined, they smoked and talked while waiting for Inspector Drench. But he never came. A telegram arrived instead stating that the fog prevented his keeping the appointment. And it also prevented Vernon getting back to his own quarters, so the Colonel put him up for the night. Next day the hunt for the criminals began in earnest.

Before Drench arrived, which he did at eleven o'clock, Professor Gail came to the Athenian Cub, where the gentlemen were waiting, and produced a wire which had arrived for Hest on that morning. He had not opened it, being afraid, but brought it intact to Vernon. That young man had no compunction under the circumstances in reading it, and found that it was from Frances Hest to her brother asking him to return home as divers matters connected with the estate required his attention.

"Sent first thing this morning," said Vernon passing the wire to the Colonel. "Poor woman! she doesn't know that her brother has been found out."

The wire was shown to Inspector Drench when he duly arrived, and he was exhaustively informed of all that had taken place. He was naturally both astonished and interested, but nevertheless expressed himself annoyed that civilians should have proceeded so far without invoking the police. Drench gave both the Colonel and Vernon to understand that if he had been on the spot Hest and his accomplice would not have escaped so easily, a view with which they privately differed, although they did not think it wise to say so. But Towton _did_ intimate to the Inspector that he was a military man and not a civilian, whatever Vernon might be. Drench declined to take any notice of this remark.

The Inspector also questioned Gail closely, but could learn nothing from him of any moment, since the old actor knew nothing and was greatly agitated over the whole affair. Finally, bidding all three hold their tongues, Drench sallied forth to search for the missing pair. He saw the Scotland Yard authorities and wired to all the ports and railway stations in the kingdom. As yet, and because he desired to keep the affair out of the newspapers, Drench did not advertise in the journals, or by handbills. Otherwise, in every way he strove to find the fugitives.

He might as well have attempted to find a shell at the bottom of the Atlantic. Day after day went by and no news was heard of Hest or Maunders, and from the moment they had been swallowed up by the fog at Isleworth nothing had been seen of them. They had not, so far as could be ascertained, passed out of the kingdom, and certainly they were not to be found in the kingdom itself. Like Macbeth's witches, they had made themselves thin air: like the children of Korah and Dathan, they apparently had been swallowed up by the earth. But, thanks to Drench, the discovery of the identity of The Spider and his subsequent escape had not yet been made public, and the Press knew nothing of what was taking place. But the time had now come when publicity was absolutely necessary.

"There's nothing else for it," said Drench, and Vernon in spite of his wish to keep things quiet, agreed with him.

CHAPTER XVII.

IN THE TRAIN.

Within a week of the episode at Isleworth Colonel Towton took Vernon with him to Yorkshire. Inspector Drench was still searching for the fugitives and was still unable to find them. True to his reputation, The Spider had covered up his tracks in a most masterly manner, and there was not the slightest clue to indicate his whereabouts. Presumably Maunders was with him, as he had not returned to his rooms in Planet Street, nor had he been seen in any of his usual haunts about town. This was to be expected, as Maunders had, as the saying goes, "gone under," and the society wherein he had glittered so gaily would henceforth know him no more. It seemed a pity that a young man with talents and good looks and social position should have ruined his life at the very outset of a promising career. But there must have been some criminal strain in Maunders, which came to the surface in prosperity instead of being revealed by poverty. He was, as Coleridge says about people with such natures, "a fool in a circumbendibus."

However, it was useless for Vernon to mourn over his old school friend's downfall. He had done his best to keep him in the straight path and had failed to prevent his feet from straying. He therefore, as there was nothing else to be done at this eleventh hour, washed his hands of him and left him, together with Hest, to the tender mercies of the law as represented by the Inspector. Now that Drench had all the threads in his own hands he resented anyone else weaving them into ropes for the necks of the criminals, as he apparently wished to secure all the glory and honour of the capture to himself. Both Towton and Vernon were rather glad that the Inspector took this view, as they wished to have nothing more to do with the matter. And, before leaving London for Bowderstyke, Vernon shut up his Covent Garden office and formally renounced his pseudonym of Nemo. As by this time he was officially recognised as his uncle's heir he could well afford to do so. Sir Edward, however, still lingered between life and death, so it was doubtful when Vernon would enter into his kingdom.

While the train was flying through the autumnal landscape Towton and his guest made themselves comfortable in a first-class compartment, which they had secured to themselves, for the purpose of uninterrupted conversation. They were still deeply interested in the case and looked forward anxiously to the capture of The Spider. It was only right that he should suffer for his dastardly crime in murdering an old and inoffensive man. As to Maunders, he was evidently hand in glove with the cleverer rascal, and would undoubtedly be given a long term of imprisonment. Thus society would be rid of two dangerous people, and those with secrets would sleep the easier, knowing that one Asmodeus was dead and the other safely locked up.

"But I don't know what poor Mrs. Bedge will do," said Vernon looking dolefully out of the window.

"Does she know anything?" asked the Colonel, throwing down the morning paper which he had been reading and settling himself for a talk.

Vernon nodded. "I saw her yesterday. She sent to ask me what had become of Constantine. I was obliged to tell her."

"Do you think that was kind or wise?"

"I think so, decidedly. It was better that Mrs. Bedge should learn the truth from a friend than see it crudely printed in the daily papers. And there it is bound to appear sooner or later."

"Drench will have to catch The Spider first," said the Colonel coolly. "No easy task, as we know. What did she say?"

"At first she declined to believe it, badly as Maunders has treated her. She kept insisting that it was all a mistake and that Constantine would appear to put matters right."

"What wonderful faith these women have, Vernon."

"Bless them, yes. They go by their hearts entirely."

"In that case," remarked Towton drily, "Mrs. Bedge must have known that Maunders is not the saint she tries to make him out to be."

"I did not say that she went by her instinct," replied Vernon equally drily; "there is a difference between that and heart-love. Because Constantine is her sister's child and her adopted son Mrs. Bedge's heart, which he has almost broken, cherishes him fondly; but her instinct must have told her long ago that the fellow is a scamp of the worst sort."

"He's a thorough-paced scoundrel," said the Colonel vigorously.

"Mrs. Bedge declined to take that view of him. She wailed that he had a tender heart and was led away because he had a weak nature. In fact, her defence was that of a man being his own worst enemy."

"Maunders certainly was. He had all the gifts of the gods, yet----"

"Yet fell because the greatest gift of honest purpose was not given," finished Vernon. "Hang it all, Towton, scamp as the fellow is, I am sorry for him."

"I'm not," growled Towton savagely.

"Ah, you did not play with him as a child, nor did you go to school with him, my friend. Although I'm bound to say that Constantine was always a selfish chap--what you would call a rotter."

"I would call him nothing of the sort, Vernon. I detest slang."

"That's a mistake. Slang frequently hits the nail on the head when the King's English misses it altogether. Slang conveys much in little, and----"

"Oh, the deuce take your philology. Go on talking about Mrs. Bedge."

"There's no more to say. Maunders has pretty well drained her, but she has enough to live on, and the Hampstead house is her own. Towards the end of our conversation, however, she let out that she was not surprised at Conny's behaviour, as she rather expected it."

"H'm! Somewhat contradictory. Why?"

"Well, it seems that Maunders' father, the Greek, Mavrocordato, you know, was rather a bad egg himself. He worried his wife--Mrs. Bedge's sister, that is--into her grave, and swindled his partner before he committed suicide."

"I never heard that before."

"No. Mrs. Bedge always kept it quiet for the boy's sake until she let it out to me in her grief yesterday. Mavrocordato--he took the English name of Maunders--bolted with a heap of his partner's money, and shot himself at Corfu, whither he was traced by detectives. Mrs. Bedge adopted the son, and did her best to train him up as an honest man. She tried her hardest, I'm certain, but what's bred in the bone, you know."

Colonel Towton folded his arms and stared straightly before him. "Poor devil. He was considerably handicapped by such a father. I wonder, Vernon, for how many of our deeds we are responsible, when you take heredity into consideration. Some sin because they like it, but many because they can't help it."

"Let us give Maunders the benefit of the doubt, and say that the sins of his father were visited on him. And, of course, we must not forget that Hest is an extremely clever and strong-minded man, who could, and did, easily control Maunders' weaker nature."

"There's something to be said there," assented the Colonel thoughtfully. "I daresay Hest entangled the poor wretch in crime before he well knew what he was about, and once committed he would be compelled to remain in the mud. But Hest himself, Vernon. What do you make of him?"

"I don't know enough about him to give an opinion. Perhaps when we see the sister she may tell us something."

"Oh, by the way, I received a letter from her two days ago, about which I intended to speak to you, Vernon. All this bother and worry put it out of my head. I left it at home, unfortunately, but I can tell you the gist of it."

Vernon looked interested. "What did she write about, and why to you?" "She wrote to me because she wants me to marry Ida."

"I really don't see what she has to do with that," remarked Vernon with a shrug; "for Ida is surely of an age to choose for herself."

"I always told you, Vernon," said Towton, deliberately crossing one leg over the other, "that Ida, being less masterful than Miss Hest, is usually guided by her, and that I objected to the guidance. Ida liked me more than anyone else before that handsome scamp came along. Then she became infatuated with him, and Miss Hest did her best to induce her to marry him. But the sad death of Dimsdale took Ida's thoughts off Maunders, and--as I judge from the letter Ida wrote me from Gerby Hall--Miss Hest tried to get her to love the man again. Failing that, she attempted to get Ida to marry her brother, only he came up to London, not feeling disposed to fall in with his sister's views. You can therefore see that Miss Hest sways Ida a great deal, and for that reason I have come to get her away from such dangerous company--doubly dangerous now that we know Francis Hest is The Spider."

Vernon shrugged his shoulders. "It's rather hard to blame the sister for the brother's delinquencies," he said judicially. "And now that he and Maunders are out of the running she will place her weight in your scale. In fact, from your late observation, she has already done so. You should be very pleased, Colonel, whereas you seem to me to be ungrateful."

"I don't want Ida to be induced to marry me by Miss Hest's representations, Vernon," said Towton hotly. "It's a liberty on her part to interfere with my wooing. Lady Corsoon comes down to-morrow with her daughter, and I shall ask her to go to Gerby Hall and bring Ida back with her. Then we will have finished with these shady people, and Ida will marry me of her own free will."

"Well, Colonel," replied Vernon pacifically, "I hope things will turn out as you expect. But what did Miss Hest write about?"

"About her brother. She asked me if I had seen him, and what was the matter with him." Vernon looked puzzled. "I don't understand. Does she suspect----"

"She suspects nothing," broke in Towton impetuously. "But she stated that she had received a letter from her brother four or five days ago saying that he intended to leave England for ever, as he was tired of civilisation. He enclosed a Deed of Gift, making over Gerby Hall and its acres to her, as he intended--so he said--to earn his own living when abroad. Naturally, Miss Hest could not understand this, and wrote asking me what was the matter."

"Did you explain?"

"No. I wrote saying that I was coming down to my own place, and would tell her all I knew when I arrived. But you can see, Vernon, that Hest is still in London."

"He was, six or seven days ago, but he may have gone away since," said Vernon cautiously. "Who drew up the Deed of Gift?"

"I can't say. Miss Hest did not explain that. Why?"

"Because if it was some lawyer we might be able to question him regarding Hest's latest movements. Humph! So Hest has bolted. Well, I'm not surprised at that. But I am rather astonished he should surrender his property."

"Oh, well. I expect his business as The Spider has made him quite a rich man. Remember, the blackguard has been blackmailing successfully for three or four years. He knows that his sister has nothing save what she makes by her reciting, so perhaps his conscience smote him, and so he made his Deed of Gift. It's a lucky thing for her, as Gerby Hall is a fine old place, although rather gloomy, and there is a decent income of one thousand a year attached to it, farms, village rents, and all that sort of thing, you know."

"It's queer Hest should have behaved so well, when he is such a scoundrel, Towton. You told me that he quarrelled with his sister, and certainly from the remarks she made about him to me, she did not seem over fond of him."

"Blood is thicker than water," said the Colonel sententiously, "and dog does not eat dog."

"I agree with your first proverb, but not with the second, Towton. Miss Hest is not of the same breed, morally speaking, as her brother, and no doubt will be horrified when she learns of his wickedness."

"Probably. You always defend her."

"I am just," said Vernon coldly. "So far as I can see, she is a clever woman of good principles, although, I admit, rather masterful. Her brother has done a wise thing in handing her over the property, whatever his reasons may be. She will be an admirable mistress."

"Oh, as to that, Hest was a great benefactor to all the villages around, and the people swear by them. If he has bolted with Maunders, Drench will have to let the matter drop. But, if he is captured, no one here will believe that he is a murderer and a blackmailer. They know him only as a good landlord and a kind friend."

"And we know him as a criminal. Strange that two such diverse natures can exist side by side."

"I daresay Hest hoped that his good deeds would pay for his bad ones," said the Colonel carelessly. "I shall be glad if he escapes, richly as he deserves to be hanged for murdering Dimsdale. It will be just as well if the whole thing is buried in oblivion. Then I shall marry Ida, you Miss Corsoon, and Miss Hest can play the lady of the manor here, as she pleases."

"What about the Dimsdale property?"

"If it belongs to Lady Corsoon she must have it; if Maunders' story is a lie, which it may be, I shall stick to it on behalf of my wife. However, we may hear from Venery of Singapore in a few weeks. My letter must have nearly reached him by this time."

"You can learn the truth of the story nearer home," said Vernon after a pause. "Miss Jewin, the housekeeper at Gerby Hall, told the story to Maunders, according to his own account."

"I shall question her, you may be sure," said the Colonel grimly; "but I want to hear from Venery also. Oh, I'm sick of talking about these things," he added with a yawn. "It's time for forty winks." And forthwith he closed his eyes, after settling himself comfortably in his seat. Vernon, not inclined to rest, lighted a fresh cigar and buried himself in a book.

It was five o'clock when the travellers reached Bradmoor, the nearest station to Bowderstyke. It was ten miles to the valley, but the road was excellent, and Towton's motor-car awaited them. In ten minutes the baggage was packed away, and Vernon with his host was safely ensconced in the back part of the machine, which was covered with a hood. Towton asked Vernon if he would care to drive, but as the offer was refused and the Colonel himself did not feel in a sporting humour, the conduct of the journey was left to the smart chauffeur. He appeared to be well acquainted with the country, and as the road was somewhat lonely, the motor travelled towards Bowderstyke at a great rate of speed. The motion was exhilarating, and the view on either side of the roadway extremely picturesque, so Vernon enjoyed himself greatly in the fresh air, after the close atmosphere and the monotony of the train. With the wind blowing in his face and the smooth, easy gliding motion, he felt like a flying bird, or at all events as though mounted on one.

The country was wild and barren, consisting mainly of interminable stretches of moorland, mounting up on either side of the road to considerable heights. Occasionally there was a dip covered with green grass and trees, already beginning to shed their leaves, but for the most part the sombre moors, darkening in the failing light, spread solemnly to right and left. It was rarely that a house or a village was passed, and only every now and then could Vernon catch a glimpse of cattle or human beings.

"This country would get on my nerves," he said to his companion. "It is like the weird landscape described by Browning in his Childe Roland poem. Those telegraph poles are the sole signs of civilisation."

"Oh, we'll come to a more cheery aspect shortly," said Towton smiling; "for my part, I love the gloom and the loneliness of our moors. Many a time in the garish Indian days, with a burning sun in the hateful blue sky, have I longed for dear old Yorkshire."

"Everyone to his taste," said Vernon with a shrug. "I prefer something much more cheerful."

"You are a cockney at heart, Vernon."

"I daresay. London is good enough for me."

Towards the end of the ten mile stretch from the station signs of civilisation became more frequent. Here and there was a village with cultivated fields around it. Cattle were pastured in enclosed paddocks, and men and women with laughing children trudged along the high road, looking after the motor with great curiosity, for the machine was yet a novelty in that lonely district. Twice the road ran directly through a village, and Vernon had an opportunity of seeing the solid grey stone houses, which were suited to the Calvinistic looks of the country. And the people themselves appeared to be what the Scotch call "dour."

And now the moors began to grow higher and to close in on the white road with a gradual menace. Leaving the comparatively broad lands, the motor glided into a valley, which grew even more narrow as they proceeded. A babbling stream prattled down the centre of this, over a stony bed, and beside it the road twisted along like a white serpent, protected by a parapet of rough stones. Already the crimson light of the sunset had died out of the western sky, but the moon was full, and, soaring high in the dark blue dome of the firmament, poured floods of light into the gully, to use a Colonial expression--for by this time it was little else. And looking upward, Vernon could see star after star peep out to attend on the majestic orb.

"What do you call this place?" he asked abruptly. Towton glanced at him in surprise. "Didn't I tell you? It's Bowderstyke."

"Great Scott, Colonel, is your house situated in this isolated, damp spot. I should think you never saw the sun from one year's end to the other, save when it was directly overhead."

"Oh, the valley broadens out further on. This is merely the entrance."

"What the deuce do the inhabitants live on? It's like living in a drain."

"Oh, confound you, Vernon," said the Colonel half annoyed. "It's one of the most beautiful places in the world. If you were a Yorkshire tyke you would admit that. There is only the village of Bowderstyke a mile away, and the inhabitants live by pasturing their cattle on the moors on the heights above. Also there is a weaving and spinning industry, the mills being driven by water power, of which there is no lack."

"This stream doesn't seem to have much water," said Vernon disdainfully.

"You should see it in winter when the snows melt on the moors," advised the Colonel. "Besides, the water from the mills comes from Hest's new reservoir, and there is a never-failing supply. This stream used to be much broader, and its bed contained much more water, but when the Bolly Dam was constructed, of course the supply dwindled. Pipes run under this road to supply the several villages you saw just before we entered the valley."

"Where is the dam which our criminal friend built?"

Towton pointed straight ahead. "Round the next corner you could see it, but we do not go so far. There was a small lake there up on the moors which fed this stream. Hest simply got engineers to dam the lake and prevent too much water going to waste down the bed of this torrent. The dam runs right across the valley a mile and a half beyond my house."

"But isn't that dangerous. If it burst this valley would be flooded from end to end, and everybody would be drowned, to say nothing of the way in which the village would be smashed up."

"Well, yes." Towton pinched his nether lip uneasily. "I've thought of that myself many a time. But I was abroad when the dam was constructed. There certainly--as I have often said--should be an outlet for the water other than the pipes which supply Bowderstyke and the villages outside the valley, capacious as those same pipes undoubtedly are. Assuredly, if the reservoir burst there would be great loss of life and destruction of property. But the Bolly Dam is very strongly built, so I have no fear of anything happening. You can see it from my house, and we'll pay it a visit in a day or two. Meantime, this is Bowderstyke village."

By this time they were passing through quite a number of small houses, from the windows of which lights gleamed cheerfully. The motor soon left these behind, then swerved to the right--looking up from the entrance to the valley--and shortly began to climb a winding road. At this point, as the Colonel had foretold, the vale broadened abruptly, and the high moors stood away so as to form a kind of deep cup. Up the side of this, the road along which they were travelling sloped upward for some distance, then turned on itself and sloped still higher. Shortly the motor attained the highest level, and in the moonlight Vernon could see the moors stretching for miles, lonely and romantic. A straight road ran parallel with the upper portion of the valley for close upon half a mile. Then appeared a miniature forest, encircled by a high stone wall. This was undoubtedly artificial, as the moorlands were treeless, and the unexpected woodland looked out of place amidst its bleak surroundings.

The motor soon arrived at two tall stone pillars crested with heraldic monsters, and passing through these, spun up a short avenue to stop before a large white house, brilliantly lighted up. Spacious lawns opened up before the mansion, interspersed with flowerbeds, now bloomless, and the whole was shut in by the fairy forest, as Vernon called it in his own mind.

"Here we are," said Colonel Towton jumping from the car. "Allow me to welcome you to The Grange, my friend."

"Thank heaven the journey's at an end," said Vernon.

CHAPTER XVIII.

AT BOWDERSTYKE.

"I hope you slept well, Vernon," said the Colonel to his guest the next morning when they were at breakfast.

"Like a top," was the response. "That journey tired me out, and your moorland air is so strong that I slept the moment my head was on the pillow."

"You will eat well also, Vernon," remarked Towton, regarding with satisfaction the attention paid by his visitor to the appetising meal. "Our air is famous as a tonic. You will return to town a giant refreshed."

"There is lots to be done before I leave here," said Vernon passing his cup for a fresh supply of coffee. "What is your first step?"

"We will call on Miss Hest this afternoon, and I can show you the village at the same time. Lady Corsoon and her daughter will come to-day, and will arrive to dinner. That is the programme."

"I'm at your disposal. And to-morrow I suppose you will get Lady Corsoon to take charge of Ida?"

"If Miss Hest will let her go," said the Colonel cautiously.

"She can't detain her, surely."

"Not by outward force; but she may use her influence to keep her. Miss Hest won't lose the chance of swaying the mind of a girl with ten thousand a year. You may be sure of that."

"H'm," said Vernon finishing the last of his coffee. "If Ida learned the secret of Dimsdale from Maunders, disguised as Diabella, you may be sure that she told Miss Hest. In that case, Ida is not worth keeping."

Colonel Towton nodded and pushed back his chair to rise. "There's something in that, I'll admit. However, we can say nothing until we interview Miss Hest. I have already sent her a note saying that we have arrived and will see her to-day."

Matters having been thus arranged, the two men lighted their pipes and strolled out into the grounds. It was a bright autumnal morning with a cloudless blue sky and a radiant sun; the moorland air was keen, and Vernon drew long invigorating breaths into his lungs. Notwithstanding the somewhat bleak surroundings, The Grange was a remarkably comfortable house, and the original Towton who had built the same had striven to render it as bright as possible, so as to contrast with the sombre moors. The Grange, indeed, was more like an Italian villa than a Yorkshire mansion, as it was constructed of white stone and every window had green shutters, while the roof was formed of cheerful red tiles. Both rooms and corridors were spacious and decorated in brilliant tints, and the furniture was of the most modern description.

"It isn't at all like an ancestral home, is it?" said Towton cheerfully. "And all the better for that, since the word suggests oak parlours, comfortable gloom, and cumbersome furniture."

"Those would suit the situation better," said Vernon, glancing at the pines and fir-trees, which formed a screen to keep away the too keen moorland winds. "Your brilliant walls and red roofs look out of place in these stern solitudes, where Nature seems to be acting the anchorite."

"I love the scenery and solitude and all that, Vernon, but I like to be comfortably housed. My great-grand-father left the original family seat, which is in the valley almost below the Bolly Dam, and built this place after a long sojourn in Italy. My cousin, from whom I inherit, cleared out all the old Victorian furniture and redecorated the house as you see it. It's all very modern, and perhaps, in contrast with the grandeur of the moors, somewhat frivolous. But, at all events, it is cheerful and comfortable. I could scarcely ask Ida to inherit a kind of Ogre's Castle like Gerby Hall."

"Where is that?"

"You will see shortly. It's a real old Yorkshire Manor House, dating, I believe, from the Wars of the Roses. There was a lot of fighting went on during those days in Yorkshire, and the original Hest procured a grant of Bowderstyke Valley from Edward IV. But my ancestors came along later and seized a portion of it and built the mansion near the dam. I understand that the Hests and the Towtons fought like cat and dog over the valley. However, the most of the property belongs to me, and I live in this very up-to-date Grange, while they' still cling to the remnants of their lands and to Gerby Hall."

"From whom does our criminal friend inherit?"

"His grandfather. Hest's father was an officer in the Indian army, and had quarrelled with the old man. Then he died, together with his wife, some spinster he had married at Simla. The twin children were sent home to the grandfather, who brought them up and left the estates to Francis. Now that he has been shown up, he has had the sense, as I told you yesterday, to hand them over to his sister. Perhaps she'll marry and carry on the family."

"And Hest?"

The Colonel shook his head. "Who knows. He may be caught; on the other hand, he may bolt to South America and become one of those Dictators we read so much about. As The Spider, we know that he has heaps of brains, and a piratical life of that description would suit him exactly."

Talking thus, Towton showed Vernon over his small kingdom, and after luncheon the two gentlemen strolled out of the grounds with the intention of taking the winding road to Gerby Hall. On the verge of the moorland they stood for some time looking down into the cup, and Vernon thus procured a bird's-eye view of the valley in the full blaze of the noonday sun.

"It's like a bead on a string, Towton," he said after a pause.

The description was an apt one, for the hollow into which they were looking was the bead, and the narrow valley, running like an irregular crack to right and left, might be easily compared to a string. From the cup upward to Bolly Dam the valley stretched for a mile and a half, and downward it ran for two miles in a somewhat crooked fashion, to terminate on the verge of the undulating plain, which stretched the further ten miles to the railway station. At the end of the valley--as Towton informed his guest--was a village called, from its situation, Gatehead, and there were four other hamlets beyond, all of which belonged to him. The Hests were reduced to Bowderstyke village alone and to a considerable portion of the moorland on the hither side.

"It puts me in mind somewhat of Blackmore's description of Doon Valley," was Vernon's remark when in possession of these facts. "I daresay in the Middle Ages it was quite a robbers' stronghold."

"With the Hests and the Towtons as robbers. Exactly. Their hand was against every man, and likewise against each other for the mastery of Bowderstyke. At the upper end the valley is blocked by a small lake, now turned by the Bolly Dam into a very large reservoir, so they were safe in that direction. Gatehead was where their vassals lived to guard the outlet, so you can see in troublesome times everything was extremely safe. From this valley the Hests and the Towtons went forth raiding, and sometimes, when not quarrelling between themselves, formed a kind of league. They struggled for centuries, but in the end my ancestors got the upper hand, and most of the property. I believe the feud and the raiding continued down to the termination of George the Third's reign, for the King's writ did not run in these wilds."

"Where is Gerby Hall?"

Towton pointed directly downward. "Under that cliff, where the moorland rises so abruptly. Like The Grange, there is a kind of artificial forest round it, so that it is concealed. But, as you can see, it is almost within the village itself."

"Right in line of the flood, should the dam break."

"I fear so; but I hope there is no chance of the dam breaking. You see," added the Colonel pointing out the topography of the valley, "the village is divided by the ancient bed of the torrent, now comparatively dry since the construction of the Bolly Reservoir. A stone bridge connects the two portions of the village, and on this side nearest to ourselves the ground begins to rise gradually. The other portion of the village and Gerby Hall lie in the hollow, and are cut off from the sunlight. I often wondered," said Towton musingly, "why the Hests, when lords of the entire valley, should have chosen to build their manor house in such a situation; for, when the torrent was in full force from the melting of the moorland snows, they must have been exposed to many an inundation."

"And now," said Vernon glancing northward to where the cyclopean wall of the dam frowned in the sunlight, "if that great body of water were let loose both the village and the Hall would be swept away."

"They are certainly directly in the line of flood," replied Towton unhesitatingly; "but both the Hall and the village houses are strongly built of dark stone. It would take some force to smash them."

"If that dam broke, Colonel, they would be swept away like straws on the surface of a whirlpool. I can't understand what the engineers were thinking about to risk such a catastrophe."

Towton laughed. "Pooh, pooh! Nothing is likely to happen. But now that I rule here I intend to see if some outlet cannot be arranged other than down the valley, so that all risk may be done away with. I objected to the dam from the first, although I admit that it is a work which is of great public utility and supplies Bowderstyke, Gatehead, and the other villages. But it spoils my view and also is dangerous, as you observe. However, we have talked enough on this dull subject. Let us descend and pay a visit to Gerby Hall. Miss Hest will be expecting us."

"And Ida," laughed Vernon with a side glance at the suddenly-flushed cheek of the soldier.

They descended by the winding road into the valley, and after pausing to glance up the valley, where the massive wall of the dam cut short the view, proceeded slowly towards the village. It was a collection of small dark houses built of moss-clothed grey stones, and looked like a colony of dwarf buildings. But the men and women who dwelt therein were tall and burly enough, and the children seemed to be well-grown. Besides the dwellings there were also two mills, the wheels of which were driven by water in a very powerful fashion. The few shops were dark and uninviting, and the chief street narrow and crooked. Secluded as it was from the sun--which never warmed the village with its beams save at noonday--it did not appear to be a desirable residence. But the inhabitants seemed cheerful enough, and frequently greeted the Colonel with gruff amiability, although he was not their landlord. That position, as Towton had informed his guest, belonged to Hest, or rather--since he had expatriated himself--to his sister.

Crossing the curved stone bridge which arched the dwindling torrent, the Colonel led his friend through several dismal streets until they emerged into an open space, to see before them a high wall built of irregular blocks of stone, covered with mosses and grasses and lichen. The massive wooden gates, which afforded entrance into the domain, stood wide open, indicating, like the doors of the Janus temple, that the Hests were at peace with their neighbours. Passing through these the visitors walked up a gloomy avenue, where the branches of the trees met overhead, and came unexpectedly upon a square stone house, the appearance of which was similar to that of the encircling wall. There were absolutely no pretensions to architectural beauty, and the mansion looked as though it had grown out of the damp, fecund ground, where rank grasses grew in profusion. Above was the slightly sloping bank of the moorland, which here was almost perpendicular, and it threw a heavy shade over the frowning dwelling, which suited its grim looks. It was two storey, with twelve windows in the front, six on either side, and three in each storey. In the centre was the door, without a porch and without steps. Only a broad flagstone formed the threshold. The trees grew up nearly to this, and there was merely a narrow gravelled path between the luxuriant grasses and the walls of the house. So amazingly dismal a dwelling Vernon had never set eyes on, and he uttered an exclamation when he beheld the desolation.

"It's the very worst place Ida could have come to," he said in high displeasure. "What could Miss Hest have been thinking of, to ask her to live in this vault."

"Ah, she will be better up on the heights in my Italian villa, Vernon."

"That is if she will come," remarked the other gloomily, for the sombre situation and ascetic looks of the Hest mansion made his spirits sink to zero.

Their approach had been seen, for scarcely had they set foot on the flagstone, and before they had time to raise a hand to the massive iron knocker, which was covered with rust, than the door was opened by a fat-faced, stupid girl dressed in brown but with a tolerably neat cap and apron.

Without inquiring their business and without speaking she signed that the two gentlemen should enter, and conducted them to a room to the left of the cheerless hall. Here she intimated that they were to wait and that the mistress would soon come to them, after which she retired sullenly and closed the door after her. What with her looks and the gloom of the room and the closing of the door, the visitors felt as though they had been bestowed in a dungeon. Anything more dismal can scarcely be conceived.

"Oh, Lord!" ejaculated Vernon with dismay, looking round at the old-fashioned furniture and the grimly-red colouring of the decorations, somewhat faded, it is true. "Within is worse than without. I should commit suicide in such a place. No wonder Francis Hest found blackmailing a more cheerful pursuit. He ought to have----"

"Hush!" said Towton sharply, and arrested Vernon's speech as the door opened to admit the mistress of the mansion. Miss Hest looked graver than she had done at "Rangoon," and more handsome than ever in her imperial, masterful way. Vernon marvelled to see how much she resembled her brother, although the disfiguring cicatrice was absent. In her plain black dress, slashed with deep orange, Miss Hest looked like a Spanish beauty, and in the damp, secluded mansion she seemed to flourish as healthily as though she dwelt in perpetual sunshine. With a smile she came forward and greeted her visitors in a most cordial manner.

"I am very glad to see you both," said Frances, sitting down when formal greetings had passed, "and especially you, Colonel Towton, as I am anxiously waiting for your promised verbal answer to my letter."

"I shall explain why I did not write you with pleasure," said the Colonel gravely, "although my explanation is painful. You may even refuse to believe me, Miss Hest."

She looked alarmed and her lips twitched nervously.

"Francis is all right, I hope?" she inquired apprehensively. "His letter and the Deed of Gift alarmed me. I think he must be crazy."

"I don't think so," rejoined Towton drily, "but before explaining, may I ask how Miss Dimsdale is keeping?"

Frances shook her head dejectedly. "The death of her father is still preying on her mind, and nothing I can say or do will make her cheerful."

"Perhaps this house----" began Vernon.

She cut him short quickly. "I quite agree with you, and I know what you are about to say. It is too damp and too dismal for Ida. She is a flower who ought always to live in the sunshine."

"Lady Corsoon is coming down to stay with me to-day," ventured Towton anxiously, "so Miss Dimsdale might come and stay at The Grange."

"It's a capital idea. You can ask her for yourself, and as I know she thinks a great deal of you, Colonel, I hope you will be able to persuade her to pay the visit. She will be here shortly, but before she comes do tell me the meaning of my brother's extraordinary conduct."

"What makes you think the Colonel can explain?" asked Vernon unexpectedly.

Frances looked at him in surprise. "Why, I wrote after I received the Deed of Gift, asking if he had seen Francis. The Colonel replied that he would explain verbally when he came down. I have no reason to think that he knows anything of my brother's private business and I was astonished to hear that he could tell me anything. I only wrote because I wished the Colonel to see Ida, and as an afterthought asked about my brother. I thought you," she addressed the Colonel, "might have seen him in London."

"I did," replied Towton gravely; "at Professor Gail's."

"I know that; he went there to deliver a message from me. But why has he made over his property to me without a line of explanation save that he was going abroad? Did he tell you?"

"No. But I am not surprised that he has done so." Frances looked from one man to the other and, seeing their grave faces, she grew white and anxious looking. "What do you mean?"

"We saw Constantine Maunders," put in Vernon.

"Well, well! What of that?"

"He was masquerading as Diabella."

Miss Hest started to her feet. "As the fortune-teller? Surely you must be mistaken? It's impossible! Why should he do that?"

"Why should he do many things," said Towton grimly. "But he has been leading a double life."

"Oh, that's impossible. Why, he was always as open as the day. I asked him down here a week or so ago and he was coming. At the eleventh hour he put me off, saying that Mrs. Bedge was ill. I fancied that something might be wrong then, but--but--oh!" she burst out, clasping her hands, "you really must be mistaken. He is such a nice young fellow."

"He's a nice scoundrel," said Vernon heatedly. "Spare your praises of him, Miss Hest. You won't think him so nice when I tell you that he accuses your brother of being The Spider."

"The Spider? Who is The--ah!" She started to her feet as she suddenly remembered all that the information conveyed. "You mean that wretch who murdered poor Mr. Dimsdale?" Her brows grew black and she clenched her hands in a cold fury. "What do you mean by connecting my brother with----"

"It is not Vernon or I who connect your brother with The Spider. Maunders made the accusation and your brother endorsed it by his flight."

"Flight! flight! My brother," she drew herself up proudly, "has not fled."

"Why has he gone abroad, then?" asked Vernon hastily; "Why has he made over his property to you? Believe me, Miss Hest, both the Colonel and myself would be glad to spare you such a blow, but there is no doubt that your brother is none other than this famous blackmailer for whom the police are searching so ardently."

The woman dropped back into her chair and clutched at her breast as though she felt a cruel pain in her heart. Her face looked grey in the dim light of the room, and she suddenly seemed to have aged. Even her confident bearing fell away from her and she crouched as though smitten to the earth. Never was there so rapid or so terrible a transformation. "Oh, for God's sake," she moaned brokenly, "for--for--my brother. Heaven knows we did not get on over well together, but that he--he--that he should--It's a lie. I tell you, it's a lie. Why, Francis has given up all his life to doing good. Everyone round here blesses his name; he was generous to a fault. And you dare to--dare to--oh!" She leaped to her feet again and strove to recover her proud hearing. "I don't believe it. Liars! both of you."

"Maunders is the liar and not us, then," said Vernon quietly.

"I never trusted him, I never liked him," moaned Miss Hest; "he is----" Then she unexpectedly fell back again into her chair, utterly unstrung and broken down, an old, grey woman, miserable beyond belief. "Francis--my brother--our good name--oh! oh! Say that it isn't true," and she wept piteously.

"I regret to say that it is," said the Colonel, extremely sorry to dash her hopes to the ground, and he rapidly related all that had been discovered. As he proceeded Miss Hest lifted her face, which grew more composed.

"And is this all the evidence you have to go upon?" she inquired with scorn; "The word of a man whom you admit to be a scoundrel?"

"You forget," said Vernon gravely, "that your brother endorsed the accusation by flight and by taking his accomplice with him."

"Such an accusation might well make a man fail to stand his ground," said the woman resolutely, "and on the spur of the moment Francis may have lost his wits. But he will return to repel this accusation."

"From what you say of a Deed of Gift, Miss Hest, that does not seem likely to happen. If your brother is innocent let him surrender himself to the police and stand his trial."

"I shall advise him to do that at once. Where is he to be found?"

"No one knows, and the police would give much to learn. But you heard last from him, since he sent the Deed of Gift and informed you of his plans."

"There was no address on the letter," said Frances, wringing her hands helplessly, "and he did not even promise to write when he went abroad. For all I know he may have vanished for ever."

Vernon made an observation: "That looks like guilt."

"Until Francis admits with his own lips that he is The Spider I decline to believe it," said Miss Hest, making a violent effort to recover her composure. "You forget that you indirectly accuse him of murdering poor Mr. Dimsdale. How can I, his sister, bear to hear that?"

"Your feelings do you credit," said Towton sadly; "nevertheless----"

"Stop!" she interrupted, holding up her finger. "Ida is coming. Not a word to her, if you please."

"Certainly not. Neither Vernon nor I shall say anything until----"

"Say nothing until I see you again," said Frances rapidly. "I shall call at The Grange and hear more. When in possession of the facts I shall go to town and----Silence! silence! Here is Ida."

Just as the name left her lips the door slowly opened and Miss Dimsdale entered. Both the gentlemen uttered exclamations of astonishment and pity at the sight of her altered appearance. From being a bright and laughing girl, rather plump than otherwise, she had become thin and careworn, and advanced with a shrinking air, quite at variance with her known character. The black dress she wore enhanced the melancholy of her appearance, and the Colonel, being very much the lover, grew darkly red at the sight.

"How is it that Miss Dimsdale looks so ill?" he asked Frances furiously.

"She is worried over something, and the air of this house doesn't suit her at all," said Miss Hest, who was trying to subdue her emotion. "Again and again I have wanted her to return with me to London, but----"

"But I won't go, I won't go," said Ida in her soft voice. "Don't look so angry, Richard." It was the first time she had uttered his Christian name, and Towton flushed with pleasure. "I am quite well."

"You look extremely ill," he replied bluntly. Ida sat down with a sigh. "It's not the fault of Frances. She has been like a sister to me ever since the death of my dear father."

"Ida, come and stay at The Grange. Lady Corsoon is coming down this evening. I am sure you will be happier there."

"I can't leave Frances."

"Nonsense!" said Miss Hest with something of her old vigour; "you will be much better with your own people, Ida. If you stay here they will think that I am after your money."

"Oh, Frances, when you know----"

"It's all nonsense, dear. The Colonel here declares that Diabella is, or rather was, Constantine Maunders, masquerading as a fortune-teller."

"Then what he said is----"

"Are you talking of a secret of your father's, Ida?" asked Vernon quickly.

"Was Mr. Dimsdale my father?" she demanded facing round anxiously. "Diabella--that is, Constantine, if what you say is true--told me that I was not his daughter. If so, I have no right to the property, and--and----" She put her hand to her forehead, "Oh, my poor head!"

Towton crossed over and took her hand. "Ida, is it this which has been so troubling you?" he asked tenderly.

"Yes! Yes! I wondered if what Diabella said was true. I could not be certain, although I _did_ want to see the lawyer and give up the property. But Frances said----"

"Frances advised delay until the truth was known beyond all doubt," said Miss Hest, now quite composed. "For this did I send for you, Colonel Towton. Ida is fonder of you than of anyone else, so you are the person who ought to marry her. Then you can look into the matter."

"But, Frances," cried Ida much astonished, "I thought that you wanted me to marry Constantine or your brother."

"Both of them are bad matches now if what Mr. Vernon says is true," replied Miss Hest bitterly; "better take up with your old love."

"What has been said?" questioned Ida anxiously looking into the disturbed face of her friend.

"Better not ask," muttered the woman, and cast a warning glance at the two visitors; "least said, soonest mended. Ida, will you go to The Grange and stay with your aunt?"

Ida ran to Frances and, falling on her knees, threw her arms round her neck fondly. "What! Would you have me leave you when I see you so sad? Something is wrong? What is it? You have comforted me, so let me comfort you."

"Nothing can comfort me," said Miss Hest in melancholy tones; "it's nothing, my dear, nothing at all. I wish--oh, I wish----" She rose suddenly and ran towards the door. "I can't stand any more."

Vernon was not surprised at Miss Hest's sudden departure. Strong-minded as she was, the terrible news that her twin brother was a robber and a murderer and was being hunted down by the police had quite broken down her strength of character for the time being. He pitied her extremely, as he had always liked her more than Towton had done. So far as he could see, she was a kind-hearted woman: masterful, it is true, but possessed of sterling qualities which that very trait enabled her to make good use of. To one of her inflexible honesty the discovery of her brother's sin must have been gall and wormwood.

Meanwhile, the Colonel, holding Ida's hand within his own, was pleading anxiously that she should visit The Grange and regain her health in the cheerful society of her aunt and cousin. "And I can explain all about the story told by Maunders, masquerading as Diabella," coaxed Towton softly.

But Ida was in no mood to listen to her lover or to yield to his wiles. She pulled her hands away hurriedly and spoke with pettish haste. "How can you bother me about such things when Frances is so ill? I must go to her at once." And she glided rapidly towards the door, evading Towton, who would have detained her.

"Ida, Ida! do listen to me."

"No! No! No! On another occasion, when I see you again--to-morrow, or the next day. But Frances is ill: Frances wants me." She opened the door quickly. "Coming, dear; coming!" and without a glance at the visitors vanished from the room. Her heart seemed to be rather with Miss Hest than with the lover who so ardently adored her.

The gentlemen looked at one another in dismay; this did not seem a propitious moment for Towton's wooing, as Ida appeared to be entirely infatuated with her friend. There was nothing left for them to do but to take a speedy departure and to return on a more fitting occasion. Miss Hest, being naturally troubled in her mind, was not likely to reappear, and Ida undoubtedly would decline to leave her friend's side. Not unreasonably, the Colonel felt very cross.

"Ida seems to be crazy about that infernal woman," he snapped irritably.

"She is very faithful to those she loves and therefore will make you the better wife," said Vernon gravely.

"I want her to be faithful to me and not to Miss Hest," retorted Towton. "It is ridiculous that she should behave in this manner. What's to be done now?"

"We must wait until Lady Corsoon comes. She has plenty of good sense and may be able to talk Ida into a reasonable frame of mind."

"I can't see where Lady Corsoon's good sense comes in, seeing that she is a gambler and has risked her husband's displeasure in pawning family jewels, Vernon. However, only one woman can talk round another, so your suggestion is a good one. Meanwhile, just ring the bell for someone to show us out of this condemned vault."

Vernon pulled the old-fashioned bell-rope and shortly--as though she had been listening on the outside of the door--a tall, lean woman with a white face and a prim, pinch-lipped smile, made her appearance. Without waiting to be addressed she introduced herself to the visitors. "Miss Jewin, gentlemen," she said with a stiff curtsey; "What can I do for you?"

At the sound of her voice Vernon started and looked at her closely, but whatever he saw he said nothing at the moment, merely intimating that he and his friend desired to depart.

"And tell Miss Hest we will call to-morrow with Lady Corsoon," said the Colonel aggressively, and stalked out preceded by Miss Jewin, still primly smiling, and looking like a white cat.

Not until they were in the village did Vernon explain why he had started at the sound of the housekeeper's voice. "That woman," he said quietly, "is the very one who admitted me into the empty house in West Kensington and who locked me in the kitchen."

CHAPTER XIX.

A BOLD OFFER.

Lady Corsoon duly arrived and duly complained of the length of the journey. The strain to which her nerves were subjected on account of the suspense she suffered regarding The Spider's blackmailing, rendered her somewhat irritable, and those around felt the effects of her temper. But Lucy, having a singularly placid nature, invariably contrived to soothe down her mother's ruffled plumes, while the two men, knowing what Lady Corsoon felt, paid her every attention. The next morning, therefore, she felt somewhat better and acknowledged that The Grange was endurable. But she resolutely refused to call straightway at Gerby Hall.

"I shall go to-morrow," she said when Towton urged the visit. "My nerves must have time to recover from the journey into these wilds. Besides, Ida should call and see me, since I am the elder."

"But I wish you to persuade Ida to take up her quarters here while you remain," pleaded the Colonel. "She is infatuated with Miss Hest and will, I am certain, not come here of her own accord."

"I'm sure I never could understand what Ida saw in that woman," said Lady Corsoon fretfully. "Miss Hest is nice enough and quite agreeable, but nothing out of the ordinary. When my poor, dear brother died Ida should have accepted my guardianship. I offered twice to look after her, but she refused--because of this Hest woman, I presume."

"You must remember, Lady Corsoon, that Ida is a spoilt child----"

"Spoilt!" interrupted the lady; "I should think so. Many a time have I implored Martin not to ruin her; but I might as well have spoken to a block of stone. You will have no easy task to manage her when you make her your wife, Colonel."

"I am quite certain that when Ida is removed from the companionship of Miss Hest I shall be able to manage her with the greatest ease," said Towton emphatically; "but the question is how to get her away. I look to you to use your influence, dear lady."

"Mine? Why, I never had the least influence with that headstrong girl, my dear Colonel. I'll go to-morrow and give her a talking to, and perhaps I may be able to induce her to return with me to London. But while she is the mistress of ten thousand a year she can defy me. Now, if The Spider can give me that fortune, as he declares, I shall soon bring Ida to see that she must behave like a sensible human being. I suppose Mr. Vernon told you of the letter I received? He hinted as much to me, though I think he should have held his tongue."

"He did hold his tongue about your business, more or less, Lady Corsoon. It was Mr. Maunders who let slip the secret."

"And what business is it of Mr. Maunders', I should like to know?" asked Lady Corsoon, putting up her lorgnette and looking haughtily at Towton.

"This much--that he wrote the letter."

"What!" Lady Corsoon bounded from her seat. "Then he is The Spider?"

"No," said the Colonel prudently, who did not intend to tell his companion more than he could help, as he placed no reliance on her tongue; "but, knowing from yourself about the first letter you received from The Spider, and anxious to marry your daughter, he made use of the blackmailer's scheme to secure his own ends."

"What audacity! Can he--Mr. Maunders, I mean--really place me in possession of Martin's money?"

"I can't answer that for the moment," replied the Colonel carefully, "but at any rate by promising to do so he hoped to marry Miss Lucy."

"He shall never do that," cried Lady Corsoon energetically; "unless, of course, he keeps his promise. Lucy must save me from----" She hesitated.

"Mr. Maunders told me about your losses at bridge, and----"

"And that I pawned certain family jewels," finished the lady. "Well, I never! To think he should discuss my affairs in this way. I have been a fool: I don't deny that I have been a fool, but there was no need for Mr. Maunders to let the whole world know."

"The world is only represented by myself and Vernon," said the Colonel drily, "and your secret is safe with us."

"But Mr. Maunders----"

"He has his hands full. You won't see him again."

"But in that case his promise----"

"My dear Lady Corsoon, I do not think he will be able to keep his promise, for certain reasons which I need not tell you now. Better give your consent to the marriage of Vernon and Miss Lucy. They love one another and he will soon have a title and an income."

"Did you invite me down with Lucy to forward that marriage?" asked Lady Corsoon with sudden suspicion.

"Partly," answered Towton coolly, "and partly because I wished to enlist you on my side as regards Ida."

"Oh, I am willing to help you, but as to Mr. Vernon--he is with Lucy now?"

"Yes. They have gone for a walk."

Lady Corsoon frowned. "Lucy could make a much better match," she said hesitating.

"With Constantine Maunders, for instance."

"At all events, he promises me ten thousand a year."

"On what grounds?"

"I don't know."

"Then, believe me, he is only bluffing."

"But he knows about my pawning of the jewels, and even if this horrid Spider creature holds his tongue Mr. Maunders may tell Sir Julius. Then heaven only knows what would happen; Julius is so impossible."

"I shall engage that Maunders remains silent if you will give your consent to the marriage. After all, Miss Lucy would be Lady Vernon."

"She could be a countess if she played her cards well. I really don't know what to say; I am in the dark, so to speak. Wait until I see Ida and then I may form an opinion."

"How can Ida help you to do so?"

"She may be able to tell me if there was a will in my favour. I really believe from that letter of The Spider's--well, of Mr. Maunders', since you say he wrote it--that Martin left the money to me and that Ida destroyed the will. I'm sure she's capable of it."

"Permit me to remind you, Lady Corsoon," said the Colonel sternly, "that Miss Dimsdale is to be my wife and that I shall not permit anyone to cast a slur on her character. If the money is left to you she will hand it over."

"What, ten thousand a year?" said Lady Corsoon beaming. "Oh, she would be a good girl if she did that. Well, I shall wait and see. In the meantime I do not mind Mr. Vernon being with Lucy."

Colonel Towton shrugged his square shoulders. He thought that the lady was making a virtue of necessity, as the young couple had taken French leave after breakfast and had vanished. And had Lady Corsoon been gifted with supernatural sight she would scarcely have been pleased had she seen the two sitting by Bolly Dam with their arms round one another. Also Lucy, the meek, the amiable, the well-conducted, was kissing Vernon in the boldest manner and swearing that she would marry him and him only.

"Mother wants me to marry Mr. Maunders," said Lucy, snuggling up close to her lover, "and papa desires me to become the wife of Lord Stratham. But I shall only marry you, darling, you. Arthur," she pressed her cheek against his breast and looked up into his eyes, "run away with me."

"Would you elope if I asked you?"

"I have just offered to elope without your asking me," she replied nodding. "I can't speak plainer, can I? Oh, dear me," she sighed, resting her head on her lover's shoulder, "how weary I am of everything. Papa is always busy in the City and has hardly a word to say to me; mamma has some secret worry about which she will not speak, and I am left to find my own amusements. Do take me away, Arthur. Isn't Gretna Green somewhere about these parts? Let us go there and get married."

"No, dear. I don't think there will be any need for a runaway match, unless it is the romance of the thing that you desire. Colonel Towton has promised to speak to your mother, and I have an idea that he will gain her consent to our marriage."

"She consented before," pouted Miss Corsoon, "and then changed her mind. Why, I'm sure I don't know. It's much better to get married quietly and then she would have to forgive us."

"My dear," said Vernon firmly, "I prefer to act honourably and openly. From a letter I received this morning it seems that my poor uncle cannot live much longer. In a month at the latest I shall be in possession of the property and the title; then I shall see your father and demand your hand. He likes me, and when he learns of my new circumstances I am sure he will consent. With him on our side your mother will be quite willing to accept me as her son-in-law."

"I'll do whatever you say, dearest," whispered Lucy fondly, "only I'll never marry anyone but you. So there!" and she gave him a kiss which her lover promptly returned. Then they sat hand in hand, looking at the view, and too happy to speak further. Love's silence is more eloquent than Love's speech.

Before them the reservoir rippled under the breath of a gentle wind, and spread like a vast blue lake toward the purple of the moorlands. Immediately in front of the lovers the massive wall of the dam stretched from side to side of the valley, which here was extremely narrow. Looking at that vast body of water, Vernon could not help doubting the strength of the protecting wall as the wavelets almost lipped its top. There was a channel on the hither side with flood-gates, but it seemed too small to carry off much superfluous water. In summer time the dam was no doubt all that could be desired in the way of strength, but when the winter snows melted on the moorlands it appeared probable--at least, Vernon, knowing nothing of engineering, thought so--that the water would overflow the dam. In that case it might break down the wall, and then the young man shuddered to think of what would happen. The whole contents of the lake, narrowed by the gorge, would shoot down the three odd miles of the valley with the force and condensation of a hose, and assuredly would sweep it clean from end to end.

"To make things safe," said Vernon aloud and giving speech to his thoughts, "there should be two channels for waste water, each broader than the single one over there. I'm sure there will be a catastrophe some winter or spring."

"Oh!" Lucy pouted again. "I speak of love and you bother yourself over this silly old puddle."

"It would prove to be anything but a puddle if the dam broke," said Vernon doubtfully. "I hope Towton will take steps to make things safer. Bowderstyke Village and Gerby Hall would be smashed to pieces if this vast body of water discharged itself without leave."

And he stared anxiously at the placid lake.

Miss Corsoon, rather annoyed by this unlover-like conduct, rose quickly and consulted a tiny jewelled watch pinned to her blouse. "It's nearly luncheon-time," she said with an affectation of indifference, "and I am so hungry."

"Hungry?" Vernon caught her hands, "when we are together."

"I can't live on love, and you keep talking of this stupid waterworks. We really must go home, Arthur, as mamma will be wondering what has become of us. You don't wish to get me scolded?"

"I'll bear half of the scolding. Hullo! Who is this?"

He shaded his eyes with his hand and looked across the reservoir to where a tall figure appeared on the broad parapet of the dam. The figure--it was that of a man--came swiftly across, but midway caught sight of the lovers. For one minute the stranger stared as if thunderstruck, and then retreated as quickly as he had appeared. Lucy caught hold of her lover's coat to prevent his following.

"Where are you going, Arthur? Who is it?"

"Hokar," said Vernon, greatly excited but pausing for a moment. "It's the Hindoo who tried to strangle me and the Colonel."

"What?" Lucy's voice sounded so terrified that he turned at once to apologise and excuse himself. "Nothing, dear; nothing. But this Hokar is a dangerous native of India whom I wish to get hold of. He went down into the valley on the other side, so I must----"

"Don't leave me! don't leave me!" wailed Lucy, desperately detaining him. "I wish you wouldn't frighten me, Arthur. Come home at once."

"But I want to follow Hokar. It is necessary----"

"It is necessary to see me home," insisted Miss Corsoon firmly. "I won't be left alone with wild Indians and strangling people."

Vernon was torn between his desire to stay with Lucy and a feeling that it was his duty to follow Hokar. He wished to meet the Hindoo face to face and force him to speak. As he was the servant of Maunders--masquerading as Diabella--he probably knew something, if not indeed a great deal, about Hest, and a few questions might intimate the villain's whereabouts. But the man had already vanished and it would be difficult to trace him, although Vernon had a shrewd suspicion that he was to be found at Gerby Hall. For a moment the young man hesitated between duty and pleasure, then, under the reproachful gleam of Lucy's eyes, pleasure gained the victory. Vernon escorted Miss Corsoon back to The Grange, comforting himself with the reflection that it was necessary to consult Colonel Towton before taking any steps to bring Hokar to book. All the way home Lucy chatted in a lively manner, but, preoccupied with his own thoughts, Vernon was somewhat absentminded, a cause of offence to the girl. But how could any man give way to the ruling passion of love when one of the villains concerned in a dangerous conspiracy against society was in the neighbourhood? Vernon wondered how Hokar had come to these solitudes and how Hest had succeeded in lulling his sister's suspicions, so that she might receive the man. For, on the face of it, Hokar must be staying at Gerby Hall.

After a merry luncheon, during which Lady Corsoon, bearing in mind her late conversation with her host, was very gracious to Vernon, the ladies departed to their boudoir, the mother to rest and the daughter to write letters. Lucy, indeed, wished to call and see Ida, but Lady Corsoon refused to let her go alone, and again expressed her determination not to pay a visit until the next day. Lucy, always anxious to keep her parent in a good temper, was obliged to fall in with this arrangement, and followed Lady Corsoon out of the room.

It could be easily seen that the wily wife of the millionaire was unwilling to leave her daughter in the too fascinating society of Vernon, and evidently had made up her mind not to consent to the match until she was certain that her late brother's fortune would _not_ come into her hands.

Left alone with the Colonel, the young man related how unexpectedly Hokar had appeared and disappeared on the dam. Towton listened frowningly and considered awhile before expressing his opinion.

"There's something suspicious about all this," he said at length. "Here is Miss Jewin, the very woman who tricked you into becoming a prisoner at that West Kensington house, and here also is Hokar, the Hindoo, so closely connected with Maunders, and, for all we know, with Hest."

"What do you make of it all?"

"It's a gang of thieves," said Towton unhesitatingly. "Hokar, Bahadur, Miss Jewin, Maunders, and Hest are all banded together under the leadership of the last as The Spider. He has vanished, and so has Maunders, so I expect he sent down the Hindoos here in order that they might be out of the way."

"And Miss Jewin?"

"She has always been the housekeeper at Gerby Hall, Vernon. But I daresay Hest got her to come to London to be used as a tool, knowing that he could trust her. She is a very old and faithful woman, and I believe was the nurse of both Hest and his sister. The people hereabouts call her an old witch, and she is credited with all manner of occult powers."

"I can understand Miss Hest not being suspicious of Miss Jewin," said Vernon thoughtfully, "as she may have gone to London ostensibly for a trip and then would have returned in the ordinary course of things. But Miss Hest must surely wonder at the presence of Hokar. I am bound to say that I did not see Bahadur."

"He may be here, or he may not," rejoined the Colonel; "We'll soon find out. To-morrow I go with Lady Corsoon to see Ida, and then I can warn Miss Hest of the character of the man. If, indeed, she doesn't know it."

"Towton, you surely don't suspect Miss Hest of knowing anything about her brother's wickedness?"

"No, I don't say that. And yet it is strange the Hindoo should be there. And why should he be lurking about the Bolly Dam? I shall go myself to-morrow, after I have seen Miss Hest, to make an examination."

"What do you mean?"

"I mean that a crafty devil like Hokar doesn't take walks for the benefit of his health, and that he may be tampering with the dam--perhaps by order of Francis Hest."

"In that case, why not have the dam examined to-day?"

"There is no immediate hurry. Hokar will find it no easy task to break down that gigantic wall, if that is his aim. Besides, the Vicar is calling this afternoon to pay his respects to Lady Corsoon. I wish to have a chat with him on the subject of Hest, and to learn what he thinks of him."

"What can he think, but that Hest is a genuine philanthropist?"

"I daresay Hest is one person here and another in London. However, it will do no harm to collect what information we can concerning him. To-morrow you can come with Lady Corsoon and her daughter to see Ida, and I shall go also. Afterwards you can inspect the dam."

"Won't you come, too?" asked Vernon.

"No. The fact is, I intend to ride to Gatehead to-morrow afternoon. I shall leave you and the ladies at Gerby Hall. My steward wants to see me about some property which requires looking after in one of the near villages. It will be easy for me to ride there and look into the matter myself. I can trust you to amuse my guests."

Thus it was arranged, and Vernon put all questions concerning Hokar and Bolly Dam out of his head. Lucy managed to evade the watchfulness of her mother when that good lady fell asleep, and the lovers had a stolen half hour all to themselves until the arrival of the vicar. After that came tea and gossip, and a very pleasant afternoon ended gleefully. But the most important event of the next twelve hours happened after dinner, when the Colonel was called out of the drawing-room to see a visitor. He left Vernon to amuse Lady Corsoon and her daughter and took his way to the library, where the visitor--who had not sent in any name--was waiting for him. To Towton's surprise, the stranger proved to be Frances Hest.

"My dear lady, why did you not join us in the drawing-room?" he asked hospitably. "I'm sure the surprise would be a pleasant one."

"Not to Lady Corsoon," said Frances quietly. "She is not over fond of me. Besides, I have come to see you privately and on a most important matter."

"Ida," cried the Colonel anxiously. "Is she ill?"

"No, no! Set your mind at rest about Ida. She has not changed since you saw her yesterday. She doesn't know that I am here, nor does any one else; not even your servant, as I gave no name when I was admitted. Is the door closed?" and she cast a searching, nervous look around.

"This room is perfectly private," said Towton, noting that she looked anxious and haggard. "Nothing mentioned here can be heard. I hope nothing is wrong."

Frances sat down and sighed heavily. "This much is wrong," she said with a gloomy look, "that I have learned the truth about my brother."

"The truth----"

"What you told me yesterday is the truth," said Miss Hest bitterly. "He is a scoundrel and--as it seems probable--a murderer. Yet I had no suspicions of him, not even when he sent that Indian down here."

"Hokar?" said Towton, secretly pleased that his doubts on this point were about to be resolved.

"Yes. Some time ago he came here with a letter from Francis, saying that he was to remain here for a time. I gave him house-room and did not pay much attention to the man, as I thought it was only another of my brother's philanthropic schemes. But, from what you said yesterday, this Hokar is connected with Mr. Maunders and my brother in their wickedness. Oh," Frances struck the table with her clenched hands, "to think that our name should be so disgraced by my brother!"

"What have you discovered?"

"That he is The Spider. Yes; there can be no doubt of that. See!"

She took a long blue envelope from her pocket and opened it to display a paper. "This is a mortgage on Gerby Hall and on all the property," she explained. "The Deed of Gift to me is worth nothing. Interest is due on the mortgage, and unless it is paid, the man to whom the money is owing will foreclose. No wonder Francis presented me with the estates. They are worth nothing and less than nothing. I am actually a pauper."

"Oh, I am extremely sorry to hear that, Miss Hest. But how does this paper prove that your brother is The Spider?"

"It proves that I am a pauper and nothing more. But I discovered amongst my brother's papers the will of poor Mr. Dimsdale."

Towton started to his feet. "What! is there a will?"

"Yes. It is signed by Martin Dimsdale and witnessed by George Venery, of Singapore, and Walter Smith, of Hong-Kong. After what you said yesterday, I made up my mind that I would no longer be in the dark regarding my brother's doings. I therefore broke open his desk, which he always kept safely locked, and found a written statement regarding Ida not being Mr. Dimsdale's daughter, but the child of a certain Mr. Menteith."

"Your brother must have learned that story from Miss Jewin," said the Colonel. "For Maunders declared that she knew the history."

"I quite believe it," replied Miss Hest. "For the statement was signed by Sarah Jewin. I have not spoken to her yet, but I shall do so to-morrow. She was in India with my father and mother and afterwards in Burmah. I expect she heard the story there, and related it to Francis. He added to it."

"Oh!" Towton remembered about the embroidery to the tale. "Then Mr. Dimsdale did not purposely delay the relief expedition which was to rescue Menteith?"

"No. He pressed on with all speed. But Francis invented that wicked lie so as to get money from Mr. Dimsdale. How Francis got the will I can't say. He certainly called at 'Rangoon' once or twice when he was in London, but I scarcely think Mr. Dimsdale would have given him the will."

"Probably he stole it. I am sorry to hurt your feelings, Miss Hest," added the Colonel hastily on seeing her wince. "But your brother is extremely clever in a criminal way, and nothing he does surprises me. I quite believe he was clever enough to get this will. Where is it?"

"I have left it at home, and if you will call to-morrow I shall give it to you. But I must make conditions."

"Conditions?" The Colonel looked puzzled.

"Ah, don't think badly of me," said Frances in an imploring manner. "But consider my position. I am without a penny, for the property must certainly be handed over to the man to whom it is mortgaged. Listen, Colonel. This will states that Ida is not the testator's daughter, and leaves everything to Ida Menteith, so there can be no doubt that she inherits. Now, Ida loves you, and although I wished her to marry my brother or Mr. Maunders, she always desired to be your wife. I am glad now that she did not yield to my persuasions, since both Francis and Constantine are criminals and exiles. So I want you to take her away to-morrow and marry her and enter into possession of the Dimsdale property."

"You are very good, Miss Hest," said Towton, who could not but acknowledge that she was acting most generously. "But your condition?"

"It is scarcely that, Colonel; merely a suggestion. I shall give you the will if you can arrange with Ida to give me eight or nine or ten thousand pounds, so that I can have something to live on."

Towton hesitated at this bold offer. "I can't say anything about that; it is for Miss Dimsdale to decide."

"Colonel, if I chose, Ida would remain with me altogether, as she loves me."

"Say rather," said Towton, somewhat unjustly, "that you have a great influence over her, Miss Hest."

"And if I have," cried Frances, rising to the height of her tall figure, "has that influence been used for otherwise but good? Instead of misusing it, as I could, to keep Ida beside me and retain command of her money, I wish her to marry you and take her fortune entirely to yourself. All I ask is for a sum to save me from begging my bread in the street. Think of my position and do not be too hard on me, Colonel."

"I admit that you have some claim," said the Colonel politely; "and doubtless Miss Dimsdale will consent to your demand. But I can say nothing. It will be better to wait."

"Until when?"

"Until to-morrow. Then, with Ida, we can talk over the matter." Miss Hest's lip curled. "You are a strange man, Colonel. I offer you a pretty wife and a handsome fortune, yet you hesitate to do me justice."

"I see no justice in giving you ten thousand pounds," retorted Towton sharply.

"Well," said Frances, suppressing her rising anger, for she felt that she was acting generously and the Colonel churlishly, "perhaps justice is not quite the word which should be used. But you spoke now of my influence over Ida as being great, and you spoke truly. She is very fond of me, and I am perfectly well able to induce her to give up all idea of becoming your wife, and to get her to remain with me. Then I should handle the sum I ask for every year instead of only once, for Ida knows nothing of business."

"See here, Miss Hest," said Towton roundly, "I love Ida and I wish her to be my wife. But she shall accept me of her own free will and without being pressed in any way. Your influence can scarcely be so great as you think, since Ida declined both to marry Maunders or your brother, although--as you admit--you urged her to do so. I am coming to-morrow with Lady Corsoon and her daughter to see Ida, and I hope Miss Dimsdale will return with her aunt to this house----"

"Not if I can prevent it," said Frances, her colour rising as she hastily wrapped her cloak round her and moved towards the door. "Ida remains with me as a hostage until I get this money, to which I am entitled."

"I fail to see that."

"Because you have an ungenerous nature," she retorted. "Were I in possession of an unencumbered estate I should ask nothing. But, as it is, I must have money, and if you are wise you will buy this will and your wife with a sincere promise--I do not even ask for it to be in writing, so confident am I in your honour--to give me ten thousand pounds on the wedding-day."

But Towton was singularly obstinate. "Wait until to-morrow," he said dourly. "What Ida says I hold by."

"In that case I have the money," retorted Frances, and left the room promptly with a dry smile and a light step, fully satisfied that she had won.

CHAPTER XX.

GERBY HALL.

Contrary to his usual custom, Colonel Towton did not mention the conversation or the visit of Miss Hest to his co-worker. And he observed this reticence for two reasons. Firstly, he noted that Vernon was too much engrossed in the society of Lucy to give undivided attention to those anxious matters dealing with The Spider and his machinations. Secondly, the offer of Frances particularly concerned himself and Ida, therefore it was useless to ask advice which probably would not be taken. As Vernon had always supported Miss Hest, he undoubtedly would urge that she should be paid if she fulfilled the conditions which she herself had laid down. Nine men out of ten would have clinched the matter at the price, so that the Gordian knot might be cut instead of unravelled. But Towton was no Alexander to adopt so hasty a course, and did not see his way to surrender a large sum for help which, in his opinion, should be freely rendered.

Moreover, as he scrupulously regarded Ida's fortune as belonging entirely to herself, Towton infinitely preferred to leave the decision to her judgment. In spite of the triumphant smile with which Frances had terminated her visit, the Colonel did not feel sure that she would gain her ends, and suspected that her boasted influence over Miss Dimsdale was less powerful than she pretended it to be. If she could twist Ida round her finger--and she intimated as much--there was no need for her to apply to Towton in any way, as all she had to do was to give the will to Ida and receive in return a cheque for the ensuing year's income. But this she had not done, and her very action in seeking him made Towton suspect that she felt her influence with Ida to be waning. The girl, therefore, would no doubt be glad to leave Gerby Hall and come to The Grange; and it might be--but the Colonel could not be certain on this point--that Frances was detaining her by threats, although what such threats might be Towton could not conjecture. And certainly, judging by the visit of the previous day, Ida was fondly attached to Frances, and was remaining of her own free will under the gloomy roof of her friend. Towton was perplexed how to reconcile Ida's evident desire to remain at the Hall with the unnecessary visit of Miss Hest.

"I can come to no decision about the matter until I have seen Ida by herself," thought the Colonel when he returned to the drawing-room. "In the presence of this woman the poor girl may be intimidated, or perhaps fascinated as is a bird by a snake. When we are alone she will open her heart to me, as I know that she loves me, in spite of what Miss Hest says.

To-morrow, if she refuses to return with Lady Corsoon, I shall remain behind when the others have taken their departure, and perhaps may get a word or two alone with Ida. I wish I could remove her from the society of that woman; I am sure it is harmful."

When rejoining his guests, Towton merely intimated that his visitor had come on business, and gave the company to understand that it was of small consequence. Then he proceeded to make himself agreeable to Lady Corsoon, so that Vernon and Lucy could have each other's company without the uncomfortable presence of a third party. He taught his elderly guest a new game of patience; but, as this proved to be somewhat dull, the young couple were called in to form a bridge party. They came unwillingly, and playing the game with but faint interest, allowed Towton and Lady Corsoon to win. As the latter individual retired to bed the winner of a moderate sum, she was in high good humour, and refrained from scolding Lucy for her philandering with the undesirable lover. And undesirable he was, so long as Lady Corsoon hoped to obtain the fortune of her niece. If Maunders failed to fulfil his promise, then the scheming wife of the financier was perfectly willing to permit her daughter to marry Sir Arthur Vernon, it being of course understood that he was to have the title before becoming Lucy's bridegroom. Certainly she would have preferred her daughter to be Lady Stratham, but as Lady Vernon, with her husband's rank and her father's money, she would shine no inconsiderable planet amongst the stars of London society, and Lady Corsoon could bask in the reflected glory. Finally, as the ambitious mother fell asleep, she reflected that Lucy being rather obstinate, it was just as well to humour her in this instance, as she was quite capable of running away with the man of her choice if permission were refused. Lady Corsoon would not have been particularly astonished had she heard that Lucy had already made the audacious proposal of flight.

Next morning, however, to enhance the value of the prize, she kept her daughter beside her, and remained in her own room on the plea of looking after certain matters connected with feminine adornment. Towton, on his part, had to attend to his correspondence; so Vernon was left to his own devices. He thought that he could not occupy his time better than by taking a walk to the Bolly Dam in the hope of stumbling on Hokar. For this purpose he strolled leisurely along the moorland path, enjoying the bright sunshine and the keen freshness of the morning air. It was a perfect day, and had Lucy been prattling by his side it would have been more perfect still. But his beloved was absent, so Vernon could only feed his hungry heart by recalling details of the delicious conversation which had taken place between them on the previous day.

He duly arrived at the dam, but could see no sign of the Hindoo. It was still early, however, so Vernon sat down on the massive stonework of the wall to wait for his possible arrival. While in this position he became aware to his astonishment that he could hear sounds extremely plainly from the mile-distant village. The clacking of the mills, the subdued murmur of the torrent tumbling under the arched bridge, the lowing of cattle, and even--but more faintly--the shrill cries of children at play; all these struck on his ear with amazing clearness, considering the distance. Certainly, a gentle wind was blowing from the village, but even that did not wholly explain the phenomenon, since the various noises were so markedly distinct. Finally, Vernon concluded, and no doubt was correct in his conjecture, that the narrow gorge acted as a kind of telephone, which, with the aid of the steady wind blowing up its length, conducted the sounds accurately. The discovery amused the young man, and he sat where he was for a considerable time trying to distinguish between the several noises. Later in the day he decided to get Lucy to sit on the dam and then from the bottom of the gorge a mile away to call out and see if she could understand what he was saying. The experiment would be both scientific and interesting.

For quite an hour Vernon waited, but no Hokar put in an appearance. He then spent another hour in walking slowly round the reservoir, and finally, without having seen a single person, he returned to luncheon. At the meal Colonel Towton mentioned that he had written a note to Miss Hest stating that the visit would be paid at three o'clock. "And I have given orders for a room to be got ready for Ida next to yours, Lady Corsoon," said the Colonel.

"I doubt if Ida will come," sighed his guest. "She is singularly obstinate in having her own way. What she can see in that woman is a puzzle to me."

"Miss Hest is very clever," remarked Lucy, "but there is something about her that I do not like."

"For instance?" queried Vernon bending forward.

"I can hardly say," said the girl thoughtfully. "She is clever and agreeable and quite well-bred. Yet she seems to be--be--dangerous."

"I think that word applies more to Maunders than to Miss Hest," observed Towton, "although I am bound to say that Miss Hest does not satisfy me in many ways. She is too masterful. Dangerous, no. I should not describe her as dangerous, Miss Corsoon."

"I should, and I do, Colonel. I may be wrong, but the first time I met Miss Hest at 'Rangoon' she gave me that impression."

"One should never go against impressions," said Vernon gravely; "They are the instincts of the soul."

"Nonsense," contradicted Lady Corsoon vigorously. "I'm sure when I first met my husband I could not bear him, and my mother had simply to drive me to the altar. Yet I married him, and I'm sure we are a most attached pair."

The gentlemen were too well-bred to smile at this statement, yet it secretly amused both. Everyone knew that the undeniable good feeling which existed between Sir Julius and his wife was mainly due to their diverse interests in life, which kept them more or less apart. Lady Corsoon was always fluttering about as a society butterfly, while Sir Julius remained constantly in the City, earning money for her to spend. It was little credit to either that they were civil to one another on the rare occasions when they met. Cain and Abel themselves would not have quarrelled when only meeting--as the saying goes--once in a blue moon But Lady Corsoon felt quite certain that she was a model wife and a typical British matron (new style), and prattled on about her domestic happiness until it was time to start for Gerby Hall.

"Vernon will escort you two ladies," said Towton, who was in riding kit, and exhibited a more youthful air than usual. "I can follow."

"You won't ride to Gatehead until you have called at the Hall," urged Lady Corsoon; "for I may need you to insist upon Ida coming to The Grange."

"I shall assuredly be at Gerby Hall in half an hour, more or less," replied the Colonel quietly. "But I should not think of insisting upon Ida becoming my guest unless she honours me of her own free will with a visit."

"Oh, nonsense," said Lady Corsoon pettishly. "When you know how infatuated she is with this woman Hest." And all the way down the winding road she lamented that Ida was so impossible, and the owner of Gerby Hall so second-rate. "For she is second-rate," finished Lady Corsoon triumphantly. "I always said so, and would say so with my dying breath."

In due time the trio arrived at the gloomy Hall, and were shown by the fat maid into the dingy drawing-room. It was less chill and dismal on this occasion, as the windows were wide open and the warm breath of the day stole in to ameliorate the damp atmosphere, as did the sunshine to lighten the darkness. In the glare of day the furniture looked quite faded, and the hangings extremely shabby; but there was something dignified about the ancient room which impressed even Lady Corsoon.

"A very quaint old place," she said surveying it through her lorgnette; "but damp. They ought to have a fire in the grate."

"They couldn't very well have it anywhere else, mamma," giggled Lucy.

"My dear, pray do not afflict me with your cheap wit. You perfectly well understand my meaning. I shall take this chair, as the light tries my eyes."

So saying she selected a seat with its back to the windows, but less to preserve her eyesight than to prevent Miss Hest from seeing too plain evidence of her age. She throned herself in the spacious chair with the air of a queen, and assumed a dignified mein as the door opened to admit Ida and her hostess. Lady Corsoon's first remark was scarcely polite.

"You _do_ look ill, Ida," she said submitting her cheek to a kiss, "and more than twice your age. Miss Hest, what have you been doing with her?"

"Trying to comfort her," replied Frances drily. "But you can scarcely expect an affectionate girl like Ida to lose her father and not show some signs of grief."

"Signs of fiddlestick, if you will excuse the expression. It's want of food and cheerful company, to say nothing of living in this vault."

"Thank you, Lady Corsoon. I find the house of my ancestors very comfortable."

"I think not," replied the visitor rudely. "Quaint, as I have already observed, old-world and interesting to an antiquarian, but I don't think anyone could call this comfortable. However, this state of things, so far as Ida is concerned, can be easily remedied. Ida, child, I have come to take you to the Grange, which stands in a much more healthy position."

Ida, who had saluted her cousin and Vernon, turned even paler than she already was and looked sideways at Frances. "I think that I prefer to remain in this house," she said timidly.

"Oh, you must not burden Miss Hest any longer," said her aunt coolly. "Ida's company is no burden to me," snapped Miss Hest, who seemed to be trying to keep her temper, "but if she chooses to leave me, she can."

"I should think so; as she is free to come and go as she wishes. Ida?"

"I would rather stop with Frances," said Ida faintly, and again sought the eye of her friend, as if seeking direction. "We are very happy here."

"Miss Hest, I appeal to you," cried Lady Corsoon, looking important. "You can see for yourself that the dear child is like a plant, she wants air and sunlight and every attention."

"Ida is free to go and come as she chooses," repeated Frances with a stealthy glance at the girl. "And perhaps it is just as well she should go. I am returning to London in a week or so."

"Frances!" Ida started to her feet, and a faint hue tinged her cheek. "You never told me of this."

"I never arrived at any decision until last night," replied Frances coldly, removing the arm which the girl had thrown fondly round her neck. "But a search amongst my brother's papers has shown me that my position financially speaking is not so secure as I thought it was. As it is necessary for me to earn my living I must go back to Professor Gail's at Isleworth, and probably I shall agree to his proposal that I should appear on the stage."

"But, Frances, I have plenty of money. Share with me."

"Ida," said Lady Corsoon sharply, "you must let older and wiser heads guide you as regards the disposition of your fortune. Besides, it may not be so secure as you think."

"What?" Ida turned to face her aunt. "Then you already know that I am not Mr. Dimsdale's daughter."

"I know something about it," said Lady Corsoon, concealing her exact knowledge and determined to appear surprised at nothing. "I received a letter stating that on certain conditions I could get the money of my brother. Whether you are my niece or not I can't say, but assuredly if the money is mine I must enter into possession of it. Of course, you may rely on my doing my best to help you."

"I want nothing," said Ida, proudly lifting her head. "If the money is yours you shall certainly have it. Am I not right, Frances?"

"Perfectly right. But Lady Corsoon's fortune--to use her own words with regard to you--may not be so secure as she thinks."

"If Ida is not Martin's daughter, and there is no will, I should certainly inherit," cried Lady Corsoon quite fiercely. "And I confess that I am surprised to hear that my brother is not the father of the girl I have always supposed to be my niece. I should like an explanation."

"You will have one to-morrow," said Miss Hest coolly.

"I want one to-day," said the elder woman rapping her knuckles with her lorgnette. "What have you to do with this matter, may I ask?"

"More than you suppose. But, after I have seen Colonel Towton, you shall be enlightened as to my exact position."

"Frances, do you mean to say that the money is really mine?" demanded Ida with a look of breathless interest.

"If it was, what would you do?" asked Miss Hest doubtfully.

"I should give you all the money you required."

Frances hesitated, then came forward and kissed the girl quietly. "You are a good child, Ida. I thought that I had lost your confidence."

Miss Dimsdale did not contradict this statement. "I shall always remember how kind you have been to me," she said, shrinking a trifle from her friend's caress. "Nothing can make me forget the past."

"Come, come," said Lady Corsoon, rising in a fussy manner. "This sort of thing will not do at all. I must understand plainly what this means. In the meantime, I request my niece to follow me to The Grange."

"I am not your niece, if all I have learned is true, and I decline to be dictated to," said Ida quickly. "To-morrow I shall come to The Grange."

"Will you leave me, Ida?" asked Frances quickly and with a look of pain.

"For a time only," muttered the girl averting her head. "But I wish to go to Colonel Towton's to-morrow."

"Many things seem about to happen to-morrow," observed Lady Corsoon walking towards the door in her most stately manner. "And as Ida refuses to obey me, I wash my hands of her. Come, Lucy. Come, Mr. Vernon. We must depart."

"But the Colonel will be here shortly," protested Vernon, and Lucy took Ida's hand kindly between her own.

"The Colonel may do what he pleases," said Lady Corsoon loftily. "I am not bound by his actions. Ida, I learn, is not my niece, and therefore I shall instruct my lawyer--since there is no will--to demand a surrender of Martin's property. Now that Miss Dimsdale--no, not that--what is your name, may I ask?" And she hoisted the lorgnette again.

Ida shrank back before that severe look, and broken down in health as she was with all she had gone through, burst into tears. Frances stepped between her and Lady Corsoon. "You are a cruel woman," she said indignantly, "and you shall leave my house at once."

"Only too willingly, only too willingly," cried Lady Corsoon swelling with pompous indignation. "But I call everyone to witness that I shall have these matters examined into, and intend to claim my rights. Ida, you are no niece of mine by your own showing, so I have finished with you. Lucy! Mr. Vernon!" and she sailed out of the room and out of the house in a high state of indignation. The fact is, the good lady was greatly perplexed over the unexpected information that she had received. She had believed that her brother had made a will in her favour which Ida had destroyed; but she had never expected to hear that the girl was not Dimsdale's daughter. In her hurry she left Vernon and Lucy behind, while she simply rushed down the short avenue and came face to face with Colonel Towton, who was riding in at the gate.

"What is the matter?" asked the Colonel surprised at seeing his guest alone.

"Matter!" Lady Corsoon halted, breathing hard with anger. "I really don't know, save that the Hest woman has insulted me. Also I have heard that Ida is not my niece, and therefore I am sure the property belongs to me. I decline to stay longer in that house, and so I am returning home. Perhaps, Colonel, you will demand an explanation. If I don't receive a satisfactory one to-night, I write to my lawyer. So there!"

Towton tried to stem the torrent of this speech, but without any result. Still talking of the way in which she had been treated, Lady Corsoon babbled her way out of the gate and disappeared. The Colonel rode up to the door, and, alighting from his horse, bound the bridle to a ring in the wall. As he stepped inside, Vernon appeared in attendance on Lucy. They had stayed behind to comfort Ida, who was weeping over the harsh treatment she had received from her presumed aunt.

"What on earth is the matter?" asked Towton, putting the same question to the couple as he had put to Lady Corsoon. "Miss Lucy, I have met your mother rushing home in a high state of anger."

"Miss Hest and mother have fallen out," said Lucy, hesitating how much to say, for she knew how Towton loved Ida.

"And Lady Corsoon has learned that Ida is not her niece," put in Vernon. "Go in and comfort her, Colonel. I shall go after Lady Corsoon with Lucy."

"That is the best thing to be done," cried Frances, overbearing, and putting her head out of the window. "Colonel Towton, I desire a private conversation."

"Do you wish me to remain?" Vernon asked his friend in a low voice.

"No, no. I must see Miss Hest alone. I understand what she wants. Go with Miss Lucy. She has already reached the gate."

"But if you want me——"

"I don't. When I return you shall know everything."

"What do you mean?" demanded Vernon anxiously.

"Colonel, Colonel," called out Miss Hest again.

"I must go. Follow Miss Corsoon and pacify the old lady," said Towton hurriedly, and hastened into the house, leaving Vernon much astonished by his behaviour. Had the young man known of Miss Hest's visit on the previous evening, he might not have been so perplexed. As it was, he hastened after Lucy, who by this time was rapidly gaining on her indignant mother, with a feeling that Towton knew more than he did concerning the present state of affairs. Which as he afterwards learned, was precisely the case.

The Colonel entered the gloomy drawing-room to find Ida weeping on the sofa and Frances comforting her. Before he could say a word, the latter turned on him indignantly. "Why did you send that insulting woman here?"

"She came of her own accord," explained Towton frowning at the speech, "and surely Lady Corsoon has not insulted Ida."

"And me. She has insulted us both," cried Miss Hest angrily. "I should have had her turned out of the house had she not gone."

"It was my fault by telling her that I was not her niece," said Ida in an agitated tone. "As if I could help that. But I won't trouble her in any way; she has never been kind to me. I shall not set eyes on her again."

"But, Ida," said Towton, taking her hand and striving to speak cheerfully, "I want you to come to the Grange."

"Not while Lady Corsoon is there, Richard."

Frances drew a long breath of relief, which annoyed the Colonel. "Are you detaining Miss Dimsdale here?" he asked snappishly, for late events had tried his temper greatly.

"Oh, no," cried Ida before her friend could speak. "As if Frances would do such a thing! But Lady Corsoon has been so rude."

"You speak of her as Lady Corsoon?"

"Naturally, since I am not her niece," said Ida simply. "When she leaves The Grange I shall be delighted to come."

Colonel Towton flushed through his tan. "I am a bachelor, Ida," he said in stiff tones. "You can't come to my house without a lady is staying there. That is unless you will marry me at once."

Ida placed her two hands on his shoulders and looked at him kindly through her tears. "If you will take a girl without a sixpence, I shall marry you as soon as you please, Richard."

"Don't put his chivalry to the test, Ida," remarked Frances in somewhat acrid tones. "Colonel Towton knows that you have ten thousand a year."

"But if this story is true----"

"It's quite true, only there is a will."

"A will?" Ida stared and flushed with pleasure. "Then poor Mr. Dimsdale did not entirely forget me."

"He did not forget you at all. I found this will--well it doesn't matter where, since I explained everything to our friend here last night. But you inherit the Dimsdale property as Ida Menteith, so Lady Corsoon will not be able to strip you of your worldly goods."

"Oh!"--Ida grew even more scarlet--"then, Richard----"

He caught her hands and pressed them to his breast.

"My dear, I would take you without a single penny."

"And that is the way in which you will have to take her," said Frances drily, "unless you consent to my demands."

"I leave that to Ida," said Towton, once more stiff and military. "Leave what to me?" asked Ida, looking from one to the other. Frances turned to her in a business-like way. "The property my brother has made over to me is mortgaged and I am penniless. If you marry the Colonel I lose your society and also the chance of being your companion at a certain wage. To make amends I ask for ten thousand pounds."

"You shall have it, of course,' said Ida promptly.

"Will you sign this document giving it to me?" asked Miss Hest pulling a sheet of paper out of her pocket.

"At once, if you will give me pen and ink."

The two women went towards a table upon which stood what was required. Apparently Frances had made all necessary preparations to get the money. "You can give me a cheque also. Here is the book," she said eagerly.

"Ida, Ida! Are you wise in doing this?" warned the Colonel, following.

"Yes," said the girl rapidly signing her name and without even reading the document. "I want to marry you and be rid of Frances."

Miss Hest sneered, while Towton started back, utterly astonished by the change of tone. "I thought--I fancied--I believed," he stuttered, "that you were deeply attached to Miss Hest."

"I was, but--there are circumstances----"

"Oh, let us have the truth," interposed Frances sharply. "You liked me well enough and I liked you until you found that I was too clever for you, so----"

Ida caught at her lover's hand and made an effort to pull herself together in the face of Miss Hest's contemptuous eyes. "You treated me shamefully, Frances," she said in tones of reproach. "I loved you dearly until you began to bully me and to make my life a burden. You got me down here in order to gain possession of my money, and have been trying to influence me into giving up not only my property but Richard also. I saw what you were ever since we came to this house, but, to deceive you, I played my part, and led you to believe that I still loved----"

"Oh, rubbish," said Miss Hest, whose eyes were as hard as jade. "You played your part very badly. I saw through your weak tricks. You were afraid of me, you know you were."

"Yes, I was," said Ida, clinging to the amazed Colonel. "Because I believe if you could have got me to sign away my property that you would have killed me. I am willing to give you ten thousand pounds, as I once had some affection for you; but now that you have got your pound of flesh I shall leave this house with Richard."

"To go to Lady Corsoon?"

"Richard will protect me. And, heaven help me!" said Ida, putting her hand to her head piteously. "I feel so dazed that I scarcely know what I am saying."

"You are not too dazed to sign a cheque."

Ida without a word stepped to the table and began to write in the cheque-book. Towton protested. "You shall not do this," he declared. "While I fancied you loved Miss Hest, I was willing you should make her a present of this large sum. But since she has treated you badly----"

"If Ida does not sign the cheque she does not get the will," said Frances imperiously. "You can save your breath, Colonel."

"You may hand over a false will?"

"If I did that I should not get the ten thousand pounds," retorted Frances. "Don't be a fool. I am acting straightforwardly enough."

"Here is the money," said Ida tearing out the signed cheque and passing it to her quondam friend.

"And here is the will," replied Miss Hest, offering a paper, which Ida took and gave to the Colonel.

Towton glanced rapidly at the document. It certainly seemed to be a genuine will signed by Martin Dimsdale and also by Venery and Smith. He felt sure that there was no trickery about the paper, since Miss Hest--now that Lady Corsoon knew the truth--would not be able to get the money unless the testament of Martin Dimsdale was above reproach. "It's all right," he remarked, slipping the precious paper into the breast pocket of his coat. "But you, Miss Hest, are little else than a blackmailer. You are the worthy sister of your confounded brother."

The woman laughed after a critical glance at the cheque and signed document to make sure that both were in order. "I am able to bear all your hard names since I have secured the money. But that Ida refused to obey me and kicked over the traces you would never have had the will."

"I thought that the money did not belong to me," protested Ida, sheltering herself under the wing of her lover, "and wanted to return it to Lady Corsoon."

Frances nodded with a sneer. "Oh, I know how tender your conscience is. You have whimpered enough about it. Only because of your silly attitude did I make this arrangement, which is the best I can do for myself. But I must say one thing, Ida, and you can take it as a compliment. Clever as I am, you with your soft over-scrupulous nature have been too many for me. Few people can say that. And now that all is over between us, you can leave my house, as I hate the sight of your insipid face."

Ida shrank back into the Colonel's arms, and he addressed Miss Hest in a voice rendered hoarse with indignation. "You are a thoroughly bad woman. I never did approve of you, and now that I see you, as Ida does, in your true colours, I tell you----"

"My true colours," scoffed the other contemptuously. "No one knows what they are. You least of all, you narrow-minded idiot."

"What do you mean?" demanded Towton, taken aback by the malignant look on her hard white face.

"Don't ask her," implored Ida, striving to pull her lover to the door, "she will only lie. Let us leave this wicked house, as I am certain that there is something terrible concealed here."

"Something terrible," echoed Towton looking startled.

"Don't talk rubbish," muttered Frances, with a dangerous expression in her eyes. "Colonel, you had better take away that fool, or it will be the worse for her. I warn you."

"I have heard strange noises," went on Ida feverishly. "People have been coming and going in the dead of night. Then that Hindoo----"

"Hokar!" cried the Colonel. "Miss Hest, how do you explain Hokar?"

"I explain nothing," snapped Frances, marching to the door in an imperious way and throwing it open. "Out you go, both of you," She recoiled. "Ah! you dare to!"--with a gasp she tried to close the door again, but Towton dashed forward and caught her arm.

"I have seen; it is too late," he almost shouted. "Maunders. Come in!"

It was indeed Maunders who stood on the threshold. He looked the ghost of his former handsome, insolent, prosperous self. Thin and haggard and worn, with his clothes hanging loosely on his figure, he presented a woeful spectacle. "What have you been doing to yourself? How did you come here?" asked Towton, stepping back much startled, with Ida on his arm.

"Ask that woman how I came here; ask her how she has treated me. But I escaped from the room she locked me in by climbing out of the window. Now I shall show her the mercy she has shown me. She is----"

Frances darted forward and clapped her hand on his mouth. "I'll kill you if you say the word. You cursed fool. Be silent or I give you up." Maunders, with a strength which his frail looks scarcely suggested, threw her off and staggered against the door. "I give _you_ up," he shrieked, wild with anger, "you thief, you blackmailer, you murderess!"

"What?" cried Towton eagerly, and grasping vaguely at the terrible truth.

"Yes." Maunders pointed an accusing finger at Frances Hest. "There is The Spider. A woman; a devil! Arrest her; imprison her; hang her on the gallows," and he sank down on the floor, his back to the door, with hatred written on his white and ghastly face.

CHAPTER XXI.

JUSTICE.

There was a long pause, a sinister lull in the tempest of passion which was raging in that quiet, prosaic room. Gasping with impotent passion, Maunders lay, resting his head against the door, an obstacle which prevented the guilty woman from escaping. Not that she attempted to escape. With a deadly white face, with steady, cold, malignant eyes, like those of a snake, and with a contemptuous smile on her thin lips. The Spider, visible at last in all her brazen wickedness, stood defiantly at bay. Towton, with Ida clinging to his arm almost terrified out of her senses, stared aghast at the evil being who had been such a curse to many. The ominous silence was like the year-long moment before the bursting of a bomb.

Ida, with chattering teeth and trembling limbs, was the first to recover the use of her tongue; but she could scarcely form the words. "Oh, God! oh, God!" she whimpered, hiding her face on her lover's breast; "it's too awful. I never thought--I never thought--oh--oh--oh!" She broke down with a strange, hysterical, choking cry, and would have fallen to the ground but that the Colonel placed her gently in a near chair.

Then he turned with military precision to face Miss Hest. "You are The Spider?" he asked in dry, precise tones, and now entirely master of himself.

"Yes," she replied coolly, and her mouth closed with a triumphant snap.

"You infernal fiend----"

"Gently! Gently! Hard names break no bones, Colonel. You should be more of a man than to throw words at a woman."

"Are you a woman?"

"Yes," gasped Maunders, raising himself on his elbow and wiping the froth from his pale lips; "she is Frances Hest right enough. Her brother is a myth invented by herself to mask her devilries. But Frances or Francis--she is The Spider!"

"I did not mean that exactly," said Towton in his hard voice; "but I asked if one capable of the enormities credited to The Spider can possibly be a woman."

"I am The Spider," said Miss Hest with a shrug. "There is your answer."

"You are a demon."

"More names! Really, Colonel Towton, you are very childish. You sink to the level of that fool," and she pointed scornfully to Ida, who was weeping in the chair as though her heart would break.

"To think that I should have been her friend," moaned Ida with a fresh burst of tears and hiding her face.

"You little fool," said Frances in a gentle, dangerous voice. "I have been a better friend to you than you think. But that I pitied you as being a poor, weak, silly worm, I would have murdered you long ago."

"You murdered my father," shivered Ida, not daring to meet the cold eyes which rested on her prostrate form.

"Martin Dimsdale was not your father."

"You--you--you murdered him."

"Yes, I did."

"What!" Towton could scarcely believe his ears. "You admit the crime?"

Frances yawned ostentatiously. "If I admit that I am The Spider it follows that I must have murdered Dimsdale."

"Well, no," replied Towton, truthfully and justly. "You may have employed Hokar to strangle him."

"That is very good of you," said Frances satirically, "but I don't place my own sins on the shoulders of others. Hokar taught me how to strangle in the Thug fashion certainly, but he did not kill Dimsdale. I did."

"Still, I don't believe that the murder was premeditated," insisted Towton.

"Upon my word," said Miss Hest good-humouredly and as coolly as though she were gossiping over a cup of tea, "one would think you were counsel for the defence. No, you are right. I did not intend to murder Dimsdale. Having got you out of the way----"

"You mean that you got Vernon out of the way?"

"Of course," assented Frances, sitting down and crossing her legs in a gentlemanly fashion; "but you must excuse my bad memory, as I have so much to think of. I got Vernon out of the way, as I overheard, and Maunders there overheard, the arrangement for a trap. We were both on the verandah."

"And I was with you," wailed Ida, shivering again. "So you were," said Miss Hest raising her eyebrows, "but you heard nothing. Maunders caught a word or two through the open window of the library and warned me. While you, my dear Ida, were talking to him I stole round the corner and listened. Knowing all about the trap, I had Vernon decoyed to the Kensington house, and at the appointed time I went into the library, masked and cloaked, as were the other guests at the ball. Dimsdale was waiting for me. I stole up behind him and slipped a handkerchief round his neck."

"Oh!" The Colonel was revolted. "And you say that the crime was not premeditated?"

"I say truly. I simply prepared to strangle him slightly should he have made an outcry. Remember, I was in a dangerous position and could not stand on ceremony. Had Dimsdale given me the money and permitted me to leave by the window I would have spared his life. As it was, he saw me in the mirror, which was directly in front of him."

"But you were masked: he could not recognise you?"

"I am coming to that. He waited for a moment, until I made my demand for the money, then suddenly threw back his hand, and before I guessed his intention he tore the mask from my face. When he recognised me I was obliged, for my own safety, to strangle him. As the handkerchief was in position I simply tightened it, and he was soon dead. Then I searched for the money, but, not being able to find it, I resumed my mask and returned to the ballroom. Maunders, of course, was with me all the time, and awaited my return."

"I did not know that you had committed a murder," said Maunders gloomily.

"No, I did not tell you at the time: it would have spoilt your pleasure. But when Ida learned the truth by entering the library you guessed what had taken place. I kept you with me for your own sake, to provide an _alibi_ should you be suspected, as I feared Vernon might be clever enough to guess that you had something to do with it. As a matter of fact, he did hint at it when he called many days later, but I was enabled to say that you were with me all the time, and so he was put off the scent."

"I remember," murmured the Colonel to himself, but not so low as not to be overheard by Miss Hest's marvellously sharp ears. "Vernon was quite satisfied when you provided the _alibi_ for Maunders. He never suspected _you_."

"No one ever suspected me," said Frances coolly. "There is no need for me to speak of my own cleverness. Anyone who can baffle the police as I have done has no need to boast."

"But why, in heaven's name, with your abilities, did you embark on such an evil course?" asked Towton amazed at her _sang-froid_.

"Fate, Fortune, Destiny: what name you will," said Miss Hest carelessly. "But you have tried to exonerate me, Colonel, and because of that you shall hear the whole story," and, leaning forward, she pulled the bell-rope.

"Remember, I shall repeat all you say to the police," warned Towton.

"I am not afraid of the police," retorted Frances with a shrug; "all my plans are made--to escape. As that fool," she pointed to Maunders lying sullenly on the floor, "has betrayed me twice I give him to you as a sacrifice. But I shall never stand in the dock, you may be sure."

"Will you kill yourself?" cried Ida, terrified at this strength of mind.

"No, my dear. I am too much in love with life. You shall know my plan presently. Meantime, you shall hear how I came to be a blackmailer, as you have already heard why I murdered Dimsdale, to my misfortune."

"To your misfortune, indeed! sharply.

"You may well say so, Colonel. I never intended to soil my hands with blood, least of all with that of a man whom I liked and who was kind to me. Don't sigh, Ida; after all, I did not shed his blood, as I merely strangled him. But that death brought you and Vernon in chase of me, Colonel, and so I am hunted down. Still, had Maunders been true, I should have been safe. You knew Francis Hest as the criminal, thanks to Maunders. I merged the brother in the sister and made everything safe. Now," she shrugged her shoulders, "I must flit."

"You shall go to prison with me," panted Maunders furiously.

"I think not," rejoined Miss Hest contemptuously. "Don't you know me well enough yet to be aware that I provide against all contingencies. Come in!" she added, raising her voice, and, when the door opened, looked at Towton. "I shall ask my old nurse, Miss Jewin, to relate the beginning of my career; at a later time I can take up the tale, and then our tumbled-down friend yonder can finish the story. Sarah, enter and close the door."

Miss Sarah Jewin was peaked-faced and white, with thin lips, scanty grey hair and cold grey eyes. She was thin and bony and very tall, so that in her plain black dress she looked like a line--length without breadth. As she entered Maunders with a groan hoisted himself into a chair. Miss Jewin had already pushed him aside when she entered the room and, in place of replying to her mistress, stood looking at his scowling, haggard face with a look of consternation. Maunders replied to the look with petty triumph.

"Yes, I got out," he said, rubbing the ragged beard which disfigured his well-moulded chin. "I wrenched a bar out of the window and climbed down by the ivy. Now the murder's out, and you and your hellish mistress are about to be brought to book."

"Don't mind him, Sarah," said Frances lazily and leaning back in her chair to light a cigarette; "you are safe and so am I. Let the fool talk. In the meantime, tell Colonel Towton here how I came to England and how you knew that Ida was merely Dimsdale's adopted daughter."

"I thought you wanted these things kept secret," said Miss Jewin in dismay and turning pale with dread at the situation in which she found herself.

"The time for secrets is past, Sarah. Shortly, thanks to your having allowed Maunders to escape and to Colonel Towton's sense of justice, the hue and cry will be out against the whole of us. Is Hokar at his post?"

"Yes. He went away when you gave orders."

"That's all right. I'll escape, sure enough, and so will you. We'll leave Maunders behind to face justice: he can declare himself to be The Spider instead of me if he chooses."

"Oh!" Miss Jewin started back looking terrified. "Do they know----"

"Maunders has told them, you dear old idiot. But there's no time to be lost, Sarah; tell your story."

"And be frank," broke in the Colonel, who was truly amazed at Miss Hest's cool composure. "If you turn King's evidence you may receive a short sentence for your complicity."

Sarah Jewin folded her arms primly. "Begging your pardon, sir, but I won't receive any sentence at all. I am quite sure that Miss Frances will save me from going to prison."

"I fail to see how she can save herself, let alone you," said Towton coldly. "My horse is at the door. After placing Miss Dimsdale in safety I shall ride to Gatehead and send for the police. You needn't chuckle, Miss Hest, and think you will escape meantime. I shall raise the village and you will be carefully watched."

"You can act as you please," said Frances coolly. "I am not The Spider for nothing, and I shall baffle you as I have baffled others. Meantime since you were so just to me, I shall satisfy your curiosity, which I am sure is very great. Sarah, tell your story."

"One moment," said Towton, turning to the prim woman, "you lured Vernon into the kitchen of that empty Kensington house?"

She dropped an ironical curtsey. "Yes, sir. Miss Frances was pleased that I managed so cleverly."

Ida stared wide-eyed at the shameless looks and speech of the housekeeper, and Towton frowned. That these creatures should so audaciously confess their crimes when they knew he would shortly summon the police puzzled him greatly. Also, remembering the wonderful craft of The Spider, he felt uneasy as to what might happen, but he could not conjecture in what way she could extricate herself and her accomplice from the trap in which they were safely caught. However, he made no comment on Miss Jewin's insolence, but merely ordered her to proceed.

"About thirty-five years ago," said Miss Jewin, plunging into her story without any preliminary explanation, "I was in India and nurse to Mrs. Hest, who was the wife of Captain Theodore Hest, stationed at Bombay. The Captain's father, who lived here, was angry when his son went into the Army, and cut him off with a shilling, but my master believed that if a son were born to inherit the estates his father would relent. When my mistress's baby proved to be a girl he was much disappointed. However, as his father was old and might die before he found out the trick, he sent home news that the baby was a boy, and had her baptised Francis."

"So you see," broke in Miss Hest who was smoking quietly, "that my real name is Francis, and by law I am a man. As a woman I am Frances, so there is merely the difference of one letter. Go on, Sarah."

"She," said Miss Jewin, pointing to her mistress, "was dressed as a boy and brought up as a boy, so that the estates might come to her. My master's father relented when he heard that he had, as he supposed, a grandson, and made a will in the boy's favour."

"The boy, you understand, Colonel, being a girl--myself," said Frances for the sake of clearness.

"I quite understand," said the Colonel frowning. "Go on."

"Then my master and mistress were carried off within a month of one another by fever," continued Miss Jewin. "They died in Burmah, where the Captain had gone with his regiment. I then took charge of Miss Hest, who was always called Master Francis, and came to Gerby Hall. Old Mr. Hest, the grandfather, just lived six months longer, but he died under the impression that his grand-daughter was a grandson. Miss Frances thus became possessed of the property."

"Didn't the lawyer know that she was a girl?" asked Towton surprised.

"No. As she had always been brought up as a boy the deception was complete, sir," said Miss Jewin, using the word with shameless deliberation. "The lawyer came here and saw Miss Frances in her boy's clothes."

"And in this way," explained Miss Hest, "it became current gossip in the village that I had a twin brother."

"A twin sister, you mean?" said the Colonel doubtfully.

"Well, you might put it that way. At all events, everyone in Bowderstyke believes to this day that there is a boy and a girl, or, rather, a man and a woman Hest. I alternately wore male and female clothes."

"Why was there any need for you to wear female clothes at all?"

"That was my fault," said Miss Jewin quickly. "When the succession to the estates was settled I could not bear that Miss Frances should masquerade any longer as a boy. I therefore dressed her in girl's clothes, to which she was entitled, and invented the twin story. Sometimes she was a boy, so that the lawyers should not learn the truth, and sometimes a girl to please me. There's the whole story."

"Now it's my turn," said Frances, throwing away her cigarette. "When I grew up and learned how Sarah had muddled my sex in the eyes of the world I decided to make use of it in order to earn money."

"Why did you need money when you had the estates?" asked Towton briefly. "Oh, those were mortgaged up to the hilt, my dear sir. I wanted to be rich and to restore the Hest family to their old position For this reason I posed as a philanthropist and spent the money I did. What with the sums I have given in charity and the buildings I have constructed, and the dam, which is my work, I think, Colonel, that the Hests can hold their own with the Towtons. I hated to think that my family was down while yours was up."

"Oh," said the Colonel with contempt, "so it's a case of jealousy merely. All your philanthropy was a fraud?"

For the first time Frances coloured and rose out of her chair to reply with more emphasis. "No; you must not say that. I really have a mixed nature, and like to help people. My good qualities are the outcome of my evil ones. I wanted to aggrandize the Hests, certainly, since they were lords of Bowderstyke Valley, until your family robbed them of their property. But also I really wished to do good and help people. I think I succeeded."

"At the cost of murder," said Ida resentfully.

"That was a mistake," replied Frances glibly, "as I never intended to murder Dimsdale. When I went to London in my woman's dress, with very little money in my pocket, I simply intended to earn my fortune on the stage, and by reciting to make Francis Hest--my other self, who was supposed to live here--wealthy and popular. I found that the reciting did not pay and cast about for some better means of making money. Alternately I lived in London as Frances, and in Bowderstyke as Francis. But I could not gain my ends by honest means, and so was obliged to take to dishonest ways. If you wish to know the devil who tempted me to eat of the Tree of Knowledge, he is before you," and she pointed deliberately to Constantine.

"It's a lie," cried Maunders, starting to his feet with a fine appearance of indignation. "I met you three or four years ago in London and you discovered that I earned my living by telling fortunes as Diabella. That was all, except," he added, scowling, "that you blackmailed me."

"Quite so," said Miss Hest quietly. "I tried my 'prentice hand on you, and the means of making money in this way was so easy that I took it up as a trade and adopted you as a partner. Go on, Maunders, you tell the rest of the story so that everything may be made clear."

"There's nothing to tell," said Maunders doggedly, and casting down his eyes as he met Ida's sorrowful look, for he was not so entirely lost to all sense of shame as were the other two law-breakers. "You made me find out all manner of secrets from my clients by hinting at things and asking questions and by----"

"I know," interrupted Towton waving his hand. "I am aware of how fortune-tellers hint at a possibility and so find out the actual truth from their too credulous clients. No wonder The Spider learned much that people would fain have kept to themselves. Who told you about Dimsdale?"

"You know," said Maunders sullenly, "that woman there."

"Yes," said Miss Jewin, still prim and shameless. "When in Burmah with my master I heard about Mr. Dimsdale's love for Mrs. Menteith and how, when her husband died, he adopted the child. But I never said that Mr. Dimsdale delayed any expedition so as to get Mr. Menteith killed."

"No. I invented that and made Maunders tell it to you, Ida, and to you, Colonel, with the additions," put in Miss Hest, with great coolness. "Also, on finding out that Ida was not Dimsdale's daughter, I became alarmed as to the disposition of the property, therefore I made myself a friend of the family and secured the free run of the house."

"You intended to get my money?" asked Ida reproachfully.

"Certainly, my dear," replied Frances, raising her eyebrows. "Ten thousand a year was far too much for a chit like you to handle. I intended to get command of the whole lot. First I hunted in the dead of night for the will, and found it in the library desk. Then I made Maunders tell you that you were not Dimsdale's daughter, after the murder, so that you might be dependent on me, since I knew a secret which could rob you of the money. I had the secret told also to the Colonel so that he might learn he would only have a penniless wife should he marry you, my dear Ida."

"Did you think so meanly of me as that?" demanded Towton, colouring indignantly.

Miss Hest raised her eyebrows. "My dear sir, my experience of human nature has shown me that there is no mean trick which the majority of men will not commit for money. You, however, were in the minority, and so was Ida, as you both were honest. This upset my calculations, as I could not provide against the unseen in human nature. You, Colonel, still insisted upon marrying Ida, and she wished to hand over the money to Lady Corsoon. For this reason I was forced to play my last card and produce the will."

"But you did not intend to be found out as The Spider?"

"No, I did not," confessed Frances calmly. "When Maunders betrayed me at Isleworth you thought that The Spider was a man, which was exactly what I wanted and what I counted upon should such an event as unexpected betrayal happen. In the fog I dragged Maunders away, and we went to the house of a friend of mine whose name I don't intend you to know. I wired in cypher to Miss Jewin here to send a telegram to Francis Hest at Professor Gail's."

"We got that," said the Colonel quickly, "and it threw us off the scent."

"I thought it would," said Miss Hest coolly. "So while you were hunting for The Spider as a man in London I went down with Maunders--he was disguised as an old gentleman and I resumed my womanly dress. Then I wrote you on the plea of talking about Ida and asked after my pretended brother to still further puzzle you."

"You certainly succeeded," retorted Towton, trying to conceal his wonder at all this clever trickery; "but Ida was here and must have known that you were absent from the house as Francis."

"Oh, no. I appeared before her twice in this room, which is, as you see, not very well lighted, in my male disguise and with the painted scar on my face. She was entirely taken in."

"The very simplicity of your disguise took me in," said Ida angrily and wincing at having been so blinded. "Had you worn a beard or a wig I should have recognised you."

"I think not," said Miss Hest quietly and with an amused smile. "As the man I wore my hair somewhat long----"

"I noted that," said the Colonel quickly.

"How clever of you. Well, then, as a woman I merely knitted in false hair. I couldn't wear false hair as a man since Ida would then have been sharp enough to have recognised me. But plenty of women wear false plaits, so I was safe on that score: she never suspected me. My sole disguise was the cicatrice, skilfully painted, and the success of the whole business lay--as Ida has submitted--in its boldness and in the belief that I had a twin brother. I have always found," added Miss Hest musingly, "that the bolder one is the safer it is: audacity always scores. At all events, I so closely resembled my own true self that no one thought I was anyone else but what I represented myself to be. As Francis I told Ida that I was taking my sister away for a week, and so slipped up to London to meet Vernon at Lady Corsoon's and to be nearly trapped at Isleworth."

"What about Hokar and Bahadur?" asked the Colonel abruptly.

"Hokar," said Miss Jewin, making the explanation instead of Frances, "was an old servant of Captain Hest's and came to England with me and the child. Later he sent for his nephew, who was Bahadur."

"Yes. And I gave them both to Maunders when I set him up in those splendid Egyptian rooms in Bond Street," observed her mistress. "They were not engaged to strangle people, as you may think, Colonel, but I merely wished them to add to the fantastical look of the place when fortunes were being told. That you were so nearly strangled, and Vernon also, was your own fault and his own. You should mind your own business, my friend."

"I am going to mind it now," said Towton with a frown; "but first tell me, since you are so frank, what about Lady Corsoon's jewels?"

"They are in this house. I gave them into Miss Jewin's possession."

"And Lady Corsoon can have them for one hundred pounds," said Miss Jewin.

"A very modest demand, Sarah," said Miss Hest approvingly, "but as the game is up I don't think you will get more. I shall leave you to arrange about getting the money and handing back the jewels. Lady Corsoon will be safe, and at a small loss. But I am glad to think that she will not get your money, Ida, dear."

"Don't speak to me," cried Ida starting to her feet. "The more you say the more I see how shamefully you have treated me."

"I have spared you," said Miss Hest coolly. "I could have stripped you entirely bare had I so chosen."

"No. By your own showing I was too clever for you."

"Why, that is true, and simply because you were honest. I always wished to keep on the right side of the law, or I could have got you to make a will in my favour, and then you would have been poisoned."

"How dare you?" shouted Towton, while Ida gave a faint cry.

"You have learned how much I dare," said Frances with an unpleasant look. "So, now the story is told, perhaps you will leave my house."

Colonel Towton walked towards the door with Ida on his arm and roughly pushed Miss Jewin aside. "I shall place Miss Dimsdale----"

"Miss Menteith," sneered Frances.

"In safety," continued Towton without noticing the interruption, "and then I shall ride for the police."

"I shall come, too," cried Maunders starting to his feet. "She will lock me up again and perhaps may kill me."

"Stay where you are," commanded Frances sharply. "I intend to----"

Maunders did not wait to hear the end of the sentence. Seeing that Towton and Ida blocked the door he made a rush at the nearest window and sprang out of it with a dexterity begotten of sheer fear. Whether Frances intended to take him with her when she fled, or whether she intended to murder him he could not say, but he preferred to trust in the mercy of the law rather than in that of the woman who had been his evil genius. Crazy with terror, he tumbled to the ground, and Towton, along with Ida, ran to the front door, to see him speeding across the grass. A moment later and Frances, with a revolver in her hand, leaped from the window in pursuit. From the expression on her face she evidently intended nothing less than murder.

Towton hastily unbuckled the bridle from the ring and flung himself on his horse. "Place your foot on my toe, Ida," he commanded; "up you get. There," he added, gathering up the reins as she sat on his saddle-bow and placed her arms round his neck; "now let us alarm the village. That poor devil will be shot if this fiendish woman is not arrested." And he rode forward at a moderately fast pace.

"She'll catch him," chuckled Sarah Jewin, who had come to the door and was looking out from under the palm of her hand. "Shoot, Miss Frances. Shoot!"

Maunders, finding that he was being chased, could not make directly for the gate and dodged behind some shrubs. Frances sighted him and fired a shot. It winged him, for he gave a yell of fear and ran directly towards her in the open. She fired another shot, which struck him in the breast, and he pitched forward at her feet. Just as she fired a third shot into his prostrate body there came a noise like thunder and a terrible cry from Miss Jewin.

"The signal! The signal! The dam's burst!" and she bolted into the house.

In a flash Towton comprehended and set spurs to his horse. Frances strove to fly, but Maunders with a last effort caught at her foot and she fell heavily, fighting for freedom like a wild cat. The next moment he had her by the throat. And in the distance a mighty roaring struck the ears of all as the flood came down gigantically.

CHAPTER XXII.

THE END OF IT ALL.

Towton could not quite understand the situation, as there was no time to consider matters. All he knew was that the Bolly Dam had burst, and even had Miss Jewin not spoken, the appalling noise would have informed him of the catastrophe. With Ida in his arms he spurred his horse frantically out of the gate and across the village bridge. He found the crooked street filled with people, called out by the unexpected thunder.

"The dam's burst: get on the high ground," shouted Towton, and with a yell of fear men, women, and children began to run wildly in the direction of the gorge and to disappear amongst the houses in the hope of gaining some level beyond the height of the down-coming flood. But there was scanty time for safety. The hollow booming sound of the waters plunging through the narrows sounded ever nearer and nearer with terrible distinctness: it seemed as though the waters were bellowing for their prey. In a moment the Colonel comprehended that it was too late to skirt the village and gain the winding road, where they would be safe. Ida gave a cry of alarm as he wrenched round the now startled horse and clattered through the village street on his way down the valley. It seemed the only chance.

"I'll save you yet, my darling," muttered Towton, setting his teeth. "We must make for Gatehead," and he drove his spurs into the animal, which now was becoming unmanageable with the roaring of the flood. Ida, almost insensible with terror, clung to her lover's neck, and the horse, making no more of the double burden than if it had been a feather, tore at top speed along the road between the torrent and the precipice. There was no safety on either side, as the precipice could not be climbed, and the dry bed of the stream merely offered a deeper grave. Fortunately, the road sloped gradually to the mouth of the valley, some two miles away, therefore the downward trend offered extra means to escape the pursuing greedy waters. A backward glance showed Towton that a tremendous flood was shooting out of the bottle-mouth of the upper gorge with terrific rapidity. The whole of the huge lake, artificial as well as natural, was emptying itself in one vast outpour, and owing to the narrowness of the valley the concentrated force was gigantic. If the flood caught them they would either be dashed to pieces against the rocks or would be borne onward--horse and maid and man--to be expelled at Gatehead, as if fired from the mouth of a cannon.

"Oh, God, save us! Oh, God, save us!" was all that Ida could moan.

"He will; He will," cried Towton, riding under spur and whip with a mad joy in the adventure, perilous as it was. "He will save the innocent and punish the guilty. Never fear, never fear, my darling."

On roared the enormous body of water, curling like a mighty wave crested with foam and glistening like a colossal jewel in the serene sunshine. It passed with a hoarse triumphant screaming over the fated village, and in a single moment Bowderstyke was not. Bearing _débris_ and bodies of cattle and men, women and children on its breast, the water rolled majestically on its destroying way. Like a wall of steel it stood up, stretching from wall to wall of the valley, and before it tore the terrified horse, warned by its instinct of rapidly approaching danger.

"We are lost! we are lost!" screamed Ida, hiding her face on Towton's shoulder. "We can never escape. It's a mile further."

"There's a crack--a path--a break in the precipice," panted the man, almost despairing of saving what he loved best in the world. "If we can gain that we can scramble up, and--and---- Great God! How it travels!"

From the sides of the valley trees were being wrenched up by their roots, and even the stones lying in the bed of the torrent were being lifted and swept onward like pieces of straw. Owing to the increasing breadth of the valley the shouting and the level of the flood had somewhat lessened, but the hoarse, steady murmur with which it smoothly advanced seemed to be even more terrible than its triumphant screaming. Nearer and nearer it rolled, towering, as it seems to the desperate fugitives, right up to the high heavens. The horse raced onward furiously, but there seemed to be no chance of escaping that rapidly approaching death-wave, which swept along with relentless speed. The man and woman were both silent, and both prayed inwardly, as they faced the eleventh hour of death.

And it was the eleventh hour, for there was still hope. Rounding a corner swiftly Towton rose in his stirrups and sent forth a cry almost as hoarse as that of the flood. A short distance ahead he saw a streak of green grass marking the ruddy stone face of the precipice, and knew that here was the crack to which he had referred. It was a mere chink in the wall, of no great width, caused, no doubt, by the volcanic action which had formed the valley in far distant ages. Many a time as a lad had Towton climbed up that narrow natural staircase to the moors above, but never had he expected to find it a means of preserving his own life and the life he valued dearer than his own. Setting his teeth, he glanced backward and then urged the horse to renewed efforts. The wall of water was almost upon them, advancing with terrible and steady persistence. The last moment seemed to be at hand.

Suddenly the Colonel wrenched at the horse's bit and pulled the animal up with a jerk. As it fell back on its haunches he slipped off with the almost insensible girl in his arms and ran desperately towards the sloping green bank, which showed itself like a port of safety between the bare, bleak stones. As he gained it the horse, having recovered itself, rushed past with a loose bridle and with the stirrups lashing its sides. But Towton paid no heed. Almost in a dream he scrambled up the bank, bearing Ida as though she were a feather-weight. With straining eyes and bursting temples, and with his heart beating furiously, he clambered desperately, dragging the girl rather than carrying her, as he needed at least one hand free to grip the tough grasses. Fortunately the slope was gradual, and had it not been there would have been no hope of escape. As it was, when they were a considerable way up the mighty wave surged majestically past, and its waters shot up the crevice with gigantic force. This was rather a help than a hindrance, as it assisted the almost broken man to mount higher. But to the end of his days Colonel Towton never knew how he saved his wife. All he could remember was straining upward, dragging the now insensible woman with aching limbs and a blood-red mist before his eyes. When his brain was somewhat clearer he found himself bending over Ida in a turfy nook, while barely three feet below him the grey water gurgled and sang and bubbled as if in a witch's cauldron.

"Safe! Safe!" muttered Towton, and dropped insensible across the inanimate body of the woman he had so miraculously saved from a terrible death.

*   *   *   *   *   *

Nine months later, when the cuckoo had brought summer to the land, and the earth was gay with flowers, two married men met unexpectedly in the viridarium of the Athenian Club. They came face to face under the peristyle, and after mutual glances of surprise and congratulation burst out laughing. Then followed a warm handshake and merry speech.

"Well, married man," said Vernon, as he sat opposite his friend at a small table and ordered a half-pint of champagne to signalise the happy meeting. "So you are back from your honeymoon?"

"As you see," said the military benedict; "and you have returned with Lady Vernon from the classic shores of Italy."

"We came back last week, and are staying in town for a few days before going to Slimthorp."

"Welcome by the tenantry, triumphal arches, addresses, dinners and speeches, and what not, I suppose?" observed the Colonel smiling.

"Oh, yes. The tenants are delighted to have a master who will take an interest in their doings and a mistress who can act the Lady Bountiful. Lucy and I are about to enter into our kingdom, so we intend to take full advantage of the satisfaction of our loving subjects."

"You are devilish lucky, Vernon. I have scarcely a loving subject left, and Bowderstyke Valley has been swept clean from end to end."

"As I saw," replied Sir Arthur with a shudder at the recollection. "By jove! Colonel, you don't know what I suffered that afternoon when I thought that you and Ida were smashed to pieces. Do you remember how Lucy fainted when you appeared coming across the moorland with Ida hanging half dead on your arm? It was a meeting of the living and the dead."

"Any woman less plucky than Ida would have died," said Towton, his face lighting up with a fond smile. "When we got beyond the highest level of the water she had fainted, and then I did. It was Ida who recovered first, and, by Jupiter, sir, she brought me round! How we climbed to the top of the moor I don't know, but she was as plucky as a man, bless her!"

"How is she now, Colonel?"

"As happy as the day is long, although I don't deny that we both feel sad when we look at our wrecked property. However, with her money we intend to rebuild Bowderstyke Village and to reconstruct Gatehead, which was also destroyed, if you remember. I daresay we'll be able to inveigle people to live in the valley by offering land at low terms. In a year or two we will have plenty of tenants to give you and Lady Vernon a rousing welcome when you pay us a visit."

"That won't be for some time, Colonel, as we have to look after our own kingdom. I am glad to see that you are looking so well. When was it that we last met?"

Towton laughed and his eyes twinkled. "You must be happy to have lost your memory so completely," he said with a jolly laugh. "Why, after our mutual wedding breakfast at Lady Corsoon's; don't you recollect? Weren't we married in great style on the same day, and didn't you go to Italy and Greece for a honeymoon while Ida and I returned to The Grange?"

"It all seems like a dream," said Vernon absently, and a cloud passed over his face, "and in my newly-found happiness I have tried to forget these sad memories. We never had an exhaustive talk over things, Colonel, and now that our wives are not here I should like to ask a few questions."

"Ask away. It's just as well we are alone. Ida doesn't care to talk of that dreadful day or of her association with Miss Hest."

"Nor does Lucy. That dreadful woman! What a dare-devil she was, and as clever as they make them."

"She was a sight too clever," replied Towton drily, "as she burnt her fingers at the last. I suppose you know that Miss Jewin was caught?"

"You wrote me something about it."

"Didn't Lady Corsoon tell you anything?"

"No. Why should she?" said Vernon with a look of surprise.

"Well, as you knew the secret of her pawning those jewels, I thought she would have told you of their recovery."

"What! Were they recovered? Who had them?"

"Miss Jewin. She escaped, but Drench caught her. She sent for me before she committed suicide."

Vernon looked horrified. "Did she kill herself, poor wretch?"

"Yes. She hanged herself by her garters in her cell. I expect she knew that she would get a long term of imprisonment, and so preferred to get out of the world. But, as I said, she sent for me and told me where the jewels were. She also threw a light on the catastrophe of the Bolly Dam breaking."

"We knew that Hokar exploded a charge of dynamite," said Vernon looking inquiringly at his friend. "Don't you remember how he could not get away in time, and confessed when dying that he had been ordered by Miss Hest to blow up the dam when she gave the signal by firing a revolver."

"Oh, yes. I remember that as it all came out in the papers," said Towton with a shrug; "and that's just the point. Listen, and---- Oh, here's the wine."

Vernon sent away the waiter after he filled their glasses, and the two gentlemen drank to their dear wives and to a happy future for themselves as married men. When this ceremony was ended, the Colonel related what he had learned from unfortunate Miss Jewin before she passed away.

"I, dragged him down in disguise to Gerby Hall, and there locked him in an upper room. Miss Jewin acted as gaoler, but in spite of her vigilance the wretched man managed to break one of his prison bars and escape. He then appeared in the drawing-room and denounced Miss Hest. Always prepared for further treachery on the part of Maunders, and never being in the habit of leaving anything to chance, Frances had arranged that she should have the dam broken down in the event of the police coming to arrest her, and so they would be destroyed."

"But she would be destroyed with them," said Vernon at this point, "and as a matter of fact she was. Don't you remember how her body and that of Maunders clutching one another in a death-grip were found when the flood subsided? She anticipated her death."

"She did nothing of the sort, sir, as Miss Jewin told me. The betrayal of her identity with Francis Hest and with The Spider came unexpectedly because of Maunders' escape. But, always making things sure, she had already posted Hokar at the dam, where he had placed a charge of dynamite under the wall. Miss Hest didn't expect trouble, as she thought she had thrown dust in my eyes by the clever way in which she had acted."

"I think she did, Colonel, and very successfully," remarked Vernon smiling.

"I admit it. She was a wonderfully clever woman and extremely unscrupulous. However, on the chance that some danger might come along she posted Hokar at Bolly Dam and told him to fire the charge when he heard the report of a revolver."

Vernon nodded. "I remember on that day how the wind was blowing up the gorge and how clearly the sounds came up from the village. Hokar heard the shots very easily."

"He heard two or three, and might have guessed that his infernal mistress was not giving the agreed signal. She was shooting Maunders, if you remember. It was her intention after we left to have escaped by a similar crack up the side of the precipice behind Gerby Hall to that which saved Ida and myself. But she didn't intend to give the signal until she was on the upward journey with Miss Jewin; Maunders was to be left behind to drown in the house. But Miss Hest forgot for the moment and let her temper get the better of her. By firing the shots she gave the signal, and Hokar blew up the dam prematurely."

"I see. But if Miss Jewin escaped why didn't Miss Hest?"

"Ah, that's where her Nemesis came in. Maunders caught her by the leg and toppled her over, then he gripped her throat, and they were both drowned."

"Serve her right, and him also," said Vernon coolly.

"I agree with you. They were a dangerous couple, and it seems like retributive justice that Maunders should bring all her carefully-laid plans of escape to grief. Miss Jewin at the first alarm caught up the box of Lady Corsoon's jewels and fled out of the back way and up the crevice, as arranged. She concealed herself for a time, and was warned by the exhaustive reports in the papers of what was going on."

"That's the worst of those papers," said Vernon with disgust, "as I found out when I was a detective. They warn the criminals of everything. I suppose Miss Jewin saw how the whole story of The Spider was set forth and appreciated the sensation it caused."

"Of course she did. I was angry at the papers myself, for The Grange was simply infested with reporters and journalists and photographers. However, after the inquest the sensation died away. Everybody has, more or less, forgotten the matter by this time. It's just as well, as neither I nor you, Vernon, wished to be bothered with questions."

"Quite so. That was why I remained abroad with my wife for such a time."

"And that was why I went back with Ida to Bowderstyke," said the Colonel. "However, to continue. Drench caught Miss Jewin and she hanged herself in her cell, as I have told you. I found the box of jewels and returned them to your mother-in-law. Thus her husband has never found out how she pawned them; so that's all right."

"I hope it has been a lesson to her."

"Not a bit of it. I dined with her a week ago, and so did Ida. Afterwards we went to a bridge drive and Lady Corsoon played furiously. She's a born gambler. But Sir Julius does not know, and never will know, how she pawned his much-prized family jewels."

"I wonder Miss Jewin didn't sell them?"

"She had enough money to live on in a small way, and, of course, lived plainly to avert suspicion. The jewels she kept as a peace-offering in case she should be arrested. She hoped to make terms by threatening to denounce Lady Corsoon. However, her heart failed her, and she handed them over to me."

"Poor woman. By the way, Colonel, what was your wife's real opinion of Miss Hest? I could never quite understand."

Towton was silent for a few minutes. "It is hard to say. Ida told me that she really liked Miss Hest for a long time, and thought that she was a genuine friend. But Miss Hest showed the cloven foot by trying to get Ida married to Maunders, and----"

"Why to Maunders?"

"Because he was under Miss Hest's thumb, and if he obtained possession of Ida's fortune by marriage Miss Hest undoubtedly would have had the spending of it."

"But this marriage to Francis. How could that be when Francis didn't exist?"

"Oh, I think that was a mere blind to make Ida fancy Francis was a real person and not Miss Hest in disguise. I can never understand," added the Colonel with a thoughtful look, "how it was that Ida didn't detect the woman under the man. Women are so quick in these matters."

"It was the very boldness of the disguise," said Vernon emphatically. "I was taken in myself at that Georgian Hall Bazaar. A less clever woman than Miss Hest would have made herself look utterly different to her natural self. As it was, she scarcely changed her looks at all save by wearing a man's dress and painting that cicatrice on her face. Anyone would have said that the supposed brother was the sister dressed up. Such actually was the case, and--well, you know that everyone was taken in. A thousand pities, Colonel, that Miss Hest did not apply her splendid faculties to better purpose. She was undeniably very clever."

"A criminal genius, as we have often said when we talked of The Spider. I must say that Professor Gail, although he admired her talents, was staggered when he found out from the papers that she was the renowned Spider. I believe he had a fit. However, he has now made up endless romantic stories about her, and actually got an engagement with his wife on the strength of having known her. It's an ill wind which blows no one any good."

"If Frances Hest had lived and could have escaped hanging and imprisonment, Colonel, she would have been engaged at a music-hall to appear at a salary of hundreds a week. This age likes romantic criminality."

"I think Miss Hest's criminality was prosaic in the extreme," said the Colonel very drily. "She couldn't earn money honestly and therefore took the left-handed path. All her philanthropy was a sham, and I really believe that she had the Bolly Dam built less to supply the villages with water than to protect herself from arrest."

"But the human lives----"

"Pooh! She thought nothing of human life, and was a kind of female Napoleon in that way. She wrung Dimsdale's neck as though he had been a chicken the moment she found her personal safety was in danger. Had he not torn off her mask and thus recognised her she would have spared him. A marvellously clever woman: she quite took me in. I never expected to find The Spider in her, and had not Maunders escaped to betray her I would have believed that the non-existing Francis was the blackguard. And more, she would have got ten thousand pounds from Ida, and perhaps in America would have started on a new career of roguery. However, I recovered the signed document and the cheque from the body, so nothing was said about that matter in the papers. I was glad for my wife's sake."

"What became of Bahadur?"

"He bolted from the country and has never been heard of. His uncle, Hokar, as you know, died after the explosion."

"And Mrs. Bedge?"

"She buried all memory of Constantine with his bones, but I think she regards him as a martyr who was led astray by Miss Hest. Yet from the lips of The Spider herself I learned that it was Maunders who induced that very clever lady to become a criminal."

"Do you think Maunders himself blackmailed his aunt?"

"He was quite capable of it. But I think Miss Hest did that to protect Maunders from possible suspicion. For no one would think that the man had anything to do with the matter of The Spider, who blackmailed his adopted mother. Simply a smart trick of Miss Hest's, Vernon, that's all."

"Have some more champagne, Colonel?"

"Thank you, no more. Come along and see my wife."

"I have to meet Lucy at Swan & Edgar's," said Vernon glancing at his watch.

"I'll go with you there first and then we can have afternoon tea together."

"Right you are, Colonel, on condition that you dine with Lucy and myself at our hotel and come to the theatre afterwards."

Towton nodded. "Well, Ida and I are up in town for a frolic, so we'll come."

"When do you return to Bowderstyke?"

"In two or three days. I'm seeing about the re-building of the Bolly Dam."

"Isn't that dangerous?" asked Vernon as they left the club. "No. I am arranging for large channels to carry off the water. Besides, had not the dam been blown up by that Indian beast the catastrophe would not have taken place. Any more questions?"

"No," said Sir Arthur after a pause. "I think you have enlightened me on every point. We'll talk no more of the matter."

"Not in the presence of our wives, at all events," said the Colonel bluffly, and stepping out smartly along Pall Mall. "But when I think of all the mystery and devilish cantrips we have had to do with, and how narrowly Ida and I escaped a dreadful death, I can only thank God that we are happily married. There's one small domestic animal, if it can be called so, Vernon, on which I can never look without a shudder."

"What's that?" asked Sir Arthur, not following his friend's train of thought.

"What, sir! What, have you forgotten the past already?"

"Oh!" Vernon laughed, but somewhat seriously. "You mean a spider."

"Yes," snapped the Colonel sharply, "I mean a spider."

THE END.

Milton Keynes UK
Ingram Content Group UK Ltd.
UKHW050652260624
444769UK00004B/238